A DANGEROUS D

"I am unarmed," Aiyana said fiercely, her chin high, her eyes burning.

"We'll see." Dutifully, Dane patted her outline. He started to shake his head, to assure Galya that Aiyana carried no weapon.

His hand bumped something large and metallic beneath Aiyana's heavy cloak. Dane's brow rose in surprise. He fumbled beneath her cloak and withdrew a full-sized rifle.

Dane met Aiyana's eyes. Her small chin lifted, defiant.

Dane continued, running his hands along Aiyana's concealed body. Another lump met his touch. He sighed, then drew out a curved sword.

Aiyana said nothing, but when Dane retrieved the saber's companion dagger, she cast her gaze upward, faintly guilty. Dane laughed when he located a whetting knife tucked into the ties of her cloth boots.

Dane ran his hands over her again, to see if he had missed anything, then stood back. "Rumors of your violence haven't been exaggerated, I see. You carry arms enough to storm a planet."

Aiyana didn't respond, but Galya appeared unsatisfied. "She must be searched thoroughly, Dane."

"What?"

"An explosive device, easily concealed, yet immensely destructive, you wouldn't find in such a gentle search. These Ellowan devices are paper-thin. They would be taped to her skin, beneath her clothing."

Dane hesitated, wanting to trust Aiyana, but . . . "I see no need . . ."

"She must be thoroughly searched."

Other *Love Spell* books by Stobie Piel:
THE DAWN STAR
MOLLY IN THE MIDDLE

The Midnight Moon

STOBIE PIEL

LOVE SPELL BOOKS NEW YORK CITY

To Natassja Voltin, my tender-hearted and beautiful daughter. I love you.

LOVE SPELL®

July 1998

Published by

Dorchester Publishing Co., Inc.
276 Fifth Avenue
New York, NY 10001

ISBN 0-505-52268-3

Printed in the United States of America.

We are as clouds that veil the midnight moon;
How restlessly they speed, and gleam, and quiver,
Streaking the darkness radiantly!
—P. B. Shelley
from *Mutability*

The Midnight Moon

Chapter One

The red sky deepened toward black, casting long shadows across the amber moon of Candor. Dane Calydon sat on a boulder, his arms folded over his knees as he watched the gas planet disappear.

"I have seen twilight on Candor a thousand times, yet it never fails to astonish me."

A small, furry head emerged from beneath Dane's cloak. "You've seen it exactly sixteen hundred and twenty-three times. And every time has been the same: red."

Dane set the lingbat on his shoulder, then drew a long breath. "I know. You're right. The first hundred times or so were interesting. In an uneventful way."

"So why do we keep coming here?"

Dane sighed again. "Because, Carob, there is nothing else to do. I came here for adventure. Instead, I've watched the Candorian Council negotiate peace through satellite communications. I've never been so bored in my life."

Carob chuckled. "Maybe you should give Selena another try."

The mention of Kostbera's elusive daughter brought a groan of defeat. "I tire of rejections, bat."

Carob adjusted his position on Dane's shoulder. "You may tire of them, but I don't. I watched you use the most ridiculous stories to woo Thorwalian women. You never failed, not once. Selena sets you back in your place."

"Sixteen hundred and twenty-three times. No, thank you. I'll just watch the planet set and the sun rise."

Far in the distance, the sun rose, fainter than moonlight. There, on an inner-system world, Dane's sister had found love and peace. He had wanted that, too. But the years had gone by, and nothing had changed. Love eluded him. Adventure eluded him.

All the while, he had practiced Thorwalian riflery, he had learned the languages of the Intersystem, and he had trained his body in the Akandan mind-body technique of TiKay. His mind was disciplined, his body had grown strong, and his skill was sharpened to prime readiness. And nothing had changed.

"Maybe it's time I returned to Thorwal."

Dane felt little enthusiasm at the prospect of returning to his homeworld. As a boy, he had been left on Candor to learn from the advanced, prosperous race. He had been left to speak for his own people, the Thorwalians. He had stayed hoping for adventure, something his staid, serious world couldn't offer.

Apparently Candor didn't offer it, either.

A white streak of light flashed across the sky. An incoming vessel. "What ship is that?"

Carob tilted his head in the direction of the ship. "Kostbera is expecting ambassadors from another system. They came through the wormhole. From what I've gathered, they're having trouble with terrorists. You might want to sit in on the meeting."

Dane considered returning to the underground city, then decided against it. "The situation will be rectified at council. What's the point?"

"I doubt this 'situation' will be rectified anytime soon. The terrorists are Ellowan. And they're notorious for not negotiating anything."

Dane looked at the lingbat. "Ellowan? You mentioned that race once before. I believe you said their women are spellbinding."

"And dangerous."

Dane didn't care. The mention of the violent Ellowan intrigued him. "I've got nothing better to do. Let's go."

The last, deep red shafts of light glinted across the Candorian desert, illuminating the pyramid gateways to the underground city of Nerotania. Carob yawned and leaned against Dane's head, then toppled off as he fell asleep.

Dane caught the bat and carried him gently. His small friend was getting old. Dane wondered how old Carob was, and how much longer he would live. Since returning to Candor, the lingbat had sired several litters, but none had his sharp, biting wit.

Dane passed through the multihued gateway and entered the colossal hallways of Nerotania. Bright mosaics covered the floor and walls, but Dane paid no attention. The wonder of the Candorian world had lost its sheen in the shadow of boredom.

Dane left Carob in the lingbat tunnels, then went to the council chamber. He stopped outside the door. He heard Kostbera speaking, her voice low and modulated, peaceful. Dane resisted irritation. The Candorian leader had probably solved the problem even before he arrived.

Another voice rose in reply, and Dane's heart took a

strange leap. ''That is all well, Kostbera. But what can Candor offer that we on Franconia cannot do for ourselves?''

A clipped voice, muffled by her life-support apparatus, yet filled with divergent emotion and bitterness, strangely compelling to Dane's ears. A woman's voice. Dane entered the chamber just to see the woman who spoke.

Kostbera sat at the head of the table, her white robe reflecting the multicolored light replacers. Her silver hair was bound in its usual twist, her expression sublime and without passion.

Dane stood in the doorway, studying the new arrivals. A young woman with light blond hair sat at Kostbera's right. Seated facing away was another being, though Dane couldn't see if it was male or female. A heavy, large cape draped the creature's body, and its head was wrapped in a protective shield.

''What can you offer us? This is not clear to me.''

That voice penetrated Dane's soul, but he endured a wave of disappointment. A creature that needed to be wrapped against the Candorian environment probably wasn't even human.

Kostbera's attention was fixed on the wrapped being. ''The Candorians offer the benefit of unbiased consideration. We do not tolerate aggression here, and seek to assuage it elsewhere, if invited to do so.''

The blond woman leaned forward, her expression desperate. ''We are in dire need, Kostbera. The Ellowans are relentless. Our civilization hangs on the brink of utter destruction.'' She paused. ''Yet the Candorians are far less numerous than we imagined. Is your power great enough to aid our cause?''

A smile formed on Kostbera's ageless face. ''We are few in number, Galya, but the power we wield on Candor is based in intellectual solutions. We can assist your needs through negotiation. Yet the Candorians never act in haste.

We know little of Franconia. Much is to be learned before we enter into your defense."

Kostbera noticed Dane and motioned for him to join the group. She rose to introduce him. "This man is Dane Caldon, from the planet Thorwal, which was once violent and barbaric, but is now in the process of civilized advancement."

The wrapped being turned. Nothing of the creature's nature was revealed beneath the protective cloak. Dane eyed her closely. "What are you?"

Kostbera winced at Dane's blunt question. "He wastes little energy on tact. . . . Dane, these are ambassadors from a system beyond the wormhole. It is known as Franconia. Galya represents the Tseirs, the most populous race of Franconia."

The blond woman smiled at Dane. "You resemble our people. You would find Franconia welcoming."

Dane bowed. "It would please me to learn of your people, Galya." Dane's attention wavered, returning to the wrapped being. He saw no eyes, but he felt a piercing intelligence assessing him. Kostbera hesitated before making the introduction.

"And this is Aiyana, of the Keiroit race. The Keiroits also are engaged in disputes with the Ellowans."

Dane studied the Keiroit. "Why are you wrapped?"

Aiyana seemed scathing even before she spoke. "The environment of your world is intolerable to a Keiroit." Her words implied she found Dane intolerable, too. "It is necessary to protect myself from the harsh factors of your climate."

Dane seated himself beside Aiyana. "My climate is much harsher than this sheltered world, I assure you. My world of Thorwal is frozen and covered with snow . . . at all times. You would not find a visit enjoyable."

"I'm not surprised." Aiyana turned back to Kostbera.

"What use is this primitive man, and what place has he at this council?"

Kostbera glanced apologetically at Dane. "I have found Dane to be fair and kind, his intellect undiluted by rash judgments and illusions. I would welcome his opinion in this matter."

A sharp, derisive laugh came from beneath Aiyana's cloak. "Undiluted by thought, you mean. This should prove interesting." She turned in her seat to face Dane. "Well, Thorwalian, what have you to say concerning the plight of Franconia?"

Aiyana's sarcasm grated on Dane's nerves. It took all his restraint to keep from insulting her in turn. "Since I know little of Franconia, I will withhold my opinion until you have explained your situation."

"I'll tell you this, Thorwalian, and that is all. Franconia is a federation of planets and moons that surpasses your simple understanding. All would be well there, if not for the Ellowans."

"That much I guessed. The Ellowans, what do they want?"

Aiyana hesitated. She seemed surprised by Dane's question, and didn't answer.

Galya bowed her head. "The Ellowans want what they've always wanted. Supreme power and control of our system. They are violent, heartless people, cruel beyond anything known in this system. They have strange powers of healing and . . . other things. As well, they are elusive, and thus their attacks have been without warning, and deadly."

Dane considered this, but he felt Aiyana's eyes on him. He wondered what kind of creature she was, what she looked like. If her appearance resembled her nature, it wouldn't be pretty.

"The Ellowans are terrorists, then. How can there be successful negotiation if they want nothing in exchange for peace?''

Kostbera nodded. ''That is a fair question. We know nothing of their demands. Before we can offer Franconia our aid, we must learn more, firsthand, of your world. We will send our own ambassador to Franconia, to learn how best we can help you. We will send Dane.''

Dane's eyes brightened. *At last.*

Aiyana stiffened beneath her cloak. ''We want advice, not a pet for the return voyage.''

Galya bit her lip in embarrassment. ''The Keiroits are blunt, but they are valuable allies in our struggle. You must forgive Aiyana, Dane. Her people have suffered much in their contact with the Ellowans. The Ellowans have swarmed the Keiroits' planet, and still ambush their ships wantonly.''

Aiyana didn't comment, but Dane guessed her ill nature began long before the Ellowan invasion. His restraint shattered. ''It appears beyond your capacity to see the situation clearly, Keiroit. Obviously the Tseirs need more sound advice than your impulsive race has given.''

''The Keiroits don't give advice, Thorwalian. We give weapons.'' Aiyana's voice quavered with suppressed passion.

So much was hidden beneath that cloak, and Dane sensed and enjoyed it. Life had been peaceful until now. Now Aiyana brought meaning to his restless soul. She brought untold aggravation. He couldn't wait for the journey to begin.

''Weapons? I will assume, since the conflict goes on, that you are less than skilled. Though I will travel as an ambassador, I would be happy to instruct you in the deadlier arts.''

Dane sat back in his seat, relishing Aiyana's reaction. He felt her scoffing beneath her head wrap. A smile curved his lips as he waited for her reply.

''And I will assume, since you are a guest of the Candorians, that you have picked up some small knowledge of their weaponry. Yet the most advanced weapons require a keen wit to use them properly. I do not see any evidence of that in you."

She was enjoying their banter, too. Dane's heart swelled with happiness. As Carob aged, his capacity for banter had faded. The lingbat offered a few barbed comments now and then, but more often than not he fell asleep in Dane's company.

"I do not claim to be from a race as advanced as yours no doubt is." Dane couldn't suppress his pleasure. His smile deepened in what he hoped was a taunting fashion. "Yet on Candor I have learned that wisdom comes from an ability to learn. From my people, I learned the strength of metal. From my sister, I learned the capacity to adapt. From her mate, I learned the power of primitive worlds. And on Candor, I have learned patience. Patience to tolerate even the most unmannered of . . . alien beings."

Kostbera gasped and rose quickly to end the meeting. "I believe the matter is settled. Dane will travel to Franconia, and devise a method of bringing peace to that system."

Aiyana placed both gloved fists on the table. "You promised to send a Candorian. This . . . primitive species is not acceptable to me."

"The Candorians are few, Aiyana. Many matters demand our attention. I have confidence in Dane's abilities."

"I do not."

Dane resisted the impulse to speak up, but it wasn't easy.

Galya rose. "I am satisfied with Dane as an ambassador. Kostbera's faith in you is strong. The Tseirs are grateful for your help."

Dane rose and faced Aiyana. He knew she smoldered with anger beneath her heavy wraps. "It seems you and I will be traveling together, Keiroit." He held out his hand. She turned away.

Galya came around the table and touched Dane's arm. "We will travel in a Franconian vessel. For your service, we will give you a craft for your return."

"Is the journey long?"

Kostbera directed her guests from the council room. "Because of the wormhole, the journey is less than the time it would take to return to Thorwal."

Aiyana passed close to Dane, then stopped. "But it is more dangerous, Thorwalian. Never forget. You may pass through the wormhole, but you may never return. Your lust for adventure may see your death."

She was warning him. Almost as if she cared. Dane watched her go, then shook his head. "The Tseirs must be in hard shape if they've allied with the Keiroits."

Kostbera waited until the Franconians had disappeared down the hall, then faced Dane. "That one, the Keiroit . . . much is hidden in her, even to me."

"What about the other, Galya?"

Kostbera's brow furrowed, an expression of uncertainty that Dane rarely saw on her face. "Galya seeks to control how we see her, what we think of her, and her situation. I do not know why. But the Tseirs are frightened, and it is a genuine fear. They fear annihilation. That much is clear to me, and moves me to learn what can be done to aid their cause. But in the Keiroit, I sense hatred."

"For the Ellowans?"

"I don't know. But it is strong and fierce. So strong it might destroy anything in its path. It is as if . . ." Kostbera's voice faded; her eyes closed. "As if that one, Aiyana, is already dead."

Dane's heart chilled; his stomach knotted. "For a dead thing, she has much to say."

"Learn what has killed her, Dane. That will be the answer to your quest."

"I wouldn't choose to spend time in her company."

"No. But my heart tells me you will. And it won't be what you expect. Remember this: In all things, there are both darkness and light, hope and despair. We Candorians do not act rashly, but we *are* capable of destroying the Ellowans. Much truth is hidden on Franconia. It is up to you to learn what action we must take, if any."

"There should be time to study the Candorian files, learn what I can about Franconia." Dane paused. "The Keiroits, in particular, require further study."

"Little is known of that system. Of the Ellowans, most is rumor and legend. It is said that they have healing abilities unique to their race, a biological way of curing injury and disease. Yet it was the Ellowans we first contacted when our wayfarers passed through the wormhole. They were resistant to outside influence, and we respected their desire for isolation."

"Apparently they were busy terrorizing the Tseirs."

"Our reports on Franconia appear to be faulty. Our research indicated the Ellowans, not the Tseirs, as the dominant culture."

Dane considered another matter. Knowing how the Candorians detested aggression, he was hesitant to broach the subject. "Shall I bring arms?"

"It is against our code to enter a world with violent intent, but you may have need of defense. You are well skilled in riflery. Used wisely, with caution, your weapon will serve you well."

Kostbera studied Dane's face and she smiled. "You have practiced long enough. I think you are more than ready for this journey."

Dane met Kostbera's eyes and a slow comprehension formed in his mind. Until now, he had considered the Candorians elusive and without emotion.

"I have watched you turn from a boy to a man. Everything has been easy for you, Dane. Study, technology, weapons. You get along with equal ease in primitive worlds and among the Candorians. For this reason, it pleases me to know that you will be tested by the Keiroits."

Dane frowned. "I can't imagine how that would be pleasing."

"She is not so easily charmed, I think." Kostbera seemed unusually pleased by this, and she chuckled. "Your ability to adapt to whatever situation you encounter will see you through. Find the reality of Franconia; then trust your heart."

"Vague advice, Kostbera."

Kostbera didn't expound on her meaning. "You may take from Candor's stores anything you need for the journey."

"There is only one thing I need on this journey. Carob could use a little adventure."

Kostbera touched Dane's shoulder. "The lingbat is old, Dane. He may not be strong enough for such a journey. But ask him. It will please his pride."

Dane didn't want to hear this. He couldn't go on the journey without Carob beside him. "I'll ask him. For one thing, I'd like to see the little fellow put Aiyana in her place."

"Her place . . ." Kostbera sighed. "I wonder where that is."

Dane returned to the lingbat tunnels, but a small, round female met him and barred the way. Dane recognized Carob's mate. "Is he sleeping?"

The female lingbat didn't understand. Carob had been given the capacity for speech by a Thorwalian mind probe. Though Dane had created a similar probe on Candor, he had found no other lingbat willing to undergo the procedure.

The lingbat flared her wings, a warning sign, and Dane turned away. After a long nap, Carob would be more likely to accept the offer of adventure.

Dane went to the library of Nerotania and searched the

files on Franconia. As Kostbera had said, little information was available. The section referring to Keiroits had even less. Dane selected an image of the creatures. What he saw turned his stomach.

Large, bulgy eyes, one larger and more dominant than the other, protruded from soft, green flesh. Octagonal scales covered a Keiroit's body, and the feet and hands were webbed. "How repulsive! I should have guessed she'd look like this."

Dane set aside the image. The Keiroits were amphibious, and indeed fragile to any alteration in climate. He wasn't sure why he felt disappointed. Aiyana's nature seemed appropriate to her appearance.

Dane left the library and headed toward the Candorian armory. Every wall in Nerotania was decorated with artwork, the remnants of a forgotten race. Little was known of the people who had founded the underground city. They had left ages before the Candorians arrived.

The art spoke of a passionate, fun-loving society. Theater, music, games, and feasts seemed to occupy their time. Their appreciation for pleasure filled every wall. Dane's eyes darkened when he spotted a scene of graphic lovemaking.

Dane's pace slowed as his body reacted to the entwined limbs. A slender, lithe woman lay on top of a man, her head tipped back, her long, black hair streaming around them both. Even in the faded mosaic, Dane felt her passion.

"I have been too long without a woman." Dane shook his head and forced himself beyond the taunting portrait of love. The corridor forked, but Dane didn't choose the route to the armory, as he had intended. Instead, he headed down a too-familiar corridor.

Through an arched doorway, he saw Kostbera's daughter taking notes. "Selena. Am I disturbing you?"

The young woman looked up, revealing no emotion at Dane's arrival. Her skin was translucent, her eyes silver and calm. Her hair shimmered between gold and silver, wound in a long twist down her slender back.

Since his arrival on Candor, Selena had intrigued him by her complete lack of interest in him.

"No, you are not disturbing me."

Selena turned back to her work. Dane looked over her shoulder, resisting the temptation to touch her. "Medical notes?"

Selena didn't look up. "It should be possible to engage various bacteria—"

"Never mind." Dane adjusted Selena's chair so that she faced him. She eyed him doubtfully, but didn't resist. "Have you heard that I'm leaving?"

"Yes." No emotion. "You will probably have contact with the Ellowans. If they don't kill you, I hope you will question them on their healing skills."

"They don't sound like very congenial people."

Selena set aside her notes. "No, they're not. They are much more likely to kill you. But before they do, you might get a chance to send a message here. Anything they've learned about healing would be valuable."

Dane remembered a time when sympathy garnered female attention. It might work. "I might never return," he said casually.

"No, you probably won't."

Apparently Selena was immune to sympathy. Dane sighed. He didn't know why he cared. Probably because of boredom. No other Candorian female appeared as young as Selena, but she treated him like a bacterial specimen.

Dane knelt before her and seized her hand. Her brow rose skeptically. "Selena, I have tried to win your favor. Tell me what I must do, and I will do it."

"Why should you desire my favor?"

Dane sighed impatiently. "I desire you!"

"For what purpose?"

Dane's jaw clenched. "Sex." There, he'd said it. "Do you know how long I've been without a woman?"

Selena appeared blank, and a little confused. "Do you mean you want to put portions of your body into mine? Why?"

"For pleasure."

Selena's eyes wandered to one side. "Is that why you visit me?"

Dane nodded.

Selena considered this for a long moment. Then she laughed. Dane had never seen her laugh before. She was beautiful when she laughed, but this wasn't the right time. Selena's mirth finally abated. She looked at him, then laughed again. Dane released her hand.

"Is it so hard to imagine?"

"Yes." Selena dried her eyes, still chuckling. "We're not even the same race. True, one day I will take a mate, but it won't be you."

Dane stood, frowning. "Why not?"

"Many reasons. You are not a member of the Intersystem. You seem agreeable enough, and your biological structure is strong, but you're quite primitive."

Dane rolled his eyes. He hated defeat. "And if I were a member of the Intersystem, would you consider me then?"

Selena shrugged. "Possibly. I suppose I have to mate with someone eventually." She swiveled her chair back to its original position. "If the Ellowans don't kill you, and if you return, and if Kostbera recommends you to the Intersystem Council, I'll consider you." She paused. "I don't know about the sex part, though."

It was enough. Not exactly a defeat. But now it was time to leave Candor and Dane wanted more. He seized Selena's chair, spun her around, and kissed her. Her lips felt cold. They didn't part or soften.

Dane drew back and she looked up at him as if a specimen had performed unexpectedly. "You put your lips on mine. Do you know that bacteria can be spread that way?"

Dane nodded, a pained expression on his face. He turned away.

"There are small crevices in lips that harbor germs."

Dane headed for the doorway.

"I don't think you should do that again."

Dane sighed. "I won't."

Dane closed the door behind him and drew a long breath. "It is definitely time I leave Candor."

"You can say that again. What a pathetic display!"

For an instant, Dane thought Carob had awakened to taunt him again. But that voice cut into him, and through him. Aiyana had appeared around a corner, somehow radiating pleasure at his humiliation.

"Do I take it Keiroits specialize in overhearing matters that are none of their concern?"

Aiyana laughed, then sauntered over to him, her hands on what passed for hips in the amorphous drape of her wrapping. "We specialize in amusing ourselves. Watching your sorry performance at seduction was well worth the effort."

"Have you been following me, Keiroit? If so, I think we need to establish some rules of good behavior before I head off to rescue your miserable world."

"Your head will be on an Ellowan stake, Thorwalian, and I'll be through with you. You would be wiser to remain here and pester your Candorian maiden."

"Shouldn't you be bathing in mud, Keiroit? I understand your scales fall off if not kept sufficiently moist."

"The environmental control beneath my wrapping keeps me in prime condition."

Dane surveyed Aiyana's outline and compared it to what he had seen in the library. "Your feet are small for a Keiroit."

"We're not cut from a mold, Thorwalian. We come in

different sizes. I see you have been studying the races of Franconia."

"I have. Yours, I might add, is exactly as I imagined."

"As it happens, I checked on your world also. There is no reference to the planet of Thorwal, other than to say it's peopled with a barbaric race fond of throwing spears at short-legged pigs."

"That information is sadly dated, Keiroit. Much has evolved since the Candorians recorded that ancient description of our culture."

"Now you throw rocks."

Dane couldn't resist smiling. Aiyana's brain seemed quick, neither literal, as were the Thorwalians, nor sublime as the Candorians tended to be.

"Thorwal is a technological world, made great by its alliance with a neighboring planet, Dakota. Together we developed space flight and progressed rapidly. Only four hundred years ago, my people were known as Ravagers, and a more bloodthirsty, passionate people never existed. Today we are logical, stoic individuals, relying on our intellect rather than our physical prowess."

Aiyana made an odd snorting noise. "I see no evidence of any change whatsoever. The term *Ravager* fits you admirably."

Several Candorians passed by, each bearing supplies for the Franconian vessel. "It seems our time of departure nears." Dane started down the hallway, and Aiyana followed.

"You are unwise to accompany us."

"You keep saying that. Why?"

"I dislike you intensely."

Dane laughed. "I find you equally repugnant. However, I take a certain warped pleasure in your company. Before we leave, I have a final task. If you wish to join me, then follow."

* * *

Aiyana stopped, resisting the desire to follow. The Thorwalian was baiting her, teasing her curiosity. She didn't care about his final task. No, she had done her part. She had warned him as best she could. If he went to Franconia, he would never return.

Aiyana stood alone in the hallway, watching the Candorians pass to and fro. Her wrapping diminished her vision, but she couldn't adjust it without revealing herself. Beneath her headdress, Aiyana frowned. She saw Dane far down the hallway. He was taller than the Candorians, and much stronger.

The Candorians looked pale, colorless to Aiyana's hidden eyes. Dane Calydon was vibrant. Alive. Aiyana sighed. The force of life flowed through him, so strongly that she almost felt it herself.

Aiyana didn't want to feel. It was too late to feel. She had to stop Dane from going to Franconia. She told herself it was for his sake and not her own.

Dane disappeared around a corner. Aiyana darted down the hall after him. He entered a dark passageway, and Aiyana followed. "Thorwalian!"

Dane stopped and waited. Aiyana saw the veiled smile on his face, the anticipation of further argument. She wondered why it pleased him. Perhaps his primitive soul found no conflict on Candor, and missed the thrill of battle.

"Aiyana. Just in time to meet your new shipmate."

"What shipmate?"

Dane pointed to a small passageway, much too small for humans to enter. "Carob! I have a surprise for you."

After a moment, Aiyana heard a strange scuffling noise. A small, round head peeked out of the tunnel, pointy ears twitching in irritation. She fought an impulse to laugh.

"What is that creature?"

The small creature pulled itself out from the tunnel and flapped itself to Dane's shoulder. "I am a lingbat. We are flightless, winged rodents, although with practice we become excellent gliders. What are you?''

''This is Aiyana, Carob. She is a Keiroit from the system of Franconia. While you napped, I accepted an assignment on that world. . . .''

Carob chuckled. ''Franconia . . . I take it you'll be dealing with the Ellowans after all.''

''Not if I can help it. We are to assist the Tseirs and Aiyana's noble Keiroits as they struggle to find a solution to the conflict.''

''We?''

''I want you to come with me, Carob. Like old times.''

Aiyana looked between the man and the lingbat. Carob seemed more like a grumpy old man than a rodent. ''He talks.''

''He does, and too much, at that. We made the mistake of applying a Thorwalian mind probe and teaching him language. I often regret it, but his advice is usually sound.''

''Always sound. But you won't be getting it on this trip. I'm too old for travel, boy. Too old for much of anything. Maybe I'll sire one more litter—''

''You're not old. Just lazy.''

Carob shook his small head. ''I wouldn't make the journey. Too much stress. Especially if you're piloting the vessel.''

''My piloting skills have neared perfection.''

''Tell that to the pyramid you nicked.''

Aiyana laughed. ''Is he a bad pilot? I should have guessed.''

Carob turned his attention to Aiyana. For an uncomfortable moment, she thought he saw beneath her wrapping. But the bat chuckled softly. ''Keiroit, are you?''

''I am.''

''Well, well.'' Carob chuckled again. ''Sorry to miss it. Don't know what he'll do without a lingbat's guidance.''

"He would be wisest to remain here."

Dane set Carob back in the tunnel entrance. "Our Keiroit ally underestimates my abilities. I must save her world to earn her respect."

"Can't do it alone." The lingbat disappeared without explanation.

"Where is he going?" Aiyana peered down the tunnel, but though she heard squeaks and scurrying, she saw nothing.

Dane shrugged. "I have no idea."

They waited, and finally Carob emerged again. Behind him was another lingbat, much smaller and weaker-looking than Carob himself. The little lingbat appeared forlorn and shy.

Dane glanced at the small creature. "What is this?"

"This is one of my last litter sons. Thought you might want to take him with you."

"What is he called, and is he willing to undergo the mind probe?"

"He's willing." Carob shot the smaller lingbat a distinctly forbidding look. "As for his name, now, that's a series of squeaks to us. Means 'He Who Flames with Courage.' "

Both the small lingbat and Dane eyed Carob with misgivings. The name hardly seemed appropriate. "We'll pick something . . . easier once he starts speaking."

Dane reached for the small bat, but it backed away. Carob swatted the little creature with a wing tip, and it moved dutifully to Dane's hand.

Aiyana cleared her throat. "He doesn't seem exactly enthusiastic. What good is such a creature?"

"You'd be surprised, Keiroit." Dane picked up the small bat and Carob fluttered to his shoulder. "We'll take this little fellow to the lab and see what he has to say for himself."

Aiyana followed Dane and the lingbats to the lab. There she watched them apply tiny probes to the small lingbat's head and body. Dane flipped through a series of dials while Carob squeaked and chirped.

As Dane worked, Aiyana studied him covertly. He was a large man, larger than the males of her world. Larger than the Tseirs. His hair was the color of the desert sand beneath a white sun. His skin was golden, darker than that of the pale Tseirs.

Aiyana didn't understand. For his size and obvious strength, Dane Calydon was surprisingly gentle. He allowed the old lingbat to tease him, to offer advice. Dane even appeared to consider the peculiar creature's comments. He smiled quickly, easily. As if life had been easy, and offered no sorrow.

"What kind of warrior are you?" Aiyana didn't realize she had spoken aloud, but Dane looked over his shoulder and smiled.

"A warrior with no battle, so far. I've been in one near-war, been imprisoned, and came here. What I hoped would be a test of manhood has been a test of patience, instead."

Aiyana didn't answer. Dane wasn't boastful. His pride didn't overwhelm his reason. Yet he seemed strong and fearless. Confident of his abilities, and more, of his ability to adapt.

Despite his size, Dane's face was almost sweet. His full lips curved easily into a smile; his fluid, strong features formed quick, teasing expressions. No, nothing had hurt this man; nothing had cut him to the quick, or destroyed his faith in life.

Something about Dane Calydon disturbed Aiyana deeply. She forced her attention back to the lingbat. "There is nothing like this on my world."

"Count yourself fortunate." Dane turned on the machine, which lit up and buzzed. The lingbat's eyes closed, and Aiyana held her breath, wondering if the probe had killed him. Dane switched off the probe and waited.

The small lingbat's eyes opened, round and surprised. The creature cleared his throat, evidently feeling the change. He coughed and sputtered, making guttural noises for several minutes. He puffed up his chest, righted himself, and hopped across the platform to Dane.

"Sir! I shall endeavor to serve you to the best of my abilities. You will not be sorry for choosing me to replace my sire as your guide."

Aiyana looked at Dane. A veiled smile softened his face, and his eyes glittered like the sun on a blue river. He obviously took pleasure in life, in strange creatures, in circumstances that provided humor. She remembered when she had been the same, and her heart ran cold.

Dane held out his hand for the bat. "What shall I call you? He Who Flames with Courage seems . . . long."

"I don't have a name, as such. But I am a lingbat, like my sire. You may call me Bat."

"Bat? Rather unimaginative, isn't it?"

The lingbat shrugged. "Then Batty. That's more friendly, isn't it? Batty. I'll just ride on your shoulder as my sire does. . . . No trouble at all."

Before Dane could speak, the bat hurled itself toward his shoulder. It flapped madly, digging in with its claws to balance itself. A small wing tip caught in Dane's hair. The bat tugged frantically, trying to free itself.

Dane closed his eyes as Aiyana stared in amazement. The claws dug into his flesh, and Dane winced. "Would you watch that?"

"Whoops! Sorry, there, sir!"

Dane stood still, his face frozen in irritation as the animal fluttered around, trying desperately to disentangle himself. Dane's jaw clenched. Aiyana suspected he wanted to smack the little rodent. The lingbat sensed his irritation, which had the effect of further upsetting it.

"Sorry, sir. Half a moment, if you please."

"Why did I do it? I might have journeyed peacefully to the comparatively sane world of the Ellowans. But no . . . Once again, I have a little winged rodent caught in my hair."

"There!" Batty freed himself and settled upon Dane's shoulder. "Takes a bit of getting used to. Used to hanging upside down, you understand."

Aiyana shook her head. "This is not promising, Thorwalian."

Dane smiled at her, then looked for Carob. The old lingbat was asleep. An expression of sorrow crossed Dane's face. He gently lifted the bat and sighed. Batty sighed, too.

"Happens all the time. I'll be on a feeding expedition with my sire, and he'll drop off. Last night he fell asleep in the middle of feeding. Insect half eaten . . . Tragic."

Dane grimaced. "I suppose your diet is similarly disgusting."

"It is, sir." Batty sounded apologetic, and Aiyana laughed.

"Wait until you learn what the Keiroits eat, Thorwalian."

"I already know. Raw fish. But that is tolerable."

Aiyana followed him from the lab. "Yes, but when we eat them, they're still alive."

Galya and Aiyana were waiting on the Franconian vessel when Dane emerged from Nerotania. Dane took one last look at Candor's scarlet sky. Batty perched on his shoulder, chirping and twitching with excitement. Kostbera held Carob, but the old bat's eyes were closed.

"I have sent word to your sister of your journey, Dane. I made no mention of the danger. As I understand it, she is with child, and needs no further stress."

"Tell her I love her. That is all she needs to know."

Carob woke suddenly. "Take care of my litter son, boy. I expect a good story when you return."

"If it follows the course of my life so far, there will be peace by the time I get there."

"That Ellowan won't give you any peace, boy. I told you once, an Ellowan female will put you in your place. It seems I was right."

"I probably won't be meeting any Ellowan females, Carob." Dane scratched behind Carob's ear, but the lingbat had already fallen asleep.

Dane sighed and turned away. The Franconian vessel was larger than any Thorwalian spacecraft. Its hull was black rather than metallic, and the power system worked silently. Inside, Dane discovered a spacious, open room.

Galya was seated near the central platform, but Aiyana stood looking out a large viewport. She didn't turn when Dane entered. "Where is your crew?"

Galya rose. "We have no crew, Dane. Our craft are completely mechanized. These systems plot the course and will deliver us to Franconia, where we will be landed by planetary guidance systems."

Dane studied the computer systems. "I have some knowledge of these functions, but this is beyond our present capacity."

Galya appeared uninterested in the workings of her craft. "We control great power on Franconia. How it works is of no importance." She glanced over her shoulder. "Aiyana, please direct the computers for our return flight."

Aiyana engaged a small panel, then seated herself across from Dane. "You were a fool to come, Thorwalian."

Dane ignored her warning. "Don't we strap in?"

"It's not necessary." As Galya spoke, the large vessel lifted from Candor's surface. Dane went to the viewport and watched the surface of Candor fade into an amber haze. In seconds, the vessel passed through the atmosphere to the outer rings.

Beyond the moon, the bright, gaseous planet of Candor took Dane's breath away. "It's magnificent, isn't it?"

Batty whistled, but seemed to be trembling. "I can't help thinking I was safer in my sire's tunnels."

"Safer, yes . . . But have you ever seen anything this glorious, Batty?"

"No. And I don't want to see it again."

"Life is for living, Batty, not for avoiding death."

Galya came to stand beside Dane. "There are many glorious sights in our galaxy. You will find Franconia pleasurable. When we arrive, there is much I can show you."

Dane glanced at Galya. He recognized a seductive light in her eyes, but his body didn't respond. Maybe the years of rejection had rendered him incapable.

Aiyana sat quietly, looking at nothing. She seemed resigned to his presence. Dane couldn't resist provoking her. He seated himself beside her. She tensed, but said nothing.

"What about you, Keiroit? Has your world wonders to show me?"

"Only if raw fish interests you. Leave me in peace, Thorwalian. When we enter the wormhole, much is rendered askew. We will lose consciousness, so it is important to be seated."

"So I've read while researching this subject. It must be hard on your soft insides and scales to endure the pressure of transition."

Aiyana didn't answer. Dane knew she didn't want to talk. All the more reason to engage her in conversation. "Tell me of the Ellowans. For all my study, I learned even less about their race than about yours."

"What do you want to know?"

"I understand they have healing powers. Tell me of that."

"They are able to heal even the gravest injuries, using a strange biological technique. That is all I know."

"It seems odd to me that a violent race like the Ellowans should possess such a skill."

Aiyana said nothing, but Galya seated herself beside Dane. "We Tseirs speculate that the Ellowan ability to heal explains their tendency toward violence. Short of death, they can quickly heal each other from anything. For this reason, fighting them has been difficult."

"Then they have no interest in negotiation?"

Aiyana answered. "None." She rose from her seat and went to the viewport. As Candor faded in the distance, a black hole emerged on the screen. In its depths, the stars didn't shine, and only faint light glowed around the entrance.

"Steady yourself, Thorwalian. Your journey begins now."

"Where are we? Aiyana!" Galya's shrill voice woke Dane from his sleep. The Franconian vessel was lowering to the surface of a small, dark planet.

Galya clutched her hands to her breast. "Our course has gone wrong. Aiyana, what happened?"

Aiyana studied the computer settings. "Our vessel has been sabotaged. We are in orbit around Keir."

Dane rose to his feet. "Keir? Your homeworld?"

"We can't do that!" Galya sounded panicked.

"Why not? The Keiroits are your allies, aren't they?"

Galya sank down into her seat. "They are. But the Ellowans overtook their planet, Dane. Most Keiroits fled to Franconia after the Ellowan invasion. The few that remain are isolated in the swamp beyond the Ellowan-held forest."

Aiyana seemed unperturbed. "We can reach the Keiroit holdings and then find easy transport to Franconia."

"What about the Ellowans?"

Dane couldn't see her face, but he knew Aiyana smiled. "We will have to avoid them."

Aiyana stood by the viewport, her concealed eyes fixed on the surface of Keir. It wouldn't be an easy landing, but she had known that all along. It had been a risk. She saw the dark Ellowan-held forest, and her quick fingers adjusted the computer setting.

The Franconian vessel lurched, then lowered. Aiyana heard Galya's harsh, terrified gasps. She glanced back toward Dane. He sat calmly, but the lingbat scurried from his shoulder and hid beneath Dane's cape. Aiyana felt a pang of sympathy for the little creature, then forced herself to turn away. She had given up sympathy ages ago.

"The landing will be rough." It had to be rough. Everything depended on that.

The vessel began to shake as it plummeted through the atmosphere. "I warned you, Thorwalian."

The computer made adjustments, and the craft slowed. Aiyana didn't move. She saw the dark green haze of trees far below. The forest stretched endlessly across the northern rim of Keir. Night moved across the rolling hills, as the last light of the white sun glinted on a high ridge.

"It must be possible to land this vessel under manual control." Dane spoke right behind her. Aiyana was startled.

"What are you doing, Thorwalian? You must strap in for whatever landing the computer makes. There is no time. . . ."

Dane's quick eyes scanned the control panel. "This was designed for manual operation, Keiroit. The computer control is the backup. I should be able to work this. . . ."

Aiyana shoved him away. "Are you crazy? There's no time."

Dane seated himself at the helm. "Where is the Keiroit hold?"

Aiyana froze, but Galya came to the viewport. "Is it possible, Dane? Can you direct this craft?"

"Possibly."

"He cannot!" Aiyana glanced down at the surface of Keir. The controls were set. If Dane fiddled with them now . . . "He must not!"

"Too late." Dane adjusted the control panel, and the vessel lurched upward. "We're too close to pull out, but I should be able to guide us to a chosen landing."

Galya clasped his shoulder. "The Keiroit hold is near the equator of the planet, below the mountain range that separates the Ellowan-held forest from the Swamp of Keir. We should be able to see it."

Aiyana's heart pounded. The lingbat had said Dane wasn't a good pilot, but his quick hands were proving otherwise. He had control of the vessel. Galya might not know the exact geography of Keir, but she was close enough. Aiyana had no choice.

While Dane focused the trajectory toward the swamp, Aiyana engaged the panel to override his attempts. The vessel spun out of control, plummeting toward the mountains.

Galya stumbled back. "Dane! You were in control. What happened?"

Dane tried his code again. "Nothing's responding. . . . The computer regained control. And we're going to crash."

A small squeak came from beneath his cloak. "I should have stayed in the tunnels. Oh, what a world!"

Dane tried again, then banged his fist in frustration. "I suggest you both strap in. I'll try to regain control. There's still a chance."

Galya obeyed his advice, but Aiyana didn't move. "This vessel is designed to protect the occupants in a crash, Thorwalian. Assuming they obey standard procedures. You must strap in, too."

Dane looked back at her, his blue eyes on fire. "I didn't

come on this journey to be protected, Keiroit. And I'd rather not land in Ellowan territory, not if there's a chance of avoiding it.''

Galya adjusted her restraints. ''He's right, Aiyana. The Ellowans kill Tseirs on sight.''

Aiyana closed her eyes beneath the hood. The vessel shook and jerked, heading for the northern side of the mountain range—For the uncertain zone claimed by both Ellowans and Keiroits. It was not the landing she had chosen.

''Seat yourself, Thorwalian. It is too late.''

''If I can rework the circuits . . .'' Dane yanked off the control panel's plastic cover and began working among the vast collection of wires and circuits. He wouldn't give up.

Aiyana knew his choice was made. Hers had been made long ago. She had to survive. She seated herself, and strapped herself in for a violent landing. Her heart beat slow and steady as the Franconian craft reached the tree line.

The high branches of the forest shattered against the black hull. Galya screamed, but Aiyana didn't open her eyes. The viewport cracked, then fragmented. She heard Dane curse.

The force of the crash snapped Aiyana forward in her seat, but the protective casing held. Aiyana shook, but she unfastened herself and shoved aside the casing. Smoke billowed and rose as the power seeped from the casing's hidden linings.

Sparks popped from the panel; broken circuits sizzled with uninsulated electricity. Ominous crackling noises sounded from deep within the vessel's power core. Aiyana looked for Dane. Nothing moved.

Galya seemed terrified as she fumbled with her own casing. ''We have to get out of here. There could be an explosion. Aiyana, lower the ramp.''

Aiyana didn't listen. She searched near the panel for Dane, but saw nothing amidst the smoke and fumes. A small, petrified squeak emerged amidst the wreckage of the Franconian vessel.

"Help!"

Aiyana followed the sound. Dane lay on his back, his sweet face calm and still, as if asleep. He had fought to the end, until the vessel crashed, trying to regain control of the vessel without realizing that she had made it impossible.

Aiyana had seen death many times. She was steeled to loss. But Dane Calydon had lived and died without finding anything he sought. Her heart quailed and she knelt beside him. To her wonder, tears stung her eyes.

"Help!"

Aiyana eased Dane's cloak back, and the lingbat emerged, trembling, eyes round as platters. Blood stained the front of Dane's white shirt, seeping across his wide chest, over his ribs. Aiyana adjusted his cloak to cover him, but her hand touched his skin, and she felt life.

Barely. But Dane was alive. Somewhere within, he clung to life, unwilling to surrender before his life truly began. Aiyana felt that. She felt him. She felt the wild power inside him, stronger than she had imagined. He didn't want to die.

Aiyana shuddered beneath the weight of her decision. Then she rose to her feet and faced Galya. "The Thorwalian lives. Help me move him outside."

Galya's mouth dropped and she glanced at Dane. "He'll die anyway. We have to get out of here before the Ellowans come. This ship is ruined."

Aiyana's expression hardened beneath the hood. "If you want the help of the Keiroits to get out of here, you will move this man as I ask."

"The Keiroits have always been unreasonable. I don't know why we continue to maintain relations."

"I do. Weapons, Galya. We fight for you. We do what you have no courage to do. We kill with our hands . . . And our teeth."

Galya grimaced, but she didn't argue. "We need your help, it's true. But what do you want with this man?"

"What we both want, Galya. We need his help, do we not? To gain the aid of the Candorians, to defeat the vile Ellowans. Isn't that why we traveled to Candor?"

Galya hesitated. "It is. Of course. If he can be saved, we must save him." Galya looked down at Dane. "That doesn't seem possible, though. Only an Ellowan could save him, and they're not likely—"

"We move him, now."

Aiyana took one of Dane's legs, and Galya took the other. "Pulling him around like this will probably kill him, Aiyana."

The lingbat fluttered to Aiyana's shoulder, still shaking. He chirped as Aiyana backed down the ramp, dragging Dane's body. "If he wasn't broken before, he is now. My sire will never forgive me if Dane doesn't come back whole."

Aiyana didn't listen. She dragged Dane from the ship, then stopped to rest. Galya looked around. "What now, Aiyana? We're in the middle of the forest, well to the north of the Keir Mountains. Look at this place. Trees everywhere, no paths. We can't drag him all the way to the Keiroit hold."

"There is no need."

Aiyana knelt beside Dane. She bent low and touched her palm to his forehead. He felt cool and smooth, a perfect strength deep inside him. Her heart ached. If she woke him, he could destroy her.

The choice was made, and Aiyana's trance began. Her hands worked over him; the essence of her body reached inside him. An ancient art swelled inside her and passed into him, finding his strength and using it to heal him.

Dane was near death. That he lived at all astonished her. He should be dead. His body had endured massive trauma in the crash. *Do you desire life? Shall I heal you?*

Aiyana heard his reply, strong and sure. *I desire life.*

It was settled. *Then yield to me. I will heal you.*

Their words passed unspoken, yet were clear. Aiyana taught his muscles to knit themselves; she taught his blood vessels to realign, his bones to mend. And he was healed.

Aiyana went weak, but she knew she had to get away. She heard Galya's sharp hiss of shock when Dane moved. She heard the lingbat's surprised, happy chirp. Her pity had brought disaster. Again.

"Sir! You made it! Thank the stars, but I couldn't have returned to my sire saying I lost you the first day."

Dane felt warm, tingly. He felt no pain. Dane opened his eyes and sat up. Aiyana sat apart from him, her head bowed. She seemed to be gathering strength.

"You're alive!" Galya sounded more shocked than pleased. "Dane, she healed you."

"I know." The meaning dawned slowly on Dane, parting the warm blur of his healing. He looked at Aiyana. Her head was still wrapped. She glanced between him and Galya, then rose wearily to her feet.

"She healed you." Galya grabbed Dane's arm as he stood up. "Do you know what that means?"

"I know."

Aiyana froze, then backed away. For a moment, Dane thought she looked too weak to run, but when she sprang away, she moved like a woodland deer.

Dane forgot his injuries as he leaped after her. Her cumbersome wrapping slowed her, and Dane bounded up behind her. He grabbed her arm and pulled her to the ground. She fell beneath him and he moved to pull away her hood.

"You can't do that!" Her voice sounded wild, desperate.

"I think I must."

"I'll die!" Aiyana twisted beneath him, her head flailing

from side to side. "I'll die. I just saved you, and you're killing me."

"I don't think so."

Galya came up behind them. Batty hopped from branch to branch and looked down. "I must be missing something. She saved you, yes, sir? That was a good thing. You were a goner, as I saw it. She's not bad, is she?"

Dane couldn't answer. His hands shook as he pulled aside the hood. More wrapping concealed the creature within. If he killed her . . .

"I can't live outside the swamp! Not even here! You're killing me, Dane Calydon!" Aiyana squirmed and fought, but her strength was less than a Keiroit's was rumored to be.

Dane pulled away the inner wrapping. The creature lying beneath him defied his imagining. The hideous beast was a young woman garbed in a cumbersome robe. Her eyes were squeezed shut. Her black, soft hair coiled in a thick braid over her shoulder, framing the most beautiful face he'd ever seen.

"Aiyana . . ."

Her eyes opened, and Dane's heart stopped. They were wide and green, tilted upward at the corners, fringed with black lashes, filled with emotion.

"You're . . . *perfect.*"

Her small, delicate features contorted in fury and disgust. Her exquisite, bowed lips pursed. With all the effort of her soul, Aiyana spat.

Accurately.

Dane closed his eyes and sighed. "Your beauty is the real disguise, Aiyana. Your nature is as scaly as I imagined."

Chapter Two

Dane held Aiyana beneath him. He had no idea what to do with her. She struggled wildly, but he pinned her arms down.

"I will kill you!"

"I have no doubt."

Aiyana's green eyes burned with fury. "Let me go."

"For a creature as small and fragile as yourself, you make many demands. Releasing you might be deemed unwise."

Galya looked down at Aiyana. "She is Ellowan, Dane. Beware. There's nothing fragile about her. An Ellowan female is the most dangerous creature of all."

"I'm not surprised to hear that."

Dane's gaze lingered on Aiyana's face. He had never seen anything so beautiful. He wanted to watch her, to study her in exquisite, painstaking detail. As her eyes closed and opened, as she drew breath, as her lips formed expressions. He thought he might kill to see her smile.

Aiyana frowned. "Know this, Thorwalian. You are on the

edge of the Ellowan hold, and you are in supreme danger from both Keiroits and Ellowans. Release me, and I will take you safely to our leader."

Dane laughed. "You have gall. It seems wiser to go to the Keiroits you impersonated, and travel as far away from your wood as we can get. But, beautiful Aiyana, what do I do with you?"

Galya's eyes widened. "What do you mean? You can't release this female! She will tell them of our visit to Candor, and the Ellowans will intensify their attacks."

Dane looked up at Galya, fighting a wave of irritation. Galya seemed feminine, but her nature had a domineering edge he found grating. "It isn't my intention to release her. Not yet. But this is her world. I suspect she traveled in disguise to learn your intentions with the Candorians."

Aiyana nodded. "That is true. And I learned the Tseirs treat with alien races to annihilate my people. You, for instance, are willing to counsel with the Tseirs, about whom you know nothing, yet you fear to enter the Ellowan hold."

Galya's expression darkened. "Beware, Dane. Much of the Ellowan female's power is in seduction. She attempts to lull you into submission. It was the curse of many a Tseir male before we realized the depth of their powers."

Cold fury glittered in Aiyana's green eyes. But Dane knew now what it meant to be spellbound. He didn't doubt Galya's claim. As he looked down into Aiyana's face, knowing she was his enemy, his thoughts nonetheless wandered to the way the dark forest reflected in her eyes.

"You can't release her, Dane. If you do, she'll bring the whole tribe of Ellowan warriors down upon us. And the Ellowans don't take prisoners."

"We don't take Tseir prisoners. Thorwalians, however, we may consider."

Dane considered releasing her. Part of him longed to set her free, to watch her run into the dark forest, her black hair streaming behind her. His rational mind overtook his imagination. "I will keep you as a hostage, Aiyana, and a guide. When we reach the outskirts of the Keiroits' swamp, I will release you to return to your people, unharmed."

Aiyana rolled her eyes, her lips curved in a frown. "How big a fool do you think me? Keep me as a hostage, Thorwalian, if you dare. But don't expect me to guide you toward my enemies. The Keiroits don't subsist on raw fish only. Their taste for live Ellowan is renowned among our people."

Aiyana chuckled at Dane's aghast expression. "They might enjoy Thorwalian meat for a change."

Galya clenched her fist. "She is lying, Dane. The Keiroits are powerful fighters, and they hate the Ellowans, but they pose no danger to us. We must reach their hold, and find safe transport to Franconia."

"They don't eat Tseirs. Why is that, do you think?"

Dane started to get up, but Galya stopped him. "She must be bound, tightly, and you must check her for weapons."

"I can't believe she would have come this far armed, Galya."

"Check her."

Dane pulled Aiyana to her feet. She stood straight and fierce, her chin high, her eyes burning. "I am unarmed."

"We'll see." Dutifully, Dane patted her outline. He started to shake his head, to assure Galya that Aiyana carried no weapon.

His hand bumped something large and metallic beneath Aiyana's heavy cloak. Dane's brow rose in surprise. He fumbled beneath her robe and withdrew a full-size rifle.

Dane met Aiyana's eyes. Her small chin lifted defiantly, and he smiled. "An Ellowan rifle, I presume."

Dane ran his hands along Aiyana's concealed body. Another lump met his touch. He sighed, then drew out a curved sword. It glowed with a pale green light. "An Ellowan saber? Naturally. And will I find a ground-hugging tank beneath these folds?''

Aiyana said nothing, but when Dane retrieved the saber's companion dagger, she cast her gaze upward, faintly guilty. Dane laughed when he located a whetting knife tucked into the ties of her cloth boots.

Dane ran his hands over her again, to see if he had missed anything, then stood back. ''Rumors of your violence haven't been exaggerated, I see. You carry arms enough to storm a planet.''

Aiyana didn't respond, but Galya appeared unsatisfied. ''She must be searched thoroughly, Dane.''

Dane glanced back at Galya. ''My search was thorough.''

Galya took a step closer. ''These weapons are nothing compared to what the Ellowan terrorists can do. They have a far more vile capacity for destruction.''

''What?''

''An explosive device, easily concealed, yet immensely destructive. Many of our outposts have been destroyed by these devices.''

''I found no explosive devices.''

''You wouldn't find them in such a gentle search. These devices are paper-thin. They would be taped to her skin, beneath her clothing.''

Dane hesitated. ''I see no need—''

''She must be thoroughly searched.'' Galya paused, as if she resisted saying the rest. ''Or it will be necessary to kill her, Dane. I don't want to do that, either. But she could destroy us all.''

''I will not kill her.''

A secret gleam lit in Galya's eye. ''Then I'm afraid you must search her.''

Dane looked into Aiyana's beautiful face. She appeared defiant, proud, but beneath that, he saw her fear. ''I don't want to do this." He didn't, more than he had realized. He couldn't strip her before her enemy.

"Aiyana, if you have these explosives, tell me, and I will let you remove them."

Aiyana's jaw hardened. "I have no explosives."

Dane wanted to believe her. The stack of weapons caught his eye, and he wavered. She had said she was unarmed, too. "Aiyana . . ."

"I have answered you, Thorwalian."

Galya clutched his arm. "You can't trust her, Dane. She lied about the weapons. These explosives are far more destructive, and far more valuable to the Ellowans. You must search her."

Dane wanted adventure. He wanted to make decisions that mattered, to have a say in the outcome of fate. Instead, he was forced to strip a sweet-faced woman to discover weapons that could destroy an outpost.

He met her eyes. "Then I will search." Her chin quivered almost imperceptibly. She averted her gaze to the treetops as he pulled off her cloak. Galya stood beside him, waiting expectantly.

Dane glanced at Galya in irritation. He wasn't sure why she bothered him. She seemed passive, reasonable. In control. That was what bothered him. She wanted to control the way every situation unfolded. The uncontrollable. She wanted to control Aiyana.

"Maybe you would prefer to do this yourself, Galya."

Aiyana tensed at the suggestion. "I will not be touched by Tseir hands. I will fight to the death first!"

Galya shook her head, an expression of sympathy on her face. "You see, Dane. The Ellowans' hatred is deep. We did nothing to deserve their anger, yet they kill us without remorse. It would be best if you administered the search."

Dane turned back reluctantly to Aiyana. She wore a close-fitting cloth bodice, laced at the front. His quick fingers unlaced the top, but he stopped before exposing her flesh. When he lived on Thorwal, he had lived in sweet, reckless abandon. He had undressed women with unmatched skill, and had taken pleasure in the act. Now, Dane Calydon thought the act would make him ill.

He drew a breath, then eased the bodice over her shoulder. She wore nothing underneath. Her skin was the color of cream, soft and perfect. Her arms were slender, but strong. He lowered the bodice quickly, exposing one small, round breast.

Before he could stop himself, he took in the rose-colored peak of her breast, the soft swell fitted to his hand. His own arousal struck him with a hot wave of shame. He wanted to cover her, to treat her with dignity, to set her free.

"Look." Galya's voice broke Dane's trance. She pointed to the side of Aiyana's breast. A sheet of fine material was taped to her skin. "The explosive device. I told you it would be there."

"So you did."

Dane peeled the explosive from Aiyana's tender skin. It stuck, and Aiyana winced. His insides recoiled as she steeled herself against the pain. He tugged, and the device came off.

"There will be more. These devices must be attached to each other before they are workable."

Dane felt sick. He felt Aiyana's humiliation, felt her resistance. And he had no choice. He lowered the bodice from her other shoulder, exposing both breasts. He closed his eyes, but her naked image was emblazoned on his brain.

Both round, perfect breasts concealed explosives. Dane peeled the other from her skin, but his hand trembled at the touch of her flesh. Small red spots emerged where he had removed the tape.

A quick glance told him Aiyana's green eyes were wet with tears. But her tears didn't fall, just hovered like mist over a forest pool. Dane's throat constricted. He pulled her bodice apart, and found another sheet of explosive taped across her stomach.

"She is attempting to arouse you." Galya's voice shattered Dane's composure, but he didn't respond. "Don't you feel it? No Tseir male has been able to resist an Ellowan female's sexual allure."

Dane saw Aiyana's small fists clench. He saw her knuckles turn white. But he was aroused. As much as he hated himself for the reaction, his blood pounded in his veins, driving heat and fire to his groin. If Galya wasn't standing beside him, nothing would stop him from lowering Aiyana to the ground and making love to her. The temptation was almost overwhelming, anyway.

Maybe she was doing this, filling his blood with lust. But Dane never blamed another for what he carried within, and from the moment he had first looked into her eyes, he had wanted Aiyana.

He tore the sheet from her stomach, feeling her pain as his own. He untied her leggings and slid them from her slender hips. He lowered himself to one knee. His heart throbbed, half in desire, and half in revulsion at his own weakness. A perfect triangle of soft, dark hair crowned her womanhood, a sweet invitation despite Aiyana's intentions.

Dane bowed his head. He knew his position echoed that of the ancient Thorwalian Ravagers as they worshiped their goddesses. He knew now what it meant to feel shame. He had never known before.

Dane's hands trembled as he pulled down Aiyana's leggings. Taped to her inner thighs were two more sheets. Dane pulled them away, feeling her tense in pain, knowing she cried within.

His throat burned. His vision blurred with hot tears. He slid his hand down her leg to feel for more explosives. He ran his hand over the flare of her bottom. Desire stabbed through him like a fiery knife.

He imagined touching her this way when it brought her nothing but pleasure. Following the trail of his fingers with kisses, sweet and gentle, worshiping her. Instead, he humbled a being so perfect. . . .

Dane checked her back, but he found no more explosive sheets. He couldn't look at her. He turned to Galya.

"Is that enough? Are you satisfied?"

His voice sounded raw, hoarse. But Galya offered an understanding smile. "Before you surrender to pity, know that this is enough explosive to destroy an entire satellite."

Dane didn't care. He rose to his feet and pulled Aiyana's cloak over her shoulders. He couldn't meet her eyes. He stood between her and Galya, protecting her. Aiyana pulled her bodice together, but her hands shook too much to lace the ties.

"I'll do it." Dane didn't give her a chance to refuse. Her vulnerability despite her pride ripped at his soul.

She lifted her chin and looked away as he laced her bodice and tied her leggings. She was trembling, her breath coming quick and shallow. She tried to back away, but Dane clasped her shoulders. "I'm sorry."

With sudden force and courage, Aiyana met his eyes. "You were right. I was armed. I bore explosives. But the Tseir is wrong. With these, I could blow up far more than a satellite. I could destroy her world."

Galya sighed. "All Ellowans are this way. We tried to befriend them, to offer them our wisdom and guidance. We tried to advise them, and they returned our goodwill with a vicious attack. Save your pity, Dane. She doesn't want it." Galya moved around Dane and leaned toward Aiyana. "Do you, Aiyana?"

"I want one thing, Tseir. I want your destruction, and I will not rest until you are gone forever."

Dane's blood ran cold. He remembered Kostbera's cryptic words before he left Nerotania. *Hatred . . . so strong it might destroy anything in its path . . . As if that one, Aiyana, is already dead.*

Dane tore a portion of Aiyana's Keiroit wrapping into strips and bound her hands. Her fingers curled, gripping the binding as if to steady herself. He should be protecting her, holding her. . . .

"You must fight your arousal, Dane." Dane cringed at Galya's remark. "She is adept at using such wiles against you."

Aiyana didn't respond, but Dane felt her anger. It seemed more likely to him that the Ellowan allure wasn't intentional. But he could be wrong. He was easily moved to sympathy. But was it more so because the woman was flawless, more beautiful than his wildest imaginings?

Dane turned away from Aiyana and studied the landscape. The planet of Keir harbored giant, ancient trees that towered toward the deep blue sky. The air smelled of pine and moss. "I've never seen trees so tall, not even on Dakota, the planet that neighbors my own homeworld."

Batty jumped from his branch and landed on Dane's shoulder. He started to topple off, but Dane caught him and helped the lingbat into place. "My sire says Dakota has some of the finest insect specimens he's encountered. Used to tell me bedtime stories about the crunchy variety. Soft, chewy middles, juicy . . ."

Dane groaned, but his heart lightened. "I trust you'll find suitable feeding arrangements, Batty . . . without sharing the details with me."

"As you say, sir." Batty sounded wistful. He looked over at Aiyana. "What are you going to feed her, sir?"

Dane glanced at Aiyana. "I believe she requested live fish." He wanted to tease her, to lighten the tension between them. His words fell flat, and Dane turned away.

* * *

Aiyana kept her gaze on her feet. She couldn't make herself look at Dane now. Her thoughts leaped and skittered, unable to form coherently after the trauma of his search. She had been prepared for such things, as all Ellowan were. Yet when it happened, when she was finally a prisoner, it wasn't cruelty, but kindness that had devastated her.

His touch had been gentle, almost reverent. Aiyana's pulse quickened. She had been exposed, naked. Her soul had recoiled. Yet she had seen tears in his blue eyes. Tears, and something else.

Aiyana had seen lust before, and it sickened her. But the desire written on Dane's face had a different effect. Her nerves tingled; her skin flushed.

Aiyana peeked up at Dane. He surveyed the land, planning the best course to the mountains. His shaggy, golden hair fell to his broad shoulders, moved by the swirling wind. "We go south, I presume."

Galya stood beside him. Too close, Aiyana decided. She saw Galya, with her pleasant face and seemingly passive demeanor, and her whole heart rose in fury.

"The sooner we find the Keiroit hold, the better. But I have never traveled here, Dane. I'm afraid I'll be a poor guide."

Aiyana stepped forward. "Tell him the rest, Tseir. Tell him about the rogues."

Dane looked at Galya, waiting. "Is there something I should know?"

Galya hesitated. "Not all Keiroits are . . . reasonable."

"Meaning you don't control them all." Galya's jaw tensed, but she didn't respond to Aiyana's remark.

"There are factions among them that are . . . indiscriminate."

"Meaning they attack anything that moves, whichever side they're on. Those are the Keiroits that roam outside the hold. They wear environmental protection, as I did, and they . . . hunt."

Aiyana took pleasure in Galya's discomfort. "For food. In the wild, a Keiroit might enjoy sampling Tseir meat."

A small squeak broke Aiyana's attention. "What about lingbat meat?"

Aiyana glanced at Batty. He was trembling violently, his eyes as round as serving saucers. Her heart unwillingly expanded with pity. "I think a creature as swift as yourself could reach a tree branch in ample time. With three humanoids available, they won't notice you."

Aiyana felt Dane's gaze, felt his surprise at her unexpected kindness. Her expression hardened. "They'll be too delighted to have a Thorwalian dinner."

Despite her cold words, Dane laughed. "We'll try to deprive them, shall we? But forewarned is forearmed, they say. We will proceed cautiously."

"You would be wise to return my weapons. We won't pass through this portion of the wood unhindered."

"Not a chance. What would stop you from turning part of your vast arsenal on me?"

Aiyana met Dane's eyes. They were warm and blue and laughing. "The same thing that kept me from letting you die."

"What was that, Aiyana?"

Her gaze wavered, and she looked away. "I want you to meet with our leader, to hear the Ellowan point of view."

"That may be possible, at a later point. For now, my mission is to meet with the Tseirs."

"So you intend to drag me to the Keiroit hold? I will not make your journey easier."

Dane smiled, slow and teasing. Aiyana's heart fluttered, for no reason that she knew. "I don't want an easy journey, Aiyana. With you around, boredom is something I need never fear again."

Dane examined her Ellowan weaponry, then fired a blast into a dead tree with her rifle. ''More power than a Thorwalian rifle, but the range is shorter. I prefer my own.''

Dane fingered her sword. ''This weapon is light, but would be well used in close combat.'' Dane attached Aiyana's sword to his belt.

''I see that theft is part of the Thorwalian instinct.''

''The ancient Ravagers of my land survived by pillaging each other. It's in my nature. The Ravagers' weapon of choice was a two-handed ax, but the noblemen carried swords.''

Dane studied the hilt of Aiyana's light blade. ''The designs resembled this far more closely than does the Candorian blade.''

Aiyana made no comment, but a cold thrill shivered through her. It was almost as if he knew . . . But that was impossible. The only connection between their distant worlds had been accidental, and ages before. It was too soon for Dane to learn of that brief history.

Dane turned to Galya. ''I suggest you carry Aiyana's rifle, Galya. We may have need of arms before we reach the Keiroit hold.''

Galya took the weapon gingerly. ''I am unfamiliar with weapons.''

Aiyana sneered. ''You'll like them, Tseir. A rifle is a fine way to exert control over others. You don't have to bother with lies or manipulation. You just blast away. Very effective.''

Galya's eyes darkened to round, black pools of anger. Aiyana chuckled and turned back to Dane. She watched as he finished affixing her sword to his belt, then slung his own rifle over his shoulder.

The wind rustled through the giant trees, turning cold and damp. Dane sighed when the first drops of rain fell. ''Night approaches, accompanied by a storm, it seems. We must leave the crash site, and find a safer spot to spend the night. There must be emergency provisions inside the craft."

Dane went into the ship and retrieved his pack. "I have one bedroll, and dried food."

Batty stuck his head inside the pack. "No bugs?"

"No bugs."

Batty made a smacking noise. "That meat looks appetizing, sir." He looked hopeful, peering up at Dane. Aiyana repressed a giggle.

Dane's eyes narrowed. "You can hunt for food, rodent. I assume you're capable of hunting."

The lingbat appeared crestfallen, but nodded woefully. "I'm a fair hunter, sir. That is a *truism.*" He dragged out the word plaintively. "Not like my sire, of course. But I should be able to make do." Batty looked around at the forbidding, dark forest. "Hate to speculate what's out there, sir. Hungry beasts who might mistake me for prey."

Dane's jaw set hard. "You'll find something."

"As you say, sir."

Galya entered the broken vessel, then emerged, distraught. "I tried to raise communications with the Keiroit hold, but this Ellowan obviously destroyed the panel."

Aiyana nodded. "I did. You won't be reaching your allies, Tseir. Though the Keiroits prowling for food will soon spot the downed vessel. How simple for them to say all the passengers died in the crash! No, I don't see any way for you to avoid joining their larder."

Galya cast a disgusted look at Aiyana, then moved closer to Dane. Her dark eyes widened in what Aiyana considered an obvious attempt to gain a male's sympathy and compliance.

Aiyana tapped Dane's shoulder. "The Keiroits are violent, but they aren't good trackers. If you are moderately cautious, you should be able to avoid them tonight. I will lead you."

Galya clutched Dane's arm. "You can't trust her, Dane. She will lead us into an Ellowan trap."

"Perhaps you will lead us then, Tseir." Aiyana paused while Galya radiated controlled anger. Aiyana cast her eyes upward, thoughtfully. "Yet the environment of the Tseir world is much different from this. Your climate is . . . controlled. Your plants grow only as you direct. How will you find your way in the wild?"

Dane eased Aiyana forward into the dense thicket. He was smiling. "My lady Ellowan has no desire to serve as Keiroit dinner. We will head south, toward the mountains, and take her advice as to sleeping arrangements."

"We may find safety tonight, Thorwalian. But the journey through the mountains is many days. And not without peril. I will guide you no farther."

"Let's consider tonight, shall we?" Dane sounded unconcerned. Aiyana drew a long breath, then walked on ahead.

"Follow me."

Dane watched Aiyana as she moved through the trees. Her motion was effortless, like fluid poured from one cup to another. Her braid had come unraveled; her hair soaked up the rain and fell loose around her shoulders, over her cloak.

"How did you accomplish the impersonation of a Keiroit, Aiyana? Of course, there may be much in common between your races. I see no scales, yet your insides might be green, your little toes webbed."

He couldn't resist teasing her. For all her beauty, the irritating creature he first met still remained.

Aiyana stopped, one hand on her hip as she waited for him to catch up. Her head tilted to the side in a haughty posture. "My impersonation was simple. I abducted the Keiroit guard assigned to Galya, and used the remnants of its protective wrapping to conceal myself."

"Can I assume that 'Aiyana' is a false name?"

"No. I *am* called Aiyana. It is not a strange name for a Keroit, for they have a habit of taking the names of the Ellowans they have killed. Partly to mock us, and also to be understood by the Tseir."

"Do the Tseirs and the Ellowans speak one language?"

Aiyana glanced at Galya, but the Tseir woman had fallen behind. "The Tseirs have spoken many languages, but their own is long forgotten." Aiyana looked into Dane's eyes, searching. "Do you find that strange? There is no remnant of their original tongue. The language they speak now is Ellowan. As do most races in this system."

Dane looked back at Galya as she struggled up the path. "She is unused to hardship."

"The Tseirs have no power within."

Dane studied Aiyana's face. Her lips curved in a frown, but nothing disguised her loveliness. "What do your people want, Aiyana?"

Aiyana didn't answer at once. Her eyes appeared haunted, suddenly distant. "We want what is forever gone."

"Perhaps, through negotiation—"

"Never. The Tseir have power. They have control. But they never rest, they will never be secure. Not while we haunt them. And we will haunt them forever."

A cold chill touched Dane's heart. "You speak as if you're dead."

"Perhaps I am." Aiyana's voice was soft, distant. As she turned away, an evening breeze caught her hair and tossed it behind her head.

Dane saw her there, the vast, giant forest behind her, her profile as exquisite as the figures on the walls of Nerotania. No woman had ever touched him this way. Yet no one had ever seemed so distant, so beyond his reach.

He touched her shoulder. "You heal others, Aiyana. You healed me. You brought me from death. Perhaps, one day, you will let me do the same for you."

Aiyana eyed Dane suspiciously, then moved away from his touch. "There is a difference between us. You desired life."

"You fought for life during the crash. Otherwise, why strap yourself in?"

"My purpose remains unfulfilled."

"What purpose is that?"

"To be a ghost, Dane Calydon. To haunt. A living ghost, in the shadow of what is forever gone."

"You suddenly speak in riddles. If you tell me the truth of your world, of the conflict with the Tseirs, I might better judge how to advise the Candorians."

"You seek peace, resolution. Some conflicts have no resolution."

Aiyana sounded old, and her head was bowed. Dane wanted to hold her, to comfort her, but she seemed beyond comfort. He knew she wouldn't willingly open her heart, but he also knew he had time to learn her secrets.

The rain eased beneath a cold wind, but the sky darkened to black before Aiyana chose a resting place. Beneath the relative shelter of a copse of trees, she stopped. "You will find no better shelter than this tonight. The Keiroit move faster in such weather. It is unwise to continue farther in darkness."

"I'll trust your wisdom in this, Aiyana." Dane set his pack down and drew out his bedroll. "I'm assuming you have a strong desire to protect your scales and green flesh."

Dane offered Galya some of the dried meat. Though Aiyana hesitated, she accepted his offering, too. "It is stale."

"It's all you've got."

Batty eyed the meat longingly, but Dane shot him a forbidding look. ''As you say, sir.'' A long, drawn-out sigh followed.

Dane unfurled the bedroll. ''Galya will sleep here. You, my lady Aiyana, will be bound tonight, but I will try to select a comfortable resting place.''

Aiyana didn't seem to care where Dane put her. He led her a good distance away from Galya, where quiet conversation wouldn't be overheard.

''I must bind you, Aiyana. But I will stay beside you lest the Keiroits come upon us.''

''If the Keiroits find us, there will be nothing you can do.''

Dane fixed a rope to Aiyana's binding, then tied the other end around his waist. He seated himself beside her. ''You underestimate my abilities, Ellowan. I spent the better part of my youth learning every weapon the people of Thorwal have ever invented. And since mine was a barbaric race, there are many.''

''I am not surprised to hear your ancestors were barbarians.'' Aiyana yawned. ''Only that they didn't annihilate themselves by mishandling their swords.''

Batty emerged from Dane's cloak. ''I suppose it's time. . . . Fine, misty night, isn't it? Damp, cold . . . Perfect.'' Aiyana and Dane eyed the lingbat with misgivings.

''Perfect for what?''

A tiny smile appeared on Aiyana's lips. ''I think he means for bugs.''

Batty nodded vigorously. ''The earth-dwelling species rise to the surface in moist weather. Those would be the soft, worm-based insects. Those require little chewing; just mull them around on your tongue, and they slide right down.''

Dane groaned. ''Perhaps we could save this discussion for later.''

Aiyana nodded. ''Good idea.''

Batty hopped up on a branch, sighting the area. ''Of course, humanoids don't have the necessary night vision. I won't have to search far. But just to your left is a prime specimen. Plumper than those I've seen in the tunnels.''

Without warning, the lingbat launched himself into the wet air and crashed to earth just beyond Aiyana. He thrashed wildly, scratched a hole in the dirt, then immersed his head. A spongy, chomping noise followed. Aiyana and Dane cringed in unison.

Batty's head popped out of the dirt. His cheeks were round and full. ''It will be a rewarding night, sir!''

''If you could hunt out of sight, we would sleep better.''

''As you wish, sir.'' Batty disappeared without another word.

''I can't think what use you find those creatures.'' Aiyana leaned back against the tree. ''But you are a strange man.''

Dane leaned back, too. He wanted to kiss her, more than he had ever wanted to kiss anyone. Selena was beautiful, but unreceptive. Even before he kissed her, he knew she would have no passion in his bed. Galya might be receptive, but he had no interest.

Aiyana might not be willing, but Dane knew she wouldn't be dull to his touch. He wondered what qualities she admired in a man. ''What are Ellowan males like?''

''Like Ellowan females with male attributes.''

''Are they large?''

''Their attributes?''

Dane's face colored, and he thanked the night for darkness. ''I mean, are they tall, big boned? You are quite delicate.''

Aiyana stiffened. ''I am not delicate.''

''You're not big.''

She huffed. ''Only because you are so large do I seem . . . smaller.''

''Then I take it your men are small.''

"Not at all! Some of our men are near your height. But their bodies are less . . . cumbersome."

"I've spent years building my strength, and now I find a woman who wants a delicate male. You would have preferred me before, when I was all bone, with no mass."

"Why do you care what I prefer?"

Dane shrugged. "I like women. For most of my youth, women liked me." He paused. "A lot."

"The Candorian maiden seemed unimpressed."

"In fairness to myself, I must point out that Selena has no interest in any male, including myself."

"Then why do you pursue her?" Aiyana hesitated. "Do you love her?"

"I fancied her. For want of anyone better. Maybe I just wanted to be in love."

"Why?"

"Love brings out the best in a man, and a woman. I have seen that with my sister."

"You speak of her with great affection."

"Nisa is older than I. Our parents were aloof. But Nisa cared for me in a way they never did. I watched her love, and hurt, and love again. Nisa and Seneca have a joy together, a bond that I envy."

Aiyana closed her eyes. "Yet if you love that way, you could lose the one you love. Then what?"

"Life would be better for the time you spent together, however brief."

"I wonder." Aiyana spoke softly, her voice sounding tired. "Maybe it would be best never to know that happiness than to lose it forever."

Dane tried to see Aiyana's face in the darkness, but she was veiled by the night. "Then you have no mate." She couldn't have a mate. Dane couldn't imagine her with another man.

"No."

"Have you ever been in love?"

"Love is for the living. I hope you find it. But you would have done better to return to your own world than to seek it here."

"Then I would never have seen you. That must be worth something."

"I can't think why."

"You are pleasing to the eye. You are argumentative and rude and difficult. I find your company enjoyable."

"You talk too much."

"I learned from a lingbat."

"Then perhaps you will go seeking worms for your dinner and leave me in peace."

"I'll wait here. With luck, the lingbat will return bearing the fruits of his labors for us both."

Aiyana bit her lip, but she smiled anyway. It was the first genuine smile Dane had seen on her face. "You are lovely when you smile, Aiyana."

"I'm not smiling."

Dane touched her face, gently lifting her chin. "I think you are. I think within you is a vast store of happiness."

Aiyana jerked her head away. Her smile disappeared, leaving instead a haunted, bitter expression. "There is no such emotion in me."

Dane didn't pursue the matter, but he moved closer to her, until their shoulders touched. "Should you seek comfort, I am here."

"I do not seek comfort."

"For all the rumors told of the Ellowan capacity for seduction, I have seen little of the trait."

"And you never will."

"Then again, perhaps I am already under your spell, and cannot see the bonds you fix around me."

"Do you believe a living thing can be truly enslaved?"

"No. Even within the most brutal slavery, we are free. And responsible for our own actions."

"I believe that, too."

"Then we agree on something."

"Our agreement isn't deep. You believe fate is fair. I do not."

"I believe we create our own destiny."

"I have seen otherwise."

"You are young, Aiyana. In years, if not in spirit. Maybe there is much you haven't seen."

"I am older than you, Thorwalian. . . ." Aiyana's argumentative tone faded into silence. A harsh wind picked up, and she peeked up at him. "Aren't you cold?"

"No."

Aiyana hesitated, chewing her lip. "The wind will grow stronger as night deepens."

"It is a fair breeze compared to my homeworld of Thorwal."

"Your constitution lacks sensitivity."

Dane studied her expression more closely. "Are you cold, Aiyana?"

"No. Somewhat."

Dane touched her hand, finding her fingers like ice. "You are not suited to this climate. Generally a species adapts more readily to its world."

Aiyana didn't answer, but her gaze drifted upward to the sky. The clouds dispersed, parting to reveal the distant stars. A large, golden planet rose above the tree line.

"Is that Franconia?"

"It is."

Farther from the golden planet, a faint sliver of a moon rose, and Aiyana closed her eyes.

"What is that moon?"

Aiyana didn't answer at once. "It is known as the Midnight Moon. Its true name is forgotten."

"Is it inhabited?"

Again, Aiyana's response wasn't immediate. "It is barren and lifeless."

Dane watched the moon as the clouds passed by, shrouding it in eerie light. He felt a strange pang as it disappeared, of loss unrecovered, of finality. "It is a sorrowful sight."

Aiyana glanced up at him. "Why do you say that?"

"I don't know." Dane touched Aiyana's hair. "It reminds me of you."

Aiyana's lips parted. For an instant, Dane saw her unguarded, astonished. She looked quickly away, but her sudden vulnerability touched his soul.

Dane placed his cloak over her. "If you are cold, then sit closer to me. Thorwalians maintain warmth in drastic temperatures."

Aiyana adjusted the cloak higher, but she still shivered. "It is unnecessary." She paused. "Your skin was cool to the touch."

Dane seized the opportunity to tease her again. "Where did you touch me? Exactly."

"Your chest." Aiyana crossed her legs and adjusted her position. "The lingbat needed assistance."

"I see. Your touch was accidental?"

Aiyana nodded. "Quite accidental."

"I'm sorry I missed it."

"You irritate me immensely."

"I'm resisting the impulse to kiss you."

"Good. You will not."

"There is a temptation to learn what you would do."

Aiyana's eyes narrowed combatively. "I would strike you."

"If your hands weren't bound . . ."

"I would find a way."

Dane chuckled. "At times you remind me of my sister. Nisa could be violent and bossy, too."

Aiyana said nothing. Dane wondered what ties bound the Ellowans. Their connections might be vastly different from the Thorwalian system. "What of your family, Aiyana? Have you sisters and brothers, or do you roam your violent world alone?"

Aiyana's jaw clenched. "I have no family."

The tone of her voice told Dane to drop the subject, but he knew he had found the source of her bitterness.

Aiyana wrapped her arms around her body, and the ache inside Dane intensified. She was strong, yet fragile—a strange and compelling combination of qualities. As Dane watched her, he realized he had never known fear. He took life as it came, and hoped for more.

But tonight, beside a mysterious and sorrowful woman, he understood fear. He feared for Aiyana. He feared she would enter his heart, then drift beyond his reach. That he would love her, and lose her. That she would die.

Dane looked back to the sky. He longed for love. He thought he would find it, and his life would emerge on a new level of adventure. Nisa told him that love was painful, but he had never truly known why.

He had nothing to lose. That was why he felt no pain. Until now. Dane's gaze shifted reluctantly back to Aiyana. He reminded himself that he fell in love too easily. He was infatuated with a beautiful, exotic woman. Nothing more.

Aiyana's teeth were chattering. Her small jaw quivered. She pressed her lips together to hide her discomfort. Dane endured an intense wave of sympathy, and resigned himself to the inevitable.

"Your lips are blue. Come here, Aiyana. I can bear no more of your suffering."

"I am not suffering." Her words came disjointedly as she shivered. Dane laughed, then slid his arm around her shoulders, gently guiding her into his embrace.

Aiyana stiffened, but Dane knew her body welcomed his

warmth. Dane eased her head onto his shoulder, and his fingers found her hair and idly combed through it. "I won't hurt you."

"You had best not."

"If you would vow the same, I would sleep easier."

"I won't hurt you either, Dane Calydon. Not tonight."

Dane glanced down. "That is not entirely reassuring, my lady."

Aiyana looked up at him, and the intensity of her bright eyes pierced his heart. "It wasn't meant to reassure. It is a warning. I hope you take it. As much as I dislike you, I have no desire to cause you pain."

Dane rested his cheek against her head, but he resisted the urge to kiss her. Despite her protestations, he knew she liked him, and he wondered why she felt compelled to deny the obvious.

"You have warned me often. It is generous, but unnecessary. I make my own fate."

"For now."

"For always."

The clouds parted high above the trees, revealing a fleeting glimpse of the Midnight Moon. The sight seemed to trouble her and she looked away. She closed her eyes and surrendered to sleep.

Dane watched Aiyana as the cold moon sent pale glimmers of light across her face. He felt no impulse toward sleep. Instead, he took a painful joy in her company, in a feeling he recognized, but had never known firsthand.

"It would be so easy to love you." Dane looked toward the silver moon. "But dangerous." He had been told, many times, that the Ellowans were a violent people, a race who placed no value on kindness, who thought nothing of killing.

Yet Aiyana had shown kindness to Batty, and to him. True, she seemed to want something from him. Dane wasn't sure what, exactly. The wistful sorrow inside her contrasted sharply with her spirited nature.

Aiyana fought, yet had no hope of victory. She lived, with no desire for life. He wondered what it would take to make him feel that way. And then he knew. It would take the end of the world.

"What a tender scene! I almost hate to disturb you."

Aiyana woke to Galya's voice, but she kept her eyes closed, her breathing slow. Her head remained on Dane's chest, his arm still wrapped around her.

Dane sighed, but he didn't move. "Galya. I trust you slept well." He offered no apologies for sleeping with Aiyana tucked in his arms. Aiyana resisted a smile of satisfaction.

"Asleep, it is hard to imagine her capable of violence. I hope you are able to see beyond her surface, Dane."

Aiyana kept her breath soft and even. Galya's patronizing tone inspired a fierce retort, but Aiyana repressed it.

"No one sees beneath the surface, Galya. We can't know the unknown, can we?"

Aiyana longed to issue approval of Dane's comment, and to add to its content. But something about Galya disturbed her. She closely resembled another Tseir woman Aiyana had known, an evil woman. Many Tseir resembled each other. There was nothing strange in that. If she didn't know that it was impossible, Aiyana would believe Galya and the woman she remembered were the same.

"We must hurry to the Keiroit hold, Dane. There is no time to lose. Both Ellowans and Keiroits must have seen the crash."

"I'm not sure which is worse."

"In the hands of the stable Keiroits, we will be completely safe, I assure you."

Aiyana waited a moment, then opened one eye. "Is she gone?"

Dane grinned. "I should have known you weren't sleeping."

Aiyana raised her brow and sat up. " 'We can't know the unknown, can we?' "

"And did you sleep comfortably, little Ellowan?"

"I barely slept at all. You are hard and uncomfortable."

"You can say that again." Aiyana's eyes narrowed, but Dane didn't elaborate on his condition. "From the way you snored, I thought your sleep adequate."

"I do not snore!"

"Not loudly. Just a low little rumble. It had its charm."

Aiyana gritted her teeth. "You were mistaken." An echo of the described noise came from Dane's other side. Dane laughed, then found Batty asleep in a scrunched-up ball.

"You see! It was your lingbat who snored. Not I."

"You both snore." Dane picked up the small creature, but it didn't wake. Dane shook his head. "He Who Flames with Courage. Not likely to warn us of a state of emergency, is he?"

"Were you expecting him to?"

"His father always seemed to know what lurked around the next corner."

The lingbat's snoring stopped, but its eyes didn't open.

"You compare this small creature to the older, grumpy bat. You expect this creature to take the other's place? You would be wiser to allow him his own place."

Dane sighed. "Batty's 'place' seems to be hiding behind my head."

"Courage doesn't come in a day." Aiyana's brow knitted, a darkness surfacing in her bright eyes. "It takes time."

"Since your courage is unquestioned, I will take your word." Dane stood, too. Batty yawned dramatically, then stretched his wings.

"Is it morning, sir?" Batty yawned again, a forced gesture. "Busy day ahead of us, sir. Are we expecting any . . . disturbance from the Keiroits?"

Aiyana rose to her feet, distancing herself from Dane. She felt sure the small lingbat had overheard Dane's comments. "Yes, tell us. What is the plan, Thorwalian? I assume you have one."

Dane turned toward the mountains. He didn't speak at once. Aiyana felt a peculiar tightening in her stomach as she watched him. She saw no fear, just calm reason. He looked tall and strong, and she remembered sleeping in his arms, safe.

He hadn't been uncomfortable. He had been warm and powerful. His masculine smell was sweet and comforting. So much so that she wondered about the taste of his skin. If she touched her tongue to his flesh, she would know.

Aiyana shuddered and turned away. Here, in her violent world, she still remembered Valenwood. She remembered the sensual nature of her people, as revealed in their art as it was in their society. Destroyed forever, yet never forgotten.

Aiyana had nothing of her own to remember. She considered herself fortunate. But Dane Calydon had awakened the sultry curiosity hidden within her. She had no memory of such a past, but she had fantasies of what might have been.

Dane glanced back at her and smiled. Aiyana frowned in return, but an irritating warmth flooded inside her. "Shall we embark on the mountain passage, or attempt to skirt the range entirely? Either way you choose should please the Keiroit rogues immensely."

Dane fingered his sword, his blue eyes flashing in the morning sun. Aiyana knew he would welcome battle. Dane shaded his eyes against the sun. "The mountain passage is most direct."

"An obvious choice. To you, and to the Keiroits."

Galya joined him, her back to Aiyana. ''We must reach safety before nightfall, Dane. We have few supplies for a long journey.''

''A wise traveler finds his own supplies.''

Aiyana nodded approvingly at Dane's remark. ''Keir is rich in supplies, if you survive long enough to obtain them. The mountain passage is most dangerous. The longer route is least expected.''

Galya's lips tightened. ''She wants us to go that way. You are armed, Dane. If we hurry, we will get through the mountains and reach safety.''

''The quick, intense danger of the mountain passage seems balanced with a journey of many days. We will take the mountain passage.''

Aiyana turned her gaze southward toward the mountains. ''It is a mistake, but you are prone to mistakes. I need not concern myself with your visit to the Tseirs. You'll never get that far.''

''Again you warn me, little Ellowan. For my own sake, or yours?''

''If you intend to haul me along with you, for mine.'' Aiyana denied an emotional reaction. She needed Dane Caldon alive. His death worked against her purposes, but his fate shouldn't concern her. ''You seem intent on throwing your life away. You neglected to heed my advice on the ship, and you ignore my wisdom now. It may please me to escape.''

Dane's blue eyes sparkled with enjoyment. ''Then it will please me to chase you down. Again.''

''I was weary then, from saving you. If I choose to run now, wings haven't the speed to catch me.''

''I have no wings, Ellowan, but I will track you down, wherever you go. I can be a patient man.''

Aiyana sensed Dane's words had a hidden meaning, but he just smiled and gathered his gear. Something about the curve of his lips tempted her to strange action. A wild, vivid image formed in her mind. Her lips on his, their breath intermingled. She would suck his lower lip, perhaps nip—

Aiyana gasped, her eyes opening wide. Dane studied her horrified expression. His brow rose when her cheeks flushed. "Aiyana?"

Her expression turned indignant, but she refrained from comment. The Ellowans were rumored to have secret powers of seduction. What if the same were true of Thorwalians? Aiyana knew, as Dane did not, that an ancient attraction simmered between their people. She knew also that Thorwalians had always inspired lust in hers. . . .

Aiyana lifted her bound hands and pointed a finger at him. "You will spare me further attention, Thorwalian. Get hence to the Swamp of Keir, and let our parting be soon!"

Aiyana refused to assist Dane's progress, but the route to the mountain passage was obvious. She said nothing, and Dane wondered what occupied her mind. A tight frown never left her lips.

She'd turned on him suddenly. He'd felt her fierce anger, but he had no idea what he had done to inspire such wrath. For an instant, he was sure he had seen pure lust on her little face. His blood still raged in response. No, he should have known better; it was fury instead.

Galya walked beside him, cheerful despite the arduous walk. "We are making good progress, Dane. You chose the swiftest path. We should reach the south hills by evening."

Progress had been good. By midmorning they had reached the lower foothills. "This is undoubtedly the easy part. The mountain passage will be more dangerous."

"If only we could establish communications with the Keiroit hold! They would send guards, and make this passage safe."

Dane glanced at Aiyana, hoping for a response. It seemed

beyond her to resist reminding Galya of the dangers. Though Aiyana chewed her lip, she remained silent.

"Our Ellowan friend has made that impossible. So we will journey through the passage, and take her with us."

No response. Dane sighed. Despite her argumentative posture, Aiyana had previously enjoyed speaking with him. Not today. She seemed determined to avoid any contact with him.

Dane led the way along the footpath. It was well-worn, and discarded fish bones told him the travelers hadn't been Ellowan. "An ominous sign."

Batty squeaked, coughed, then moved closer to Dane's head. "Maybe they're full, sir, and not interested in passersby."

Aiyana's silence shattered. "Keiroits don't kill for food. They kill for pleasure."

Batty squeaked again. "Perhaps we might stop to rest for a while, sir. . . . Maybe you'd like to go on ahead and check out the area."

The lingbat's voice quavered and Dane wished again that Carob had accompanied him. "Maybe you'd like to maintain silence and use those highly developed ears of yours, Batty. You should be able to hear—"

"Stop!" Batty fluttered his wings madly, then chirped. "I hear something now!"

Aiyana eyed the bat doubtfully, and Dane sighed. Galya clutched her rifle. "What is it?"

"I hear . . . hissing, sir. And a croak." The bat's voice was barely audible. "It sounds evil, sir."

Aiyana's brow furrowed. "Keiroits don't hiss or croak. On the prowl, they make no sound at all. Listen for silence, Batty. When the animals fall still, when the birds fly in haste . . . that is when we must beware."

"Sound advice." Dane adjusted the lingbat farther down on his shoulder, away from his hair, and started off.

The path narrowed, cutting between large boulders on either side, and Dane's own tension grew. Birds still flew above, diving for prey, and he saw a rabbit on the path ahead, but his unease didn't abate.

Aiyana moved soundlessly beside him, but Galya labored to maintain the swift pace. A shallow stream raced down from the mountain heights, cutting a narrow gorge toward the northern lowlands. Dane followed the path, but he couldn't help thinking that the Keiroits would find the water welcoming.

Dane stopped and refilled his flask with water. From this vantage point, he could see the northern forest, a gray-green haze stretching endlessly from the mountains. The giant evergreens grew more sparsely in the higher elevation, but taller.

"The slope is highest from here. In other circumstances, I would suggest we rest, but that seems unwise today. We have few provisions, but eat now, and drink. We won't stop again until we reach the other side."

"Or until we're attacked." Aiyana seized Dane's flask and drank. "You'll never cross these mountains in a day, Thorwalian. We'll have to stop at nightfall, or be lost. Many paths here lead nowhere."

Dane considered her advice, but he feared trusting Aiyana. "I have a keen sense of direction, even in the dark. We will go onward."

Aiyana shook her head, but she didn't argue further. They started off again, but soon the sound of their footsteps seemed loud, echoing against the rising slopes. Dane stopped to listen. Nothing. Only the slow, steady beat of his heart, and his even, deep breathing.

Dane glanced at Aiyana. She was listening, too. Galya sank down to rest, but Batty trembled on Dane's shoulder. "Sir, should we be stopping?" The lingbat cranked its head around, searching nervously. ''Good place for an ambush, wouldn't you say, sir?''

Aiyana nodded. ''He has a point. Up ahead, the path grows narrower still, and many boulders offer hiding places.''

''You speak as one who has used those places.''

Aiyana's eyes gleamed. ''Many times, Dane Calydon. The Keiroits are hunters. But we are hunters, too. Did you not know?''

''I guessed. But we have no choice. We go on.''

As Aiyana said, the path narrowed to where they could walk only single file. Dane led, with Galya at the rear. She glanced back often, but Dane knew the real danger lay ahead. Again he stopped, surveying the land for strategic opportunities.

Dane's gaze fixed on a lone evergreen, nearly dead, the branches decayed. ''Batty . . . climb that tree and check out the path ahead.''

Batty gulped, and his eyes grew round. ''You want me to go up there, sir?''

Dane nodded, fighting impatience. ''Yes. Up.''

The bat hesitated, shifting its weight closer to Dane's head. ''Now, lingbats have superb hearing, sir, but sight . . .''

Dane drew a restrained breath. ''Go.''

''As you say, sir.'' With painful reluctance, Batty edged down Dane's shoulder. ''I'll just be on my way up then.''

''There's no need. They are coming.'' Aiyana spoke calmly, without fear. Batty dove for Dane's neck.

''Who?'' The squeak was high and terrified.

''The Keiroits. They are around the bend. A large group, twenty or more.''

Dane retrieved his rifle and started up the path. ''Stay here.''

"What about me?" Batty flapped his wings, but Dane ignored him.

Aiyana raced after him. "You can't hold them alone!"

Dane stopped and met her eyes. "I don't mean to hold them, Aiyana. I mean to destroy them."

"You need me."

Dane glanced back toward Galya. "We need to find a defensible position."

"The best strategy against the Keiroits is attack. Make them fear you, or they will never relent. They must think there are many of us."

"And how do you propose we create that illusion?"

Aiyana huffed impatiently. "The Ellowans are well skilled at battling Keiroit rogues. Return my weapons, and I will help you."

"I can't do that."

Galya joined them, her rifle held in shaking hands. "What do we do?"

"There is little coverage here. Back down the path there were better hiding places."

Aiyana shook her head. "You can't hide forever. We have to fight."

"She may be right, Dane. The Ellowans know how to fight Keiroits."

Dane turned to Galya. "Can you fight?"

"My skill is in diplomacy, not in weapons. It may be wisest to give her the rifle. Put her in front, where she will be forced to defend us."

Galya's suggestion surprised and annoyed Dane, but Aiyana offered no objections. "You won't succeed without me, Thorwalian. Let me fight." He suspected she was right.

"Sir! I hear them now. Oh, help!" Batty entangled himself in Dane's hair, and Dane gritted his teeth in irritation.

"Galya, take shelter behind that rock. Aiyana and I will go on ahead, but we may be forced to retreat here."

Aiyana held out her bound hands, and Dane cut the tie. "My weapon."

He handed her the Ellowan rifle, which Aiyana seized without preamble. She moved stealthily up the path, her weapon poised in her small, steady hands. Aiyana gestured to a flat rock, then effortlessly leaped onto another. She knelt, her rifle ready. Dane took the other position, aimed his rifle, and waited.

He heard them now, a heavy shuffling just around the bend. His first real battle, yet he felt none of the thrill he expected. Looking across the path at Aiyana, Dane knew why. She was fearless, and she was in danger. And she mattered to him. More than any woman had ever mattered.

"Aiyana . . ."

"Hush!"

Dane smiled at her abrupt command. "Take care."

Aiyana glanced over at him, her brow furrowed, her lips curved in annoyance. Her expression softened as if against her will. "And you."

"What about me, sir?"

"Off my shoulder, Batty. I need both arms to shoot straight."

"Where do I go, sir?"

Dane's patience shattered. "Anywhere!"

Batty scrambled from Dane's shoulder, then flapped to a nearby branch. Small squeaks burst from the little creature as he hopped higher and higher up the tree.

"Oh, no! Help!"

The Keiroits appeared around the bend, large, squat figures, wrapped as Aiyana had been. They moved in unison, wielding heavy rifles and forked spears. Aiyana hesitated, waiting until they were nearly upon her.

Dane fought the desire to shoot, to protect her. She knew what she was doing. His finger twitched on the trigger. Dane studied the enemy as they approached. The Keiroits were more orderly than he imagined of rogues. They uttered commands, brutal-sounding but still controlled.

Something felt wrong. Aiyana's rifle shot a line of blue plasma, and a Keiroit fell lifeless. Before Dane aimed his rifle, she shot again. Rather than panicking, the Keiroits formed an ordered resistance, backing away, and assuming defensive positions.

Aiyana moved like a woodland creature, higher, then shot again. The Keiroits clearly assumed many assailed them. Guessing her strategy, Dane fired, moved onto a higher rock, then fired again. The Keiroits blasted toward Aiyana's position. Dane tensed, then leaped down from the boulder, bounding toward them as he fired.

Startled by his assault, the Keiroits fled back up the mountain path. Aiyana rose from her shelter and stood motionless, her mouth open. Dane stared back at her, the soft forest wind lifting her hair, lifting his. She was safe, alive.

Aiyana scrambled down from her position, shouldered her rifle, and faced him. Her breath came in quick gasps beneath her snug bodice. "You have obviously not evolved far from your spear-tossing ancestors. What kind of fool charges twenty armed, amphibious warriors?"

"The kind of fool who sees you in danger."

Aiyana's chin lifted. "I am capable of withstanding danger."

"You're not capable of surviving a shattered boulder landing on your head, and that's just what would have happened after another blast."

Aiyana appeared skeptical, so Dane aimed his rifle, shot at the rocks above her position, and watched the cliff side crumble. He turned a satisfied, knowing gaze back to Aiyana. Her lips twisted, but she made no further argument.

"It appears my position wasn't entirely secure."

"Indeed." Dane waited for some gesture of appreciation. Receiving none, he assessed the fallen as Galya emerged from her hiding place. His eyes narrowed as he studied the fallen Keiroits. "They wear the same garb. Almost like uniforms."

Aiyana glanced at the Keiroits and shrugged. "What of it? They are gone."

"Easily defeated."

"I led them to believe they had happened into an Ellowan ambush. They have no courage to face us."

"Is that it, Aiyana? I wonder."

"What about me, sir?" Dane looked up and saw Batty high up in the dying evergreen.

"It appears the battle is over, Batty. Come down."

"Can't, sir. Up too high."

Dane's jaw twitched. "Find a way, rodent."

"I'm not a flying creature, sir." Batty's voice grew higher still, and revealed a distinct tremor.

Aiyana aimed her rifle at the tree, the bat squealed, and the branch shattered. She caught the lingbat as he dropped. "He appears to have fainted . . . *sir.*"

Dane sighed and shook his head as he took the bat and stuffed him in his pack. "My hero."

Galya hurried up the path behind them, but her face blanched when she saw the fallen Keiroits. "These aren't rogues! Dane, these are Keiroit soldiers! They wear the Franconian mark. She has led you to defeat our rescuers."

A cold wash of anger began in Dane's heart. He turned to Aiyana slowly, his jaw tight with restraint. "Once again, you have led me into error, lady."

Aiyana didn't deny Galya's accusation. She smiled, and Dane's anger surged. He stepped toward her. "Give me your weapon, woman."

"Or should you hand over your rifle, Ravager?"

Dane's blue eyes glittered. He rarely felt anger, but it boiled inside him now. He drew his sword and held it at her throat. "Then kill me, Aiyana, for I will not let you go."

"Too late."

From the path ahead, a loud, disorderly group of Keiroits appeared. Galya gasped. "Those are rogues, real rogues. Dane, shoot!"

The second band of Keiroits contrasted with the first. They ambled without precision, without caution, and they conversed loudly. Dane shoved Galya behind him, then aimed his rifle.

"If you shoot, you'll be sorry, Ravager." Aiyana positioned herself between Dane and the new attackers. Dane realized that the animosity between Ellowans and Keiroits had been fabricated to serve Aiyana's secret schemes.

She calmly walked toward them, that irritating smile still on her face. Among the new Keiroits were several taller specimens, all hooded, but Dane's heart chilled.

He knew he should shoot; he knew he had been betrayed. Aiyana greeted them, and the tallest Keiroit pulled back his hood. Dane's breath caught, but his heart turned to stone. A tall, dark man appeared, his long, golden hair tossed around his shoulders.

The Ellowan resembled Aiyana so closely that Dane assumed the man to be her kindred. He embraced Aiyana, then turned to Dane. "You bring prisoners, *damanai.* Which is the Candorian?"

"Neither. The woman is Tseir, but the male . . ." Aiyana hesitated. "He represents Candor, but his homeworld is Thorwal."

The Ellowan appeared stunned by this, and Dane wondered why. "Thorwal? A strange chance . . . "

Aiyana cut him off. "Chance it is. He speaks for Candor, and that is all that matters."

"Do you consider him worthy, *damanai?*"

Aiyana hesitated, then glanced over at Dane. "He will suffice."

"Then kill the Tseir, and take him."

Galya gasped, but Dane shouldered his rifle. "Unless you intend to kill us both, I suggest considering that more carefully."

Galya moved closer to Dane, grasping his arm in terror. The Ellowan watched Dane dispassionately, ignoring Galya. "Strange that a Thorwalian should guard the Tseir . . ." Aiyana caught his eye and shook her head, and Dane wondered what she concealed from him this time.

The other Ellowans removed their hoods, revealing faces impassive and proud, though none quite as beautiful as those of Aiyana or the Ellowan leader. The shorter attackers remained hooded, and Dane looked to Aiyana for explanation.

"What are those?"

Aiyana's green eyes glittered. "They are the Keiroit 'rogues.' They refuse Tseir domination, and have in secret become our allies."

"Another deception."

"They do eat live fish."

Dane's gaze shifted to the Ellowan man. "Who are you?"

"I am Arnoth of Valenwood, prince of the Ellowans."

Even Arnoth's voice resembled Aiyana's, although his eyes were brown rather than green and his skin was darker. "Are you Aiyana's brother?"

"I am her mate."

Ice gripped Dane's heart. His face felt numb. He couldn't speak. She had lied about this, too. His shock gave way to slow anger. "Indeed. I had thought otherwise." He turned his cold gaze to Aiyana. She looked subdued rather than smug.

Arnoth didn't seem to notice the undercurrents, nor Dane's mood. Perhaps his faith in his mate was strong. Dane endured a stab of bitter envy.

"Thorwalian . . ." Arnoth paused. "By what name are you called?"

"Dane." Dane's sullen tone embarrassed him. "Dane Calydon."

Arnoth's dark eyes narrowed with interest. "The House of Calydon . . ." His voice caught, fading as if under the weight of emotion.

Dane looked between Aiyana and Arnoth. "You know much of Thorwalian terms. Calydon indeed refers to the house of my ancestry. A member of my house has led the Thorwalian Council for generations. Before that, a Calydon chieftain ruled as overlord, from a time when small kingdoms raged in battle for supremacy."

Neither Arnoth nor Aiyana responded. Aiyana appeared uncomfortable, but Dane felt certain Arnoth was troubled, even sorrowful. Why?

Arnoth turned away, almost as if the sight of Dane caused him pain. Even his pain resembled Aiyana's. Dane's hurt from learning Aiyana loved another gave way to a strange chill.

"Relieve the Thorwalian Dane of his weapons." Arnoth checked Aiyana. "Did you take them captive, *damanai?* You are armed still, I see."

Aiyana hesitated. "Not exactly. He restored my rifle when the Keiroit guards came upon us."

Dane watched as they exchanged a silent look. "Your . . . mate led me well astray. Again."

Aiyana's mouth twitched into a slight frown, but she didn't meet Dane's eyes. "He took the Rurthgar strips. They are in his pack."

Arnoth's face hardened. "The strips . . ." His gaze turned in accusation to Dane. Dane supposed Aiyana's mate guessed how the strips were found and removed. He felt a twinge of guilt, then shoved it away as he recalled her deception.

Arnoth's dark eyes burned into Dane's. "For this, your life might be forfeit, be you Thorwalian or not."

Dane's gaze didn't waver. "I have no apology. So be it."

Aiyana touched Arnoth's arm. "He was not . . . unkind."

Aiyana's hesitant defense was enough. Arnoth relaxed and his gaze shifted. Dane wondered why. If someone had stripped Nisa, he would be tempted to kill him, too.

"What devices has he? Anything for communication?"

"I saw nothing of that sort."

"Recording devices?"

"I don't know."

"We will check." Arnoth seized Dane's pack and opened it. A sharp squeal startled him and he dropped the pack.

"Help!"

Arnoth's mouth dropped as Batty emerged. He looked at Aiyana for explanation. "It is a lingbat. It talks."

Arnoth watched the rodent as it scrambled to Dane's shoulder, half-hidden in his hair. Dane sighed, but didn't comment.

"Nervous little fellow, isn't he?" Arnoth placed his hand on the lingbat's small, round head. Batty relaxed at the touch.

"Sorry, sir." Batty addressed Arnoth pleasantly. Dane glanced at the rodent from the corner of his eye. "Didn't realize you were friendly, sir." *Trying to endear himself to the enemy.* "Startled me, you did. I was having a bit of a rest."

Dane cleared his throat. "You fainted."

Batty assumed a pained expression, but he didn't argue.

Arnoth laughed, then picked up Dane's pack. He rummaged through it. Nothing caught his eye but a small, flat box. "What is this?" He didn't wait for an answer. His quick fingers touched a latch, and the box popped open.

"An image recorder. We keep images of our loved ones in these devices."

Arnoth looked at the picture and his face went white, sick. Aiyana looked up at her mate, bewildered by his reaction.

"What is it?"

Arnoth didn't speak, but she peeked around his shoulder. Dane watched as her face formed a sudden mirror of Arnoth's. "That is my sister, Nisa. She is now high councillor of Thorwal."

Aiyana closed her eyes, and Arnoth snapped the image recorder shut. He handed it back to Dane and turned away. "We start for Valendir." His voice sounded thick, strained.

Dane glanced at Aiyana for explanation. Her lips looked tight, and tears sparkled in her eyes. Her pain stabbed into his heart, despite her deception. "She is very lovely, your sister."

"Yes."

"She looks strong and happy."

"She is both."

Dane's words seemed to crush Aiyana like blows. He had no idea why. He wanted to ask, but her pain seemed too brutal to touch.

Arnoth spoke to the Keiroits, who gathered around Galya. "It is my wish to give you this Tseir, my friends. Yet today our purpose is otherwise. Forgive me."

The Keiroits muttered and growled as Galya's face drained of blood, but they seemed to acquiesce. One of them chuckled, then poked at Galya with its large, blunt hand. "Maybe later."

Galya looked desperately at Dane. He felt sympathy for her, for the first time. "She walks free, beside me, or I will fight you."

Arnoth glanced back at him. "I took your weapon."

"I don't need a weapon."

Arnoth shrugged. "She walks free, then." His dark eyes fixed on Dane's. "You are kindhearted. I was kindhearted once, too."

Arnoth started away, but his words left a foreboding sense of doom. Dane didn't understand why. Arnoth made kindness seem like . . . Dane's heart chilled. Like the end of the world.

Chapter Three

Arnoth led his group through the dark trees, along narrow paths that twisted deeper and deeper into the forest. Dane walked beside Galya, but he watched Aiyana. He tried not to focus on her relationship with Arnoth, but their interaction compelled him to scrutiny.

Batty kept his gaze fixed on the Keiroits. "Don't like the look of them, sir." His high voice quavered.

"I don't know why, Batty. You can't see them under those wraps."

"Yes, sir. But I suspect they're . . . green."

Arnoth glanced back at the lingbat. "They are green."

"They look hungry."

A broad, squat Keiroit passed by Dane, grumbling. "We *are* hungry."

A choked squeal followed. Batty waited until the Keiroit took the lead before questioning Arnoth further. "They don't consider winged creatures . . . succulent, do they?"

A smile flickered on Arnoth's lips. "They consider winged creatures sacred. You are safe."

Batty relaxed and moved down Dane's shoulder, closer to Arnoth. "Not that I'm afraid, of course. I just have to gauge the danger to my . . . to Dane."

"I can see that you are a wise friend."

Dane rolled his eyes, but didn't comment.

With a mad flutter, Batty transferred his position to Arnoth. *There's loyalty for you.* Dane felt certain that Carob wouldn't have absconded to the enemy's shoulder.

"So you're a prince, are you? Very interesting. I enjoyed some of your forest's offerings last night. Had to forage for my own meal, you understand." Batty paused to cast a meaningful look Dane's way. "Found several specimens the like of which I've never encountered."

Arnoth nodded, seeming both interested and concerned for the rodent's welfare. "Deeper in the forest, moths are abundant. We would welcome your assistance in reducing their population."

Dane fought an urge to groan loudly at this. Aiyana laughed at Arnoth's offer. "Don't say that until you've heard him eat. We may end up with a colony of hungry lingbats."

"After witnessing the Keiroits on a fishing expedition, how bad can it be?"

Aiyana grimaced. "I was awfully afraid they'd give me live fish to eat when I was in disguise."

"In the line of duty, *damanai* . . . "

Dane listened to their exchange with mixed feelings. Besides his own jealousy, he sensed something wrong. Something out of proportion to reality.

If Arnoth hadn't told him otherwise, Dane would have been certain Arnoth was Aiyana's brother. They reminded him of his relationship with Nisa. He saw love and compassion, but something was missing. Something Nisa shared only with Seneca.

Aiyana and Arnoth spoke in the manner of people who have known each other for a long time. A very long time. Maybe their passion had faded. No. No man could lose passion for Aiyana, no matter how long he lived with her.

Dane frowned. Aiyana seemed too young to have lost passion for her mate. Especially a mate like Arnoth. Dane's frown deepened, his eyes narrowed to slits, his clenched jaw twisted to one side.

He couldn't resist. He lengthened his stride and caught up with Aiyana.

"Dare I ask where you're taking me?"

She didn't look at him. "We're taking you to Valendir, our hidden village." She tried to walk faster, but Dane kept pace.

"It seems I was wrong about you." He waited for her response. When she glanced up at him, he smiled, but he felt no warmth.

"In what way?"

"I had almost come to believe your attraction wasn't intentional. That you didn't mean to affect me."

She stopped, glaring. "I did not!"

Dane stopped, too. The other Ellowans passed on ahead, paying no heed. The Keiroits ambled along, just behind Galya. "Why did you lie, Aiyana?"

"About what?"

"Which lie, you mean? You told me you weren't mated. Why?"

She wet her lips, then drew a quick breath, but she didn't answer. Dane refused to accept her silence. Anger coiled inside him.

"Well, Aiyana? If not to encourage my wayward affection, then why?"

Her green eyes widened into what appeared to be genuine surprise. "Is that what you think?"

"Yes."

"It's not so!"

"Why did you lie?" His voice grew more cold, more controlled. Aiyana seemed to recognize his mood and she averted her gaze to her feet.

"I didn't lie exactly."

"What then? Did it slip your mind, Aiyana?"

She hesitated, chewing her lip. "Well . . . yes."

Dane shook his head and walked on as Aiyana scurried beside him. "I almost believe you."

Arnoth's group reached a river, and the Keiroits left the others, hunting loudly along the bank. The Keiroits removed their protective wrappings, revealing squat bodies, indeed green, covered with small scales that sparkled in the fading sun.

"They're not quite as ugly as I imagined."

Galya eyed Dane doubtfully. "You are generous. These rogues are quite unlike the loyal Keiroit guards. These are the undisciplined few. I assure you, their behavior and lack of restraint isn't typical."

Aiyana's lip curled in irritation. "No, but it's refreshing."

As the Keiroit fed on small fish, Arnoth strung a rope bridge over the river.

"We will cross to the other side, then rest to take nourishment. We are used to these bridges. Can you cross?"

Arnoth ignored Galya, addressing all his comments only to Dane.

"I can, but Galya may have trouble."

Arnoth's eyes narrowed. "She will have no trouble." He nodded at a Keiroit, who spat fish bones from its wide, flat mouth. "Take the Tseir across."

"Can I dunk her?"

Arnoth chuckled, looking tempted. Dane started to speak, but Arnoth rolled his eyes. "Not just now."

Galya backed away from the Keiroit, but before Dane could react, the creature seized her and lifted her over his head. The Keiroit ignored the bridge and splashed through the water.

"Dane! Help me!"

Dane started after her, but Arnoth caught his arm. "Look. She is unharmed."

The Keiroit dropped Galya unceremoniously to the ground on the other side, then headed back into the river. He reached beneath the dark surface and yanked up a twitching fish, which he bit into with particular vengeance.

Batty made a gagging noise. "Disgusting." He flapped himself from Arnoth's shoulder back to Dane. "Thought you might need guidance in balance, sir. The Ellowan prince looks agile, but you . . ." Batty gulped and coughed. "I didn't mean . . ."

"Never mind." Batty's pity irritated Dane more than it should have. A lingbat's opinion of his abilities shouldn't matter. It was the unfavorable comparison to Arnoth that annoyed him most.

Irritated, Dane went on ahead of the Ellowan. *Balance, in everything*. Dane remembered Seneca's advice. He had learned it well. He fixed his eyes on the path beyond Galya as he crossed over the rope, over the swirling, dark river, and to the other side.

"Whew! Didn't think you had it in you, sir!"

Dane knew the lingbat meant to compliment him. Unfortunate choice of words, perhaps. "Thank you, Batty."

"My sire said you landed a fighter craft upside down more often than right. Figured you'd never get over that rope."

"Quiet, rodent."

Aiyana laughed. Behind him. Dane drew a long breath of

pure exasperation. ''Were you following me?''

''I, too, considered your agility questionable.''

''Thank you both.'' Dane noticed a coiled rope gripped in Aiyana's hand. ''Is that for my benefit?''

She blushed. Dane couldn't imagine her blushing, but her cheeks were pink. She peered off into the forest, casually. ''I thought I'd have to pull you out. The current is swift here. You could drown.''

''Thank you.''

Aiyana's blush deepened. Dane felt an intense wave of satisfaction.

The other Ellowans crossed over, then seated themselves while the Keiroits splashed in the water. In their dark gray cloaks, the Ellowans blended with the forest.

The Ellowans took small wafers from their packs, and Arnoth gave two wafers to Dane. ''Take this, Thorwalian. It appears light, but you will find it substantial.''

Dane accepted the wafers, but his impatience grew when they ignored Galya. ''Galya requires sustenance also.''

''We do not feed Tseir.''

Dane passed Galya a wafer. ''Yours is a stubborn race.''

''We are now.'' Arnoth rose and stood alone by a tree, tall and regal. An empty pit formed inside Dane as he watched Aiyana join Arnoth, as she touched his shoulder.

Dane seated himself beside Galya, trying not to watch Aiyana and Arnoth. He took a bite of his wafer. ''It tastes better than it looks.''

Galya ate hers, but Dane noted that she had no reaction to the unusual flavor. His attention wavered, returning to Aiyana as she sat cross-legged beside her mate. ''I don't understand them.''

''Don't try, Dane. Their cruelty is beyond understanding. But this Arnoth, he is known among our people. He is evil, relentless. I had heard rumors that his mate was equal to him in villainy, but it surprises me that he would send her on such a mission."

Dane glowered. "Maybe she was the best person for the job." Best, indeed. Who else possessed her matchless allure? He wondered if Arnoth had used his mate deliberately.

"Their outward appearance is deceptive. You have no idea what they're capable of, Dane."

"They won't hurt you, Galya. I give you my promise in this."

"You're the only reason I'm alive. Dane . . ." Galya moved closer to him, resting her hand on his arm. "Do you know why they want you?"

"I have no idea."

"They want to influence you against us. They fear the Candorians."

"They should. Candor wields great power."

Galya's gaze intensified. "I saw little evidence of their strength. Maybe their diplomacy has carried them beyond the need of weaponry."

"Candor is capable of defending itself."

"The Ellowan woman intends to seduce you for her own ends. For her mate's ends. Perhaps he even instructed her to do this."

Dane glanced toward Aiyana. "So far, she's hidden her intentions well."

"She may tell you lies about Franconia."

"She has already."

"I'm glad you realize that, Dane. But if you don't agree to whatever it is they intend to demand, they'll kill us both."

"That seems likely."

"You must agree, in order to free us."

Dane considered this. "It may be necessary in order to gain our freedom." He owed the Ellowans nothing. He owed Aiyana nothing. "Dishonesty is preferable to death."

"A noble sentiment." Aiyana's voice startled both Dane

and Galya. Her green eyes flickered with anger, her small jaw seemed clenched to restrain fury. Her stance indicated jealousy.

Dane rose to his feet. "You should know, my lady. You've chosen lies over truth to gain your ends . . . many times."

"One does what one must."

Arnoth joined them, his hand on Aiyana's shoulder. Dane considered it a comforting gesture rather than a possessive one. "We draw close to Valendir. The Tseir will be blindfolded, but you may walk free."

"Blindfold us both."

"As you wish." Arnoth readied a black cloth for Dane, but gave the other to a Keiroit. "We do not touch Tseir."

The Keiroit made a lip-smacking sound as he moved to bind Galya's eyes. It occurred to Dane that the Keiroit's action was based more in humor than in actual intent. Cruel humor, but humor nonetheless. Galya didn't notice this discrepancy. She moved close beside Dane.

"I'm frightened."

Dane took her hand. "Bind us together, so that I may know Galya is safe, and to reassure her."

Arnoth exhaled a long breath. "Do it." He tied the black cloth over Dane's eyes. "This path you walk down, Thorwalian . . . I have walked it once, too."

Despite the darkness, Dane knew Aiyana remained beside him. "He speaks cryptic words, your mate. As if he's warning me. You did this also. Why?"

Dane heard Aiyana sigh. "Because we know what you do not. You need warning."

"We have arrived in Valendir."

Arnoth removed Dane's blindfold, again leaving Dane to untie Galya's. They were deep in the forest, but the dwellings weren't as primitive as Dane expected. Wooden homes were built above the ground, secured to living trees.

Small, green hovercraft glided in and out of the darkness. Unlike Thorwal's round, white craft, the Ellowan machinery was sleek and dark. The green color seemed imposed over black. Like the Franconian flight ship.

"We use the craft little outside of our city, lest they be traced to our village. But in Valendir, you will find comfort and ease."

"What is the purpose of bringing me here? What can you say in this dark wood that couldn't be said before?"

"Not all the Ellowans have to say can be spoken in words."

Dane wearied of Arnoth's veiled statements. "You are their leader. If you have something to say to the Candorian Council, I will hear it. If not . . ."

"I am not their leader."

"Who is?"

Arnoth hesitated. "It depends on which portion of Ellowan society you address." Dane repressed a sigh of irritation at this, but he allowed Arnoth to continue. "You will be taken to our high priestess."

"Why?"

"She'll tell you that."

"And then?"

"That is for you, and her, to decide."

Dane looked around. "Where is Aiyana?"

"She is not here." Arnoth's eyes twinkled.

"I see that." Dane resisted pursuing the matter. Arnoth had no intention of telling him Aiyana's whereabouts. If she were his mate, he might keep her whereabouts secret, too.

"At this point, the Tseir can go no farther. Never has a Tseir walked free in Valendir, and never will one."

"If you harm Galya, I will prove to you what kind of enemy I can be."

"She will not be harmed, but she will not enter Valendir. She will remain under Keiroit guard."

Galya clung to Dane's arm. "They'll kill me, Dane."

"That is not acceptable, Arnoth."

Arnoth's lip curled in distaste. "She will not be harmed. In this, you have my promise."

"Ellowan promises are suspect."

"We need your assistance . . . beyond Valendir. When you leave this place, the Tseir will go with you. Believe me, if we intended to kill her, we would have done so already."

"I will agree to nothing while Galya is held captive."

"You pity her fear. Pity is blindness." Arnoth didn't wait for Dane's response. He motioned to a Keiroit, who drew out a sponge and placed it over Galya's nose and mouth. She dropped to the earth.

Dane knelt beside her, checking her pulse. It remained strong and even. "What have you done?"

"Pity her no more. For the duration of your visit, she will sleep."

Dane rose to his feet, but Arnoth didn't let him speak.

"Take care for what threat you make here, Thorwalian. This matter is deep to us, too deep for even a Ravager to dislodge."

"I am not a Ravager." Dane wondered how Arnoth knew about Thorwal's violent past, and why he referred to that ancient history as if it were current. "You speak of a distant past. My people now are stoic and logical."

"You've threatened me twice already." Arnoth was smiling. Dane's jaw clenched as he imagined using Seneca's TiKay to knock Arnoth flat. But Arnoth's smile faded, leaving instead a haunted sorrow. Dane's violent impulse stilled, but he hated his own pity. "Your sister, is she logical, too?"

"She can be." Dane faltered. "Sometimes. I'm not entirely sure what her mate would say on this point."

"I am."

Arnoth turned away and motioned toward Galya. The Keiroit tossed her over his shoulder and carried her back into the woods.

"If anything happens to her, Arnoth, I will return to Candor, and I will advise the Candorians to destroy you."

Arnoth glanced back over his shoulder. "Another threat. That would be three." Arnoth's smile returned and deepened. "When they are spoken by a Ravager, I believe them all."

A sharp wind gusted through the forest; the ancient trees creaked as they bent to its weight. Dane noticed that the Ellowan hovercraft remained unaffected by the gusts. "Well-made machinery."

"Cold wind." Batty shivered and dug himself closer to Dane's neck. Dane didn't feel the cold, but the Ellowans drew their heavy capes tighter around their bodies. Even Arnoth pulled his hood over his head.

Arnoth motioned to a shuttle, which stopped before them. "Perhaps you will find the craft of interest, Thorwalian."

Dane climbed in and examined the controls. "As I thought . . . These are the same design as the Franconian vessel. Stolen, I presume?"

"Stolen, yes." Arnoth paused. "But from whom?"

Dane wasn't sure what Arnoth meant, but Arnoth said no more on the subject. "I assume Aiyana has gone on ahead to inform your priestess of my arrival." Dane settled himself in the dark craft, reluctant to allow Arnoth the controls.

Again, that infuriating smile. "Aiyana has gone on ahead." Arnoth guided the hovercraft forward, then looked over at Dane. "You are concerned for her welfare. She is not far from your thoughts. Can it be your thoughts of her are those of a lover?"

Dane cringed. He'd never dallied with another man's mate, nor wanted to. But Aiyana was different. Dane reacted as if she were his mate, and Arnoth the interloper. Arnoth laughed.

"Never mind. It was an unfair question."

Batty perched on the edge of Dane's shoulder, then hopped again to Arnoth. "Thought he was going to take the female for himself, until you showed up. My sire told me humanoid sexual function was complex."

Dane longed to swat the lingbat from the craft, but Arnoth only laughed again. "It is, indeed."

The hovercraft stopped—none too soon, to Dane's thinking. His face felt hot, and he blessed the Ellowan preference for darkness. Only small lanterns lit the center of their hamlet.

Dane left the hovercraft and looked around. They were on a platform that led into a sleek, narrow building. Unlike the wooden huts Dane had seen, this building was crafted from the same black material as the Franconian vessels.

"It's a flight ship."

"It was."

"Your village reminds me of Dakota."

Arnoth glanced at Dane. "Dakota?"

"Since you know so much about my system, I assumed you knew of Thorwal's neighboring world."

"No."

"My sister's mate rules in Dakota."

"The daughter of one world, the son of another. Two powers become stronger united into one."

"Maybe. But Nisa and Seneca mated for love."

"Sometimes it is so. Fortune favors the few . . . and the doomed."

Arnoth walked away, leaving Dane standing alone. "What is going on here?"

"Morbid fellow, isn't he, sir?"

"In an irritating way, yes." Dane paused. "Not unlike Aiyana."

"I thought that, too." Batty fell into a contemplative mood. "Don't see any young, any small Ellowans."

Dane looked around. "No." Every Ellowan he had seen appeared to be similar in age to Aiyana and Arnoth. His own age, young. Young, but with another element that eluded his understanding. No, they weren't young, but ageless.

Dane wanted to find Aiyana, to question her. In comparison to Arnoth, she was a fountain of information. From all over the village, hovercraft arrived at the platform, docked, then made way for the next. The other Ellowans proceeded into the dark building. Dane followed.

He entered a narrow passageway, then stopped. The black wall inside the transformed flightship was decorated with mosaic art. Candorian art. But not Candorian. Ellowan. A cool rush swarmed Dane's senses. Candor had been founded by the Ellowan.

"That's where I've seen her before."

"Who, sir?"

"Aiyana." Dane scrutinized the wall art, and saw images of sexual intimacy, of sensual detail, of dancing and feasting and pleasure. The people were clearly Ellowan, dark haired, lithe. Beautiful.

Batty chuckled, and Dane eyed him suspiciously. "You knew."

"Knew what, sir?" The high chirp indicated a lie. Dane's cold stare intensified. "Oh, that. About the Ellowans . . . I didn't *know*, per se. Just a theory formulated by our old ones."

"What theory?"

"Legend passed down from lingbat to lingbat. Similarities in what the Candorians found out researching Franconia and what we remembered. Only we didn't call them Ellowans. We called them Elves."

"So Candor was an Ellowan outpost, was it?" Dane

watched the Ellowans file into main hull of the ship. "Yet these are too few in number. . . . Even Galya says they are few. How could they build an outpost?"

"That was ages ago, sir. Before the Candorians arrived, while your people were . . ."

Dane recalled Aiyana's words. "Throwing spears at short-legged pigs."

"Were they, sir? Seems like an awful waste of time."

"Not if you're hungry." Dane started down the hallway again, determined to get answers. His eye caught a discordant image and he stopped. There, on the wall of faded mosaic, was a tall, blond man. A man holding a two-handed battle-ax. A Ravager ax.

Arnoth appeared at the door. "The priestess awaits you, Dane Calydon."

Dane tore his gaze from the image. His heartbeat became strange and heavy as he joined Arnoth and entered the dark room. There was no light, though he knew many Ellowans filled the room. Arnoth led him through an unseen aisle.

"Whew! What a crowd! Now, there's the group that escorted us here." Batty could see in the dark. Of course.

"Do you see Aiyana?"

"No."

"What about this priestess?"

"Don't see her, either."

Arnoth made no comment as he led Dane through the crowd. There were no murmurs, no sound. "Does it have to be this dark, Arnoth? We're inside."

"The priestess always begins ceremony and ritual in darkness, for it is darkness that surrounds us. Once, this act was performed in light."

A small glow began behind Dane. It grew and spread, then formed a point in front of him. He saw that a woman knelt before him. She wore a sheer purple dress, trimmed with deep purple. She rose, and he knew her.

"Of course." Dane's dry voice broke the respectful silence. "Aiyana."

"I am Aiyana Nidawi, high priestess of Valenwood."

"I thought it was 'Valendir.' Keep the names straight to avoid confusion."

Dane felt satisfied for successfully flattening the moment. Her lips tightened in irritation. "Valenwood was the home of our . . . ancestors. Valendir is this hamlet. *Dir* means, in the tongue of our people, 'shadow of.' "

"I see. The shadow of Valenwood. Then this place is an Ellowan outpost." Dane paused for effect. "As was Nerotania on Candor. Go on."

"Thank you." Her voice was low and strained. "You speak for the Candorian Council. They represent the Intersystem to which Franconia does not, nor has it ever, belonged."

"An excellent recap."

She twitched. "It is your purpose to learn on their behalf whether or not to intervene in Franconia's troubles."

"To learn whether or not to aid the Tseirs against you, yes."

"We ask that you do not."

Dane hesitated at this. Aiyana waited. "Do not what?"

"Do not come to Franconia, do not aid the Tseirs."

Dane nodded impatiently. "That request, I assumed. Go on."

"That is all."

"What do you mean, 'that is all'? You brought me here, Aiyana, you and your gloomy mate. What do you want of me?"

"We ask that you pass our request on to the Candorians."

Dane shook his head to clear his senses. "Just that? You want them to mind their own business, is that it?"

Aiyana nodded.

Dane shrugged. "All right. I'll pass it on."

"Thank you."

"There's nothing else?"

"You may stay here until tomorrow. At that time, we will give you a hovercraft, and you may take the Tseir to the Swamp of Keir."

Aiyana bowed slightly, then turned away. Dane caught her arm. "Aiyana, I want answers. Believe me, this visit and my encounter with you and your crazy people has given me far more questions than answers."

Aiyana peeked over her shoulder, hesitating. "What do you want to know?"

"Who are you?" He spoke loudly, his patience strained.

"I just told you—"

"Yes, I know. Aiyana Nidawi. I like that, by the way. It suits you."

"What do you want to know?"

"Explanations, Aiyana. For this . . ." He waved his arms, gesturing at the room. "Why did you bring me here? Why not travel yourself, in the open, to Candor with your request? Why the subterfuge?"

"We haven't the means to travel to Candor."

Dane's eyes narrowed with distrust. "Hijacking doesn't seem beyond you."

"We wished to learn the Tseirs' intentions. We brought you here to make a formal request. It is our way."

Dane seized Aiyana's arm and led her down the aisle, past Arnoth, past her people. He wondered why Arnoth didn't try to stop him.

"What are you doing?" She tugged to free herself, but Dane led her forcefully to the mosaic wall outside the door. He pointed at the final scene.

"Explain this."

Aiyana drew a quick breath. "What do you want me to explain?"

"What do I want you to explain?" Dane made a growling

noise, his fingers tightening around her arm. "This is a Ravager, Aiyana. You may consider me a fool, but I know my own people. He bears a Ravager ax. He wears a Ravager tunic. We have a record of history, you know. A Hall of Ancients that depicts these things quite clearly."

"Oh, that." Aiyana winced at his icy expression.

"Yes, *that*. What's he doing there, Aiyana? A Ravager, on your wall. Here, in the Franconian system."

"He was king. Long ago."

Dane nodded. "Perfectly understandable." He drew and exhaled a long, taut breath. "Who was he, and how did he come to be king of the Ellowans?"

"His name was Hakon. In the ancient times of your world, an Ellowan priestess—"

"Your ancestor?"

"Yes, she was my ancestor. She crashed her flightship on Thorwal."

"Thorwalian history seems to have overlooked that."

"I don't believe your people recorded history then."

"We had oral history, passed down in song and story. A crashed flightship would show up in legend. Or certainly be discovered later."

"Only one person saw the ship before it burned up in the crash."

"This Hakon?"

"Yes."

"How did he come to be king of the Ellowans?"

"When Ariana was rescued, she brought him with her. He was a good king."

"Why did she bring him?"

Aiyana averted her eyes. "They fell in love. The Ravagers were at war; Hakon's brother wanted him dead—"

"Hakon! Not Hakon *the Betrayer*?"

Aiyana made a fist. "Hakon the Magnificent!"

"Ha! If he is the same, Hakon the Betrayer was a villainous rogue who turned on his brother—Haldane, the rightful leader of the Calydon line and my own ancestor. Hakon led a force against his brother, then deserted the battle effort against him."

"You know nothing of your history, Thorwalian. For one thing, he didn't desert. He left your planet and went with Ariana to Valenwood. And he had no choice but to fight. Hakon's fiendish brother tried to take my . . . ancestor, and when Hakon refused . . ."

Dane angled his jaw in a stubborn posture. "In those days, it was the chieftain's right to claim any woman he desired."

"A foul practice. Ariana didn't want to be 'claimed.' She loved Hakon."

"Ariana . . ." Dane studied her face while Aiyana fidgeted. "I suppose she looked like you."

"Perhaps."

"No wonder they went to war. Does this mean you, my sweet lady, have Thorwalian blood in your veins?"

"Distantly."

"That explains the light eyes. Well, well."

"Is there anything else? I have explained the Ravager on the walls."

"Arnoth's reaction. Why does the mention of Thorwal, and my sister in particular, cause him pain?"

Aiyana hesitated, and sorrow flickered in her eyes. "Since Hakon's time, there have been a few Ellowan who resembled Thorwalians. My sister was one."

"Your sister?"

"Arnoth's first mate."

A cold pain of understanding washed through Dane. "Your sister resembles Nisa."

Tears appeared around Aiyana's lashes and she swallowed hard. "She did."

"She died."

"Yes."

"In warfare against the Tseirs?"

Aiyana clenched her teeth. "You might call it that."

"I am sorry, Aiyana. I will tell the Candorians your request, Aiyana. But unless you're prepared to negotiate—"

"We are not!"

"Then I don't know what I can do." Dane paused. "How did your people lose their power? The Ellowans must have been dominant once, to have outposts as far as Candor."

Aiyana held his gaze for a long while. "We were kind." She gathered her long skirts and turned away, leaving Dane standing by the mosaic.

Dane watched her hurry away, and his heart quailed. No wonder the mention of Nisa brought them pain. This explained her friendly but passionless union with Arnoth. They were joined together in grief, not desire.

Batty uttered a long, drawn-out sigh. "Sad tale, wasn't it? They don't make much sense, do they, sir?"

"No."

Arnoth approached the wall, assessing the image of Hakon before he spoke. "She told you."

"Yes." Dane hesitated, feeling uncomfortable. "I am sorry."

Arnoth didn't look at Dane, but kept his gaze fixed on the wall. "Your people, so filled with life. So strong."

"We are, perhaps."

Arnoth turned, his dark eyes filled with sudden emotion. "Hakon believed in destruction. He believed in destroying the enemy before they struck. We did not. We were wrong."

"The Ravagers nearly destroyed each other with that philosophy. Yet negotiation tends toward peace. Dakota and Thorwal neared war, but it was successfully averted."

"This Dakota, was it stronger than your world?"

"In some ways. We were stronger in others."

"Did they hate you?"

"No. They were afraid of us. Maybe we were afraid of them, too."

"There are other kinds of war, Dane."

Dane saw a glimmer of hope. He seized Arnoth's shoulder, hoping to will logic into the Ellowan prince. "Then give up your hatred. If you abandon your emotion, your concepts of each other, you'll see what's really there." Dane felt powerful, and he knew he was right. This was what Kostbera wanted of him.

But Arnoth laughed bitterly. "We rid ourselves of emotion, Ravager. We rid ourselves of concepts. We saw what's there. . . . Too late, what we saw there was only hate."

Dane started to speak, but Arnoth held up his hand. "You need us, Thorwalian. Candor needs us." He leaned closer, his dark eyes as bright as Aiyana's. "Your sister needs us."

"Why?"

"That, you must learn for yourself. Go to Franconia, for all the good it will do you. But the Candorians would be wiser to offer no aid. They may need it for themselves one day."

Find the reality of Franconia . . . Dane wondered if Kostbera had any idea how difficult a task that might prove. Asking didn't seem to get many answers. "What now?"

"We eat. I will bring you to our feasting hall. Come."

Dane shrugged, then followed Arnoth to the platform that lowered to the ground below. Arnoth led Dane to a long, low building. The other Ellowans waited outside the entrance, all gray-caped and silent. Aiyana stood among them, but she didn't meet Dane's eyes.

Dane sighed and looked around. The Ellowans were waiting. An oppressive gloom settled over the glen, gaining entrance into Dane's heart. "What are we waiting for?"

"Midnight."

Dane wanted to strangle Arnoth. "Midnight." The Ellowan prince seemed incapable of a straight, informative answer. "Why?" Dane growled the word.

Arnoth's dark eyes twinkled, an infuriating response. "Because, *Ravager*, there is a ritual before feasting."

Dane wondered how Arnoth knew so easily how to annoy him. He seemed well practiced in the art. A strange premonition circled around his heart. Perhaps Aiyana's sister had the same looks and temperament not only as Nisa, but as Dane himself.

Dane chewed the inside of his mouth as he pondered this possibility. He didn't consider himself violent. Certainly not akin to a Ravager, as Arnoth seemed to indicate. He was restrained and logical, the most skilled technician Thorwal had ever produced. Hardly violent.

Dane's impatience soared. "Look, Arnoth . . . your wafers may have had more flavor than I expected, but I could use a real meal."

"Silence."

Dane gritted his teeth. *Yes, TiKay might prove useful here. Curse Seneca's instructions to use the art only in defense! Sometimes, attack is more satisfying.*

Arnoth laughed as if he read Dane's thoughts. Dane felt the impending heat of battle. *Feed me or die* seemed an excessive response, so he forced restraint over his impulse. It wasn't easy.

Arnoth looked up into the sky, through a small clearing in the thick branches. His teasing expression faded to the same haunted, sorrowful look Dane knew from Aiyana's face. Despite himself, Dane felt pity.

"It begins . . ." Arnoth left Dane and took his place by Aiyana. The Ellowans formed a semicircle around them. Dane stood outside the circle, watching. Seeking anything that would broaden his understanding of their peculiar race.

As one, the Ellowans turned their gazes to the sky. Dane followed the direction of their gaze into the stars. There hung a thin sliver. A sliver he knew. The Midnight Moon.

The dark moon shimmered in the sky, partially obscured by the clouds over Keir. Aiyana chanted soft words, repeated by Arnoth, then the other Ellowans.

"We remember, forever." Over and over, softer and softer, until their words faded into a whisper. The chant echoed in Dane's mind. *Remember, forever.*

A terrible longing sounded in their voices, devoid of music, yet still lyrical, poignant almost beyond endurance. The open space between the high branches was small. The Midnight Moon offered only a glimpse, then disappeared behind the black canopy of trees.

Dane stared into the sky, though the other Ellowans turned away and headed into the building. Arnoth glanced at him thoughtfully, then passed by, leaving Dane alone with Aiyana.

She stood beside him, silent, waiting.

"Do you know what it is now?"

Dane nodded, his heart chilled to the core. "It is the home of the Ellowans . . . Valenwood."

"It was."

"This is why you brought me here, isn't it? To see that moon."

"Yes."

"Curse you, Aiyana. Why didn't you tell me? Why don't you tell me now?"

"Would you believe me?"

"I might."

"And you might not. Words are just words, expression of a greater form. And that form might be deceit."

Dane nearly succumbed to violence again. He wanted to pick Aiyana up and shake her. "Is it a trait of the Ellowan to say nothing that is clear?"

"Do we say too little, or too much? I do not know."

Dane's only response was a rumbling growl. "Do you

think I'm incapable of a rational decision? Do you think I'm such a fool that you must toy with me this way?"

Aiyana laid her hand on his arm. "No. I think you're kind."

Dane clasped his hand over hers. "I do want to understand you, Aiyana."

She smiled, and his frustration faded in the face of her charm. "I think you do, more than you know. You think we're different. The truth is more complex. We're too much the same."

"In what way?"

"We're both hungry." Her smile widened, a teasing glint in her bright eyes. She might as well have reached inside him, seized his heart, and ripped it from his chest.

Dane shook his head. "Maybe I was wrong. I am a fool, after all."

Aiyana brought Dane into the feasting hall. She took her place beside Arnoth, seating Dane on her other side. Dane considered the placement awkward, but neither Arnoth nor Aiyana seemed to notice.

Batty sat on the back of Arnoth's chair, awaiting his portion. "Any bugs?"

Arnoth glanced over at the bat. "No bugs. You may sample what we have, as you wish."

Batty leveled a long, meaningful stare at Dane, then turned back to Arnoth. "Thank you. A true prince, you are, sir."

A large, squat Keiroit entered the hall, then seated himself beside Arnoth. He wore protective wrapping, and Dane wondered if the Ellowans served live fish. "This is Rurthgar, leader of the rogue Keiroits."

"Rurthgar?" Dane turned to Aiyana. "Isn't that what you called your explosive devices?"

"It is. In fact, it was Rurthgar who designed them. He is

an able technician.'' She paused. ''Like yourself, perhaps.''

''Technician, are you? Ha!'' Rurthgar made an odd sputtering noise beneath his wrapping. Aiyana had mimicked the Keiroit behavior well. ''Humanoids know squat about technology!''

Dane frowned. ''There is nothing made by hand—or fin—that I can't divine and better.'' He sat back in his seat, resisting a twinge of regret over his rash boast.

An older Ellowan woman laid a large platter of food in front of Arnoth. She chuckled at Dane's words. ''There's a Ravager for you. Boasting even before he's drunk.''

Dane clenched his teeth, warm with anger. ''For the last time, the Ravager period in Thorwal's history is long past. True, once my distant ancestors sat around their great halls and drank and bragged and generally wreaked havoc, but we evolved beyond that. . . .''

Rurthgar drew a flat, pronged instrument from his cape and passed it to Dane. ''Prove yourself, Thorwalian. What is it?''

Dane examined the instrument. He made no comparisons to other objects; he didn't generalize or seek to find its answer from another's form. ''It's a feeding device. A fork.''

Rurthgar snatched the fork back. He stabbed it into a sliver of roasted meat and stuffed his portion beneath his wrapping. ''Should have given you something more complex. Thought I'd trick you.''

''You failed.''

Arnoth set a blunt, metallic flute on the table in front of Dane. ''When they weren't drinking or pillaging, the Ravagers played music.''

Dane fingered the instrument. ''A Thorwalian flute . . . Hakon's, I presume. It appears authentic, forged in our subterranean mines. My uncle was well skilled at this. When I was a boy, he taught me a few old songs.''

''Play.''

Dane shrugged, then picked up the flute. "It's been a while." He tested the instrument, tried its notes. "Well tended . . ."

Aiyana watched as Dane breathed life into the Ravager flute. Her heart clenched with a longing so strong that it obliterated her reality. She remembered who she had been, long ago, and what she wanted. . . .

It was an old song, one she had heard before. In Dane's music, she heard the sonorous glory of the Ravagers as they had been; strong, valiant, proud, and filled with fire. Arnoth rose from his seat and retrieved a small Ellowan harp from the corner of the hall. Without a word, he passed it to Aiyana.

She touched the harp, and it sang. Dane stopped, his blue eyes wide. When he realized she played the same song, he smiled, and added his music to hers. Tears stung Aiyana's eyes as their music filled the hall. She saw in her mind a memory, a man and a woman whose love changed two worlds, who had played music that filled a giant, sparkling hall of light. . . .

The song ended and Dane set his instrument aside. "I take it Hakon passed his people's music to his mate's world."

Aiyana fought her emotion and lay the harp at her feet. "The Ellowans love music."

"You blend well together." Arnoth took his flute and put it back in his cape. Dane appeared uncomfortable, and Aiyana wondered if Arnoth spoke of music only. He knew her well. He knew her old dreams.

"In Valenwood, it was said that if a man and a woman played music well together, they would be well mated. If discordant . . . the match was doomed to fail."

Arnoth took a bite of his dinner, but his eyes sparkled. A smile twitched at the corners of his lips. Aiyana cast a reproachful glare his way, but his smile only widened. She checked Dane's expression. His brow was furrowed, and his eyes were slits of confusion and suspicion.

Aiyana cleared her throat. "Music is for its own sake . . ."

"An expression of a form." Arnoth chuckled. "Sometimes that form is love. Sometimes sorrow." He glanced at Dane, then Aiyana. "Sometimes . . . pure, untarnished lust."

Rurthgar belched. "Humanoids are disgusting. Sex, sex, sex."

Aiyana repressed a giggle as Dane eyed the Keiroit. Batty made a slight chirp that sounded like a fake cough. "My sire did mention a certain fixation on the act."

Dane's brow rose, his lip curling. "He should know. He sired enough litters during our stay on Candor to populate this world and several others."

Batty looked surprised, then contemplative. "Now, that *is* a truism, sir."

Arnoth laughed. "And you, Rurthgar, you have sired . . ."

"Sixty-two eggs this year. Seventeen hatched. Ate the rest."

Arnoth nodded, his face serious. "Those eggs weren't fertilized on their own."

A chortling noise came from beneath Rurthgar's wrapping. "Not exactly, no."

Aiyana felt relieved that the conversation had shifted away from her relationship with Dane. "Arnoth is better skilled than I at the harp."

Dane leaned back in his seat and folded his arms over his chest. "If he plays like he talks, the music will be vague and without a point, and deliver us nowhere."

Arnoth took it as a challenge. He seized Aiyana's harp and set his long fingers to the strings. Aiyana had heard him play a thousand times, yet his music never failed to stir her heart. But gone tonight was the endless sorrow that permeated Arnoth's usual music. He played from a time before darkness. He played to desire. He played from Valenwood.

Aiyana resisted the images that fought entrance into her mind. But the music cascaded and wafted, lifted and penetrated, and her inner senses stirred to life. The song was teasing and passionate, nearly touching, then retreating. It was sexual and contemplative.

Aiyana's gaze drifted to Dane. He felt it, too. His sweet, sensual face was a veiled mask of desire, his eyes darkened beyond blue, deep and fiery. His blond hair hung over his eyebrows, to his shoulders, around his face.

Aiyana endured a wild impulse to touch him, to tangle her fingers in his soft hair and kiss him. As if he read her thoughts, his lips parted. Aiyana squeezed her eyes shut, but Arnoth didn't end the song. It went on, building and building. Promising.

Just as she thought she would perish from longing, Arnoth stopped abruptly and set the harp aside. He went back to his meal, pleased with himself. "You'll have to finish the rest on your own."

Dane's jaw dropped and Aiyana cringed. Was that what she had wanted? Dane ate his meal in silence, and Aiyana avoided meeting his eyes. He would never understand the Ellowan way, nor what stirred between them. Only Arnoth understood.

"Well, sir, where do we sleep?" The lingbat's cheerful voice indicated that he had missed the undercurrents of tension between the humanoids. Rurthgar burped again.

"I'd think you'd want time away from humanoids, little fellow," Rurthgar observed.

Arnoth set aside his plate. "A good suggestion. Take the lingbat to your hold, Rurthgar. He should find hunting in the marsh a success beyond his wildest dreams."

Batty's claws scraped the chair nervously. Arnoth patted

his head. "The Keiroits will defend you. As I told you, winged creatures are sacred to them."

"Are they?"

Rurthgar rose and bowed before the lingbat. "You do us great honor by visiting our hold."

" 'Hold,' sir?"

"Well, it's a small marsh outside Valendir, but you'll like it."

Batty turned toward Dane. "Shall I, sir?"

"As you wish, Batty. Just see that you're back in time to leave tomorrow."

Batty seemed hesitant. Arnoth rolled his eyes, and Aiyana wondered why he wanted the bat out of Valendir. "You may find the Dwindle Bats of interest. They're smaller than yourself, and they speak only in their own tongue, but because of this, they will find you majestic." Arnoth paused, his dark eyes shining. "Especially the females."

This perked Batty's interest. "As you say, sir. I'll check out this marsh, and report back any finds of interest."

Dane's brow angled. "What would you expect to find in a marsh that could possibly—"

Arnoth held up his hand, silencing Dane. Dane glared. "It would be of great service. Communicate as you see fit, and perhaps shed new light on the Dwindle Bats' viewpoint."

Aiyana eyed Arnoth doubtfully. He'd never expressed an interest in Dwindle Bats before.

Dane sat back in his seat. The more time he spent with the Ellowans, the more confused he became. He felt certain now that Arnoth was crazy. Dwindle Bats. Dane shook his head, but his gaze wandered back to Aiyana.

He hadn't misconstrued the look on her little face this time. He knew desire when he saw it. It was the same look he had noticed in the woods, only stronger, fed by Arnoth's pulsating, erotic music.

If it didn't seem so preposterous, he'd be certain Arnoth was offering him his mate. From the art on the Candorian wall, Dane guessed that the Ellowan were uninhibited, rarely bothering with privacy to consummate their bliss. Maybe they took some odd pleasure in sharing their mates.

Dane's blood stirred at the thought. His own ancestors had been the same. Many a frozen night was spent in drunken orgies in the old Ravager halls. No, he wouldn't share Aiyana—Dane caught himself. She wasn't his to share. She belonged to Arnoth.

With any other woman, he might consider it. He could imagine the pleasures of sexual freedom. But when he looked over at Aiyana's small, lovely face, he knew he wanted more. Anything less would hurt too much.

Arnoth rose from the table and faced Dane. "You may rest now, Thorwalian. Tomorrow you will be given a hovercraft, and the Tseir, and you may depart Valendir."

"I will hold you to your word."

"Or fight me . . . Yes, I know." Arnoth took Aiyana's hand, and Dane's heart constricted. "There's something we need to discuss, *damanai*."

She nodded, but she didn't speak. Dane noticed that she carefully avoided his eyes as they left. Dane's mind pounded him with agonizingly erotic images. She would go with Arnoth to some mystic room they shared, and they would make love to the rhythm of Arnoth's music, while Dane lay alone, longing for her, a woman beyond his reach, beyond his understanding.

"Curse you. Curse you both."

"Sir?" Batty's small, hesitant voice broke Dane's painful concentration. "Are you all right, sir?"

"Fine, Batty." His voice came lower, huskier than normal.

"Perhaps you'd rather I stayed to guard you, sir."

"That won't be necessary, rodent." Batty winced at Dane's harsh tone, and Dane felt a twinge of remorse. "Enjoy the role of sacred winged being tonight, Batty. But keep your head if these 'Dwindle Bats' decide to crown you king. Tomorrow we leave this place . . . and not a moment too soon."

"I want to live."

Aiyana knelt before Arnoth's seat, her hands on his knees. He looked away, into the darkness of his chamber. Very gently, he touched her hair.

"I know, *damanai*."

"We both know why the Tseir went to Candor. It is the strongest planet in their system, but it's not populated. They dwell on the fringe of the Intersystem." Aiyana's fingers clenched. "Arnoth, someone must go. Let it be me."

"Can you stand the pain, little one? Do you know how much it hurts?"

"Yes." Her voice quavered. "But I can't go on this way anymore. I want an ending."

"It is your right to choose. It may be the only way. We need the Thorwalian aligned with us. He wants you."

"He says so." Aiyana frowned. "Sometimes I question this. He desired a Candorian woman, too."

Arnoth smiled gently. "He wants you, *damanai*. It has been a very long time since I felt that, but I remember wanting."

Aiyana looked up at him, tears streaking her cheeks. "I didn't expect to feel this way."

"You didn't expect to meet a Thorwalian. But I remember a child, long ago, who told me she intended to take a ship through the wormhole and capture one for herself."

Aiyana's heart warmed and constricted simultaneously at the memory. "But they aren't Ravagers anymore."

"From what I've seen, the Ravager impulse is as strong as it ever was. Perhaps more so now that it's tempered with logic. Your Dane, he professes reason, but he is quick to battle."

"I noticed that. He enjoys battle."

"He enjoys life."

Aiyana nodded, but her throat clenched. "Yes."

"Then it's up to us to see that his life, and his world's life, continues."

Aiyana's eyes met Arnoth's, steady and sure. "I believe the Tseirs are prepared, even now."

"Evidence suggests this, yes."

"If that is so, we have no other choice. If I can't convince Dane . . . Arnoth, someone must destroy their central command station. And there is only one way to do that."

Arnoth's jaw hardened, but he didn't argue. "It will only set them back for a while, and it will mean the loss of an Ellowan."

"Let it be me."

For a long while, neither spoke. Then Arnoth nodded. "It is your choice. If the Thorwalian's nature proves more 'civilized' than Ravager, there will be no other way. The Candorians, are they capable of destroying the Tseirs?"

"If they so desired, yes."

"Would they listen to a Ravager's counsel in this matter?"

"The head of their council, Kostbera, holds Dane in high esteem. She left the matter to him. I believe they would take his word."

"Then it is necessary that he be bonded to you. He will not take our word otherwise. Do you know what this means, little one? Are you prepared?"

"I am." Aiyana quivered, fear and hope and need inside her, breaking to life. "I want him, too."

"I wouldn't willingly see you endure such pain, Aiyana.

If we fail, you know his fate. His world's fate."

"We can't fail."

"That will mean your death, then. I won't be there to heal you. You will be alone."

"But I will have *lived,* Arnoth. I would prefer it to this endless existence."

Arnoth sat back, studying her face. Aiyana looked up at him. She saw his eternal pain, and she saw his eternal youth. She wished his life could develop again, grow. Maybe someday, beyond this endless war, he might find something to relieve the pain of his past.

"You and I are the best of friends."

Arnoth touched his long finger to her cheek. "We are the same, *damanai.* We always have been. I fear for you, but I won't deny you the power of what you seek."

Aiyana pressed her damp cheek against his hand. "I will take the chance."

Arnoth bent and kissed her forehead, though she saw tears in his dark eyes. "Then I release you."

Chapter Four

Dane stood in the Ellowan guest chamber, staring out a wide window into the night. The door opened silently. In the reflection on the window, Dane saw Aiyana. She fiddled with her dress. She looked nervous, her hands clasped in front of her body.

Dane glanced over his shoulder, but he didn't turn. "What do you want, Aiyana?"

"I . . ." She drew a tight breath. "I thought you wanted me."

Dane's brow furrowed as he eyed her in confusion. "No." She still wore her priestess dress. It was cut low over her breasts, snug at her waist. She was too beautiful. Dane turned back to the window.

"Oh." She sounded despondent, but she didn't leave. "I thought, from your behavior, from the things you said . . ." She was rambling, making no sense.

Dane turned around, his arms folded over his chest. He studied her like a technician. "What do you mean, 'wanted you'? I didn't call for you, nor did I request your presence.'' He paused. ''That is what you meant, isn't it?''

Aiyana puffed a small breath of frustration. ''No, it's not what I meant.'' She cleared her throat. ''I thought you wanted me . . . as a woman.''

Dane laughed. His brow lifted, and he laughed again. Aiyana lifted her chin, fiercely. ''Very well. I see that you do not. I will trouble you no further.''

She aimed for the doorway, but he caught her and drew her back. ''Have you lost your mind, Aiyana?'' Dane released her and paced around the room, separating her from the exit. ''Want you? Are we talking about the same thing here?''

''Possibly.''

Dane seized her arm again and positioned her in front of him. She refused to meet his eyes. ''Sex, Aiyana. If I didn't know better, I'd think you were offering me your body.''

She didn't answer, enough of a reply to shock him into silence. His grip on her arm relaxed. He backed away, but his heart moved in odd, erratic jerks.

''And your mate . . . Arnoth, what does he say about this?''

''Arnoth has released me.''

''Just like that?'' Dane's voice grew louder. He pointed his finger at her, shaking it. ''The Ellowans make the Dakotans look sane. And that's not easy, woman.''

Dane turned around in a full circle, then faced her again. ''Maybe I don't understand the customs of your people. Maybe it's usual for a man to share his woman with guests. Maybe you learned it from Hakon—''

''Hakon never shared Ariana!''

''It was an old custom among the Ravagers.''

Her mouth formed an indignant pout. ''Not here.''

Dane studied Aiyana's small face, hoping to see some flaw, something he could focus on and forget her strange appeal. His heart had turned to her when they met. Learning she belonged to another had wounded him, but he respected her bond with Arnoth.

Yet here she was, apparently offering herself to him. "Why?"

She looked confused now. *Good.* "What do you mean?"

"Why would you surrender your 'virtue,' shall we say, for me?"

"Do I need a reason?"

"Yes."

She looked at her feet, shifting her weight. Fidgeting. Dane resisted a mad impulse to draw her into his arms and comfort her. "Well?"

"I thought . . . it might be pleasant."

"It might. Curse you, woman. It might, indeed." Dane fought the image. "So, Arnoth grants me his lovely mate for the night. A generous man."

"I am no longer his. I told you—"

"Yes, I know. He released you. I've never even kissed you, Aiyana."

"No." She still didn't look at him. She was trembling, visibly. "You said you wanted to."

"I do." Dane touched the side of her chin. He tilted her face up, though her eyes remained cast to the side. He bent and touched his lips to hers, briefly. Her lips were soft and warm. He allowed himself no other impression as he drew back from her.

"There. I have kissed you."

She looked up at him. The fire in her dark green eyes sent a thrilling vibration along his nerves. "That wasn't a kiss." Something changed in her face. The haunted expression was gone; the vagueness disappeared. She looked fierce enough for battle.

Aiyana seized Dane by the hair, entwining her fingers in it as she pulled his face down to hers. Her parted lips met his; she ran her tongue along the outline, tasting. She sucked his lower lip. She nipped.

Dane's restraint shattered like a burst dam. In his mind flashed the image of Thorwalian lava flows, shattering the ice, rending his world. . . . "Aiyana . . ."

Her soft mouth left his; she kissed his jaw, his face, his neck. She kissed his throat as her quick fingers parted his shirt. He felt her lips on his chest, felt the little darts of her tongue as she tasted his flesh.

Dane fought to regain control of his senses. He knew she wanted something from him. He couldn't flatter himself enough to think it was just sex. "Aiyana, if you would tell me the truth—"

She bit him. A small bite, painless. Her tongue laved the spot. Dane's pulse surged. "If Hakon endured this, I see why he betrayed Thorwal. . . ."

Aiyana rested her cheek against his bare chest, leaning against him. Dane supported her, his heart thundering as she leaned against him.

She looked up at him. "You said once you would give me life. Then give me life now."

He didn't know what she meant, but he saw deep passion in her eyes. "I misjudged your capacity for seduction, my lady. I should have known it would prove more than I could resist."

Aiyana reached her trembling hand to touch his face. She touched his mouth, then closed her eyes. "I don't mean to seduce you. I want to be with you."

Dane caught her hand in his, then held it to his heart. "Why?"

"Because you're everything I was once. You're everything I wished for, before . . ." She faltered and looked away.

"Before the war with the Tseirs?"

She hesitated, then nodded. Dane kissed her hand. "I

didn't realize there was a 'before.' I thought that the Ellowans had battled the Tseirs for ages. Maybe since Hakon was your king."

"It has been since that time."

"There is much you keep to yourself, my lady. Much you don't say. You ask me to take a stranger to my bed."

Aiyana peered up at him, her eyes narrow. "Is that something you've never done before?"

A reluctant smile curved Dane's lips. "When I was young, I was unrestrained in my pursuit of pleasure. But those encounters that idled my time then meant nothing, Aiyana. Nothing except flattery to myself, to my skill."

"I will flatter you."

"That's very reassuring."

Dane's heart ached as he looked at Aiyana, her slanted green eyes sparkling, her lips parted and moist. He imagined taking her as she offered, loving her to exhaustion, cradling her head on his shoulder and drifting into sleep . . . together.

"I want more from you."

Her brow furrowed in confusion. "You have only to teach me."

Dane held her small hands against his mouth. He closed his eyes and kissed the backs of her fingers. "Aiyana, some things can't be taught."

"Then what do you want of me? Tell me, and I will do it."

"I want your love."

Aiyana rolled her eyes. Dane winced inwardly, though he kept his expression straight. How could love mean so little to her? He didn't understand the Ellowan race, nor their peculiar interaction. But he'd never met a people so compelling.

"I've loved you since I met you." Aiyana sounded impatient. Dane's eyes widened.

"You have?"

"Of course. It was my fate to love someone like you."

Dane released her hands, stood back, and assessed her carefully, like a scientist. "Because I'm Thorwalian?"

She nodded. "You are."

"So are two million other men! Aiyana, is that all you see in me? Am I some shadow of an ancient king, or a man in my own right?"

She looked surprised. "You resemble Hakon. You are strong and good and brave."

Dane's jaw tightened. "Then you would be wise to remember that I am not Hakon's descendent, but his brother's. The clan of Calydon traces its line to Haldane the Bold, not Hakon. Hakon is considered a traitor, one whose ambition and pride nearly destroyed our race."

"That is inaccurate." Dane read her stubbornness from the set of her small chin. "Hakon was a great man, wise and strong."

"You speak of him as if you knew him. That was distant history, Aiyana. You know him no more than I do. Although he must have done something to earn the continuing loyalty of the Ellowans."

Her green eyes blazed. "If we had listened to him . . ." She stopped, and Dane wondered why. She looked away. "Much would be altered this day."

Tears puddled in her eyes. Dane watched, helpless to comfort her when he didn't understand the cause of her pain. "Aiyana . . ."

She looked up at him, stubborn and proud. "Will you make love to me, or not?"

"No."

For an instant she looked vulnerable, hurt. Her eyes glistened; her lip quivered. Then she turned away and nodded.

"Do you want to know why?"

Aiyana shook her head. "It doesn't matter." She sniffed. Dane touched her shoulder.

"Because I love you, too."

She looked back at him. "You make no sense."

"Good. That makes us even."

Her eyes wandered to the side as she considered this, then shot back to him with fierce intensity. Dane noted that her small hand formed a fist. "You will explain."

Dane cupped her tense face in his hands, longing to kiss her, to meld with her. "If I cared nothing for you, Aiyana, I would take you, I promise you. I would fulfill every ache I've developed since I left Thorwal. Every cursed longing I've endured looking at Ellowan art—which is incredibly erotic, I might add. I think I might kill to learn what you'd do in my bed."

Aiyana opened her mouth to speak, then closed it again. As if she wondered, too.

"I would take you for the sake of your beauty, to see your face in pleasure. Believe me, it's an image I've entertained before now."

"Then why . . . ?" Her voice faded; she bit her lip. She looked as confused as she made him.

Dane's thumbs stroked her cheek, over her mouth. He bent as if to kiss her, but their lips didn't touch. "Because I love you. I've loved you since I first saw you. I felt drawn to you even before, when I thought you were green flesh and scales."

Dane paused and rested his forehead against hers. "I thought love would be simple. . . . Stars know why. I thought it would be a resolution, an ending of sorts. The culmination of trials and endurance. I see that I was wrong. It begins everything again, and nothing is the same; the old rules are shattered. Nisa told me this, but I didn't understand. I couldn't understand then. But I look at you, and I know."

Aiyana slid her arms around his waist. Dane drew her into his arms and cradled her head on his shoulder. "I will protect you, Aiyana. I will give you all my heart. When you need me, I'll find a way to be there for you. And when you're ready to let me see inside your darkness, I'll be there. But I want all of you, not a shadow of a lover."

"I'm afraid I have nothing else to give you."

"When you're ready, you'll know. We'll both know." Dane kissed her forehead and she peeked up at him.

"Does this mean you want me to leave you now?"

"No. I enjoyed your company last night. If you wish, stay with me here." His smile deepened. "I might even kiss you again."

They lay together on Dane's bed, hand in hand. Both stared at the ceiling. "Everything tiled, mosaic. Your craftsmen have great skill."

Aiyana stared up at the ceiling, at the ancient figures woven in and out of the patterns. "When one is gone, the whole collapses."

Dane looked over at her. "Yours is a gloomy race, Aiyana. Yet I see no sense of doom, no foreboding, in those designs. In fact, your ancestors seemed to prize pleasure above all things."

"We . . . They loved art. Once, music filled every hall, the Ellowan danced, they sang. We staged grand performances, mainly comic. We were unskilled at tragedy."

Dane studied her small, knitted face. "Your skill for tragedy is matchless now."

"You said you would kiss me again."

"I said I might." Dane watched as her green eyes widened, then lowered his mouth to hers. He kissed her gently, his lips teasing hers, tasting her. Her breath quickened; her fingers clenched, gripping his shoulders.

His body burned to satisfy itself; he longed to bury himself inside her. Dane drew back, then lay on his back again. *What kind of fool turns aside the thing he wants most?*

"I like kissing you."

Dane tried not to look at her. "Thank you." He saw her out of the corner of his eye. Her hair fell over one shoulder, coiled like a slow, dark river. Her eyelids were low, seductive, her lips parted as she contemplated his kiss.

"Did I do it right?"

"Do what right?"

"Kiss."

Dane laughed. "Too right, woman." He paused. "Don't you know?"

She shrugged. "It felt right to me."

"What does Arnoth say on the matter?" Dane wished he hadn't asked. He had no right to ask. But Aiyana just looked confused.

"What matter?"

"Kissing."

"I suppose he approves of it." One brow angled as if Arnoth's opinion on kissing had nothing to do with her.

"You're mated, Aiyana. Generally, as I understand it, mated couples do quite a bit of kissing."

A small smile started on Aiyana's lips. "You're jealous."

Dane considered denying the obvious, then sighed. "I'm jealous."

She leaned a little closer to him and kissed his shoulder. Even through the fabric of his shirt, Dane felt the warmth of her lips. "There's no need."

"I almost believe you." He hesitated before pursuing the subject further, afraid to learn something that would shatter his hope. "Tell me of Arnoth. Your bond seems one of friendship rather than passion. He wouldn't have passed you to me otherwise. Why did you form your union, if not for love's sake?"

"I love him. . . ." Aiyana's voice trailed off and she sighed heavily. For a reason Dane didn't understand, her pronouncement of love didn't trigger his jealousy. She rested her head on Dane's shoulder, and he sifted her hair through his fingers.

"You love him as I love Nisa . . . like a brother."

"Yes. I have known him all my life—I know him so well. We share the same memories, the same pain. We understand each other."

"That doesn't necessarily mean you're well matched. Why choose him for a mate?"

"It was my duty, and his. The power of the Ellowans is passed from female to female, through the line of the priestess. This line has never faltered. But the priestess takes to mate the highest-born son of the high tribunal, and he is the prince, who becomes king when they are joined."

"Is that what Arnoth meant by many leaders?"

"Yes. Arnoth was prince. My sister was his mate. When she died, he and I had to bond for the sake of the remaining Ellowans. Our mating has never been . . . formalized. It is understood."

Dane tried to remain analytical, but he couldn't restrain his relief. "You wed for practical reasons. But it is clear that he loved your sister."

"They were betrothed in childhood."

"Romantic."

A sorrowful smile appeared on Aiyana's face. "You wouldn't have thought so then. They loathed each other. They were the same age, and they fought constantly. Elena devised elaborate schemes to torment him, and Arnoth did likewise. I thought they would kill each other before they ever mated. When they were children, they even fought physically."

Aiyana sighed, an admiring glint in her eye. "Elena always wound up on top. My grandfather had to pull her away, kicking and screaming."

"This isn't the way I envisioned her . . . or Arnoth. I would have thought you were the violent one."

Aiyana's eyes clouded over, her expression turning distant. "Not then."

"Had they no choice? Were they forced into marriage?"

"Not exactly. My grandfather was king at that time. After a particularly fiendish prank concocted against him, Arnoth refused to take Elena as his mate. He said he would wait for me to reach womanhood instead, because I was a proper Ellowan, not an uncivilized Ravager harpy. That's what he called her. The king locked them in Elena's bedchamber together and said if they emerged the next morning and still wished to dissolve their union, he would grant it."

"I take it they changed their minds."

"We heard a few crashes, then silence. They didn't come out until the following evening. They wed that night."

Dane squeezed Aiyana's hand. "She was dear to you."

Tears flooded her eyes, but she didn't cry. "Elena was as vibrant as a star, filled with mischief. I learned to spit from her."

Dane laughed, though his heart constricted with pain. "So I have her to thank."

"Elena often enlisted me in trouble, usually against Arnoth. He was so quiet and serious, cerebral. He was always in the library, studying."

"Arnoth? We're talking about the same man who ordered Galya killed on sight, aren't we?"

"When he was young, he was different."

"Young? Aiyana, he is no older than myself. No one changes that much. But perhaps the change was sudden."

"It was."

"When your sister died?" Dane knew he delved into dangerous waters, but he had to understand.

"Yes." Aiyana swallowed hard. She closed her eyes, though tears glistened on her lashes. "She had been . . . brutalized by the Tseirs, but she wasn't dead." Aiyana's voice faded until she spoke in a strained whisper. Dane watched her, helpless to spare her pain, wishing he hadn't asked. "Arnoth was given the chance to save her. They gave him this chance to torment him, you see."

Dane's blood ran cold. Aiyana's hand felt limp in his. He squeezed it tight and pressed it to his lips, but she didn't respond.

"He formed the bond with her, to heal her. Arnoth is the greatest of the living Ellowan healers. But when he asked if she desired life, she said no."

Dane saw his own sister in his mind. Nisa, strong and willful, ready to twist life to her will, to make it right. He saw her with Seneca, in love, young, tender. "Why didn't he heal her anyway?"

Tears ran down Aiyana's face, over her temple, into her dark hair. "The Ellowan respect the right to choose, no matter how painful. But even if we wished to inflict life despite another's wishes, it isn't possible to heal an unwilling person. When you were injured, I asked you the same question. Do you remember?"

"Yes."

"You desired life, so I could teach you to mend. Elena refused. Her life was shattered beyond healing. She died in Arnoth's arms. He has never gone beyond that moment."

Dane's eyes burned with tears. Tears for a strange and mystical people, for the woman he loved. For a man who should, by rights, be his enemy.

"Aiyana, war is cruel. The Ravagers proved this again and again. Their propensity for torture and mayhem was unmatched. They took glee in violence. But there must be some bridge to build with the Tseirs."

"We thought that once, too. We were wrong."

"I know little of them, it's true. But Galya seems . . . bland."

Aiyana turned in bed, propping herself up to look down

into his face. "If I told you the Tseirs are evil, would you believe me? If I told you the only chance against them is to strike first, would you do it?"

Dane hesitated. He felt cold inside. . . . Doomed. "There must be a way to reason with them, to seek peace."

Aiyana laughed, a raw and bitter sound, then sank back onto the bed. "I thought as much. You don't know them. But there's something about them, something the Ellowans have never understood." Aiyana bit her lip, struggling to explain. "There is a mystery to the Tseirs, one we never uncovered."

"What mystery?"

"Where they came from, who they are, *what* they are."

"I assumed they were another Franconian race."

"No. They came to Franconia an age ago, from another system."

"When Hakon was your king?"

"Just before, yes. The Tseirs came as 'dignitaries' from another world. They told us they were terrorized and ravaged by a vile race in their system. A system we never were able to verify. The Ellowan Tribunal allowed them to settle on Franconia, which then was only a sparsely inhabited Ellowan outpost. It was then that Ariana returned with Hakon. He distrusted the Tseirs at once, though his reasons never satisfied us."

"What were his reasons?"

"They had no children."

"I noticed the same about you. I see children in your art, but not in your village. Where are they?"

Aiyana didn't answer at once. "Once they were the focus and joy of the Ellowans."

"And now?"

Aiyana hesitated long enough for Dane to feel certain her answer would be incomplete. "The Ellowans have greater control over our biological functions than other races. As we heal each other, we control the time of our fertility.''

''Convenient. How has your race survived?''

Again, hesitation. ''When it is necessary to reproduce, we will do so. But this is no place for children.''

''So Hakon found the Tseirs' absence of children suspicious?''

''He did. He didn't trust them, because they were too quick with answers, too quick to ingratiate themselves. He said they didn't respect truth. He said they clouded truth for their own ends. He saw no evidence that they owned their own power. They had flightships, with no skill at tending them.''

''I noticed that. Galya knew nothing of the Franconian vessel, nor cared to know. As if it's easier to replace them than to fix them.''

''That can't be, Dane. The flightships are made of a rare material. It's not easily replaced.''

Dane paused, considering the significance of this. ''Arnoth said Hakon wanted to attack. To 'strike first.' ''

''He did.'' Aiyana bowed her head, perhaps beneath the weight of grief.

''If he were king, why didn't the Ellowans follow his command?''

''The Ellowans don't follow commands. The tribunal was hesitant. The Tseirs pleaded that their actions had been misunderstood.''

''What were their actions?''

''They overtook Franconia, killing or enslaving the Ellowans who lived there.''

''Hard to misunderstand that.''

''So said Hakon.'' Aiyana's eyes brightened at Dane's reaction. ''But the tribunal remained divided. Two members of the leadership believed in negotiation. They couldn't imagine attacking without giving the enemy a chance to withdraw.'' Aiyana's eyes glazed over, and Dane's heart took a strange, heavy beat. "They were fools."

"What happened?"

"The two Ellowans who believed in peace traveled to Franconia, answering the Tseirs' plea." Aiyana's expression darkened as if a shadow had fallen upon it. "They were enslaved, and while they were held captive, their world was annihilated. Annihilated by their own defensive weaponry."

"A vile story."

Aiyana's eyes burned into his. "Then you see what must be done."

"I would be reluctant to advise the Candorians to assist them."

"No! You must convince the Candorians to destroy them! Now, before it's too late."

"I can't do that. Aiyana . . ."

She sat back, despondent. "I would expect no other answer. Go to Franconia, and see for yourself. Maybe you will see something I did not. Maybe the Ravager blood is stronger in you than it seems."

"What has Ravager blood to do with this matter?"

Aiyana looked stubborn again. "That remains to be seen."

"So you want me to destroy them, or have the Candorians do it, without a reason?"

"If I gave you a reason, would you then?"

Dane hesitated. "It depends upon the reason."

She didn't look at him. She stared at the ceiling, at the fading tiles. "The world of the Ellowans is gone, Dane Caldon. You see before you, around you, ghosts. The shadow of what was. We are the remaining few. A hundred at most, from a population of millions."

"So a few Ellowans survived to carry on a lost battle?"

"No. To prevent another."

"Aiyana, you speak in riddles. How can you expect me to answer you when I don't know the truth?"

Still, she didn't look at him. She spoke as if she didn't expect to convince him. "I believe the Tseirs intend to overtake your system, Dane. Because Candor is powerful."

Dane sat up in bed, pulling Aiyana up to face him. "Why?"

"Because the powerful, the advanced . . . those races are also kind. They negotiate. They believe reason will find a way of solving all matters. I know. The Ellowans believed that, too."

"Aiyana, the Ellowans have been known for almost four centuries as relentless terrorists, beings without mercy."

"We are now."

Dane studied Aiyana's face. "You're keeping something from me."

"Haven't I told you enough?"

"That's no answer, Aiyana. I'll assume you've told me the part of your story that you want me to know. I know what you want of me; I know what you want of Candor. I will keep that in mind when I visit Franconia. Beyond that . . ."

Dane fell silent. What did he want? It hadn't occurred to him. He wanted to be useful, to help a troubled system find balance. But he saw no balance to be found. A sudden hope flashed in his mind and he took her hands.

"Aiyana, come back to Candor with me."

"What?"

"Return with me; leave this place. Bring your people." He paused, frowning. "Even Arnoth."

Aiyana smiled, her expression soft and sad. "I can't do that. My duty is here."

"Why? Your world is gone. Come with me, and add your gifts to another world. A peaceful world. You deserve that. Maybe Arnoth deserves it, too. Maybe he'll find another mate on Candor."

Dane paused, wondering why he cared if Arnoth ended

up happily mated or not. He shook his head, banishing his unwilling affection for his adversary.

"Candor was Ellowan; we could live there. Or if you prefer, we'll make a home on Thorwal. If that's too cold, then Dakota. You'd like Dakota. It's warm and beautiful. The Dakotans are an entertaining race."

"For how long?"

Dane heard her answer in her level tone. "What do you mean?"

"How long will your system be so pleasant, so untarnished by strife? I've told you, Dane. The Tseirs mean to take your system. When they do, nothing will be left but what you saw in the sky tonight. . . . Midnight."

"I won't let that happen."

"You don't really believe me. You entertain what I've told you as a possibility. For me, it is real. The Tseirs destroyed my world. They will destroy yours, too."

"They destroyed your planet, but your race survived and still retains the capacity for tormenting the Tseirs, it seems."

"It seems so, yes."

Dane fell silent, considering all Aiyana had told him. What could he do for her? He came to the Franconian system to learn its hidden truths. His purpose changed with his heart. The stakes were raised, like some vile Ravager's gamble. He had to save Aiyana.

"I must go onward to Franconia. . . ." Dane's voice trailed away as he met her eyes. "I will learn what can be done, what they're willing to do."

"They will tell you lies."

"Galya said the same about you."

"And one of us is lying." Her chin raised, quivering slightly. "You think it's me."

"I didn't say that."

"You didn't have to." Her lips formed an angry pout, her delicate brow furrowing. "I suppose I can't blame you."

"No, you can't. Aiyana, I have told you I love you. Can a man trust his judgment when he loves?"

"If not then, when else?"

Dane slid his hand over her shoulder, his fingers touching the soft skin at the nape of her neck, and she closed her eyes. "Do you have any idea how much I want to believe you? If only to assure myself you love me, too."

"You doubt that, too."

"Your appeal to my heart is strong. It might be that I would forgo my reason to do your bidding without question, all for the sake of your favor."

Aiyana leaned her head against his shoulder. "You have my favor, Dane Calydon. Whether you act for the Ellowans or against us. Love is sacred. It doesn't change for the sake of reason."

Dane longed to believe her. It was the answer he wanted to hear. But he was intensely aware this night that he was far away from home. The Franconian stars looked different from those in the Thorwalian sky. Maybe truth was different, too.

No. What is real remains. Dane looked down at her. *She either loves me or she doesn't. Nothing will change for the sake of my wanting.*

Aiyana ran her hand across his chest. "I cannot form the future. I learned that many long years ago." She paused, looking up at him, her eyes soft and warm. "I have told you what I could. You are right. You must decide for yourself. Hakon taught us to look for what's really there, not what we think is there. We learned too late, but we learned. Kostbera said something like that about you."

"Yes, I remember. 'Intellect undiluted by rash judgments and illusions.' And I remember your response."

"I tried to warn you, Thorwalian."

"I've never understood why."

"Because Franconia is dangerous. Should you join us, your life will be in grave danger."

"You couldn't have known a Thorwalian would speak for Candor."

"It was a great shock. We expected to deal with a Candorian. Maybe that would have been easier."

"Not if you intended to convince them to attack the Tseirs."

"I didn't mean that. . . . I care for you. Arnoth cares for you."

"I find that hard to imagine."

"He loved a Ravager."

"Your sister's Ravager blood was thin and distant."

"She was a Ravager. Had you seen her pinning Arnoth down and attacking him, you would know. But those qualities that infuriated him were the same that he loved most. He can't help but care for your fate."

"Curious . . . I can't help but care for his, either."

"That is because you are a good man."

"Or a fool."

Aiyana watched Dane as he contemplated what she had told him. He was so beautiful, strong, and kind. He was everything she imagined a Ravager lover to be. As if he came out of her childhood dreams. But he came too late.

Aiyana didn't want to talk anymore. She had told him all she could, and he would decide for himself. Maybe she would lose him. Maybe she would die. Maybe he would learn her intentions and never forgive her.

"You leave tomorrow. I would spend tonight wisely."

"I will come back for you, Aiyana. You have my promise in this. When I have finished my task for the Candorian Council, I will return here, and I will serve as your most humble servant if you ask it."

"Many things I have asked. One in particular." Aiyana

ran her hand up and down his strong arm, then settled her hand on his chest.

What she knew of men and women came from art; it came from Elena's descriptions. Aiyana remembered the glee of the older sister telling the small one the horrors of reproduction. She remembered the dewy-eyed sighs as a mature Elena told her she had been wrong. *It's the best thing in all the world,* damanai.

Aiyana fiddled with the tie of Dane's shirt, seeking the touch of his bare skin. Dane's eyes were closed, his flesh heated. Aiyana wanted to taste him, to meld with him. She wanted to hold him and believe for a while that her old dream had come true.

"A Ravager of my own . . ." she whispered against his skin, then pressed her lips against his shoulder.

She slid her finger down his chest to his hard, flat stomach. He quivered beneath her touch, and her blood flamed. She peeked up at him. He was biting his lip. The seduction he accused her of became strangely appealing. *I wonder if I could. . . .*

Aiyana peeled Dane's shirt apart. She held her breath as she uncovered his shoulder. "You did this to me . . . Perhaps it is my right to see you also unclothed."

"The circumstances were different." Dane's voice sounded odd, constricted. Aiyana licked her lips.

"But the sight didn't displease you." His gaze shot to her, dark blue and powerful, making her feel powerful. "I think it aroused you."

He held every muscle tight; he trembled. "I think you're right."

Aiyana fixed her gaze on his bare shoulder. The muscle was well defined, broad and strong. His skin was smooth and golden. She swallowed, then pushed his shirt over his other shoulder, baring his chest and his back.

Aiyana felt a new hunger, and she ran her hand over his

skin, over the broad muscle that spanned his chest, to his other shoulder. "It's like a feast."

She settled herself in front of him, kneeling as she studied his naked torso. Dane groaned, but he made no move to stop her, nor to forward her interest.

"You are beautiful." Aiyana felt giddy, weak and strong at the same time. She tugged his shirt away and tossed it aside. She watched it slither from the long, low bed onto the tiled floor. "So goes your restraint, my love."

"You do this with a certain violence, my lady." Dane's voice sounded hoarse. Aiyana wondered why.

"I don't mean to hurt you. I want only my due as your . . . opponent."

A visible tremor ran through Dane and he moaned again. Aiyana placed her hands on his shoulders, then down his arms, savoring the feel of him. She felt warm, moist, deep inside. She squirmed to seat herself closer to him.

Dane seemed to recognize the feeling, because he drew her onto his lap, his large hands supporting her waist. Aiyana flamed within. "This is . . . pleasant." Her breath came swift and shallow, almost gasping. She tried to steady herself and failed.

"Yes."

His voice sounded even more odd. She sat back and studied his face intently. "Am I hurting you? You sound strained."

"I *am* strained." He tipped his head back and drew a long breath. Aiyana noticed a faint sheen of perspiration on his throat. Compelled by impulse, she pressed her lips to his neck and tasted him.

"You are sweet."

Dane uttered a Thorwalian curse that Aiyana didn't understand. His fingers clenched around her waist. She wondered if he thought he had hurt her, because he moved his hands lower to her bottom.

His hands felt warm, even through the heavy fabric of her dress. ''Your touch is gentle.'' Aiyana paused to catch her breath. ''I noticed that the first time.''

''The first time I had no choice. My touch was for necessity's sake. Tonight it is for pleasure only.''

''Mine or yours?''

''Both.''

This satisfied Aiyana. ''Does my touch bring you pleasure, too?''

''Too much.''

''You said that about kissing. I will test it.'' Aiyana ran her hands down Dane's taut sides, over his close-fitting leggings, until she touched his bottom. ''You are firm.'' She explored further, skimming her touch along his hard thighs. ''And hard.''

A low groan emanated from deep in Dane's throat, but he didn't comment on her observations. Her gaze fixed on his concealed male organ. It looked large. Very hard. She could see the outline of its shape, long and thick, blunt at the tip.

She caught her lip between her teeth, then hesitantly touched him there. His whole body seemed to clench and she drew her hand away in surprise.

''Did I hurt you?''

''No.''

''I have seen this portion of a man in images. It is often displayed in our art.''

''I've noticed that.''

''Your voice grows more and more odd. Are you sure you're well?''

''Couldn't be better.''

Aiyana shook her head, confused. ''In those images, I have seen women holding this . . . portion in their hands. I have seen them kissing it—'' Dane's harshly intaken breath interrupted her. ''I have seen them seated astride it.''

The Thorwalian curse was repeated, more forcefully.

"At one time, Ellowan females were taught explicitly of its nature. Later that was deemed disrespectful to women, and they were encouraged to find out on their own."

"Like this?"

"I expect so." She paused. "But in earlier times, the female was given to a well-skilled male, who taught her as he saw fit."

"Oh." Dane cleared his throat.

"Sometimes he taught several females at once."

Dane bowed his head and issued a long, defeated moan.

"We are told it was a popular vocation."

"I'll bet."

"It is hard to tell from the art what happened once the female takes the male's portion in her hand. Elena only told me 'a lot,' and I never dared question Arnoth on the matter."

"Good. A man's restraint only goes so far."

Aiyana scoffed. "Arnoth has no such interest in me."

"Maybe not then, when he had your Ravager sister to keep him occupied. But now . . ."

Arnoth didn't want her. He *couldn't* want her. He couldn't want anyone. His eternal quest depended on that. "Now his focus is elsewhere."

"If you start asking about what to do with 'portions,' woman, his focus may shift."

"I will not ask him." She paused, a tiny smile on her lips. "As long as you tell me."

"You touch the man's . . . 'portion' and move your hand in a manner mimicking lovemaking."

"Up and down?"

"Yes."

"What about the kissing?"

"A similar act."

"Only moister, because of the mouth's involvement."

"Yes."

"Now your voice is high. Almost a squeak."

Dane laughed. "Woman, I am in agony."

"I don't want you to suffer. How do I relieve you of this pain?"

"You allow me to relieve you of yours."

"I'm not in any pain."

"I didn't call it pain. I called it agony. You will soon learn the difference."

Dane studied Aiyana's expression. She looked curious, young, and aroused. His pulse surged. Her innocent questions tantalized him with the possibility of teaching her pleasure.

"I am not certain I wish to experience agony, Dane Caldon."

"It is sweet agony."

"But how—" Dane stopped her question with a kiss. His tongue parted her lips, gaining entrance, sliding over her uncertain tongue. She shivered in his arms.

He pulled up her skirt slowly, brushing his knuckles along the length of her leg. His fingers grazed her firm, round bottom as he lifted the garment to her waist. "I did this to you before, my sweet lady. Know that my touch worshiped you then, just as it does tonight."

"I knew it then." Her voice was a small, breathless whisper.

Dane drew a breath, then pulled the dress over her head. He tossed it to the floor beside his shirt, then allowed himself to take in the sight of her body. The perfection of the shape emblazoned on his brain hadn't been exaggerated. She was slender and lithe, her breasts round and firm.

"You are more beautiful without the explosives, my lady." He smiled, then ran his finger across her collarbone, then lower, over the swell of her breast. "Here, and here."

He circled the small peak, not touching the summit. It firmed and tightened, and she caught her breath.

Dane trailed his finger down one arm, down the other, up her stomach, beneath her breast. Her skin tensed where he touched, and she quivered.

Dane ran his finger over Aiyana's mouth. "I had no idea. . . ."

She sighed, her eyelids heavy with desire. "I thought you knew."

"Not this, Aiyana. There was a time when I touched for the sake of conquest. 'Touch here, and the woman responds. Touch here, and she moans. Smile when she hesitates, and she will surrender.' "

"You do have an appealing smile."

"Love changes everything. I could touch you all night, just for the sake of touching."

"Our positions aren't equal. You are still partially clothed."

Dane glanced down at his pants. "So I am." With his eyes on hers, he rose from the bed and unfastened his waistband. Slowly. Aiyana waited expectantly, her white teeth sinking into her lower lip.

He'd taken his good looks for granted. On Thorwal and Dakota, he used his appearance to enamor women when his lust needed slaking. But it mattered now. He wanted Aiyana to burn for him, as he burned for her. He wanted to please her.

He stripped away his pants, freeing himself to her sight. A small gasp escaped her parted lips as her gaze fixed on his "portion."

"It's larger when viewed in person." She sounded nervous. She gulped, but her eyes whisked over him and a smile grew on her lips. "You are magnificent to look upon. How is it that a technician appears so bold and so strong?"

Dane laughed and seated himself beside her. "The technician had a lingbat who delighted in reminding him of his frailty.''

''You were never frail.''

''Carob felt otherwise. And in truth, I wasn't strong.''

''You are now.'' Aiyana reached hesitantly to touch his arm again.

''Seneca taught me his mind-body art, TiKay, and I've practiced for years. I built my strength on Candor, though I came to wonder if I'd ever need it.''

''It is welcome tonight.''

Dane turned on the bed so that they faced each other, both kneeling, both naked. His heart opened wide; he had longed for this moment—to truly love, to be loved. They faced each other, and he saw her heart in her eyes.

A tremor of doubt disturbed his joy. Aiyana kept too much hidden; she had purposes he didn't know. Dane realized that his actions tonight were based on hope. He wasn't looking for the truth; he was leaping over reason for the sake of love.

''Aiyana, I want to trust you.''

A sorrowful light flickered in her eyes, then passed. ''What is the desire to trust? The Ellowans wanted to trust the Tseirs. . . .''

''Not an entirely favorable comparison.''

''No, but an accurate one. You want to trust me so you can be sure of what will happen in the future. The future isn't written. We have now, and that is all.''

''Sometimes you sound like Seneca. Strange, because he is the most trustworthy person I've ever known.''

''You speak of him with love.''

''I emulated him as a child. I admired him as a man. Other than the gloomy nature, Seneca resembles Arnoth.''

''Ah, but your Seneca didn't lose his mate to his own folly.''

''His own folly? Why should Arnoth blame himself for

your sister's death?'' She didn't answer. ''Do you blame him, too?''

''I blame myself.''

Dane's heart chilled. Here was the crux of Aiyana's tragedy, and Arnoth's. Here lay concealed the secret of the Ellowans. ''Why?''

Aiyana didn't answer at once, and Dane knew she wouldn't tell him. Her eyes drifted from his and she sighed. ''It doesn't matter now.''

At least she hadn't lied. Dane took slight encouragement from that. ''No, I guess it doesn't. I'm sorry, Aiyana.''

She looked back at him, her eyes piercing and bright. Searching. Dane wondered what she searched for that she couldn't request from him directly. ''There is light between us, you and I. Yet the darkness looms larger. Will it always be so?''

Dane took her hands and bent to kiss her forehead. ''I can't answer that, love. You're right . . . I can give you nothing but tonight.''

Tears glistened in her eyes. ''That is what I want from you.''

Dane sensed danger. He knew he could lose her. He knew her darkness was large, and it might destroy what they had found together. He knew his strength might not be enough to save her. Even as she sat before him, unclad, *his*, Aiyana seemed to drift away.

His heart took a demanding beat. In the back of his mind, he heard Arnoth's music. He recognized a desperation in the rhythm. *Seize life now, for it will soon be gone.* Despite his own hope, his own faith, Dane couldn't resist the image. It sat before him, a young and delicate woman, the image of hope utterly destroyed.

Dane's most primal core rose in rebellion. For the first time, he knew what it meant to be a Ravager. When Thorwal was thrust into a sudden ice age, the Ravagers fought and survived. That battle still raged in his soul. It was a battle he would not lose.

Dane lowered Aiyana to the bed beneath him, and she gazed into his face. Her heart moved in odd, erratic beats. A swift pulse, a pulse eager for life. Even her cells seemed eager for change. She drew a quick breath. Fear waged battle against excitement. "Do you think . . . have you changed your mind?"

"On what subject?"

He knew, and he was teasing her. "On the subject of . . . union."

"Sexual union?"

He sounded serious, solemn. Aiyana couldn't gauge his mood.

"Yes."

A tiny smile flickered on his lips. "Tonight, my lady, I would prefer to tease you."

"What?" Aiyana struggled to sit up. "I don't wish to be teased!"

Dane chuckled and eased her back beneath him. His flesh felt hot, his muscles tight. Aiyana frowned. She felt . . . combative. Her eyes narrowed. "We will see about that, Thorwalian. I will tease you back!"

She slid her hand down his stomach until she felt the hard staff between them. Her gaze fixed firmly on his and she wrapped her fingers around his length. She saw his surprise and the dark flash of lust that contorted his sweet face. She beamed with satisfaction.

"Up and down, you say? We will see if it works." She moved her wrist and Dane uttered a low, rumbling groan. The position was awkward. Her grip felt feeble. Aiyana stopped and squirmed from beneath him. "Roll over."

Dane's eyes widened and he hesitated. Aiyana shoved him onto his back. He laughed. "As I thought . . . violent."

"I have only begun." With fierce intensity, she seized him again, this time with freedom of motion. *Up and down* . . . It worked admirably. His breath came short and hoarse, his hips moved with her growing skill. Aiyana felt weak inside. Hot liquid seemed to pool in her secret depths.

"Aiyana . . ."

"Again, your voice is quite unnatural." She squeezed tighter around him, moving her hand more rapidly. "I believe that means you are teased."

"You could say that . . ." Dane's voice trailed away into a moan of pleasure.

Aiyana loved her power. She loved the harsh gasp that escaped his mouth when she fingered the blunt tip of his erection. She loved the mask of desire that changed his sweet face into a Ravager's raging lust.

"Aiyana, my control is weakened. I can bear no more. . . ."

"Maybe I shouldn't let you speak at all." She leaned down to kiss him, still stroking his length. She touched the tip of her tongue to his upper lip, then slid it along his clenched teeth. Dane groaned, and she slipped her tongue over his, teasing.

His body spasmed; his back arched into her hand. She kissed him more fiercely, nipping his lip as her hand's pressure increased. He belonged to her, here. He returned her kiss, heat like a raging fever soaring between them.

His hand locked in her hair, holding her close as he kissed her, as she kissed him. He moved into her hand, and Aiyana knew what lovemaking would be. He would do this inside of her. . . . She whimpered against his mouth, answered by a deep, primal growl. He must have seen the image in her mind. Something shattered inside him. She felt it happen. He cried out, hoarse and triumphant.

She felt the heat of him spill into her hand; she felt him shaking. His male organ throbbed with power as the sensation overtook him. Aiyana watched his face in wonder. She'd never seen anything so beautiful as Dane Calydon in ecstasy.

His rapture eased and abated, and he lay still beneath her, his eyes closed. She stopped her erotic ministrations, but she couldn't take her eyes from his face. Suddenly she frowned, feeling cheated.

"You were supposed to do that inside me!"

Dane opened his eyes and looked up at her. She could tell that he tried not to laugh. His repressed grin inflamed her further.

"You cheated."

The laugh burst forth. Dane laughed until his eyes watered, while Aiyana fumed. "You weren't taught this by a 'well-skilled male,' were you?"

"Taught what?"

"You just drove me into oblivion, my lady. And then you accuse me of cheating. You have only yourself to blame."

Aiyana's pout eased. A small trace of pride surfaced instead.

"I was successful, wasn't I? You thought to tease me, and I defeated your purpose."

Dane propped himself up on one elbow. "Not entirely." He reached to touch her cheek, trailing the tip of his finger down her throat, stopping at the swell of her breast. "Lie down."

"I will not." She paused. "Why?"

"Must you always be so argumentative?"

"You said you liked that about me."

"I do. But just now, I think I'd like your silence. I suppose unquestioning obedience is out of the question."

Aiyana's lips curved in a frown, one brow angled. "It is." She paused as she debated her actions. She didn't want to obey, but she didn't want to miss anything he might do, either. "I have decided to lie down, but only because I am weary from teasing you."

"I don't think you understand the concept of teasing, lady. It generally involves the withholding of satisfaction."

Her brow furrowed. "Does it?" Dane nodded as she considered this. "You appeared satisfied."

"I am satisfied."

She thought about this awhile, too. "As I said, you cheated." She lay back, stiff, and watched him suspiciously. Waiting. Dane didn't move. Aiyana puffed an impatient breath. "Well? What are you going to do?"

"Tease you."

Aiyana's frown deepened. "Then get started."

Dane didn't respond, though a smile flickered on his lips. She fidgeted. He licked his lips, moving slightly nearer to her, but he didn't touch her or speak.

Aiyana twitched. She felt curiously tense inside. The warm, inner pool of excitement hadn't subsided with Dane's satisfaction. In fact, it seemed to grow, leaving her irritable and . . . tense. Very tense.

She tried not to look at him. She sucked her lower lip, then chewed it. She glanced at him to see if he was doing anything yet. He wasn't. His hair hung over one eyebrow in a particularly annoying way. His full, sensual lips curved in a smile. A teasing smile.

"You will commence teasing at once, or I will strike you!"

His blue eyes glittered with amusement, his brow rising in mock fear. Aiyana quivered with irritation. Suddenly her budding fury turned against her. A small giggle erupted instead. *I love him.* She felt dizzy, even lying down. "You toy with me."

"Umm."

Aiyana peeked over at him. The liquid pool seemed to writhe and boil inside her. His eyelids looked heavy, sleepy, yet the blue was very dark. For a reason she didn't understand, this triggered an even fiercer yearning inside.

She wet her lips and caught her breath. He didn't do anything. Maybe he smiled a little. He didn't look at her body; he just watched her face. Just as she realized this, his eyes whisked along the length of her, then back to her face. Those blue eyes looked darker still.

"Aren't you going to touch me?"

"Where would you like me to touch you?"

An annoying question. Aiyana clenched her teeth. "I was simply curious. . . . Anywhere!" Her voice sounded tense, too.

She should have known he wouldn't touch anything . . . vital. Just her wrist. "Here?"

Aiyana rolled her eyes. "That is not sufficient."

She barely felt his touch as it eased up the inside of her arm. But her whole body tingled. "Is that all you're going to do?" *How odd!* Her voice sounded like his had, husky and uncertain.

Dane chuckled. He must have noticed the difference, too. He ran the tips of his fingers to the soft skin beneath her tense shoulder, just grazing the side of her breast before slipping away. Aiyana moaned, a soft, shivering sound.

He did it again, this time with even less pressure. She held her breath as he again grazed her breast. She released a shuddering sigh when his hand drew away. She adjusted her hips. Why, when he touched her arm, did the spot at the juncture of her thighs feel . . . attended?

As Aiyana pondered the connection, Dane bent and touched his lips to her wrist. She gasped and watched in astonishment as he trailed his lips along the same path. The touch of his mouth was almost as light as his fingers had been.

When his fingers sought a new path along her side and across her stomach, she froze in anticipation. How could a man move so slowly? She bit her lip hard as his fingers wended their course to the far side of her other breast.

She peeked at him, waiting, her heart slamming fiercely beneath her breast. He smiled again, that torturous, leisurely smile. . . . He kept his eyes on hers as he bent to follow the course again with his mouth.

No. Not his mouth. His tongue. Aiyana groaned, more loudly than she intended. Her heart beat way too fast. Faster than in battle, faster than when she was running.

He didn't settle back this time. He remained poised above her, his large body shadowing hers. He looked down at her. She wanted to grab his hair and yank him down, to kiss him severely. But she couldn't move. Breathing was hard enough.

He kissed her, but only lightly. She couldn't get a firm grip on his lips before he drew away. A muted, frustrated whimper burst from deep in her throat. It seemed to please him. A lot. Aiyana felt his male portion, stiff and hard against her thigh.

She was quivering violently. She couldn't stop. Her muscles twitched wherever he touched. He made small circles around her breasts, which felt full and engorged. They'd never felt that way before. She wanted to question him on the matter, but when her mouth opened, no sound came.

His lips replaced his fingers, circling her breast. "Oh, no . . ." Aiyana wondered if she could stand it longer. And if she couldn't, what then?

"Such a beautiful little peak . . ." Aiyana's eyes shot open and saw that he focused on the tip of her breast. "So sensitive. So . . . female."

She held her breath, her heart throbbing. He moved so slowly that she wanted to hit him. With one finger, he touched the very tip, so lightly that she barely felt it. Desire stabbed through her. He withdrew his touch, then lowered his mouth.

She bit back a cry, but his lips didn't touch her. She felt his breath, warm and swift. Then the smallest tip of his tongue. Her heart beat with enough fury to burst free from her chest. His tongue wavered, touching and not touching.

Aiyana twisted beneath him. His tongue flicked out and swept across the small peak, and she arched her back toward him. "You will cease this torment. . . . You will—"

"What, love?" His tongue circled the peak. "This?" He drew it between his lips and sucked gently. She felt his teeth just grazing.

"This . . . ?" Her voice was so low and so hoarse that it sounded like another woman's. He moved his attention to her other breast. His soft hair grazed her skin as he moved.

As his tongue laved the other peak to the same excruciating pleasure, his hand slid down her side. Aiyana wondered what more he could do. This teasing was already unbearable.

His fingers ran lightly along her hip, then down her thigh. Her attention wavered between his hand and his lips. He touched the inside of her thigh, then drew back to brush his lips back and forth over the peak of her breast.

He stopped long enough to look into her eyes. She couldn't control her breathing; she just stared back at him, astonished at what he had done. That teasing light glimmered ever brighter in his eyes. He was watching her for a reason, to see her reaction.

His fingers played upward between her legs. He found the triangle of dark hair and drew his fingers in outline. He slipped his finger slowly between her legs. When he felt how damp she was, he groaned.

Aiyana endured the gentle pressure; she endured his teasing finger as it glided around her feminine juncture. She gnawed at the inside of her lip as he parted the soft folds and delved inward. But when he discovered her tiny, concealed bud, she could bear no more.

"Please, Ravager, I can stand no more without . . ." Her throat clenched. His touch centered there. "Without . . ."

"Without what, love?"

Her head angled back and she surrendered to whatever he would do.

"Without this?" His touch intensified on the tiny spot. The man was a demon at teasing. She'd had no idea. Deep in the impassioned fog of her mind, she vowed to do the same to him one day.

His finger slid back and forth, then circled, over and over until her hips moved with his touch, until her every breath was a cry and a plea for release. His lips returned to her breast, sucking and nipping.

Aiyana's fingers clenched in his hair; her whole body writhed. "Should I stop now? Are you well teased?"

She screamed. "Do it and die, Ravager."

He stopped her threat with a kiss. His whole hand moved over her woman's mound. She arched beneath him, squirming to increase the friction. The erotic tension spiraled so tight that she thought she would die of it. It burst into shards of blinding pleasure, undulating waves that consumed her entire being.

For an eternal moment, those waves transported her to realms unknown. Then gradually they subsided, leaving her shaking and shocked. And *alive.*

She opened her eyes and saw him looking down at her. She saw wonder. The same wonder she felt when she watched him . . . "The same thing happened to you." She caught her breath and touched his face. "Now I know. . . ."

"What?" Dane gathered her quivering body into his arms. He kissed her forehead, then lay down beside her.

Aiyana closed her eyes and sighed, content. "What Elena meant by 'a lot.' "

Chapter Five

Something sharp and cold pushed at his throat. How irritating! It almost pierced his skin. Dane fought the heavy blanket of sleep and lifted his hand to push the object away.

"Awake to battle, Ravager. Your time has come, and this deed will not go unpunished." A soft, low voice.

Dane opened his eyes and blinked twice to clear his vision. Arnoth stood beside his bed, holding a sharp, narrow sword.

Dane blinked again. Arnoth positioned the sword at Dane's throat, not quite piercing the flesh. "What . . . ?" Small puffs of air touched his shoulder. Aiyana's breath.

Blood drained from his face. *Aiyana.* He had taken Arnoth's mate to bed. But hadn't she assured him . . . ? "What's going on, Arnoth?"

"Quiet, Ravager. You'll wake Aiyana."

"You'd prefer to kill me in silence, then?" Dane sat up, heedless of his nudity. He'd forgotten how irritating the Ellowan prince could be.

Arnoth chuckled, then lowered his rapier. To Dane's astonishment, Arnoth seated himself casually on the bed. "Perhaps I won't kill you just now."

Dane studied Arnoth's expression. "I wouldn't blame you if you did."

"Had you touched my first mate this way, I would kill you slowly, bit by bit. But your claim on Aiyana is greater than mine. You own her heart."

"Then why are you armed and threatening to kill me?"

"Well, you *did* bed my woman."

Dane clenched his teeth. "I understood that you 'released' her."

"Not formally." Arnoth's dark eyes twinkled in an increasingly familiar and infuriating manner. He leaned over Dane to examine Aiyana's sleeping form. "She is unclothed also." He made a chastising sound with his tongue as he eased the covers over her shoulder. "I'm afraid you must assume responsibility for this outrage, Ravager."

Despite his words, Arnoth sounded unaffected. Dane shook his head. He was lying in bed with another man's mate. Maybe. That man now sat on the edge of his bed, cheerfully and casually announcing that Dane must now suffer the consequences.

"You're crazy, Arnoth." Dane adjusted the blanket tighter around his waist. "I suspected it before now, but you've convinced me beyond any doubt. You're crazy."

Arnoth appeared unperturbed by Dane's diagnosis. "That may be. Out of curiosity, why do you say so?"

"Why? Oh, I don't know." Dane glanced over at Aiyana. She slept through their conversation, a small smile on her lips. "I spent the night pleasuring your woman, as you call her. I have to wonder, somewhere in the back of my mind, why you haven't done it yourself. Living with Aiyana, with all her curiosity about 'portions' . . . That would have done it for me. As a matter of fact, it *did* do it for me."

Arnoth's brow furrowed doubtfully at this. "Portions?"

"Erections, you idiot. If you'd ever taken the time to talk to her, you'd get an earful."

Arnoth appeared a little pained. "I was afraid of that."

Dane huffed. "Were you?"

"She has a very erotic edge to her, my little *damanai.*" He stopped and sighed. Dane fought the desire to punch him.

" '*Damanai.*' You've called her that before. What does it mean?"

"It means 'my treasure.' It was Elena's name for her. Later, my own."

"She isn't yours." Dane nearly growled the words.

Arnoth didn't argue. "So she lived up to it, did she?"

"That—" Dane struggled to speak through a constricted throat—"is none of your concern."

"It is. She's my mate. So she's good at it. . . ."

Dane eyed Arnoth's cast-off rapier. He could snatch it away and skewer Arnoth. "I understood you had no interest in her."

Arnoth glanced over at Aiyana. "She's beautiful. Lively. But it would be a dance of grief between us, not passion." He hesitated. "Although it might have been pleasurable."

Dane clasped his hands to his head. "I can't believe we're discussing this. Look, Arnoth, either kill me and get it over with, or remove yourself from my room."

"You're in my village. Thus, this must be considered *my* room."

Not for the first time, Dane contemplated strangling the prince. Slowly. "What do you want?" He spoke in a clipped, abrupt voice, but Arnoth paid no attention to Dane's budding rage.

"I believe I've conveyed that. I want to exact revenge and punishment from you for this. . . ." He waved his hand absently at Aiyana. ''For this vile act of betrayal. As her mate, and as prince, it is my right.''

''Is it? Well, do it, and have done.''

''After breakfast.''

Dane's fists clenched. ''Whatever you do, Arnoth, know that I won't give her back.''

Arnoth rose from the bed and sighed, casting a final look Aiyana's way. ''It's probably for the best. I don't need the temptation.''

Dane heard authentic regret beneath Arnoth's light manner. He wondered why Arnoth resisted when real desires obviously stirred somewhere beneath his dark surface.

''The harder you resist, the harder you'll fall.''

Arnoth's brow knitted at Dane's comment. ''What are you talking about? I 'fell' once. I will never fall again.''

''You don't want to fall, Arnoth. You're afraid to. Despite your gloomy manner, you reminded me of Seneca. You look alike. But I was wrong. You're more like Nisa. Nisa, when she was terrified to love again, because the first time had been such a disaster.''

Arnoth's jaw hardened. Dane watched as the dark prince attempted to resist further inquiry. Finally, ''What happened?''

''Love found her anyway.''

''Ah . . . but I'm not here for it to find.'' Arnoth refused to hear any more of Dane's insights. ''Bring my mate to breakfast, Ravager. On second thought, I'll have it sent in here. It may take you a while to pull yourselves together. After that, you and she will face the tribunal. Your fate, and hers, will be decided there.''

Dane sat staring at the closed door, a cart offering a full breakfast beside the bed. ''He's crazy. He's the craziest man in the universe. Why do I bother?''

Aiyana stirred beside him, yawned, and opened her eyes. "Were you talking to me?"

"Arnoth."

Aiyana squinted and looked around the empty room. "Arnoth? Arnoth isn't here, Dane."

"He was. By the way, your mate has insisted we face the tribunal. Whatever that means."

"It means we must publicly atone for our crimes."

"Crimes?"

"Again your voice sounds high." Aiyana noticed the breakfast tray and seized a fat, square roll. "Don't worry." She spoke thickly, around the roll. "It's a formality of sorts. Arnoth presides."

"Wonderful! He almost killed me."

Aiyana took a sliver of dried meat and ate it. "When?"

"Just now. While you slept."

"He must have done it quietly."

Dane hesitated. "Yes."

"You appear unscathed." She turned her attention to a pot of steaming liquid, then slapped dark purple jelly onto the roll. She offered the roll to Dane. "Try some. The jelly is made from nettle-grapes. They're found in the Swamp of Keir. Once they were abundant, but now they're rare."

Dane shook his head at the proffered roll, wondering how she could eat when their fate hung delicately in Arnoth's balance. "Had I been armed, your former mate would be carved into small, bloody, quivering pieces."

Aiyana grimaced. "And you deny your Ravager nature. . . ." She set aside her breakfast, then looked around to find her dress. "I suppose I must wear this. No, I'll go back to my chambers and find my real clothes."

"Your real clothes?"

"My warrior's garb."

"It is a pleasing sight, actually. In particular, I like the way your leggings fit so . . . snugly."

"I like that about yours, too."

Dane felt a new rush of warmth. "Your bodice, also, fits well. Just enough of a cleft . . ." He stopped and threw up his hands. "What am I saying? My life has been threatened, and I'm to go before the tribunal, and here I am, hungry for you again."

"It is a good morning, isn't it?" Aiyana pulled her dress over her disheveled head and flipped her hair behind her back. "Dress, and attend to your hair." She ran her fingers idly through his tangled blond strands. "You're quite messy this morning." She sighed, sounding smitten. Dane's heart felt swollen in his chest. "You're beautiful messy."

"Like you, my love."

Aiyana kissed his cheek. "I'll meet you back here. We'll go together."

She started to leave, then turned back to kiss him again. "I'll miss you."

"Not if you hurry." Dane kissed her, too.

"I'll hurry."

Aiyana returned, again dressed in her warrior's clothing. Dane paused to admire the snug fit. He liked the way her boots were bound with narrow thongs. He liked her small, narrow feet.

"Are you ready to face the tribunal's inquisition, my love?"

Aiyana slipped her hand in his. "I am." Dane felt blissful, as if the world could crash around him, and he wouldn't notice. A sudden, dark premonition told him the world was about to do just that.

"You took this man . . . this Thorwalian to your bed. What have you to say, Aiyana Nidawi?"

Arnoth sounded surprisingly grim, considering his cheerful morning demeanor. Dane stepped forward. "It was my doing, Arnoth—"

"Silence!" Arnoth actually seemed to mean it. Dane's anger doubled.

"The fault is mine. And yours for letting her go." Dane felt stubborn. He hadn't obeyed Arnoth's commands yet, and he wouldn't start now just because the entire armed Ellowan camp stood around him.

Arnoth ignored Dane's protest. "Once again, the high priestess of the Ellowans has wronged her rightful prince for the sake of a Ravager's primitive appeal."

Dane leaned toward Aiyana. "What does he mean, 'once again'?"

"Ariana was betrothed to the highest-born son of the tribunal, too. When she took Hakon, it was considered a betrayal."

Arnoth nodded. "Rightfully so."

"How was the situation rectified then?"

"It was decided that each of their offspring should marry. But the prince failed to marry until late, and by that time Ariana's daughter had married another Ellowan, who was also highborn."

Dane's brow furrowed. "This grows complicated. Two princes."

"For a time. The matter settled itself. Ariana's daughter and the other prince were killed soon after the birth of their second child."

"By the Tseirs?"

"No. Accidentally."

"So who married who?"

"The first prince's son married Ariana's granddaughter. They were the same age."

The Ellowans listened silently, and Dane felt their collective gloom. They seemed far more intensely interested in their distant past than were the Thorwalians. "So do we promise our future offspring to Arnoth's children?"

Arnoth held up his hand, blocking the suggestion. Maybe blocking the possibility as well. "I will have no children."

"When you're an old man, Arnoth, gray and feeble, probably toothless—something that will please me to no end, by the way—then I'll take your word in this. Until that time . . ."

"I will have no children." Arnoth spoke sternly, with anger. Dane's brow tilted. At last, he had irritated Arnoth as much as Arnoth irritated him.

"We'll see. Be that as it may, I took your woman; you want revenge. What now?"

"You will maintain silence while I question my betrayer." Arnoth turned to Aiyana. "I will hear of your misdeeds, female."

Aiyana seemed unperturbed, so Dane trusted that she knew Arnoth's capacity for revenge better than he did. Aiyana cast her gaze upward as if searching her memory.

"What do I tell you?"

"What you did with this . . . Ravager."

"We kissed. On the lips. With tongues."

Dane shifted his weight from foot to foot. He felt the intense, dark stares of the Ellowan Tribunal. It wasn't entirely comfortable.

"What else?"

"We touched."

"Where?"

"Oh, everywhere." She sounded casual. Dane squirmed inwardly, but he kept his expression impassive.

"Clothed or unclothed?"

"Both."

Arnoth nodded, thoughtfully. "I must therefore accuse you of sensual union with another man."

"Yes."

"Did he say anything to provoke you?"

Aiyana considered this. "He said he was in pain."

Arnoth's brow rose as Dane cringed. "Pain?" Arnoth cast a knowing glance Dane's way. "*Pain.* Well, well."

"Actually, he called it agony."

Dane caught Aiyana's arm. "I don't think we need to share all these small, insignificant details with your tribunal, Aiyana."

Arnoth looked grave. "It is necessary." His brown eyes glittered. "And amusing."

"Is it? If you'd pronounce whatever judgment you intend to render—"

"Not so fast. Aiyana Nidawi, were you coerced by the Thorwalian's plea of agony?"

"No. Not after he gave me agony, too."

"How did he do this?"

"He took off his clothes and—"

Dane coughed. "Aiyana . . . A bit much, don't you think?"

"I'll sum up, shall I?"

"Good idea."

Arnoth grinned. "Don't leave out anything vital."

"He taught me teasing. . . . How to touch slowly, for the purpose of increasing anticipation. One feels very tense, and then . . ."

Arnoth cleared his throat. "Maybe you should sum up, after all, Aiyana."

Dane recognized Arnoth's masculine discomfort at the subject. "The harder you resist, the harder you'll fall, Arnoth." Arnoth glared at Dane's lyrical tone, and Dane felt a deep surge of satisfaction.

"There was no penetration of his male portions into my female spots." Aiyana appeared completely unaffected by what Dane considered excruciating revelations. "Only the finger."

Arnoth looked a little flushed. Dane enjoyed the Ellowan

prince's reaction. *Good. I'm not the only one.* "Did he attain orgasm?"

Aiyana glanced at Dane. "Is that what happened when you—"

Dane coughed again to silence her. "Yes."

Aiyana turned back to Arnoth and nodded. "Yes."

"And yourself?" Arnoth's voice sounded somewhat strained.

Aiyana looked at Dane again. "Is that what it was?"

"Yes."

"Yes." She paused. "I liked it very much."

Arnoth sat back in his seat and drew a long, taut breath. "Well, that's enough for me! I've been thoroughly betrayed."

"Yes."

Dane wondered why Aiyana didn't remind Arnoth of "releasing" her. Every man in the meeting hall appeared strained, though the women looked calm and unperturbed. *A strange lot, they are.*

"Dane Calydon, Ravager and seducer of this female . . . step forward."

Dane took one step. "What now?"

"You entered a sensual union with this female, my mate. What have you to say?"

"I love her."

"Love is sacred. Will you abide by those words?"

"I will."

"I can't keep a woman who has fiddled with another man's . . . 'portions.' " A laugh seemed to infect Arnoth's voice and he paused to clear his expression. Dane wondered if he were dreaming. "But I must know that my claim has been superseded by a better one."

"How do—?"

Arnoth didn't wait for Dane's question. "Will you take her as your mate?"

This was the true purpose of the tribunal. Dane felt an odd rushing sensation. Happiness. "I will."

"Then do so."

Dane hesitated. He couldn't control his smile. "How?"

"Take her hands and accept her as your mate."

Dane turned. Aiyana was looking up at him, still calm and placid. But beneath, Dane sensed . . . regret. "You do want this, don't you, Aiyana?"

"More than anything."

She meant it. But the regret remained. Dane had no idea why.

"I want you as my mate, on this world and any other. I'll protect you and love you for all time to come."

Tears glistened in her eyes. "No matter what happens, no matter how wide the darkness, I am yours."

"Not an entirely cheering promise, Aiyana."

She didn't rescind it. Doubt tugged at Dane's heart, but he shoved it away. She was his. "Well, Arnoth? Is that sufficient to amend our 'crimes'?"

"She is yours."

"Good . . . Now, if you'll leave us in peace."

"The tribunal isn't finished, Thorwalian." Something in Arnoth's tone sent a cold chill down Dane's spine. He didn't want to hear this.

"Is this really necessary, Arnoth?" Dane knew Aiyana held her breath. What Arnoth was about to say, she already knew. Had known all along. An icy numbness spread through Dane's limbs, shooting toward his heart.

"It's necessary. You are going to Franconia."

"I am." His throat felt tight. *No* . . .

"Franconia is forbidden to the Ellowans. We are considered a threat."

"For good reason. Arnoth—"

"You travel as a Candorian ambassador. Your mate is free to travel with you."

Dane couldn't move; he couldn't respond. His breath came slow and labored. He couldn't look at her, but he felt her beside him. Dane's jaw set hard. His heart labored. She had lied. Again. She had recognized his wish for love, and she'd given it to him. Beyond his dreams, beyond hope, she'd given him love. And it was a lie.

Curse you, Aiyana. "I see."

"Aiyana will go with you to Franconia. We must learn, firsthand, what you will do that influences our course."

Dane stood motionless, his face blank. It had been a lie. Another in a long series of lies. All designed to send a young and lovely terrorist into the land of her enemy.

"And if I refuse?"

"Then I will kill the Tseir, and imprison you until you change your mind."

"Why not kill me, too?"

"You walk in the shadow of one I loved. You walk in the shadow of our greatest king."

"Your words might be true. They might not. For all I know, you had no Ravager king, no Ravager wife. Maybe you used your mate last night as a whore. . . ."

He heard Aiyana's sharp breath, but he didn't stop. "Tell me, when she goes to Franconia, will her soft flesh be covered with explosives? Would you share her with the Keiroits if it served your purposes? Would you share her with the Tseirs?"

Arnoth rose slowly from his seat. He walked to Dane. Without warning, he slammed his fist into Dane's jaw. Dane staggered backward. He could use TiKay to defeat Arnoth, but he had no heart for battle. His heart felt like cold metal in his chest.

"You're a fool, Thorwalian."

"That much has been proven beyond doubt. You've given me little choice. Free Galya, and I will bring my . . . mate."

"Treat her as such, Thorwalian."

"I will treat her as I see fit. She is no longer your concern, Arnoth. She is mine."

Dane couldn't bring himself to look at Aiyana, but he knew she was shaking. "I will not bring her anywhere while there's a possibility she bears explosives."

"I do not." Her voice shook, too. Dane's heart had turned to ice. He felt nothing beyond numb pain and anger.

Dane rolled his eyes, his lip curling in distaste. "I've heard that before."

"You require proof. I will give you proof." Aiyana fixed her gaze on his, then tore open her bodice. Her hands shook, but she ripped it away and dropped it at her feet. She yanked down her tight leggings, then fumbled with her boots. She lowered them, too.

"It is impossible to attach explosives to feet, but I will show you my feet as well, if I must."

Arnoth turned away, but the Ellowan women moved closer around her, a silent support. Dane didn't back down. His gaze moved over her slowly. "Turn around."

She did, giving him enough time to see that her back was clear. She turned back, her leggings tangled around her feet. The tips of her breasts shrank into small peaks in the cold room. Reminiscent of desire, and yet so far removed.

"Are you satisfied? I am unarmed. I will go to Franconia, because it is my duty, and I will go without weapons, because there is no other way. I am your mate, because you agreed with our tribunal's demand. You don't know our truths. Perhaps you never will, but it was your choice."

A heavy silence filled the room as they faced each other. Before this moment, Dane had felt only a shadow of anger. This was different. It was deep and strong. He didn't know what to do with it. He didn't know how to assuage its power, or resolve its fury. It threatened to take over everything. Including Aiyana.

"I accept it, Aiyana. You are mine. I am satisfied that you are unarmed. Dress."

Aiyana tugged up her leggings and tied her boots. A woman handed her the bodice, which she assembled quickly. When her body was again covered, Arnoth came to stand beside her. He touched her shoulder, then turned her to face him.

"I warned you, *damanai.* Are you strong enough for what comes next? There is still time. . . . There is nothing pronounced at this tribunal that I can't change."

Aiyana looked up at him, and Dane's anger boiled at the affection between the two. "It's too late to alter our course now. I will do what I must. Yes, the pain is greater than I imagined. But we've both suffered that before, haven't we? I can endure."

Arnoth's long fingers squeezed around her slumped shoulders. "I want more for you, *damanai.*"

Tears streamed from her eyes. Aiyana rose up on tiptoe and kissed his cheek. "You have been my treasure, too. I wanted you to know."

Arnoth took her hands in his and kissed her clenched fingers. "We are now, and always will be, the best of friends."

Dane's anger splintered. He seized her arm and yanked her away. "Touching, but too late, Aiyana. You are mine. Your treasured mate gave you to me, and I intend to make good use of you."

"What do you mean, 'use of me'?"

"I would have thought from last night that you understood the concept quite well. If not, you will learn it soon."

Arnoth positioned himself between them, but Dane refused to release her arm. "Beware what you do in your rage, Ravager. Love is sacred. If you defile it, you may suffer something much worse than injured pride."

Dane laughed. "Sacred! Nothing is sacred without truth, Arnoth."

"Truth is here, beneath the surface. You don't see it, but it's there. It's there whether you see it or not."

"I tire of you, Arnoth. I tire of Valendir. Bring Galya, and a hovercraft, and I will depart."

"Your lingbat hasn't returned."

Dane released a long, weary groan. "I should leave without him."

Aiyana tugged her arm free of his grasp. "You can't do that! It would hurt his pride."

Dane eyed her irritably. "His pride? What pride?"

"Save your cruelty for me, Thorwalian. You accepted responsibility for the small lingbat. You must offer him adequate care."

"Must I?"

"Galya is held in the marsh also. It would save time if we took the hovercraft to Rurthgar's marsh, where the Dwindle Bats entertain your lingbat. Unless you prefer to return to Candor without him?"

Dane didn't want to relent, nor agree with any of Aiyana's requests. If she asked it, he would do the opposite.

Aiyana seemed to guess his intention. "I don't think the old lingbat would appreciate your abandoning his litter son."

"Carob . . . I suppose I'd have explaining to do."

"You would."

"Then we will go to the Dwindle Bats." Dane paused, his lips curved in perpetual irritation. "Dwindle Bats . . ."

Aiyana cast a quick look at Arnoth, who shrugged. "It will delay your journey to the Swamp of Keir." Arnoth paused. "But perhaps that is a good thing. Rurthgar's marsh is northwest of here. From there, head directly south rather than returning here. The trees are less thick in that direction, though you'll find it colder. That shouldn't trouble you, Thorwalian."

Aiyana sighed. "I'll bring two capes."

"I want sufficient blankets and food for Galya." Arnoth started to object, but Dane cut him off. "Don't consider denying me this, Arnoth. I've accepted your treachery, and I've honored my word to you. But I will go to Franconia as I planned, as is my own duty, and none of you will stand in my way."

Aiyana lifted her chin. "We asked that you deliver our request to the Candorians. Nothing more."

"You had something better planned. I should have known. But I was a fool. I trusted you. I wanted to trust you. I won't make that mistake again." He didn't wait for a reply. "Bring the hovercraft, Arnoth. The sooner I leave your cursed village, the better."

Arnoth started away, then turned back. "You're right, Ravager. You are a fool. I lost my world long ago, because I was a fool. I hope it won't take the same for you."

Arnoth kissed Aiyana's forehead, then left the meeting hall. The other Ellowans followed in silence, leaving Dane alone with Aiyana. He took her arm, but she didn't look at him.

"Well, my lady, are you ready? It seems we'll be traveling together again. All your guises are ripped away. Your scales and green flesh, your innocence, and your love. What's left?"

Aiyana met his cold eyes. "Duty."

"For us both." He hesitated, but dark anger replaced the spasm of pain. "I would have given you anything, Aiyana. We both made choices, didn't we? You chose to lie."

"I don't owe you anything, Thorwalian. Not truth, nor trust, nor anything. Neither do you owe me." She paused as if fighting emotion. "I told you I love you." He winced, but he didn't stop her. "I didn't lie. Love is sacred to the

Ellowans, whether you believe it or not. I told you I would be yours through all darkness. But I never imagined the darkness so wide. . . ."

His grip on her arm intensified. "It has only begun."

Dane waited while the Ellowans loaded supplies into a sleek, dark green hovercraft. He checked everything first, to be sure nothing concealed weapons. When he was satisfied with the contents, he entered the narrow shell and awaited Aiyana.

She stood with Arnoth, silent and wistful, beautiful in the shadowy morning light. Arnoth wrapped his arm around her shoulder, speaking softly. She nodded, then hugged him. Dane's heart turned to ice and he looked away.

She had slept in his arms. Dane closed his eyes. He saw himself holding her hand, entering the tribunal's meeting hall like a lovestruck fool. He remembered his fool's joy when he learned she was really his. All the while . . . a lie.

Aiyana kissed Arnoth good-bye, a tender farewell beyond Dane's hearing. He hated his jealousy, hated knowing he cared. He hated knowing she would be with him, and that never, not as long as he lived, would he ever be free of her memory.

Curse you, Aiyana. . . .

Aiyana entered the hovercraft, seating herself beside him. She didn't speak. Her eyes glistened with tears, her lips pressed together. *Touched by Arnoth's loving farewell, no doubt.* Dane turned his attention to the hovercraft's controls.

His technician's skill hadn't failed him. "Simple . . ." The hovercraft lifted with more power than a Thorwalian vessel. Its design allowed it to maneuver above the trees, or through, more mobile than his own craft, or those used by the Candorians.

Dane fiddled with the controls, then guided the craft up through the trees. The filtered sunlight sharpened, and he squinted in the light. The craft's dark hull seemed to absorb the light, reflecting nothing.

"The craft can be programmed." Aiyana sounded tense. Dane glanced at her. She looked tense, too.

"I prefer manual operation."

They reached the treetops, and Dane leveled the craft. From this viewpoint, the Ellowan-held forest stretched endlessly, showing no sign of Valendir. Far to the southeast, Dane saw the mountains that concealed the Swamp of Keir.

"Rurthgar's marsh is also hidden. It's just there." Aiyana pointed to a spot where the trees seemed lower. "The Tseir is kept just south of the marsh."

"So I was told. Don't bother me with conversation, Aiyana. I prefer your silence."

"Do you? I don't recall anyone making you my master."

Dane clenched his teeth. "Arnoth gave you to me."

"And you gave yourself to me! Perhaps you must do *my* bidding, Thorwalian."

Dane glared. "You will maintain silence."

"And if I don't?" She looked so smug. Her eyes were narrow, combative. Her lips curved in a tight, infuriating smile.

Dane couldn't think of a proper rejoinder. He couldn't think of anything. His brain failed him. Why? Because of his anger. *Yes. Ravager fury.* Dane considered this. Passion had nearly destroyed his race, until they discovered logic. Discipline.

"Speak as you wish, Aiyana. I reserve the right not to listen."

That felt better. Much better. He was in control. Until she leaned over and nipped his ear. The hovercraft dove, then swerved to the side, barely avoiding an evergreen tip.

"The lingbat was right about you. You are a very poor pilot."

His logic vanished. "If you touch me again, woman . . ."

Her slanted green eyes met his in challenge. She reached one slender, tapered finger toward him, slowly, then touched his shoulder. "I shall touch you as I please, as long as you are in reach." She sat back, pleased with herself.

Dane quivered with repressed violence. "I'm warning you, Aiyana. If you insist upon antagonizing me, I'll . . ." He faltered. *Cut you into quivering pieces forever to lament your fate* seemed excessive.

"You'll what?" She crossed her arms in front of her, waiting. Her little face bore the most infuriating expression he'd ever seen.

Dane punched the controls and the hovercraft plunged. Her eyes widened as they banked downward through the trees. She gripped her seat as the craft dove, barely avoiding branches.

"What are you doing?"

Dane brought the craft to an abrupt stop on the forest's rough floor, then turned to face her. "Get this straight, woman. You're here because you betrayed me. I had no choice but to bring you, but—"

"You could kill me."

He hesitated. "What?"

"You have a choice. You could kill me. The Ellowans aren't here to protect me. Arnoth isn't here to heal me. It would be a simple matter. Kill me."

Dane swallowed. She sounded serious. But she knew. He'd sooner die himself than harm her. "Curse you, Aiyana. You know better."

"You will not dictate my behavior simply because I've angered you, Thorwalian. If you wish to silence me, you'll have to kill me."

"I could bind and gag you."

"I will fight you."

Dane looked around for something to honor his threat. He

spotted a blanket and ripped off a strip. Aiyana seized the other end of the strip and held fast. "Let go, Aiyana."

"So you can gag me? I don't think so!"

Dane tugged, and she jerked toward him. Her long, soft hair coiled around her arm, around his. Dane pushed her back, but she still didn't let go. He was getting aroused. Of all times! He dropped the strip, and she snapped back, bumping her head.

"You did that on purpose!" She rubbed her head, glaring back at him. Dane shoved open the hovercraft's shell and got out. "Where are you going? Come back here!"

Dane walked in circles, banging his fist into trees as he passed. Aiyana hopped out after him and stood with her hands on her hips. "Of course, I don't care if we reach the marsh or not."

He stopped. "Don't you? Something tells me you want to get to Franconia a lot more than I do. I shudder to think of the reason."

"Your poor, sleeping Galya must be getting hungry."

Aiyana's taunt burned away the last of Dane's restraint. He went toward her, and she backed away. She stumbled on a tree root and he caught her. His fingers clenched as he gripped her arms.

"You do it deliberately, don't you?" He closed his eyes, fighting rage. "Everything . . ." His eyes snapped open as he realized the depth of her scheme. "Even the explosives."

"What are you talking about?" Aiyana trembled, but Dane felt no pity this time.

"Why didn't you tell me, Aiyana? I gave you the chance."

"I don't know what you mean."

"You wanted me to strip you; you wanted me to fall at your feet, and hate myself for the cruelty I inflicted on you. It made me weak, and had the added benefit of giving me a fine look at your perfect little body."

Her mouth dropped open. "How dare you!" She struggled in his grip and she tried to kick him. He evaded her and yanked her close. His arousal hadn't subsided. It burned and demanded.

"Your plan worked, Aiyana. I've never known such hunger. I've never wanted anything like this. Even now, when I could kill you . . ." He stopped, and his expression changed. "Why not? You're mine. You've done everything in your power to arouse me, to make me as crazy as your precious mate. Why not?"

"Why not what?"

Dane backed her against the hovercraft, then pinned her hands back at either side of her shoulders. Aiyana tried to push him away. "Stop that!"

"Some things can't be faked, Aiyana. Last night, whatever your purposes may have been, you wanted me. I've never touched a woman so ready."

Aiyana slumped back as if her knees wouldn't hold her up. He didn't let her fall. "I wonder if you're ready now?"

"I am not!"

"I am." Dane dragged her small hand down between them and placed it on the evidence of his desire. Her fingers clenched, squeezing around his length, and he shuddered. She gasped and released her grasp, as if she hadn't intended to respond.

"You can't mean . . . You can't do this."

"Why not?" His gaze ran over her, stopping at the swell of her breasts beneath her snug bodice. He dropped her hand and ran his finger along the neckline. With sudden violence, he tore the garment apart.

He spread the bodice, freeing her breasts. They were round and firm, the pink tips taut and ready for his touch. He cupped one small breast in his hand, then ran his thumb over the little bud. Aiyana struggled, but her body was responding just as he wanted.

Dane kissed her mouth fiercely, sucking, nipping, as he tugged her leggings down. He lowered his own, and pressed his full length against her stomach. Desire was stronger than anger. Aiyana kissed him back, her hunger equal to his.

"I will have you, Aiyana, and it won't be sweet and tender. You'll satisfy me, again and again, until I tire of you."

This fired her resistance. He wanted her resistance. He didn't know why. "You will not!"

Dane chuckled, then slid his fingers between her legs. She was slippery and wet, and he laughed again. "You played innocence well, my lady. But I want to see the well-skilled female that you are."

She met his eyes evenly. Her expression changed. A tiny smile formed on her lips, and his heart wrenched. "Take what you want from me, Ravager. You're right. I want you, too."

Her response inflamed Dane further. He lifted her from her feet, his hands gripping her waist as he positioned himself between her thighs. He probed upward, slick and hard. He moved her back and forth, sliding her over his staff.

Aiyana shuddered with raw, female pleasure. She kissed his neck, his shoulders. Her fingers gripped the muscle of his arms. His staff rubbed over her small peak and she moaned.

"You do like this, don't you? That much, at least, is true between us."

"When we're together, you'll understand." She sounded young and trusting, as if she believed sexual union would erase the distance her betrayal had wrought. Her innocence was feigned. But her desire wasn't.

Dane moved his hips, thrusting against her, and the wild tension spiraled between them. Her head tipped back and he kissed her throat. "I want you, Aiyana, whoever you are, no matter what you want from me."

"I want you. I am yours."

"You are, whether you want to be or not."

His staff felt near bursting as it pressed against her damp entrance. He ached—all the fire of his anger and pain centered there. Here, he would find relief. Dane gripped her hips and thrust inside her.

Her body resisted, then gave way to his thrust. Aiyana gasped and froze. "It hurts!" She wiggled and fought, but Dane didn't move. He just stared, shocked beyond speech. "You did it on purpose. You hurt me!"

She tried to kick at him. The motion caused her further pain. "Aiyana, stop."

"Remove yourself from my body, Thorwalian. I never dreamed you'd really hurt me." She was crying. Dane's blood ran cold at his error.

"You've never done this before."

Aiyana rolled her eyes, though tears ran down her face. "I have now. And I don't like it. This isn't like teasing at all."

"Aiyana . . ." His body filled hers. He felt her pulse, surrounding him. A warm rush centered around his length. Her body responded to his invasion, but fury and hurt sparkled in her eyes.

"Get out." Her voice shook. Dane's eyes glistened with tears, too. Aiyana stopped fighting. "Did it hurt you, too?"

A single tear fell to his cheek. "No."

He softened inside her as his heart plunged with remorse. He lifted her gently, and their bodies separated. She looked confused, as if she didn't understand her own warring reaction. "I'm sorry, Aiyana."

Dane fastened his belt again and turned away as she pulled her bodice together. She bent to pull up her leggings. She examined a small stain of blood on her thigh. "I'm bleeding!"

"That is expected the first time." His voice came low, strained.

"Well, I didn't expect it."

"I know." Dane sank down onto the forest floor, his head in his hands. Aiyana hesitated, then sat down beside him.

"I almost believe you didn't mean to hurt me."

"Not physically."

"You did."

"I know." He didn't look at her.

"Why did you cry?"

He looked at her now, his face stricken, the anger gone. What he felt instead was worse. He felt defeat, endless and certain. He'd killed whatever hope remained between them. Until now, Dane hadn't realized how much his anger had obliterated hope. It had been there. And he killed it. Just as Arnoth warned.

"I hurt you. Aiyana, I hurt you."

Her eyes puddled with fresh tears. "Why do you care? That's what you wanted, isn't it?"

"No. It's not what I wanted. I don't know you, Aiyana." He paused. "Well, I know one thing now. You didn't lie about your relationship with Arnoth. Obviously he never touched you."

"He's touched me. Just not there." She hesitated. "What now?"

Dane sighed heavily. "We go on." He rose to his feet and helped her up. "You and I, we can't seem to stop hurting each other. We'll go on together, because we must. But don't tease me, Aiyana. I can't take it."

"I liked teasing you."

She didn't know what she was saying. Because she was innocent. Truly innocent. "If you'd restrain yourself, this would be easier for both of us."

"You're going to leave me, aren't you?"

Dane's heart clenched. He couldn't tell if she feared his

answer, or desired it. "When I've completed my task for the Candorians, yes."

"You said you'd come back."

"That was before, Aiyana, when I was floating in a fool's dream."

She bowed her head, but Dane thought she was crying. "Will what we just did make a baby?"

"No, it shouldn't. I didn't reach release."

"As you did in my hand?"

Dane hesitated, uncomfortable with her bluntness. "Yes."

"I've never bothered to learn these things. There has been no need for so long."

"There won't be a need. I took you in anger. It won't happen again."

Dane held open the hovercraft shell, and she climbed in. She glanced at him briefly, her expression more curious than angry or hurt. She looked at him as if seeing him for the first time. Dane couldn't imagine her new impression could be positive.

He sighed, then entered the craft beside her. He wondered if he'd really lost her at the tribunal. Maybe his Ravager fury had destroyed something he really hadn't lost at all. Until now.

They said nothing to each other as the hovercraft rose again through the dark trees. Dane adjusted the controls toward Rurthgar's marsh and Aiyana looked out the window. She wanted to tell him that her pain was gone, but she didn't dare broach the subject.

She felt warm and congested in her secret depths. Well, not secret anymore. She wondered if it would always hurt when he entered her, then remembered with a cold wash of misery that she'd never know.

"Elena never told me that it hurt." Aiyana hadn't meant

to speak aloud, but the matter of coupling needed resolution. If not physical, then verbal would have to suffice. "Perhaps that falls under the term, "a lot."

Dane responded slowly. "Perhaps what happened afterward made her forget the pain."

Aiyana's brow furrowed as she speculated what this might mean. "She did mention that at first she thought Arnoth's male extremity too large to fit inside her."

Dane made an odd, weak noise, and Aiyana looked over at him. "Must you share these details with me, Aiyana?"

"Why not? Of course, I've never seen that portion of Arnoth's body. Though I always thought favorably of his chest and shoulders."

"Quiet!"

Aiyana liked Dane's reaction. "His bottom—the buttocks—is also admirably formed. And those pretty brown eyes . . ." Aiyana paused to issue a calculated sigh of appreciation. "You're very different in appearance, you know."

"That happens when a race evolves on a different planet in a different sector of the galaxy."

"And his hair. Arnoth has beautiful hair. Long and thick."

For some reason, this description brought an indignant huff from Dane. Aiyana had no idea why. Dane had good hair, too. "Ellowans don't have curly hair, but I've seen library images of curly-haired aliens, from a distant world that once contacted Valenwood. I thought them beautiful. Of course, the library didn't survive Valenwood's destruction. Are there curly-haired Thorwalians?"

Dane's brow knitted in irritation. Aiyana remembered that he didn't want to talk. "Well, are there?"

"No. Maybe a few, from the rare times when a Dakotan mated with a Thorwalian. Seneca's hair has a slight wave."

Dane paused, then shook his head. "Why are we talking about hair, Aiyana?"

"I thought you preferred that to a discussion of sensual intimacy."

"Where were we? Hair . . . Seneca. He keeps it long now, so it's fairly straight."

Aiyana chuckled. "You're right. It is a tedious subject. I thought your portion was too large, too."

"Shouldn't we be landing about now?"

Aiyana leaned forward and looked down at the forest. "Not yet. What was I saying? Oh, yes . . . Are Thorwalian women perhaps more substantial in their female spots, so as not to be rent asunder by your inordinate size?"

Dane jabbed at the front panel and the hovercraft sped forward.

"This craft is best kept at an even speed. You're going too fast. I suspect your erratic skills explain the collisions the lingbat mentioned." She watched him. He swallowed several times. His breath appeared rapid. His face looked flushed. "Well?"

"Well what?"

"You were explaining the nature of Thorwalian females' spots."

"I was not."

"How do they bear the pain?"

Dane drew a tight breath. "I have no idea. I suppose they clench their teeth and suffer through it."

"They must be more stoic than I. I should prefer to fight you rather than endure that again."

Aiyana watched Dane struggle with his desire for silence and his need to correct her. "It only hurts the first time."

"How do you know? You're not female."

"I've been told!"

"No doubt they told you this to appease your vanity. So . . . you've bedded many virgins, have you?"

"A few."

"Then you're well versed at causing pain."

He turned in his seat and glared at her. "I've never heard any complaints until now."

"Because they were busy clenching their teeth."

"They were writhing in bliss!"

"Ha! Writhing in agony, more likely."

"If you don't mind, woman, I would prefer not to discuss this subject further."

Aiyana hesitated. He wanted to distance himself from her. Because she had deceived him. He didn't want the passion between them. Maybe that was his right.

"Very well, Thorwalian. I will trouble you no further."

Dane glanced at her doubtfully. "You will trouble me forever, Aiyana. And you know it."

Dane kept his attention on the control panel, but it wasn't easy. She'd finally abandoned her excruciating line of questioning, but his blood refused to cool from their thwarted encounter. He tried to imagine Aiyana with green flesh, covered in scales. It didn't work.

It was different when he knew his arousal was fueled by her own. Now she seemed to consider sex a vile nuisance. *What have I done? I should have taken her gently, with love. . . .* Dane glanced over at her. She was looking out the front window, unaffected by their torturous conversation.

Yet in her eyes, he saw sorrow. And something more. Whatever she wanted, she accepted that it might elude her. Because so much had eluded her throughout her life. Dane looked away. That, too, could be a lie. But her virginity wasn't.

Maybe I shouldn't have stopped. I should have shown her pleasure, at least once. . . . Now her inclination would be to fight him. At first. He hardened at the thought.

"Stop that at once." Her sudden, sharp order startled him.

Dane looked over to see her gaze fixed on his trousers.

"I don't have much control over this, woman."

"Apparently not." She paused, looking contemplative. "It felt better in my hand."

"Especially when you talk this way."

"I suppose it doesn't matter now."

"No. It doesn't."

"You will never touch me again. You said so."

"True."

"You've missed the landing space. You must circle around and go back."

"Why didn't you tell me that earlier?"

Aiyana looked surprised, and a little superior. "You were rattling on about your male portion, so I couldn't tell you."

Dane whirled the hovercraft in a reverse direction, jarring them both. "You've lived with Arnoth too long, Aiyana. I've never known two more infuriating people. And that includes lingbats."

Rurthgar's marsh was darker than Valendir. Dane hadn't noticed flies before, but small, black bugs swarmed the area. "Batty must be delighted."

They left the hovercraft on the outskirts of the marsh, but Dane already noticed noxious, stagnant odors arising from the bog. Dane hesitated. "Can't they bring Galya out to us?"

"It's not a long walk." Aiyana swatted a fly and adjusted her hood. "Swamp flies. They'll go away soon, because it's getting colder. But their bites leave a fearsome itch. Cover yourself, Thorwalian."

Dane's cape had no hood, so he slapped at the flies as he and Aiyana walked toward the marsh. Spirals of marsh steam rose, creating a greenish haze over the brown surface. Dane stopped at the border of the stagnant bog.

"What's to stop us from disappearing in this rotten quagmire?"

"There are paths." Aiyana indicated a row of torches that led inward along a curved path. "The Keiroits dwell deep in the marsh, but the Ellowans enter at times."

"What times?"

"When Tseir patrols search Keir."

"How have you avoided them?"

"Most of our huts are wooden, easily moved, easily replaced."

"What about the central hall? It is, or was, a flightship, made of the same material as the hovercraft. Black."

"It is obsidian. But despite its appearance, it is still a workable craft."

Dane fought his curiosity. "Shall we proceed?"

"Follow." Aiyana started into the marsh, but Dane shook his head.

"You can be a very bossy woman."

She glanced back. "Someone has to lead. Why shouldn't it be me?"

Dane shrugged, then started after her. "Did you treat Arnoth this way, too?"

"Arnoth has always been wiser than I. Yet he never fails to hear my thoughts and wisdom." She paused. "Unlike yourself."

"If he's so wonderful, why aren't you occupying yourself in his bed?"

Aiyana chuckled. "Calm yourself, Dane. I find you wonderful, too. Most of the time."

Dane twitched with irritation as she walked on ahead. Even picking her way through the marsh, she looked graceful. Her feet left little imprint. Her dark hair swayed back and forth as she moved. He sighed.

She cast a knowing glance over her shoulder. "Almost as wonderful as you find me."

"In appearance, you are flawless."

"When you entered the Candorian chamber, I thought the same of you."

"Did you? That would be just before you called me a 'pet,' wouldn't it?"

Aiyana chuckled, pleased with the memory. "Just prior to that, yes. I didn't say I considered you intelligent. Just well made."

"Indeed." The path wasn't wide enough for him to walk beside her. Dane disliked following.

"I also thought you were arrogant, too sure of yourself, and probably very vain."

"I'm not vain."

" 'They were writhing in bliss.' That sounds like a vain assumption to me."

Dane fought an urge to trip her from behind. "It was an accurate assessment."

"Ha!"

"There is a temptation to prove this point beyond argument."

She stopped, turned, and faced him, her hands on her hips. "How? By stabbing that"—she pointed at his groin—"that weapon of flesh into me?"

Dane winced at her choice of words. "A poor comparison, Aiyana."

"An accurate assessment."

"Did you feel no pleasure?" *Curses!* He sounded wistful. And he'd given her a perfect opportunity to insult him further.

She licked her lips, and he held his breath. "Not at first." She paused, reflecting. "But just before you removed yourself . . . when the pain abated . . ."

"Aha! So it did ease."

She hesitated. "A bit."

"Well?"

"I didn't think I liked it at the time. But afterward . . ."

"Yes?" Dane folded his arms over his chest, feeling smug again.

"It wasn't entirely disgusting." She turned and proceeded down the path. Dane's pride deflated.

" 'Not entirely disgusting.' Didn't you say something about flattering me last night?" He muttered his comments under his breath, but she heard.

"I did. I didn't realize then what a leap from truth flattery would be."

That was it. Dane bounded forward, caught her in his arms, bent her backward, and kissed her. She gasped in surprise, then struggled. "Release me."

He kissed her again, slowly, reining in his desire. He teased her clamped lips into softness, then apart. She relaxed in his arms and caught his hair in her fingers. His tongue slid over hers. When she answered his kiss, he stopped, then set her abruptly upright again.

"There! Tell me you disliked that, woman!" Dane didn't wait for an answer. He marched on ahead, following the line of flickering torches deeper into the marsh.

"Kissing is one thing. You do that well, I admit. But the other . . ."

"Don't tempt me in this, Aiyana." He walked faster.

"Don't worry."

Dane's jaw tightened angrily. "I made a mistake. I see no reason for you to torment me into eternity."

"You hurt me."

He stopped and waited for her to catch up. "I'm sorry. I didn't think I was the first."

"You should have known."

"I thought you were lying, to make me love you."

"Does that mean you wouldn't love me if Arnoth had placed his male portion inside me first?"

"Must you be so graphic?" Dane sighed. "That's not the

point. It's the deceit and manipulation that bother me."

"Is that all?"

"No. It's knowing that any man who represented the Candorians would have faced your seduction. Had a female been sent, I suppose Arnoth would have seduced her and made her the same kind of fool you made me."

The sudden flash of anger in Aiyana's face astonished Dane. He nearly stepped back. "You're right. You are a fool."

She said nothing more. She shoved him aside and retook the lead. Dane endured a moment of remorse. *Why do we hurt each other?*

Dane caught up with her, though she walked surprisingly fast. "Aiyana, please wait."

"We're almost there. If you'd be silent for a change, you would hear the Keiroits ahead."

"I don't care about hearing Keiroits. Aiyana, I'm sorry. Again. I might have been wrong."

"You might." She wasn't relenting. Her small jaw was set, her green eyes cold and unyielding.

"Maybe you're telling the truth about a Ravager king. Maybe you do bear my race some peculiar tenderness."

"It's fading fast, Thorwalian." She started away, but Dane drew her back. She refused to meet his eyes. He waited silently until she peeked up at him. He smiled. Slowly. Her eyes widened, and she puffed a fierce breath.

"And you call me manipulative!"

"What are you talking about?"

"That!" She pointed her finger into his face. "That smile. You know what you're doing."

"What?" He tried to sound shocked, innocent.

"You're trying to make me feel giddy about you again. Well, it won't work. In fact, I think you know a lot more about seduction than any Ellowan ever did. Ariana said the same about Hakon. She said he would smile and look innocent and sweet, and the next thing she knew, she was on his lap, making love in a roomful of people."

"What?" Dane's mouth dropped. "A roomful of people?" His voice was small and high.

Aiyana nodded. "After he saved her from her crashed flightship, he brought her back to his brother's great hall. Apparently Ravagers had a tendency to while away their hours with uninhibited sensual union."

"Orgies. So we're told. Go on."

"Why does this subject always increase the pitch of your voice?"

Dane shrugged, and Aiyana shook her head. "There might have been a time when the Ellowans behaved likewise, but by Ariana's time, we were far more reserved. Hakon, however, thought nothing of it. So he seduced her in front of a large group of drunken Ravagers. Unfortunately, his brother was one."

"Oh." Dane nearly doubled over with this image. "No wonder they went to war!"

"Hakon refused to share her. He said it had never bothered him before, but Ariana was different."

"How do you know these things about a king who lived centuries ago?"

Aiyana hesitated, awakening Dane's suspicions. "His life has been recorded. He wrote a great deal."

"He wrote? Ravagers didn't write. They had runes, but rarely used them to convey much."

"Hakon did. He turned the Ravager runes into a well-developed language."

"Where he recorded his orgies . . . Let's go, Aiyana. I can bear no more."

The marsh water bubbled beside the path. Dane started as a green head emerged. Rurthgar pulled himself out of the water and nodded pleasantly at Aiyana before turning his round eyes to Dane. He held a half-eaten fish in one webbed paw.

"Still here, is he?"

Dane eyed the Keiroit in distaste. "I am."

Rurthgar took a bite of the fish, then held it toward Dane. "Want some?"

"No."

Rurthgar chuckled. "Here for the lingbat, are you? Well, good luck getting him to leave."

"I came to retrieve Galya. If the rodent wants to stay, I have no problem leaving him here throughout the passage of eternity."

Aiyana jabbed her elbow into Dane's side. "Please take us to the lingbat, Rurthgar. Dane requires his assistance."

A loud whirring noise erupted in the branches of the marsh alders. The sky darkened with tiny bats. Dane stared in astonishment and Aiyana covered her head. "They have a tendency to lodge themselves in hair, Thorwalian."

"Perfect. If one of the miserable little rodents comes anywhere near me—"

"Duck!"

Dane ducked. The bats swarmed in circles around Dane and Aiyana, but Rurthgar bowed. Dane looked for Batty. "Where is that cursed beast?"

The bats fluttered to a low branch, hanging by their toes. Something hopped from branch to branch above them. The bats issued peculiar squeaking noises.

"Dane. What took you so long?"

Dane looked around slowly. Then he turned his attention to the higher branch. "Batty."

"Dane."

Dane clenched his teeth, but Aiyana giggled. "If it would please you, rodent, to get down here, we might start for the Swamp of Keir. Or have you been made king of the esteemed Dwindle Bats?"

Batty hopped down to another branch. Aiyana moved closer to Dane. "I wonder what happened to him? He looks different. Arrogant . . ." Aiyana peeked up at Dane, a smile flickering on her lips. "He reminds me of you."

Dane ignored her teasing. Batty hopped lower. Aiyana was right. The rodent's chest looked puffed out with self-appreciation.

"Not king . . . 'honored master,' roughly translated. Of course, seeing a specimen as massive and majestic as myself stunned them at first, but I used my wits and calmed them down."

"Did you?"

Aiyana chuckled. "No doubt he had them 'writhing in bliss.' "

Dane glared, recognizing her comparison. "Agony, at this point, seems more appropriate."

"You should know."

Batty hopped down among the Dwindle Bats, who made further squeaking sounds. "So, Dane. Did you convince this female to mate with you? If not, I'd be happy to give you a few pointers at impressing the opposite"—Batty made a smacking noise—"sex."

Dane's sudden movement startled both Aiyana and the Dwindle Bats, who flapped madly higher into the tree. He caught Batty by the neck, then held him at eye level. "You've got a choice, rodent. Stay here and play honored master, or wipe the smirk off your puckered little face and continue on our mission. What will it be?"

"Dane—"

"That would be 'sir' to you, rodent."

Rurthgar tapped Dane's shoulder. The Keiroit drew forth a stout sword. "Sacred."

Dane rolled his eyes. "Lingbat."

"Sir." Batty's squeak was almost too high to hear. Dane released his grip slightly.

"Yes?"

Batty twisted his neck and gasped for air. "Sorry, sir. Let it go to my head."

"I can see that."

"Sorry, sir."

"If that means you intend to continue on with me, let us speak of it no more."

"Yes, sir. Sorry." Batty's chest looked deflated and sunken as he scrambled to Dane's wide shoulder. He cast a forlorn, longing look upward to the Dwindle Bats. "They'll probably get along fine without me, but still . . ."

"They seem to have done well enough without you so far." Dane glanced up at the hordes of small bats. "There's certainly a multitude of them."

One very tiny bat hopped back down the branch and issued a plaintive squeak. Batty squeaked back, a lower, deeper sound. Aiyana and Dane exchanged a doubtful glance.

Aiyana had a sympathetic, feminine expression on her face. "Who is that, Batty?"

"She Who Leaps High." Batty paused to sigh. "Just entering her first breeding cycle. Of course, that means she's forbidden territory."

Dane eyed the tiny bat. "Why?"

"A female's first cycle is sacred, sir." Batty spoke as if everyone knew this fact. "For both the ling and Dwindle varieties of batdom."

Aiyana turned away quickly. Dane suspected she was fighting laughter. Dane remained both bored and irritated. "I take it your species are related in some way?"

"Closely, sir, now that you mention it. We did some speculating, She Who Leaps High and myself, that the earliest Candorian lingbats may actually have come from Keir, maybe brought by the Ellowans."

Aiyana turned back and nodded. "It could be, Batty. The

Ellowans love animals. Especially exotic, majestic ones.''

Dane looked at Aiyana, wondering if she'd lost her mind. ''Shall we proceed?''

Aiyana and Batty exchanged an impertinent glance, then spoke together. ''Yes, sir.''

Chapter Six

‘‘Where’s Galya?’’ Dane settled his pack and Batty to the marsh floor and looked around. The damp air had turned cold, and evening raced inward through the eastern alders.

‘‘Got her somewhere.’’ Rurthgar mumbled something unintelligible to another Keiroit, who shrugged and looked around.

‘‘Where is she?’’ Dane fought to maintain control of his temper.

‘‘I don’t know.’’ Rurthgar sounded both put out and disinterested.

‘‘Arnoth told you, at least in my presence—stars know what his real instructions were—that you were to keep her safe.’’

‘‘She’s safe. Somewhere.’’

Dane’s patience faltered. He drew out his Thorwalian rifle and aimed at Rurthgar’s bulgy left eye. ‘‘Fetch her or die, Keiroit.’’

Rurthgar looked over at Aiyana, who shrugged. ‘‘So this

is the Ravager temper, is it? Can't believe your king carried on like this."

Aiyana sighed. "He didn't."

"I'll put a bite on the Tseir." Rurthgar gurgled, then flapped away.

"He'd better not mean that, Aiyana."

"Rurthgar likes jokes. He's been that way since just a hatchling."

"You've known him since he hatched?"

"Not quite. Keiroits are called hatchlings until they reach full maturity. But he was mated and leader while still a hatchling."

"Must be younger than he looks."

Aiyana didn't comment on Rurthgar's age. "I'll speak to the Keiroit for you, if you'd like. I suppose you're eager to depart."

"Do so."

Aiyana started after Rurthgar, leaving Dane standing amidst noxious pools of stagnant water. Batty clambered up his leg and returned to his shoulder. "Odd . . ."

"What, Batty?"

"What the Ellowan female said, sir."

Dane battled his raw patience. "Speak clearly, rodent. If possible."

"About the Keiroit's age. Funny she should remember him as a hatchling."

"Why?" Dane stared absently into the rising fog. The sky darkened early and the temperature dropped. "Reminds me of Thorwal before a storm."

"Yes, sir. Ice droplets will commence before the sun sets."

"How do you know?"

"Lingbats sense weather, sir." Batty hesitated, looking guilty. "Actually, the Dwindle Bats told me, sir." His expression turned to downcast shame, but Dane's mind wandered.

"You were saying something about Aiyana being odd. Not that this should surprise me."

"Yes, sir." Batty sounded relieved that Dane chose to overlook his momentary deceit. "She took me aback a bit. The Keiroits have long life spans. Their hatchling phase is at least fifty years."

"What of it?"

"Well, their leader is generally the oldest among them, and they live what you'd call three hundred years, or more. Rurthgar is oldest here."

Dane considered this, decided it made no sense, then shrugged. "So this time they made an exception. These are rogues, Batty. Outside the norm for Keiroits. Whatever the norm is."

"As you say, sir. Odd, though. Since I heard it from the Keiroit himself."

"Probably lying to impress you. I noticed Rurthgar was boastful."

Batty sighed. "Just what he said about you, sir."

Dane gritted his teeth, but Aiyana appeared with Rurthgar. The Keiroit was dragging a long sack behind him. A suspiciously humanoid-shaped sack.

Dane positioned his rifle and went to meet them. "Galya, I presume."

"It's her." Rurthgar gurgled again and broke into a hacking wheeze.

Dane fought to keep his voice even. "What is she doing in a sack?"

"Not much."

Dane noticed Aiyana's sparkling eyes as she fought laughter. She covered her mouth and pretended to cough.

"If she's dead, Keiroit . . ."

"She's not dead." Rurthgar paused. "At least, I don't think so. Wasn't last time I checked."

"When was that?"

"Just about when I shoved her in the sack and dropped her in the mud."

Dane drew his sword and cut open the sack. Galya lay motionless, but breathing, unaware of the Keiroit's haphazard treatment.

"Wake her."

Aiyana groaned. "Now?"

"Yes. Now."

"Can't we just bring her along like this until we reach the Swamp of Keir?"

"No, we cannot. Wake her, Aiyana."

"Ellowans don't touch Tseirs." Her voice dropped, low and adamant.

"So I've heard. Rurthgar, you'd better know how to reverse the substance you applied to her."

"Sure."

"Do it now."

Rurthgar turned to Galya and gave her a hard kick. Dane winced, but Aiyana chuckled. Galya stirred, then woke. "Dane . . ."

Dane knelt beside her. "Don't try to get up, Galya. You'll need time for the effects of this 'sleep' to wear off."

"You saved me."

Aiyana rolled her eyes and coughed loudly. "Right. From what?"

Dane decided that Aiyana had reached an even more irritating level of behavior. She threatened to surpass Arnoth in infuriating him. He wondered if the loss of her virginity contributed to her annoying manner.

"You're safe, Galya."

Galya tried to sit up. "My side. . . . I've been injured, Dane. I don't think I can walk."

Dane glared up at Rurthgar, who eased back. ''Might have kicked her a little hard. Tseirs usually bear up better than that.''

''It's hard to breathe, Dane.'' Galya clutched his arm. ''What have they done to me?''

''Just prodded you a little, Tseir. With this.'' Rurthgar held up his foot. It was large, and webbed between the splayed toes. Galya grimaced, but Aiyana sighed happily.

Dane rose to his feet and faced Aiyana. ''You know what I want. Galya's injury is your fault. Yours and Arnoth's, for leaving her in the 'care' of these. . . . reptiles.''

''Amphibians, sir.'' Batty adjusted his position on Dane's shoulder. ''Not reptiles.''

''Whatever. Aiyana, you can heal her. Easily.''

Aiyana met his angry gaze without flinching. ''Ellowans don't touch Tseirs. Not now, not ever. Not even for you, Thorwalian.''

''If her ribs are broken, and they probably are, Galya could die.''

''Dane, help me. I feel so weak.''

Dane's gaze intensified. Aiyana's expression turned colder still. ''I will die first.''

Dane started to speak, but she held up her hand. ''Say what you will. Ellowans do not touch Tseirs.'' Aiyana turned her back to him and rummaged through her pack for wafers. She sat down and bit into a wafer in a manner resembling the Keiroit's vengeful intake of fish.

Dane started after her, but Rurthgar placed a cold, webbed fin on his shoulder. ''Watch your step, Thorwalian. You don't know what you ask if you demand that an Ellowan heal a Tseir.''

''I don't understand them, Rurthgar. Their hatred is so strong, yet Valenwood fell centuries ago. But to Aiyana, and Arnoth, it seems recent past.''

''You see a discrepancy?''

"I do. I don't know which is true. And I have to know, to make the right choice."

Rurthgar assessed Dane quietly, then nodded. "Sometimes there is no right choice."

Dane's irritation flared. "You've listened overmuch to Arnoth."

"You haven't listened enough."

"I would appreciate, just once, a straight answer from someone, somewhere in this system."

"Don't you know, Thorwalian? Do you ever listen to your heart's voice, or do you distrust it so much?"

"What are you talking about, Rurthgar? Which is true? If you know, tell me."

"Both." Rurthgar slapped Dane's shoulder in what was probably meant to be a friendly gesture, then flapped from the path. He dove beneath the thick, green surface and disappeared.

"What did that mean, sir? 'Both?' How could it be both?"

"I'm not sure, Batty."

"It's a mystery, sir."

Find the reality of Franconia. "What do I do?"

"Are you asking me, sir?"

"No, Batty. I wasn't really asking anyone. Maybe there is no answer."

"We'll find an answer on Franconia, sir. That's what Kostbera said. You're doing what you think is right. That's the only way, sir. My sire always said so."

"What if I'm wrong, Batty? What if I make the wrong choice?"

"You won't make it until you know. My sire said that, too."

"I hope he knows me better than I do."

Dane turned back to Galya. Odd, how easy it was to forget her. He felt a pang of guilt at the sight of her, sitting in mud. Yet oddly composed. Controlled. For someone who'd spent days unconscious in a sack, she looked unaffected.

Dane knelt beside her. "I'm sorry, Galya. I'll have to carry you back to the hovercraft and bind you myself. I couldn't persuade Aiyana to use her skills on your behalf."

"I knew she wouldn't. Our pain means nothing to them. They make sport of our deaths. No doubt they kept that side of their culture from you. But their leader, Arnoth, excels in torture."

Galya paused, looking hard into Dane's eyes. "I was fortunate that you were with me when we were captured. It terrifies me to think what he would have done otherwise. He is known for rape."

Dane didn't respond, but he couldn't imagine Arnoth going that far, even in vengeance for his wife's death. If Arnoth killed, it would be swift and sure. Remorseless, but not cruel. *Ellowans don't touch Tseirs.* In this, Dane knew both Arnoth and Aiyana spoke the truth.

Galya glanced over at Aiyana, who spat out a portion of wafer and wiped her mouth on her sleeve. Dane warmed with affection.

"What happened with the Ellowan, Dane? Why is she here?"

Dane hesitated. "I'm afraid Kostbera selected the wrong ambassador. I didn't prove myself immune to temptation."

Galya's eyes went back to Aiyana. "But you're here. They didn't convince you to support their cause."

"No, they didn't. It is my intention to continue my mission to Franconia. But you should know that while 'visiting' Valendir, Aiyana became my mate."

Galya's lips tightened, then formed into a tender smile. "I knew she would try. But what is an Ellowan mating to an outworlder?"

"My word binds me. For now. To secure our freedom, I

had to agree to bring her with me. As I understand it, the Ellowans aren't permitted on Franconia."

"They haven't been on Franconia for centuries."

"Centuries?" Dane glanced over at Aiyana. Another lie was making itself known. His warmth faded, leaving icy emptiness again. "Not even Ellowan prisoners?"

"We haven't been able to take any Ellowans captive. They are sly, devious. Now that I've learned they are allied with the Keiroit rogues. . . . I don't know how much longer we can endure their attacks. With the help of the rogues, they can inflict horrible damage. They always seem to elude capture."

"Arnoth claims to have been held prisoner on Franconia."

"Then he's lying, Dane."

Dane sat back and studied Galya's face. She looked bland, but sincere. "How was Valenwood destroyed?"

"Don't you know? The Ellowans destroyed their homeworld themselves."

"That can't be."

"It's hard to imagine, I know. The Tseirs came to this system desperate, in dire need. They promised us aid, then enslaved us. We soon realized they were vicious and warlike beyond comprehension."

"Aiyana says the Ellowans were peaceful until the Tseirs destroyed their planet."

"Like Arnoth, she lies, Dane. No, they fought amongst themselves, and finally detonated a power core, which devastated their atmosphere, poisoning it."

"That much is true, then. Nothing lives on Valenwood."

"No. It is barren, lifeless." Galya sighed. "A tragedy."

Dane considered Galya's words. The discrepancy widened. "If they destroyed themselves, then why the eternal hatred for your people?"

Galya looked down, sorrowful. "We've never understood

their hatred. We did nothing to deserve it. We tried to help them, to offer counsel, wisdom. I believe our prosperity angers them."

"Then for generations, the Ellowans have survived in small numbers fixated on terrorizing the Tseirs?"

"That is true, Dane. You must beware of the Ellowan woman. She seduced you into a mating to secure her passage to Franconia."

"So it seems." The truth sounded stark spoken aloud. For the first time in his life, Dane felt old.

"There is a way to end this, Galya. I'll return to Candor and send another in my place. Another whose susceptibility to the Ellowan allure is less. . . . primitive."

Galya considered Dane's offer. "You have proven yourself, Dane. You endured the Ellowans' persuasion, and live to speak honestly to me. I can't think of a better ambassador than you."

Dane nodded, but he didn't understand Galya's reasoning. Another factor that made no sense. He rose to his feet and looked over at Aiyana. She watched them intently, probably guessing the nature of their conversation.

The lies were cleanly drawn. He had to search out the truth from among the mired deceit. No one had told him the full truth. Dane felt certain that the Tseirs weren't as uninvolved as Galya claimed. But he wouldn't know more until he reached Franconia.

Aiyana watched as Dane gently lifted Galya into his strong arms. Her annoyance surged. Aiyana couldn't resist. She hopped up and joined them. "What horrible affliction does the Tseir suffer? Weak knees?"

Dane carried Galya carefully along the marsh path, Aiyana close at his side. "Her ribs may be broken."

"Ha! What led you to that conclusion?"

"She's in a lot of pain."

Galya leaned her head on Dane's shoulder, and Aiyana made a noise that closely resembled a Keiroit gurgle. A smile flickered on Dane's lips.

"Well, then. . . . She's probably right. *If* her ribs are really broken, she'll be spitting up blood by morning. Probably entrails, too."

Galya cringed, and Aiyana wiped her hand across her mouth, removing imaginary spittle. She expected Dane's anger, but he seemed to be fighting laughter.

"I don't know much about medical practices, but as it happens, I endured several broken ribs once. I should be able to recall how the Dakotans bandaged me."

Aiyana studied Dane intently. "Did you crash?"

"No, I didn't crash. Most of my crashes happened as a young man, and they were relatively harmless. To my person, anyway. My craft were less fortunate."

Aiyana bit her lip, but she smiled anyway. "The ribs, Thorwalian. What happened?"

"A revolutionary attempted to take over Thorwal, and I was imprisoned. His guards weren't particularly gentle."

Aiyana realized she knew very little about Dane Caly-don's life. She knew much more about his distant ancestors, the Ravagers. "How did you escape?"

"With the help of a tyrannical lingbat and a sister who specialized in the art of TiKay. . . . I was lucky."

The sky darkened as they emerged from the marsh. Ice droplets fell, mingling with snow. Aiyana shivered, but Dane paid no attention as he lowered Galya to the ground. Maybe he liked the cold weather. Hakon said it was the one thing he missed from Thorwal.

Aiyana positioned herself by the hovercraft, watching as Dane prepared to bind Galya's ribs. She saw the Dwindle Bats flock into the alders, and her heart softened. Dwindle Bats. Some value remained in life. Dane and Batty, facing off in the forest. Rurthgar kicking Galya. . . . Life was still worth living.

The Dwindle Bats offered a final chorus in honor of Batty, and Dane grumbled. Aiyana's pain eased. *There is life beyond me. What I do, I do for you. . . .*

"They're a fine lot, aren't they, sir?"

Dane didn't look up. "If you say so."

Batty sighed. "You may not believe it, sir, but I'm considered small on Candor."

Dane glanced at the bat doubtfully. "Why wouldn't I believe that?"

Aiyana winced. "Dane is so large that anything else seems small to him. But I've often felt too much bulk slows the thought processes. You're very swift, Batty. The Dwindle Bats must have been impressed."

"They were, at that." Batty looked proud, but Dane shook his head. He searched through his gear, then tore strips from a blanket.

Galya waited while Dane prepared the strips, but Aiyana thought the Tseir looked wary. "What's wrong, Tseir? You don't mistrust your 'ambassador,' do you?"

"Of course not. I just hope it relieves some of the pain."

Dane assembled the strips and turned to Galya. "I'll have to check your side, Galya." Galya nodded shyly, and Aiyana rolled her eyes, irritated as Dane pulled up the Tseir's red shirt.

"It's bruising."

Galya winced, holding her breath in what Aiyana considered an exaggerated fashion. "It's painful, Dane."

"I don't think your ribs are broken, Galya. Cracked, possibly. More likely they're just bruised. But a bruise can cause more pain than a break, if it involves pulled muscles."

Aiyana looked on appreciatively. "You know something of medical treatment, it seems."

Dane bound Galya's torso with the strips, but he flashed

a quick, teasing smile at Aiyana. "My doctors were female. They were trying to convince me that movement wouldn't hurt me."

"Did it?"

"Let's say I contented myself with teasing."

Her lips parted as her own jealousy rose to the surface.

Dane laughed. "Verbal teasing." He secured the strips around Galya's ribs. "This should hold until you reach the swamp. We may have to stop tonight, if the storm worsens."

"I feel better already."

Aiyana issued a derisive snort. "It's all in your mind, Tseir. Everyone knows a Keiroit's foot has no bones. Just cartilage. When traveling with the Ellowans, they wear support shoes made from metal."

"Yours is a peculiar world, Aiyana Nidawi. Support shoes!"

"No stranger than talking lingbats."

Dane laughed. "You've got a point there. Shall we go?" He didn't wait for an answer. He popped open the craft's hull and helped Galya into the first seat. He cast a quick look at Aiyana. "You'll have to take the smaller space behind mine."

"I could operate the vessel, and *you* take the rear."

"I don't think so."

"Just thought you might kill us all. Your skills are suspect in balmy weather. In a storm . . ." Aiyana shook her head, then swung herself easily into the hovercraft, taking the rear seat.

"I didn't need Carob along. You're worse."

Batty chirped. "You know, you're right, sir! For the longest time, she's reminded me of someone. It's my sire!"

"Wonderful. I'm in love with the likes of a lingbat."

Aiyana's breath caught; her eyes widened. She popped

her head out of the craft and stared at him. "You still love me?"

Dane met her eyes. He smiled, that slow, sweet smile that wrung every drop of feeling from her heart. "Of course. Did you ever doubt?" Ignoring Galya's dark gaze, he reached to touch Aiyana's face. "Or did you never believe in the first place?"

Tears stung Aiyana's eyes. "Both."

Dane climbed into the hovercraft. "A man can love, and still be a fool."

"A woman, too." Aiyana settled back into her seat. The ice droplets pummeled the front window, but it seemed comforting. Dane's love hadn't changed. She sighed. He glanced back at her, still smiling. Aiyana felt giddy.

Dane guided the hovercraft through the trees. He tried to take it higher, but the hovercraft jerked in the storm's gusts. "I told you to keep it low, Thorwalian. But I suppose you'll have to learn from experience."

"I was just thinking the same thing about you."

Aiyana caught his reference, and her mouth dropped. He was teasing her. With words.

Galya reached over and touched Dane's arm. "You obviously have great skill, Dane. My pain is much relieved."

Aiyana tapped Dane's shoulder from behind. "Mine, too."

He snapped around, wide-eyed, and she allowed herself a slow, sensual smile. She had learned the art from him. It worked. He drew a quick breath as if to calm himself, then turned back to the controls.

Galya's presence served to heighten the tension between them. Aiyana felt it, centered low and warm inside her body. She knew the meaning of that spot now. Here, Dane's body entered hers. It felt warm because it prepared itself for him.

That thought made her warmer still. She wanted him. Now that she knew his initial entry would hurt, she would be ready. She would clench her teeth, as he said, and wait for it to ease again. Then . . . he would do what he had done in her hand.

She wondered what it would feel like inside. She recalled the way his hips, had thrust, and she gasped. Dane looked over his shoulder and seemed to recognize her expression. Aiyana blushed.

His eyes darkened. He must have known exactly what she was thinking. He chuckled, then turned back.

"The ice is turning to heavier snow. We may have to stop."

"Hovercraft don't 'stop,' Thorwalian. You'll have to land."

"We'll go on awhile yet. Until dark, perhaps."

"We can't all sleep in this small craft."

Dane glanced back at her, his eyes twinkling. "I know."

The heat inside Aiyana increased. "It will be cold."

"There are ways of maintaining warmth, Aiyana. Galya will stay in the hovercraft, with Batty. You and I will have to find another way to endure the elements."

Galya's eyes narrowed, though her expression remained benign. "I can't be so selfish, Dane. Surely we can all find some comfort in this craft."

"The seats can be adjusted to form a bed. You'll need that, Galya."

Gray light still lit the sky above the Ellowan-held forest, but Dane seemed eager to land. Aiyana wondered why. She leaned forward and peeked over his shoulder. "Is there something wrong with the hovercraft controls?"

"They're a little . . . sluggish."

"Sluggish? That doesn't make sense."

"Quiet, Aiyana. If I say they're sluggish, they're sluggish."

Aiyana sat back, but her pulse raced in a peculiar way. "Oh."

Dane eased the craft to the forest floor. It skidded on the ice, but he stopped its motion just before they impacted with a giant evergreen. Aiyana exhaled. "That was close."

Dane appeared unconcerned. "Perfect landing." He turned to Galya. "Rest will serve you well, Galya. I'll adjust the interior for comfort."

Galya seemed reluctant. "What about you? It will be a cold night."

"I brought sufficient supplies. Even a small tent."

"What about me, sir?"

"You can stay here, Batty."

Batty smacked his lips, hesitating. "Thinking of supper, sir. No bugs flying in this weather, sir."

Dane snatched his pack and seized a container of wafers. "Here. These should hold you." Batty's eyes widened. "And don't eat it all, rodent. Leave some for the rest of us."

"Yes, sir."

Aiyana didn't speak. Her heart pounded too fast. Dane held open the hovercraft shell, waiting. He still smiled. Snow fell around him, but he didn't notice. Aiyana winced in the cold.

"Are you sure about this, Thorwalian? Ellowans don't endure low temperatures very well."

"Ah. But Thorwalians do." Dane held out his hand. Aiyana hesitated, biting her lip.

"That's all very well for you."

"Are you going to argue, or trust me in this?"

"I'll trust you. For the time being. Until I commence freezing."

He didn't lower his hand. She drew a short breath, then put her hand in his.

"Where are we going? I don't understand why we're walking this far from the hovercraft." Aiyana's foot slipped on the snow-covered ice, but Dane caught her arm and kept going.

"I'm looking for shelter, my lady. Where I can assemble this tent to best advantage."

"What's wrong with this spot?"

Dane glanced back, then shook his head. "I can still see the hovercraft."

"So?"

His eyes met hers, glittering. "I want privacy."

Her insides tingled. She held her breath. "Why?"

Dane stopped and analyzed her appearance. "Your voice sounds unnatural, Aiyana. Why is that?" She knew from his tone that he fully understood her condition. Aiyana's eyes narrowed.

"I'm cold."

Dane took her hand and guided her further through the trees. "We'll have to see what can be done to warm you up."

They reached a gully, and Dane looked back over his shoulder. "Far enough."

Aiyana looked back, too. "I can still see the craft."

"Yes, but nothing can be heard from this distance."

"Heard? What would be heard?"

He grinned. "That remains to be seen."

Aiyana's nerves tensed beyond endurance. "You will cease this . . . this . . ."

"Teasing."

"Yes. You will cease at once and explain yourself."

He moved closer to her. "You know."

She caught her breath. "I do not." Her voice shook.

He reached, slowly, to touch her chin. "I think you do."

She gulped. "Not at all!"

"Umm."

Aiyana squeezed her eyes shut. "Behave." His lips

touched hers. She felt the tip of his tongue. Her own lips parted, but he drew away.

"The tent, Aiyana."

Her knees seemed shaky. Aiyana hesitated, then decided to occupy herself helping him. Her hands shook, too, and she dropped the assembly rod. Dane chuckled and completed her task. He placed a mat inside the tent, then arranged the blankets.

"I don't think those blankets are enough."

A smile flickered on his lips, tightening Aiyana's nerves. "We'll see."

"What if it snows all night? That happens on Keir, Thorwalian."

"Then the tent will be covered by morning. But it won't collapse. This, like everything else Ellowan, is well made."

"True."

Dane stuffed his gear into the tent, then held open the flap for her. Aiyana steadied herself, then crawled in. Dane followed. She felt so nervous. She tried to deepen her breathing to calm herself. "Normally we supply them with heaters."

"We don't need heaters."

"You don't, maybe." He touched his finger to her mouth, stopping her words.

"We don't need heaters."

Her chest rose and fell with small, swift breaths. Breaths made visible in the frosty air. "Thorwalian . . ."

"Do you want me, Aiyana?"

"What?"

"Again, you squeak. Do you want me, Aiyana?"

Aiyana couldn't breathe; she couldn't speak. He sat before her in the fading, shadowed light, and she thought she'd never seen a more beautiful sight. His lips curved, slightly, and she longed to kiss him.

Snowdrops clung to his hair, and she longed to tangle her

fingers in their place. The droplets melted on his warm skin and trickled down his neck. She wanted to lick them away.

"Dane . . ." She grabbed his shoulders to steady herself. Her fingers dug into his muscles and she buried her face in his neck. "I want you so, I think I might perish of it."

Dane's arms closed around her, and she felt his warm breath, felt the heat of his body. "I know."

Aiyana pulled back and looked up at him. "You know? Is that all you're going to say?"

"What else would you like me to say?"

"That you want me, too!"

"What do you think?"

She frowned. "You'd better."

"I want you, too."

Aiyana's temper had the reassuring effect of calming her nerves. She felt stronger now. She settled herself against him, her head on his shoulder. "I am still cold."

"You won't be."

"You keep promising warmth, Thorwalian, but I don't feel it."

"Don't you?"

Aiyana started to disagree, but Dane parted her cape, then ran his finger along the line of her bodice. "Not even here?"

"That is a warm spot, anyway. Just above the heart."

"What about here?" His finger slipped down farther, beneath the bodice. To the swell of her breast.

"That is warm also."

Dane nodded and withdrew his hand. Aiyana wondered if her argumentative nature might injure her own purposes. "I am cold in other places."

"What places?"

She hesitated. "My stomach is cold." She paused. "And my legs. The thighs in particular."

"The thighs? Hmm."

Aiyana tensed as Dane settled his hand over her thigh.

He was right. He was warm. "One spot of you at a time . . . I'm not sure I can warm you that way."

"Have you another suggestion?"

"Yes." Dane lay back, looking comfortable on the thin mat. "Come here."

She hesitated. "What do you mean, 'here'?"

"Lie on top of me, Aiyana."

"Oh . . . very well." She positioned herself above him, then lowered herself. She didn't know what to do with her legs. Straddling him seemed suggestive. She positioned herself to balance upon him. Dane wrapped his arms around her waist, but he didn't move.

"Shouldn't we . . . undress?"

Dane's brow angled. "In this weather? Even a Thorwalian doesn't lie naked in snow."

Aiyana fell silent. Dane's heart thumped beneath hers. Strong and sure, like everything else about him. She adjusted her position. His body was longer than hers. She wondered if his male portion was in a state of arousal. She couldn't feel it.

Aiyana wiggled again, more deliberately. Maybe his breath came more quickly than before. She wasn't sure. "Well?"

"Well what?"

Aiyana propped herself up and looked down at him. "What now?"

"Are you hungry?"

"No!"

"We could sleep."

"Sleep? You said you wanted me."

"I do."

Aiyana's patience grew more and more strained. "What are you going to do?" He opened his mouth to speak, but Aiyana's temper flared. "And don't you dare say, 'What do you want me to do?' Or I'll make you very, very sorry."

"I wouldn't dream of saying that." He said nothing else. Aiyana quivered. She chewed the inside of her lip. It felt raw. From too much chewing, no doubt.

She was waiting for him to tell her. Waiting for him to dictate what happened between them. Aiyana considered this. She remembered his teasing. He did it very well. He touched her and made her writhe. She wanted to do that to him, too.

"I think I shall kiss you, Thorwalian." She paused. "If you have no objections."

"Not a one."

Aiyana held her breath, then lowered her mouth to his. He didn't respond, though his lips felt soft. She played with his lips; she touched her tongue to the corner of his mouth, dipping slightly, then withdrawing. Her heart made quick, uneven beats.

Aiyana slid her fingers into his hair, balancing herself. The position gave her more leverage. She squirmed farther up his body, then kissed him more firmly. His lips parted this time; his tongue met hers. Like a dance. Touching and parting.

Aiyana moved her attention to his face. She kissed his jaw; she kissed the spot beside his mouth, the spot that dimpled when he repressed a smile. She kissed his cheekbone. He closed his eyes, and she kissed his eyelids, then his wide, smooth forehead.

She stopped and looked at him. "I have kissed your face."

"So you have."

"I shall move on to new spots now."

"As you wish."

Aiyana sat up, her curled legs on either side of his rib cage. "It requires that I open your shirt."

Dane nodded, looking serious. "Go ahead."

Aiyana untied his shirt and loosened the throat to expose

his chest. "It would be easier if you removed it entirely." She seated herself beside him.

Dane sat up and pulled it over his head. "Better?"

Aiyana's eyes fixed on his chest. "It is a beautiful chest."

"Thank you." Dane lay back down, his arms folded behind his head. Watching her.

Aiyana climbed back onto his stomach, resisting the impulse to seat herself lower. She ran her hands over his chest. Her hands looked smaller than usual, narrow, the fingers delicate. She liked the contrast. She slid her palm over his flat, male nipple, and he shuddered.

"Does that please you, too?"

"Sensitive spot."

Aiyana beamed, then bent to kiss him there. She laved the smallest tip of her tongue across him, then pressed her cheek over his heart. The pounding within him had intensified. Aiyana sat up.

Her eyes on his, she slithered down over his hips. She felt him now, large and hard. Her breath caught as she moved herself back, over him. She knelt between his legs. His arousal defined itself beneath his snug pants.

A tremor of fear returned at the sight. His portion was indeed large. No wonder it hurt. But she would clench her teeth, and it would ease. . . .

Aiyana drew a hurried breath, then examined his belt. "This is an inconvenience to me." She didn't request permission this time. She tore open his belt.

Dane lay suspiciously motionless. Aiyana realized he was holding his breath—as she did when excitement mounted beyond endurance. She watched his face as she placed her hand carefully over the bulge.

His eyes rolled back in his head. He leaned back. *Good.* She moved her hand slowly over his length. His jaw clenched. *Even better.* Aiyana turned her attention back to undressing him.

"Raise your hips."

"What?"

Aiyana indicated his hips. "So I can remove your pants."

Dane lifted his hips, and she tugged them down. His arousal rose, standing straight out from his body, a pillar of masculine strength. The sight made her nervous, but curiously compelled. She forced her gaze away and yanked off his low boots, tossing them aside.

"Are you too cold?"

"No."

"Nor am I." Aiyana turned her attention back to his arousal. She remembered the feel of it in her hand. It hadn't injured her then. She touched his shaft and felt his rapid pulse beneath the tight, silken flesh. She wrapped her fingers around its base and slowly eased her hand up.

"Does this please you, Thorwalian?"

"Yes."

She slid her hand to the hard, blunt tip. He groaned. Aiyana circled her fingers around the tip until his hips lifted from the mat. "This is teasing."

"Yes."

"You're not saying much."

"No."

Aiyana studied Dane's expression. His neck muscles looked strained; his head was angled back, his jaw clenched. His stomach quivered, every muscle drawn tight. Like a bow.

"Relax, Thorwalian. I'm still teasing you."

Dane muttered a Thorwalian curse, but he didn't resist. Aiyana wondered how to increase the level of her teasing. Ellowan women knew such arts once; they learned and they practiced. "Oh! Of course!"

Aiyana bent and pressed her lips to the tip of Dane's staff. His curse gave way to a deep, rumbling groan of pleasure. Aiyana touched her tongue to the sleek surface. His groan became a harsh gasp. She made small circles with her tongue, then followed his length downward. Back again.

She took the blunt end between her lips and tried suckling gently. The curse and the groan and the gasp came all at once. Dane's fingers clenched in her hair.

"Aiyana, come here."

"I'm not finished."

"I am!" Dane seized her shoulders and pulled her up along his body. He positioned her so that his shaft slid between her thighs.

"Didn't you like it? But you didn't give me time for practicing. . . ."

"Do you know why Thorwalians stopped worshiping their goddesses?"

Aiyana's brow furrowed, wondering what primitive rites had to do with lovemaking. "No."

"I'll tell you, woman." Dane paused to draw a shuddering breath. "It was said that the goddesses sought out mortal men and drove them mad . . . like this!"

"Oh." She still didn't understand. "Does that mean I should stop?"

"No. It means I should start." He didn't explain. He flipped her over, then positioned himself above her. "I think history recorded Ariana's landing, after all."

"Why?"

"The last goddess of Thorwal had black hair, and drove men crazier than all the vixens before her. She stole a prince, and disappeared."

Aiyana smiled. "Hakon the Betrayer."

Dane lowered his mouth to hers. "The Magnificent."

Aiyana wrapped her arms around his neck and returned his kiss. His lips played over hers as he nibbled her lower lip, then tasted her tongue. She felt his hand moving up her side, then under her short bodice.

He kissed her throat and made wide, slow circles over

her breast with his palm. Her nipple pebbled beneath the snug fabric. Dane centered his touch there, teasing her until she moaned and arched beneath him. He grazed his mouth over the hard little bud, then his teeth.

"This is . . . pleasurable." She whimpered when he laved the covered peak, then suckled it through the fabric of her bodice. The damp cloth clung to her flesh, a sensation of cold mingling with the hot fire striking her blood.

"I'm still dressed, Ravager."

"You won't be."

Dane opened her bodice, baring her round, firm breasts. He ran his palm over each breast, making her weak with wanting. He sat back and removed her leggings. The cold air played over her sensitized flesh like wind on an ember.

He untied her boots and kissed her toes. He ran his hand along her calf muscle. "Do you have any idea how I longed to touch you this way? That first day, when I searched you . . . Aiyana, I wanted nothing more than to love you like this."

"I know that." She propped herself up on her elbows, looking down the length of her body to him. She was aware of her own body for the first time. She knew that propping herself up this way exaggerated the fullness of her breasts. Her lips parted and she drew a quavering breath.

"Your touch didn't displease me then. But now, when I know the pleasures you bring . . ."

Dane's eyes darkened at her inviting posture. "Even here, in a tent, in the snow?"

"Wherever you are. Perhaps it was in just such weather that Hakon first showed these pleasures to Ariana. It is right between us."

"It is."

Aiyana shivered, but she didn't feel the cold. The night darkened outside; the snow fell. Nothing existed but them. Dane lowered himself above her, his warm skin barely touching hers. She lay back, naked before him, her hair splayed out around her head as he bent to kiss her.

"I love you, Thorwalian."

"I love you, too."

"My spots are ready for you, you know."

Dane chuckled. "Are they?"

"If you touch me, you'll know."

He took her words as a request. He slid his hand down between them, then between her legs. "Sure enough." He found the secret peak and circled it lightly, until she squirmed against his hand.

Aiyana closed her eyes and surrendered to whatever Dane Calydon wanted to do.

Aiyana's reaction to his lovemaking fueled Dane's desire beyond anything he'd ever known. His pulse throbbed so loudly that he heard it ringing. His erection felt full beyond endurance. It rubbed against her thigh and she tensed beneath him. Now, when he needed to be gentle, his body demanded raw, primal satisfaction.

A Ravager wouldn't wait. He would drive his swollen length deep inside her and take his fill of her. He would thrust until she grew moist, until she writhed—not in agony, but in mindless pleasure.

For an instant, Dane looked down into her delicate, flushed face. He imagined taking her as a Ravager would. As his own ancestor, Haldane, had tried to do to Ariana. Dane wondered briefly how he knew this to be true. But he knew Haldane had loved Ariana, and became reckless when she fled with his brother.

Dane couldn't banish the image, though it disturbed him. He would possess her, this exquisite, black-haired woman. He would make her moan and whimper his name. She was female, and she burned with desire.

Dane looked into her eyes, and he knew Aiyana resembled her ancestor. Ariana, who inflamed the Ravager king to war. Just as Dane himself resembled . . . not the sweet and wise Hakon, as Aiyana believed, but his reckless brother, Haldane. *I am not a Ravager.*

Aiyana loved him, Dane. Despite her fear, she lay beneath him, ready to trust him. To endure whatever pain might come for the promise of what lay beyond. Love wrenched his heart.

Ariana belonged to Hakon. But Aiyana belonged to Dane. For a reason he didn't fully understand, he felt Haldane's soul had reached its destination. Dane kissed Aiyana's forehead, his heart filled with love.

"You know what I'm going to do, Aiyana."

"Yes."

"If you want me to stop, I will."

"I know."

Dane positioned himself between her legs, moving inward until his tip touched her liquid warmth. He fought his desire, sliding against her. Her body felt tense, her pulse rapid as he kissed her throat. He turned his face to hers and kissed her mouth.

He broke away and looked into her eyes. She touched his lips. "I do like kissing you."

"I know."

He moved against her, back and forth, his eyes still fixed on hers. He watched her need increase, felt the heat of her inviting him inward. He allowed his tip to meet her entrance, just parting the soft folds.

Aiyana lifted her hips to meet him, but he restrained the need to take her, to satisfy himself. He let her move against him, seizing pleasure, building need. Slowly, with perfect care, he eased himself inward.

Aiyana stopped and her eyes opened wide. "Wait! I almost forgot. . . ."

Dane watched in wonder as she squeezed her eyes shut

and clenched her teeth. "I'm ready now." He didn't move. He waited until she peeked with one eye.

"I can't keep clenching for long, Thorwalian. It hurts the jaw."

"Look at me."

She did. Then her eyes drifted to one side, confused. She relaxed her jaw for a moment, then resumed clenching.

"Do you love me, Aiyana?"

She nodded, still clenching.

Dane touched her cheek. "Stop that."

She looked surprised, but she stopped. "I'm avoiding pain."

"You're causing pain in the jaw. Aiyana, if I hurt you, tell me, and I'll stop."

"I don't want you to stop. When the hurting stops, it might be pleasant." She clamped her jaw shut again.

Dane shrugged. "We'll test your theory." He pushed inward. She tensed and he held his position. He leaned down and kissed her throat, then her chin, then the corner of her tight mouth.

He ran his tongue over her lips. Then between, to her clenched teeth. "Stop that! You're distracting me."

He moved a little, barely in, then out. Her eyes popped open. Her mouth opened, too. Dane seized the opportunity to deepen the kiss. Aiyana hesitated, then kissed him back. He slid his tongue in and out, mimicking the action of his body.

Her tense muscles eased beneath him. She sighed and sucked gently on his tongue. Desire flooded through him and over him, but he restrained his need.

"Wrap your legs around me, love."

She hesitated, then slid her legs over his. Before she clenched again, he kissed her. He wanted to drive himself inside her, bury himself, but instead he moved with infinite tenderness. He felt each fraction of motion as her body opened for him. He felt her heat and her tightness encasing him.

She didn't wince or cry out. She just moaned softly. Her legs clamped around him and her hips arched, drawing him over her inner threshold. Dane groaned and caught his breath. Her beautiful head tipped back, a sensual smile on her lips.

"Are you all right?" She didn't answer. "Aiyana?"

"Thorwalian . . ." She grabbed his hair and pulled him down to kiss her. "You talk too much."

Dane kissed her, then drew back, angling his pelvis between her legs. Her slender hips moved beneath his, and Dane's restraint shattered. He braced above her, then sank himself deep inside her.

"Look at me."

She opened her eyes, wide and shocked. "You're in me."

"I am."

"I like it."

"I know."

Dane took her hands and held them to his chest as he moved inside of her. Her fingers clenched around his. She answered his thrusts with perfect rhythm. Dane remembered Arnoth's words about a well-mated couple making music together.

"I guess he had a point."

"Who?"

"Never mind."

"This is better than I expected. . . ." He drove deeper, and Aiyana's words trailed away in a hot wave of pleasure.

Aiyana watched Dane, and he was watching her. His face changed, softened by bliss. She matched his thrusts, wanting more. He seemed . . . careful.

"You're not hurting me, Thorwalian."

"No?"

"No!" She squirmed to increase the sweet friction. Dane seemed to be withholding something. She arched beneath him. Again he withdrew just as . . . "Stop that!"

His brow arched, surprised, but she knew that look. "You're teasing! Even here!"

"Your accusation stings, my beloved."

He was inside her, and infuriating her. Aiyana snatched her hands from his and seized his hips for better leverage. She untangled her legs from his, dug her heels into the mat, and thrust upward, drawing him deep inside.

"You are a wild and violent creature, Aiyana Nidawi." She knew from his raw, hoarse voice that she had won. She smiled triumphantly, but Dane's eyes darkened. He grabbed her hands and pinned them over her head.

"Not yet, love." He held her beneath him, deeply embedded, unmoving. . . . He bent and brushed his lips over one engorged breast, then the other.

"Thorwalian, I warn you. . . ."

He didn't respond. He touched his tongue to the aching peak, then suckled.

"Dane . . ."

He answered her plea and moved. Very slightly. She squeezed tight around him, but he held her down, refusing her motion. She squeezed tighter.

"I thought it would be a battle between us. . . ." He nipped at her hard nipple, then suckled again. She felt him, thick and full inside her, refusing to move. She felt his pulse. She thought she might burst from wanting.

His kiss moved up her chest, along her throat. She turned her face, waiting, desperate, and he kissed her mouth. He slid his tongue between her lips and teased. Aiyana sucked fiercely on his tongue, and he began to move, so slowly at first that she didn't realize he was really moving. It seemed like imagination.

But he moved deeper and harder. Her body quaked. He

whispered Thorwalian words into her ear, words she almost understood, but not quite. Words that spoke of primal desire, of raw power. And she knew that she had found what had so long been denied her. *I've found my Ravager. . . .*

He drove hard and deep, and she answered. What he gave, she took. He moved from side to side, drawing her with him. He cupped her bottom in his hands and guided her in wild motion. He pulled her legs up over his shoulders and filled her with raw, demanding thrusts.

Aiyana knew when his motion cascaded beyond his control. His neck strained; his breath came in moans. She saw every muscle draw tight. He carried her with him. Fierce little stabs of pleasure surged around his length, spreading through her loins, down her legs. Her toes curled.

She knew this feeling. She knew where he took her. It was stronger now, centered around him, fueled by him. A wild current twisted inward toward bursting. Life and forever after meant nothing. Only now. The tension shattered into shards of blinding pleasure. Waves followed waves as she clung to him, as he buried himself deep in her.

The waves crashed and joined; Dane's whole body tensed, then spasmed into sweet release. He lowered himself above her, keeping his weight off of her as he buried his face in her outspread hair.

Aiyana's pulse raced, every nerve tingling in the aftermath. She wrapped her arms around his shoulders, then ran her fingers through his hair. "You have beautiful hair." She sighed. "Long and thick."

Dane chuckled, though Aiyana couldn't guess why. "Now would be a bad time to mention Arnoth, woman."

Aiyana's brow furrowed, but some things about men must be beyond comprehension. She kissed his warm, damp temple and hugged him. "What happened to the pain? Was it the clenching?"

Dane rolled to the side and pulled her on top of him again. ''Must have been.''

''Will I always have to clench?''

Dane considered this thoughtfully as she anticipated his answer. ''I'm not sure. Were you clenching at the end?''

Aiyana smiled. ''Not in the jaw.''

''Did it hurt?''

''No. It felt very good.''

''Then I think the need for clenching has passed.''

''Good.''

Dane pulled the blanket around them, then his cloak.

''What are you doing? I'm not cold.''

''I want to keep it that way.''

''Can I sleep on top of you?''

''You're small. I'm large. Why not?''

She yawned. ''I'm not small. It's your inordinate size that makes me seem . . .''

''Smaller.''

She nodded. ''Exactly.''

The last light faded into darkness and the wind stilled. Night came silently to the forest. Aiyana lay close beside Dane, tucked peacefully in his arms. Dane kissed her and sifted her soft hair through his fingers. She pressed her lips against his chest, then settled her head onto his shoulder.

''What happens tomorrow, Dane?''

''We'll go to the Swamp of Keir then find a way to Franconia.''

''The Keiroit guards will accommodate you, if Galya requests it.''

''Why do they remain loyal to the Tseirs?''

''I'm not sure. But they aren't real Keiroits. That's what Rurthgar says. He says they aren't normal. They don't mate, you know.''

''That is odd.''

"Yes, because at first there were only a few Keiroits in the Tseir guard. Now there are thousands upon thousands. The swamp teems with them. They drove out the older Keiroits."

"Was Rurthgar leader then, too?"

Aiyana didn't seem to notice the inconsistency of this "hatching" she remembered. "Yes. He is a fine leader. Not exactly gentle, maybe. But the Keiroits' disloyalty wounded him. His mate was killed in battle with those guards, back when Rurthgar tried to retake the swamp. He has never taken another mate. Keiroits form strong bonds. I think that's why Arnoth befriended him."

"I thought he said he'd . . . fertilized a vast number of eggs."

"Yes. He does quite a bit of . . . fertilizing." Aiyana sighed. "Keiroits are like that. They take life mates. But sex, or whatever they do, is considered insignificant. Although it does involve an immense squawking. You don't want to be near the marsh during their mating season."

"You're telling me more than I want to know, my dear."

Aiyana chuckled. "About Keiroits, I *know* more than I want to know. About us, I knew nothing. Until now . . ."

"You learn quickly, my love." Dane kissed her forehead. "How long have you been allied with the Keiroit rogues?"

"A long while now. At first the Ellowans were wary of them, as they were of us. But the Tseir-controlled Keiroits became our common enemy. All three—Rurthgar's forces, the swamp Keiroits, and Arnoth's Ellowans—faced each other in battle, long ago. We knew we either joined or perished."

"How did you gain their confidence?"

"Arnoth . . ."

"Ha! I should have guessed . . ." Dane paused, irritated and jealous, and feeling foolish for reacting that way. "I suppose he was heroic beyond measure."

"He was."

Dane sighed. "Couldn't you tell me that he quivered in fear, then dissolved in hysteria while you allayed the Keiroits?"

Aiyana giggled. "I could, but it wouldn't be true. You wanted truth, as I recall."

"Not in this instance."

"Very well. He hid under his bed and wept."

Dane laughed, and Aiyana kissed his cheek. "The real story, woman."

"He laid down his weapons and entered their camp—which was Rurthgar's marsh. Rurthgar caught him by the throat. At that time, the Keiroits saw no difference between the Ellowans and the Tseirs. And Rurthgar hated the Tseirs for subverting his people. He said all humanoids look alike. We thought the same of them."

"Ah! The story of the ages, war from lack of understanding. As you were saying . . . Rurthgar had Arnoth by the throat. I liked that part."

"You'll be pleased to know that it gets worse. He dragged Arnoth into the swamp. . . ."

"Into that stinking, stagnant quagmire of putrid water?"

"Yes."

"A good mental image. Thank you for sharing that, Aiyana."

Aiyana eyed him reproachfully. "Arnoth fought him and won, then dragged Rurthgar to the surface—they were both covered in reeds and blood and slime—"

"Good, good . . . Go on."

"Arnoth healed him, and then Rurthgar listened to our story."

"Noble." Dane's lip curved in a tight frown, but he couldn't help a swell of admiration.

"He has been our ally ever since. The Ellowans heal the rogues when they're injured. In return, they help us hide our hamlet, and they risk themselves as spies. This is how I was able to impersonate a Keiroit guard, you see."

"You did it frighteningly well."

"Thank you."

She settled her head back onto his shoulder and sighed. "I feel quite peaceful, Thorwalian. It's odd, because I thought life would be desperate. That's the way I remember it in Valenwood. . . ." Her voice trailed off, but her words triggered a strange premonition in Dane.

As if that one, Aiyana, is already dead . . . "You speak often of death, Aiyana. Why?"

She seemed to be drifting toward sleep, barely hearing him. "Death? No . . . There are many kinds of death. Life, and not life. Growth, and not growth." Her words quieted into another yawn. "I like this growth. I'd forgotten. . . . I wonder if Arnoth has forgotten, too?"

"Aiyana, what are you talking about?"

She didn't answer. Dane angled his head to look at her. Her eyes were closed, her expression peaceful. But her mumbled words left a foreboding chill in his heart. He closed his arms tighter around her and she sighed. "Sleep well, my love."

Chapter Seven

Dane woke to bright sunlight. Even through the dark tent canvas, it stung his eyes. Aiyana slept peacefully beside him, snoring in small, rumbly rhythm. He listened for a while, liking the sound. He didn't want to wake her yet.

Despite the glory and magic of their night together, dark dreams had tormented his sleep. Not of Aiyana, but of Arnoth. Arnoth confined in a small, dark room. The dream had wavered between Arnoth and Seneca, as if deep in his soul, Dane loved Arnoth just as he loved Seneca.

Or maybe it was because Seneca had been imprisoned once, too. Dane preferred this explanation.

He rose and looked outside. Only a thin layer of snow covered the forest floor, melting already in the morning sun. He thought of Thorwal, perpetually frozen, always white. Unchanging. Warmed only where the subterranean lava flows broke to the surface.

Aiyana's world knew no balance. Frost gave way overnight to warmth. But the Ellowans weren't native to Keir.

Their world was Valenwood, the Midnight Moon. Dane closed the tent flap and sat back. Valenwood. Gone, but never forgotten. A barren, lifeless world that hung in the night sky like a beacon of doom.

"Aiyana . . ." Dane brushed her hair from her face and kissed her cheek. "Wake up."

She opened her eyes and groaned. "Leave me be, Thorwalian. It is still night."

Dane laughed. "The sun speaks another tale."

"So speaks the moon. Sleep." She closed her eyes and rolled over. Dane lay down again beside her, curling his body around hers. She snuggled back against him, her bottom perfectly aligned with his groin.

The darkness of his dream fled as his body responded to the possibilities. He hardened. Aiyana murmured and leaned back against him, curving her arm to touch his hair. "You please me, Thorwalian."

"I've barely begun." Dane lifted her tangled hair and kissed her neck. He slid his hand over her rib cage to cup her breast. The small peak pebbled against his touch; her breath quickened. She started to roll over, but Dane gripped her shoulder, holding her in place.

"Stay there."

"I thought you wanted . . . I thought we might repeat what we did last night."

"Not exactly."

Aiyana eyed him suspiciously, but he smiled—an ever-reliable tool—and charmed her into agreement. "Very well." She lay back, tense, as she awaited what he might do.

Dane did nothing, just lay close to her, his palm over her breast, his length against her bottom.

"I will not tolerate teasing this morning, Thorwalian. Do something."

She smiled, no doubt expecting him to tease her well past noon.

Dane reached down, parted her thighs, and drove himself inside her. She cried out with the suddenness of pleasure. He buried his face in her hair, his breath warm on her neck as he thrust, then withdrew to thrust again. He held her still as he moved inside her. He kept nothing back this time, showed no hesitation.

Aiyana arched her back to deepen his penetration. He rolled her over onto her stomach, keeping himself barely inside her. He gripped her shoulders as he began to move again, this time deeper. She gripped the blanket to brace herself.

Dane looked down at Aiyana's slender body beneath his, impaled by his. Her head tipped back, her eyes closed, her lips parted as she drew swift breaths. Her long, black hair splayed out over her shoulders, down her back like a shimmering curtain.

He saw her round bottom, muscles tight as she invited his thrusts. He moved deep within her, slowly, watching her reaction. She whimpered, a small but demanding voice. Her bottom tensed, seizing him from within.

Dane stopped and withdrew from her tight, fiery sheath. She sputtered in frustration and he laughed. "Roll over, love. I want to see your face." He guided her onto her back. Her green eyes sparkled; her face was flushed, her lips puffy and damp.

He held his shaft just above her feminine mound, waiting. His pulse thundered; he ached for release. She arched beneath him, but he held himself back.

"Now you tease!" Her small face knitted in determination. She seized his length, wrapped her legs around his waist, and maneuvered herself closer. She sank down over him, drawing him inside.

He felt her inner passage close around him, tight and hot.

Dane fought his need and let her move, her hips twisting, then easing into a mindless rhythm as she pleased herself with his length.

Dane watched her, mesmerized as she gave herself over to the pleasure. Her little toes curled as, she clamped her legs tight around his waist. Her back arched, her head tipping back. Wild, shuddering moans escaped her lips. He felt her spasms, the contractions that squeezed around him.

His own release crept in on him slowly, tiny tremors that erupted with sudden violence and glee. Ravager glee. He caught her hips and drove deeply inside her. His sudden motion sent her into a second wave, and she writhed around him as he poured himself inside her.

He stilled, and she went limp, eyes closed, her breath coming in gasps. Her legs relaxed and dropped on either side of his. Dane didn't move; he just watched her. "Your satisfaction is a beautiful sight, Aiyana Nidawi."

She opened one eye. "I am satisfied." She sighed happily. "I never knew satisfaction before you."

"Good." Dane couldn't bring himself to withdraw from her body. She was warm inside, and he could feel her racing pulse. Here, they mingled. Nothing separated them.

"Sir!"

Batty. Dane groaned. "Not now, rodent." He didn't want to move. If he gave it a minute, they might make love again. Slower this time.

"Sir! Is that you?"

Aiyana waited expectantly, a smile on her lips. "Well? *Sir.*"

Dane groaned again. "Who else would it be?"

"Thought someone was killing you, sir." Dane winced at the scraping noise of claws on the tent.

"No."

"Awful racket in there, sir."

Dane withdrew from Aiyana's body, glaring. ''How did you hear us from the hovercraft, rodent?''

''Lingbats have superior hearing.''

''I'd forgotten that.''

Aiyana cringed. ''How embarrassing!'' She fumbled for her clothes, then shoved Dane's tunic into his lap. Dane pulled it over his head, still glaring.

Batty poked his head through the tent flap. ''Mating, were you, sir?''

Dane tied his belt. ''How and by what stretch of the imagination would that be your concern, Batty?''

Batty eased into the tent, shivering. ''Wondered if there'd be little sirs coming along soon.''

Dane's dark expression faded as he contemplated this possibility. ''Little 'sirs.' An interesting notion, Batty.''

Batty squirmed under one edge of the blanket. ''How many would you have in the first litter? Six is average for lingbats, but maybe humanoids have more.''

''Humanoids don't have litters.'' Dane glanced at Aiyana. ''Do they?''

''An Ellowan female spawns at least twenty in her first litter.'' Aiyana watched Dane's face pale, then patted his arm. ''One, Thorwalian. Twins are rare among my people.''

Dane breathed a sigh of relief. ''Twenty 'sirs' might be too much.''

''Especially if they took after you . . .''

Dane took her hand and kissed it. ''Twenty crazed Ellowans might be hard to handle, too.''

''Think I should leave you alone again, sir? A lingbat must mate several times to ensure fertilization.''

Batty made no motion to depart. Dane tore his gaze from Aiyana. ''How is Galya this morning?''

''Guess she's fine. Doesn't talk much. In fact, doesn't talk at all.''

Dane pulled on his leggings. "Probably couldn't get a word in edgewise."

"I tried talking with her. But she didn't talk back. Not like you, sir. When you start talking, it's hard to stop you."

Dane shot a forbidding look Batty's way. "Is it?"

"That's all right, sir. I don't mind. My sire warned me that you're a talker."

Dane's eyes narrowed to slits. "Did he?"

Batty nodded, missing Dane's dark tone. Aiyana chuckled and patted his shoulder. "I don't mind either."

Dane seized Batty and put him outside the tent. "Go back to the hovercraft, rodent. Aiyana and I will be along shortly."

"Very good, sir." Batty started away, hopping and bounding over the slush. Dane snapped the tent closed.

Aiyana started to rise, but he caught her arm. "Wait, love. We may not get another chance to talk privately."

"I suppose not. What do you want to talk about?"

"Franconia . . ." Dane paused. "I dreamed of Arnoth last night."

"Truly? He wasn't covered in slime, was he?"

Dane laughed. "Unfortunately not. He was imprisoned. Maybe it's just that I was imprisoned once, too. Or because of Seneca. Arnoth resembles Seneca. Maybe my subconscious mind confused them. But something doesn't fit and I have to know, before we reach Franconia."

"What do you want to know?"

"Galya insists no Ellowan has been on Franconia in centuries. Certainly not Arnoth."

Aiyana met his eyes steadily. "Do you believe her?"

"I don't know, Aiyana. I love you. My judgment is biased. She also claims that the Ellowans destroyed Valenwood themselves."

"Right! Why?"

"Her reason wasn't convincing. Mainly because you're

crazy, always have been, and have battled each other since the dawn of time.''

''There's a deviation from reality to boggle the mind. The truth is the opposite. We were too peaceful. Unlike your Ravagers, the Ellowans never warred. Never.''

Dane remembered Ravager history. He thought of Haldane and Hakon. Conflict between people seemed inevitable. ''That seems implausible.''

''Our earliest culture made a ritual of blending our darkness and light, from the time when the People of the Elf Wood met and married with the People of the Desert. From this history comes our culture, and that is why the high priestess of the Elf Wood takes the prince of the Desert Tribunal as her husband.''

Aiyana paused and sighed. ''Together they built the White Tile City by the golden sea. It was our most beautiful creation.''

''Does this mean Arnoth's ancestors were Desert people?''

Aiyana nodded. ''That is why his skin is darker than mine, and his hair has a slightly more golden tone. You may have noticed that his hair has pleasant flecks of light.''

Dane frowned. ''I hadn't noticed Arnoth's hair.'' He paused. ''Not gold, really . . . More red, I should say.'' He stopped himself and shook his head. Aiyana's brow angled pointedly.

''Because we embraced our capacity for evil, we also accepted our inclination for good.''

Dane considered this. ''I believe that is where Thorwalian evolution is now.''

Aiyana's bright eyes glittered. ''Then it's an evolution doomed for destruction. The Ellowans believed in embracing that same capacity in other races, and that their inclination would be the same.''

"So your people cast aside that ancient learning and became warriors?"

"We did. Too late."

"Maybe. But it seems you've stuck to it for generations."

"It has been centuries since Valenwood fell, yes."

Dane sensed evasion, but he couldn't pinpoint its source. "Was Arnoth imprisoned, or not?"

"He was."

"How did he escape?"

"I freed him."

"You were there, too?"

"I was. Arnoth and I were captured together. He sacrificed himself so that I could get away. Though I was terrified, I hid in the Tseir embassy, searching for a way to free him, too. I had no idea how. I was too scared to try, at first."

"What about Elena?"

"I don't know why she was there. Arnoth didn't know, either. The Tseirs must have captured her." Aiyana stopped and closed her eyes. "You see, I learned too late. I was trying to steal keys from a guard when I heard screams. Ellowan screams. I couldn't believe it was my sister. She wasn't supposed to be on Franconia." Aiyana paused and drew a painful breath.

"I was high above the courtyard, in the guard's tower." She stopped, fighting emotion. "I couldn't see the courtyard below, but I could hear her. And then I saw them drag her to Arnoth's cell, and I followed—" Her voice broke and she leaned against him.

Dane held her and brushed the tears from her face. "I'm sorry, Aiyana. I shouldn't have asked."

"You have the right to know. It happened long ago. . . . It's been so long, Dane. But it hurts as if it happened yesterday. It never eases."

"How did you escape?"

Aiyana sat up and looked into Dane's eyes. "It isn't a pretty story. Do you really want to know?"

Dane touched her face. "I have to know."

"It was the darkest day of my life, and it changed everything. When I saw what they'd done to my sister . . . I loved her so. . . ."

Aiyana's words trailed away, her small face knitted in dark anger—anger that smoldered, undying. "The guards threw Elena's broken body into Arnoth's cell, and he tried to save her. When I saw that she refused, because of what they'd done to her . . . She was always so much stronger than I. But I learned that hate can make you strong. That day I learned to kill."

"You had reason, love."

"Yes, I had reason. The guards were outside Arnoth's cell. They were laughing. I walked right up to the nearest guard and I grabbed his rifle—he was shocked to see me. I shot him, and when he fell, I shot the others. He had a section of my sister's dress tied to his belt, as a trophy."

"The Tseirs could teach the Ravagers new crimes."

"The Ravagers were passionate and violent. Maybe they were cruel. The Tseirs are different. I can't explain the difference. The Tseirs don't seem to feel. They use others for sport, as if nothing of their own matters."

"Kostbera said she sensed real fear in Galya."

"Yes, they have fear. We taught them fear."

Dane looked into her face, into her green, unfathomable eyes. She had seen so much, suffered more than he could imagine. In so brief a time . . . "So you rescued Arnoth."

"I did. He didn't want to go at first. He held Elena's body, and he wouldn't leave. And then . . . And then something changed in him. I will never forget. He kissed her forehead and he stood up. He took a rifle from a dead guard, and he told me we would fight.

"He told me we would fight and fight, and never give

up. The Tseirs will never forget the Ellowans, and they will never know peace. Arnoth and I fought our way through their dungeons. We stole Tseir weaponry along the way, until we escaped from the embassy. We fought because we wouldn't let them beat us. And they didn't."

Dane listened to Aiyana's story with a haunting chill of admiration, all the while knowing it made no sense.

"We stole a flightship."

"The flightship . . . your meeting hall?"

"Yes."

"So you returned to Keir?"

Aiyana hesitated. "Eventually." Dane knew she had gone somewhere else first, with Arnoth. He wondered why she didn't tell him where. But the Ellowans had lived on Keir for generations. Valenwood had been lifeless and barren, its atmosphere uninhabitable for ages before. It made no sense.

"You told me Valenwood was destroyed in Hakon's time."

Aiyana studied his face a long while without answering. Dane knew she concealed something from him. "That is true."

"That was ages ago. What happened to your race after that time?"

She looked away. "Our race died."

"You survived, Aiyana. Arnoth survived. You've mentioned grandparents. Some Ellowans must have lived on."

She didn't answer. "Our race died when two fools believed in peace, and begged Hakon to let them negotiate. After that, we have been nothing but ghosts."

Dane started to speak, but Aiyana shook her head. "It is time to head for Franconia, Dane." She rose to her feet, then looked down at him. Dane felt as if she looked at him from a great distance. Maybe an insurmountable distance.

"You and I met at the twilight of time. I wish it had been

the morning.'' Aiyana gathered her gear and left Dane alone in the tent.

He'd never known such contentment as their night had given him. He'd never felt so certain of love. But her words struck an icy chord of doom in his heart.

Aiyana was waiting by the hovercraft. Batty perched on the top of the craft, chattering. Dane saw Aiyana nod in response. The morning sun gleamed brightly through the trees, glistening off ice-covered boughs, through droplets of melting snow. Their last conversation seemed unreal.

Dane carried the folded tent to the craft and stuffed it into the back.

''If you're hungry, Thorwalian, Batty has left us a wafer to share.''

Dane turned slowly to the bat, who hopped back to the far side of the hovercraft. ''To *share?*''

Aiyana passed him a half-eaten wafer. ''They're filling.''

Batty nodded enthusiastically. ''They are, indeed, sir! I won't have to eat for days.''

Dane fixed his gaze on the lingbat's stomach. It looked suspiciously round. ''You, rodent, are the size of a clenched fist. Your share would have rightly been a crumb. Yet you've left *one* wafer to split between us?''

''Lingbats burn a great deal of energy, sir.''

''How?''

''Flight, sir.''

Dane's eyes narrowed to slits. ''What flight?''

''Hopping, sir. Bounding from branch to branch.''

Dane opened the craft's shell quickly, dislodging the bat. Batty skittered down, claws scraping, then flapped himself to Dane's shoulder. Dane noted that the claws dug into his shoulder with particular vengeance.

Galya was waiting inside the craft, still seated as she had

been the night before. "I hope you were comfortable, Galya."

"The hovercraft controls provide an optimum climate, Dane. It's good of you to worry about me."

Aiyana climbed into the craft and took her seat behind Dane. "I don't recall the subject coming up last night."

Galya looked back at Aiyana as the hovercraft lifted from the forest floor. Aiyana met her gaze, and Galya turned back to Dane. A tremor of unease settled around Dane's heart. Both women held secrets. Until he discovered those hidden truths, no peace would last for long.

Aiyana settled back in her seat and folded her arms behind her head. She looked smug and satisfied. "Perhaps you should tell Dane a little about your planet, Tseir. Maybe brief him on your customs."

Galya cast a dark glance Aiyana's way. Aiyana matched her expression, then smiled falsely. "For instance, where will he be housed? In the barracks?"

"In our embassy, naturally. In a suite reserved for our most prominent guests."

"I think one of your associates offered Arnoth the same suite."

"Our people live in terror of your leader. We would certainly never accommodate him as a guest."

"Your terror is well founded, Tseir."

Galya turned in her seat, a smile on her lips. She looked kind. Tolerant. "I invite you to set aside your prejudice, Aiyana. You will be traveling to Franconia as Dane's mate. Perhaps you should consider that an honor."

Aiyana made a gagging noise and Dane shook his head. "She has a point, Aiyana."

"Steer straight, Thorwalian. You must take care over the mountains."

Dane turned his attention back to the hovercraft controls. Neither Aiyana nor Galya told him the truth. At least, not the complete truth. If Aiyana was right about the Tseirs, then Galya's lie made sense. She was distorting the purpose of her people to gain something. Control. Of Franconia . . . and maybe of Candor, too.

Aiyana was hiding something, too. But what? And why? What could there be that she couldn't say, that he couldn't understand? Dane drummed his fingers on the control lever.

"If you don't elevate our position, we'll soon be meeting a mountainside . . . too close for comfort."

Dane elevated the position. "What's to stop the Keiroit rogues from shooting us down?"

"These hovercraft aren't armed, and we don't use them when attacking. They'll assume we're Tseirs."

Dane glanced back. "I take it you've traveled this route before."

"Many times. For now, Thorwalian, you and I are safe. For now."

The Swamp of Keir stretched flat and long from the southern face of the mountains. Green and brown and purple intertwined in endless, twisting patterns.

As Dane lowered the hovercraft, he saw that Aiyana had been right. The swamp buzzed with activity. Hovercraft maneuvered over the surface, circling around myriad structures below.

"What are those buildings?"

Galya looked composed. "Those are workstations where the loyal Keiroits assemble our craft."

Aiyana tapped Dane's shoulder. "And weapons."

Galya glared back at Aiyana. "We need weaponry to defend ourselves against your attacks."

"You do. But before you consider attacking Valendir again, know that Arnoth will have moved our village already."

"He is devious. We know that too well."

"Yet your Keiroit technicians aren't working on a way to rid yourselves of the Ellowans. Why is that, Galya? What are they working on?"

"You can't expect me to divulge sensitive information to you."

Dane ignored their bickering and slowed the craft. "Where to now?"

Galya studied the landscape. "The central command post is on the far southwestern corner. We will find interplanetary shuttles available there."

"Not flightships?"

Aiyana leaned forward, peeking out Dane's window at the swamp below. "We use flightships for travel through the wormhole. Shorter travel requires only shuttles." She sat back and eyed Galya. "But perhaps the Tseir can tell you more. They are Franconian vessels, aren't they?"

Dane glanced at Galya, but she didn't respond. Aiyana nodded as if this imparted proof of her claims. "I suggest you angle the hovercraft to blend with the others, Thorwalian."

Dane set his course lower, level with the Keiroit craft. He aimed south and west, though the structures prevented him from seeing far. They were constructed above the marsh, on tall metal pillars.

"It was more scenic from above."

Aiyana nodded. "There was a time, ages ago, when this swamp was indeed a thing of beauty. Tiny flowers grew; birds filled the trees. Probably Dwindle Bats, too. The Keiroits simply thrived, then. Now they dominate, and the swamp is polluted with the filth of their workstations and the excess of their waste."

Galya smiled. A patronizing, forced expression. "As always, you exaggerate, Aiyana. The swamp is in far better condition now that it's tended and controlled."

"You like control. I don't."

Dane circled around a partially constructed station. Keiroits worked on the frame. They didn't look up as he passed by. They just worked.

Batty hopped from Dane's shoulder to the viewport. "Odd, isn't, sir?"

"What, Batty?"

"Didn't think Keiroits did much during the day. Rurthgar says they're nocturnal by nature."

Galya glanced quickly at the bat, then turned her smile to Dane. "You mustn't judge the Keiroit race by that band of rogues. Our Keiroits are disciplined, hardworking individuals."

Aiyana coughed. "Individuals? Where's the evidence for that, Tseir? They all look the same to me. Of course, so do the Tseirs. Why is that?"

"We take pride in working as a unit. Perhaps the Ellowans could learn from our example."

"We learned from you, Tseir. We have never forgotten."

Galya ignored Aiyana, but her facial muscles appeared tense. "The central command station is there, Dane. The largest building on the left."

"A sight to behold, isn't it?" Aiyana whistled.

Dane stopped the hovercraft and assessed the building. Gray metal, which looked less substantial than the obsidian craft. No windows. "And I thought Thorwalian housing lacked imagination. . . ."

"It's not meant to be beautiful, Dane. Its purpose is to house the Tseir representatives. On Franconia, our structures are much grander and more luxurious."

Aiyana leaned over Dane's seat, her fingers dabbling in his hair. "Ah, but you didn't build on Franconia, Tseir. Those structures are Ellowan."

Galya licked her lips, then resumed smiling. "Perhaps we built on the sites of Ellowan antiquity. But our buildings can hardly be called Ellowan now."

"They are forever tarnished. But they're still Ellowan. Except the dungeons. Ellowans never constructed dungeons."

"Our containment centers are precautionary."

"And dark."

Dane looked back at Aiyana. She looked smug, as always. Galya would never get the last word with Aiyana nearby. "We've arrived, Aiyana. Please remember that you travel as my mate. And behave yourself."

Her brows angled doubtfully. "When have I not?"

Dane laughed. "When have you, woman?" He opened the hovercraft shell and got out. Metal beams formed walkways above the swamp, but the smell seemed worse than in Rurthgar's marsh. Less organic. Fumes mingled with chemicals.

Aiyana hopped out beside him. "Stinks, doesn't it?"

Batty scrambled to Dane's shoulder, then broke into a fit of coughing and gagging. "Oh, sir . . . After the sweet aroma of the marsh, this is foul. Foul beyond words, sir."

Dane eyed the lingbat with misgivings. " 'Sweet aroma?' That's not quite the way I'd refer to Rurthgar's bog. But it was preferable to this."

Galya reached for Dane's hand as she left the hovercraft. She didn't seem to notice the smell, though both Aiyana and Dane covered their noses. "This way, Dane. I'll show you to the Tseir headquarters on Keir."

Aiyana hung back as Galya led Dane down the metal walkway. She glanced about, probably seeing spots worthy of explosion, Dane thought wryly. "Come along, Aiyana. If you remain out here, you're likely to keel over from the fumes and I'll be carrying you to Franconia."

"And me, sir."

"I'm not carrying you, rodent. Brace up."

"As you say, sir."

Dane waited for Aiyana to catch up, then followed Galya

into the Tseir building. Tseir guards stood in the corridor. They wore identical white helmets and visors covering their faces, obscuring their identity. They wore red shirts, similar to Galya's, but less well made. Shoulder badges indicated rank.

They didn't move or look toward Dane and Aiyana. Dane wondered why. An Ellowan in their midst should create a stir. Galya stopped and looked back. "This way, Dane."

Aiyana slid her hand into Dane's. He glanced over at her. She looked small beside him, small and nervous. A cool tremor crawled through him. Aiyana was afraid. Dane closed his fingers solidly around hers. She squeezed back, but her eyes remained fixed on the guards.

"They don't seem to notice you, love."

"No. They never do."

Galya stopped by a door and motioned to Dane. "Here I will introduce you to the Keir commander. She will arrange our passage back to Franconia."

Dane nodded. Aiyana still held his hand. She stood close to him, but silent. Batty seemed to sense her mood, and he trembled, too.

"Relax, both of you. I won't let anything happen to you. Either of you."

"Thank you, sir." Batty and Aiyana spoke at once.

The door opened, and Galya stepped back. A woman emerged, and Dane caught his breath. She resembled Galya closely enough to be her twin. Aiyana peeked up at him, a knowing look on her face. "What do you make of that, Thorwalian?"

"Sisters?"

"If so, there are thousands."

The woman assessed Dane with the same bland expression. "Galya. We heard that you had crashed in the Ellowan-held forest. We feared the worst."

"It was the result of Ellowan sabotage, Drusalla. This

Ellowan posed as a Keiroit and threatened our entire mission.'' Galya turned to Dane. ''Dane, allow me to introduce Drusalla, the commander of Keir. Dane represents the Candorians, although that is not his homeworld.''

Drusalla's expression resembled Galya's. ''It is my great honor to welcome you to the Franconian system, Dane.''

''Thank you.'' Dane felt hesitant. ''I hope I will be of service to . . . all concerned.''

Drusalla's gaze shifted from Dane to Aiyana. She noted their clasped hands. ''You bring an Ellowan. A prisoner?''

''My mate.''

Drusalla looked quickly to Galya. ''An Ellowan trick, Drusalla. Arnoth used his mate to seduce Dane. Yet Dane withstood their treachery and remains true to our purpose. The female is here because Arnoth vowed to kill me otherwise.''

Drusalla and Galya exchanged a silent look. ''He is fond of her, then?''

Galya hesitated, but Dane stepped forward. ''I am. Whatever the conclusion of this negotiation, Aiyana is my mate. I ask you to treat her as an ambassador. Maybe she can be persuaded to speak for the Ellowans.''

''I will not. We have nothing to say.''

Dane pulled Aiyana to face him. ''Quiet, woman. If I say you're an ambassador, that's what you are.'' He waited while her eyes narrowed. He hoped she would hear his veiled warning. Apparently she had. Aiyana shrugged.

''Very well.''

Drusalla watched their interaction, then glanced at Galya, who nodded. ''Though we resist allowing an Ellowan on Franconia, I see it can't be avoided. We hope that you, Dane, will realize the threat she poses and guard her carefully.''

''I will. Aiyana will do no harm to your people during our visit. In this, you have my word.''

Aiyana tensed beside him, but she didn't argue. A pit formed low in Dane's stomach. From her reaction, he guessed she had intended to do some damage. No doubt that had been her purpose all along.

"You have our trust, Dane. We will give you a shuttle, automated for Franconia. The embassy representatives will handle the matter from there."

Aiyana released Dane's hand. She drew a quick, tight breath before speaking. "Galya stinks. From her stay in the marsh, I suspect. Perhaps she could alter her attire before we depart."

Dane's pulse moved slowly, labored. He knew her so well. He knew what this meant. Galya hesitated. "I am injured as well. Dane bandaged me, but I could use tending before we leave."

Drusalla nodded. "Come this way."

Galya removed her coat and gave it to a guard. "You may dispose of this garment."

The guard said nothing. He took the coat and started away.

Aiyana stepped forward. "I need use of your private facilities also."

Dane watched, but he said nothing. He watched it unfold, knowing it unfolded, but unsure as to how. . . .

"There is a changing station around the corner. While Galya washes, you may make use of the private chambers."

Aiyana glanced quickly at Dane, though her eyes shifted. "I won't be long."

Drusalla moved back to allow the guard passage. "There are guards all over this station, Ellowan. Should you attempt any subterfuge, you will be apprehended."

Aiyana didn't answer, though she frowned. Drusalla went with Galya, and Aiyana hurried after the guard. She didn't meet Dane's eyes at all. He felt numb. He stood a moment, then followed her.

"What's going on, sir?"

Dane stopped and removed the lingbat from his shoulder. "Stay here, Batty."

Batty looked small and forlorn stationed in the center of the corridor. Maybe the bat was the only real thing in Franconia.

Aiyana disappeared into a chamber, and Dane concealed himself behind a wide, metal pillar. Across the hall, the guard tossed Galya's stained garments into a disposal bin. Dane held his breath as the guard continued down the hall.

The chamber door opened a crack. Aiyana peeked out, then looked furtively up and down the hallway. Dane watched her emerge, then move stealthily across the corridor to the disposal bin. She withdrew a small can of liquid, an oil can, and squirted it on the hinges.

Professional. Dane knew he watched an expert at work. The bin opened without sound and she reached in. She pulled out Galya's coat and tore the lining open. Her quick fingers worked beyond his sight, but Dane knew.

"Clever."

She jumped, then shoved the coat back into the bin. Her expression told Dane far more than he wanted to know. "You followed me!"

Dane didn't answer. He grabbed her small hand and squeezed until her fingers opened. "Rurthgar strips." His whole chest felt heavy, as if a great weight came to bear over his heart.

"Dane . . ."

"Don't say anything, Aiyana. I might be fool enough to believe you."

"I wasn't going to use them. Unless . . ."

He turned, so angry that she stepped back, her face pale. He stuffed the strips into his pack, then caught her chin in his hand. "I don't want to hear anything more from you."

She tried to twist free from his grasp. Dane let her go

suddenly, then backed away. "You don't understand. I must—"

"Destroy your enemy . . . You sicken me."

Her eyes widened, shocked. Then she bowed her head and turned away. "Then I have failed."

"You have failed. But not as you think, Aiyana. You're coming with me to Franconia, and you will face your enemy. Unarmed. Without power. You deserve that. Maybe the Tseirs deserve it, too."

Blood drained from her pale face and she swayed. "You don't know what you're saying."

"I know exactly. I won't alert the Tseirs to your scheme. I will guard you myself."

Her small chin lifted. "It seems you did that already. You followed me. You doubted me."

Her defiant words drove like splinters into Dane's heart. "With reason, my lady. You have ever been treacherous. Tell me, was this your idea, or Arnoth's?"

She maintained silence.

"Rurthgar must have been involved, to apply the strips to Galya's clothes while she slept. A foul band of rogues you are. Every one of you."

"If that is how you feel . . ." Aiyana looked away. "So be it."

"So be it."

Drusalla came around the corner with Galya. Aiyana held her breath. "Is everything all right, Dane?"

"It is now. Has a shuttle been prepared?"

"It awaits us. Follow me."

Aiyana sat beside Dane in the front seat of the shuttle. He didn't look at her or speak. She felt sick, and her heart ached. *Curses!* Why did he have to follow her?

The shuttle maneuvered by automatic piloting. Aiyana watched through the viewport as they lifted from the docking bay and rose into the sky. It was nearly dark. That morning, she had awakened in Dane's arms. She had never felt so alive, nor imagined that life could be that way.

She had experienced life in all its splendor. She had experienced Dane. Life flowed through him with power and faith and joy. Aiyana closed her eyes. *I love you so.* Maybe it was enough, to have felt that love at all, to have shared his body, his life.

It had been a risk. She had taken it, and failed. Now she would be at the Tseirs' mercy. And they had no mercy. She traveled as Dane's mate, and she had angered him once too often. She doubted they would allow her to stay at his side.

Aiyana rested her head against the seat. She felt so tired. She closed her eyes and imagined Arnoth's cool fingers on her temple, relieving her of pain, relieving her of life's misery. Then she would do the same for him.

"Arnoth . . ."

Dane tensed beside her. She had whispered aloud, not meaning to. He wouldn't understand. Aiyana refused to look at him.

"It seems he failed you, too."

She clenched her teeth, but the pain continued and grew. "No. I failed him."

"Curse you, Aiyana."

Aiyana heard anguish in Dane's voice. His pain struck her like cold wind. She sat forward and looked at him. "I hope someday you will understand. I can't explain. You wouldn't believe me anyway."

"No, I wouldn't."

Aiyana forced her gaze to the viewport. Black space swallowed the shuttle. Then, ahead, loomed Franconia, A desert world, a golden orb in space. Beautiful, like a jewel on a black velvet tablecloth.

"In the Ellowan tongue, Franconia meant 'gem of the sky.' Because it looks golden."

Batty eased from Dane's shoulder to Aiyana's lap. Her heart constricted at the comforting touch. She scratched gently behind his twitching ears. Batty leaned against her hand. "How will it be for foraging?"

"Do you mean for insects?"

Batty nodded vigorously.

"I'm afraid Franconia can't offer you the wealth of bugs that you found in Rurthgar's marsh, Batty. But they have small insects, beetles, and such. Beware the more beautiful specimens, those with bright colors. Those have poisonous stings."

"Advice well heeded. The same might be said of the Ellowans."

Aiyana didn't respond to Dane's comment. She turned her attention back to the viewport, watching Franconia swell before her. As if to taunt her, the distant, dark shape of Valenwood appeared beyond Franconia. A shadow, a ghost, forever haunting.

"The Midnight Moon." Dane's voice contained a bitter edge. "A dead world, for which you sacrifice everything. I hope it's worth what you've lost, Aiyana."

Aiyana didn't answer for a long while. "I hope so, too."

"Welcome to Franconia, Dane." Galya rose from her seat. "It's been a long journey since we left Candor, but I think you'll find it rewarding."

Aiyana glared beside Dane. "It's been a joy from beginning to end. But this isn't the end, is it, Tseir?"

Dane caught Aiyana's arm. "Enough, Aiyana. Keep your barbed remarks to yourself. You're here as my mate. Ludicrous as that may be, I intend to hold you to it."

Her expression indicated that she wanted to fight. Dane prepared himself. But instead, she sighed and looked away. Defeated. Maybe it was easier this way. He couldn't endure her rejoinders now. He just wanted it over.

Galya waited by the door. "I've communicated our arrival to the first command. They'll be waiting to greet us. Though it was night when we left Keir, it is only midmorning in our central city. We will soon dine with the first commander."

Dane nodded, but the thought of polite, diplomatic conversation seemed unendurable now.

The door hissed open, admitting a breath of hot, dry air. "Hakon hated the Franconian climate. He wanted to alter its orbit to encourage snow."

Aiyana spoke wistfully, but Dane tried to ignore her sorrowful tone. She sounded . . . odd. "Being Ellowan, Ariana preferred the heat. The climate control in their chambers was always a subject of discussion."

Dane fought his interest. She spoke of Hakon and Ariana as if she knew them. Maybe the Ellowans kept better historical records than Thorwalians, but his suspicions were raised. Something hovered just outside his understanding. The mystery of the Ellowans, just beyond him. If he had the time . . .

"This way, Dane. The first commander awaits you."

Dane banished his curiosity about Aiyana and followed Galya down the ramp. He still gripped Aiyana's hand, lest she escape and do damage that he couldn't yet fathom. Batty puffed in the hot air.

"Whew! It's hot, sir. Now, the lingbat tunnels are warm, but this is dry heat."

"You'll get used to it, rodent."

Dane stopped at the bottom of the ramp and looked around. The shuttle had landed in a central square. Earthen buildings circled the square, designed as if carved from living rock. Just beyond the rock-hewn buildings were sharp hills.

Aiyana stood beside him. "This center has existed for a thousand years. It was the first Ellowan outpost."

"It is beautiful."

"It was."

The Franconian sky was light blue, cloudless. The only plants were sleek, upright domes, covered by sharp thorns. Bright pink flowers bloomed on the shiny surface.

Galya motioned to Dane. "This is the central square of Franconia, site of the Tseir embassy."

"It is . . . impressive."

Aiyana made a small, sputtering noise. "Naturally. It's Ellowan. You don't want to see the cities the Tseirs design for themselves. On the other hand, you have already. In the Swamp of Keir."

Galya ignored Aiyana and positioned herself at Dane's other side. "Our first commander awaits you."

Dane noticed several women standing near a silent fountain. Not all Tseir women resembled Galya. Though of a similar height and age, two of the women had pale blond hair and blue eyes. The leader had reddish blond hair and was somewhat larger than the others.

However, the Tseirs did seem designed from a limited mold. Their outward appearance seemed differentiated to designate rank rather than individual personality. The woman at the center wore a long red robe, and her hair was covered in black netting.

Galya approached the group. "I bring the Candorian representative, Dane Calydon. Due to Ellowan treachery, this female accompanied us also."

The leader faced Dane, then glanced at Aiyana. Dane sensed no fear, nor hesitation. Why? Galya insisted the Tseirs were in dire need of protection from the Ellowans.

The leader smiled, that same forced smile Dane recognized from Drusalla and Galya. "We welcome you to Franconia, Ambassador. I am Rattan, first commander of Franconia. It pleases me that you survived the journey and its hardships."

"It was not uneventful, Rattan. But I am here now. By

sabotage, I learned the Ellowan point of view. I am eager to hear the Tseirs' response, and to learn what Candor can offer."

"We will open our session soon. There will be wine provided for you there. I hope you will find it . . . pleasant."

Dane sensed sexual interest from Rattan. Her eyes swept slowly and appreciatively over his body. He saw no men other than the guards. They all appeared uniform in size, though he couldn't see their faces beneath their helmets and visors. Maybe the Tseir women hungered for variety.

"First we will show you to our guest facility, and allow you to rest."

"Rest would be welcome. Thank you, Rattan. I am indeed weary."

Rattan returned her gaze to Aiyana. "Unfortunately, I'm afraid the Ellowan must be detained."

"Detained?"

Again, that smile. "We can't allow an Ellowan to walk free in Franconia. The threat is simply too great. You've heard of their explosive strips."

"I have. She bears no strips. I searched her myself."

"I trust you, of course. But the Ellowans are devious beyond measure. Who knows what new devices they have conjured?"

Galya nodded. "I bring dark news, also, Rattan. During my captivity, I learned that the Keiroit rogues are allied with the Ellowan. Much sabotage can be explained by this."

Rattan's face hardened, her demeanor of pleasantness fading. "They are few, yet deadly. We must take extra precautions." She turned back to Dane. "You do understand, then, why we must keep this Ellowan under guard."

Dane hesitated. Aiyana stood close to him, and he felt her fear. Maybe it was only his weakness that made him imagine her distress. "She is under my protection."

''You may check on her, as you wish, so that you know no harm has come to her.''

Dane looked down at Aiyana. She stood very still, stiff, trembling almost imperceptibly. She was terrified. Or did she want him to think so to encourage his fool's pity? Ice formed around his heart.

''What you offer is more than the Ellowans granted Galya. If I may have access to her, and can check on her . . .'' Dane paused. *Aiyana . . . My treasure . . .* ''When I leave, she goes with me. She will be returned to her people . . . to her rightful mate.''

''Of course,'' Rattan answered quickly. Too quickly, perhaps.

''Know that I will not leave without her.''

''There's no need for concern, Dane. While you are with us, speaking on behalf of the Candorians, she must be kept under guard. When you're ready to leave, we will place her again in your care.''

Dane turned to Aiyana. She looked very pale; her eyes were round, her jaw clenched. *Avoiding pain.* ''Nothing will happen to you, Aiyana. But you must be kept from . . . mischief. I'm sorry.''

She swayed slightly. He caught her arm to steady her. She trembled, every lithe muscle drawn tight. Pity stabbed at his heart. ''Nothing will happen to you.''

She didn't speak. Her lip quivered, and she bit it hard.

''Our guards will escort her to the containment facility.''

Aiyana backed away. Rattan motioned to her guards, who surrounded Aiyana, closing in. She looked like a wild forest creature pursued by hunters. Dane saw panic in her eyes.

''I will go with her.''

Aiyana stopped and turned to face him. The change in her expression shocked him beyond words. ''Stay here, Thorwalian, with the Tseirs. I have no need of you. Have you forgotten? I've faced these guards before.''

She whirled away, heading across the courtyard. The guards hurried after her, armed, but they didn't alter her direction. She went to a high, narrow door and stopped. A guard opened the door, and she disappeared inside.

"What is that place?"

"That is the entrance to the containment facility. It is just below our embassy."

Dane said nothing more, but he reeled as he realized what this meant. Aiyana had known the exact location of the containment facility. She needed no escort. She had been there before.

Chapter Eight

Aiyana sat alone in the Tseir cell. A dim, blue lamp shed the only light. Nothing had changed since Arnoth had been imprisoned here. She wondered if they had placed her here on purpose, to remind her of her sister's fate.

The dungeon had been dug beneath the embassy. The Tseirs had disguised their intentions from the resident Ellowans, digging their dungeon in secret, preparing. . . . The Tseirs had no skill at building. The cell was not much more than a scraped-out hole. It hadn't been improved over time.

The dry heat sucked the life from the underground air, and Aiyana's breath came labored. If she slowed her pulse, she would use less air. The guards paced across the floor above her; she heard their even steps, back and forth. Then silence. Then movement again. They moved in perfect regularity.

A door creaked above; someone was coming to her cell. Aiyana braced herself. It had to be Dane, fulfilling his word to check on her. The guards entered the dark hall, then made way for Galya. Aiyana looked beyond her, but Dane wasn't there.

"I trust you are comfortable, Ellowan."

Aiyana didn't answer. Galya smiled, but without the pretense she used in Dane's presence.

"You did well to get this far. It surprises me, though, that you would choose to return here of your own free will."

Aiyana drew a quick breath, then rose from the metal bench. "You knew. You've known all along."

"Of course. Do you think we are such fools that we could forget you or the sweet prince of Valenwood?"

Aiyana felt chilled despite the radiant heat. "I have seen you before, Galya. But that was long ago."

"Let's just say the Tseirs share a common memory."

"The woman I remember murdered my sister."

Galya laughed. "Not before sharing her with our guards. We have to reward them somehow."

Aiyana clenched her fists, but her limbs felt weak. Tears stung her eyes. "You are evil, Galya. You and every lookalike Tseir that exists. We will never relent until you are gone."

"One Ellowan at least will relent. You. True, I considered using you to lure Arnoth back to Franconia. But since you've bedded the Thorwalian, I doubt you mean that much to your prince."

"What I mean to him, you could never imagine."

"It doesn't matter, Ellowan. We may not 'enjoy' Arnoth, but we will destroy him. Now that we know the location of the rogues' marsh, we will attack. Arnoth will defend them, and he will die, too. Unless we're fortunate enough to capture him alive."

"Have you shared this information with Dane?"

"Your Thorwalian provides interest of his own. It's a shame I can't force the issue. Rattan, also, has expressed interest in his physique. Perhaps we will share him."

"You didn't have much luck convincing Arnoth."

"If we had waited to kill his precious mate . . ."

"Your eagerness for blood defeated your purpose. But a man must feel desire to perform as you wish. And I don't see that a Tseir female is capable of inspiring desire."

Galya's face contorted with anger. "The Ellowans specialize in sensuality. You made it an art. How that trait disgusted us when we first came to this system! Your women wore almost nothing; your men displayed their bodies without shame. If not for the cold climate of Keir, I think you would do it still."

"I have no shame."

"You willingly displayed yourself to the Thorwalian. It worked; he pants at your feet. But he bears you little loyalty, beyond the base desire to mate."

"What do you want, Galya?"

"I have come to warn you, Ellowan. We desire the Candorians' cooperation. Dane Calydon must return to them, confident of our plight. You stand in our way. It might be that his affection for you would alter his course."

"It might."

"I can't allow that. Rattan can't allow it. So you will convince him otherwise, let him know that you have used him, and betrayed him."

Aiyana angled a brow and seated herself, cross-legged. "I don't think so, Galya. Convince him yourself."

Galya's dark eyes hardened with secret hatred. "You will do exactly as I ask, Aiyana. We need Dane's compliance, but we can maneuver without him. Should you resist my suggestion, his fate will be no more pleasant than Arnoth's."

"I see. I either alienate him further, or you'll kill him. Simple and direct. Tseirs lack subtlety."

"We don't need subtlety, Ellowan. We've grown more powerful than you can imagine. But such things, such as colonizing outward, must be done delicately.''

''You can't have grown more powerful, Tseir. You lack the capacity to develop.''

Galya's expression turned mocking, evil. ''Do you think the Tseir rule is limited only to this system? Our empire is vast beyond your understanding. Many such colonies exist. Another colony had a brilliant success in expansion, and brought new destructive technology to our empire.''

Aiyana shuddered, but Arnoth had warned her of this possibility. Galya wouldn't be telling her this if she intended to free Aiyana. ''You're nothing but parasites, dependent on the creations of others.''

''What we take from others becomes our own. That is wisdom, Aiyana. You have Dane. We want him. You will see that we get him.''

''So I'll convince Dane that I'm evil, that the Ellowans are violent and dishonorable, and then you'll kill me. Is that it?''

''Honor is your weakness, Ellowan. It always was. You're ruthless now, but too late.'' Galya's mocking tone intensified. ''We rely on your honor. You won't let the Thorwalian die.''

''He'll die either way, Galya. Now, or when you invade the Candorian system.''

''Maybe. But you have faith in him, don't you, Aiyana? You have faith in Arnoth. You think, even if you die, they'll find a way to defeat us.''

Aiyana didn't answer, and Galya laughed.

''Hope is your enemy, Aiyana. The Ellowans have fought us, a constant irritation, since your planet fell. You fought because you believed you could stop us, because of hope. But you'll comply now. I have no doubt.''

''What do you want me to do?''

''I will bring you to the guardroom above this cell. I don't want Dane to see these squalid conditions. You will assure him that you're well, and that you want nothing more from him. You will express your anger and outrage. Then you will try to kill him."

"I will not."

"Don't worry, Aiyana. The weapon you'll seize will be set on stun."

"Of course. Why should I believe you in this?"

"Because we need Dane, as I told you. We want him alive."

"You want him. But you'll never have him, Galya. His desire is a delicate thing. It requires skill to activate."

"He will be weakened by your betrayal. He will need . . . comfort."

"I hope you'll allow me to live long enough to hear his laughter." Aiyana watched Galya's anger twitching just beneath the surface. "For Dane, I will do what you ask. But life is unpredictable, Galya. The more you attempt to control its outcome, the more it leaps beyond your grasp."

"The outcome is already secured." Galya nodded to a guard, who unlocked Aiyana's cell. "When Dane has left Franconia, you will meet your sister's fate. Do you see this guard, Ellowan?"

"I see his helmet and uniform. I assume there is some element of a man beneath."

"Tseir men aren't quite as composed as our women. They lust. Ellowan women always drive them to lust." Galya licked her lips, and Aiyana's skin crawled. Galya reached to the guard's groin, then rubbed her hand over his concealed manhood.

Aiyana watched, horrified.

"Do you see how you arouse him, Aiyana? The guards above have been wagering already on the first to make use of you. We will not kill you as swiftly as your sister. You will be an amusement for our most faithful guards for as long as they want you."

The guard grunted when Galya removed her hand. "I have tired of their rutting, you see. It is so base, force without skill."

"And without result. I have never seen a Tseir child. In fact, I can't imagine you as a child, Galya."

"Yet there are millions of us, Ellowan. We far outnumber you. Come, Aiyana. Dane has already requested to see you."

Aiyana followed Galya up the jagged stairs. Daylight stung her eyes and she winced. The guards walked just behind her, saying nothing, marching in file. Galya led them through several small rooms, down a corridor, skirting any view of the courtyard. Aiyana guessed that she didn't want Dane to see her moved.

Galya opened an arched door. An Ellowan door. "In here, Aiyana. Dane must believe you are held here, in comfort. Should you indicate anything else—"

"I know." Aiyana pushed past Galya and entered the room. The structure was Ellowan, clay walls, round windows. Still beautiful. The furnishings were stark, metal . . . Tseir. There was a small metal bed, a table for dining, seats.

"Hardly more comfortable than my cell, Galya. You might as well have shown Dane in there."

Galya ignored Aiyana and turned to a guard. "Bring the Thorwalian. When you return, see that you position yourself near the Ellowan, with your rifle disengaged."

The guard bowed, but said nothing. Aiyana shook her head. "Not a chatty group, are they?"

"They serve their purpose. Now, sit down and await your lover. If you value his life, you'll make your act convincing."

Aiyana didn't answer, though she seated herself. Let Galya worry over the outcome; let her wonder if her domination had succeeded. Galya looked nervous. *Good.*

Aiyana heard the guards returning. She heard Dane speak, and receive only a monosyllabic answer. She heard Batty chirp. *What do I do?* She couldn't alert Dane to the Tseirs' plan. He probably wouldn't believe her, anyway. But she couldn't follow Galya's orders either. There had to be another way.

A guard held the door open and Dane entered. Batty sat on his shoulder. "Aiyana? Are you all right?"

She swallowed. "Your interest is touching, Thorwalian, but unnecessary. You chose to take the Tseirs' part over the Ellowans'. I have nothing more to say to you."

She spoke in a flat tone, without emotion or passion. Galya wanted passion; she wanted Dane to see the violence of the Ellowan.

Dane didn't respond. He looked around the room, then nodded. "Nonetheless, I feel responsible for you." He paused. Aiyana held her breath. They were fencing, silently, each trying to learn the other's intention.

"There is no need. You were no more than a toy to me. A pretty toy . . ." She saw a chance and seized it. "But I much preferred Arnoth in my bed."

Aiyana watched Dane for his reaction. He revealed none. Galya was waiting.

"I cannot allow you to enlist the Candorians against us. Since you refuse to heed our demands for weaponry, I must stop you."

Still, no reaction. Aiyana hesitated, but she saw Galya's warning glance. The guard stood close beside her. She saw his loose rifle. She had one final chance to warn Dane of Tseir subterfuge. Two hints might have gone astray. The third . . .

Aiyana seized the rifle and fired. . . . Her shot grazed his hair.

Aiyana heard Galya's false scream of terror. "Stop her!"

The guard leaped toward her and clamped a moistened

cloth over her nose and mouth. Darkness swallowed her, and Aiyana sank to the floor.

Dane started toward Aiyana, but Galya grabbed his arm. "She's all right, Dane. Our guards are well trained, and act quickly. But the substance is the same as Arnoth used on me." Galya motioned to the guard. "Please, set her gently to the bed. We'll let her sleep."

The guard lifted Aiyana's small, limp body and set her onto the bed. His hand lingered on her thigh, and Dane's heart chilled. "I will check her, Galya."

Dane knelt beside the low bed and touched Aiyana's forehead, then felt her pulse. It was strong and swift, though her skin was cold. She looked pale, more vulnerable than he had ever seen her.

"I'm sorry, Dane. It was my negligence. I should have warned the guards to conceal their weapons. I just didn't think."

"I'm fortunate that she missed."

"I never dreamed she'd try to kill you."

Dane touched Aiyana's limp hand, then squeezed gently. He rose to his feet and turned away. "There's no need to apologize, Galya. Nothing the Ellowans do surprises me, but they are an unpredictable race. Don't concern yourself."

Galya moved closer to Dane, touching his arm. He recognized her desire, but it was stronger now. Maybe she felt more confident since Aiyana had revealed her treachery. "I'm glad to see you're handling her betrayal so well, Dane. But it must be a sorrow to you. Perhaps we can find ways of distracting you from your loss."

Dane hesitated. "Perhaps. I've learned of Ellowan women. . . ." He forced a smile. "Yet other women, from other races, may have . . . appeal."

Galya's eyes darkened, her lips parted. "I'm pleased you consider the possibility."

"I am a man, Galya." For some reason, this statement of obvious fact brought a swift gasp from Galya. Dane wondered why. He'd seen far more male Tseirs than female. "While I enjoy beauty, sexual intimacy means little to me beyond the physical release." The gasp came again. Galya's skin flushed with desire—beyond desire; lust.

Dane glanced back at Aiyana. "The little Ellowan didn't understand that. She thought that by luring me to her bed, she could change my decision." Dane paused to laugh. From the corner of his eye, he saw Batty looking aghast, puckered mouth dropped, shaking his small head.

"This pleases me, Dane. Your stay will be so much more . . . rewarding."

"I hope so."

Galya turned to the guard. Her breath was swift and shallow. "Leave us, but prepare to stand guard over the Ellowan."

The guard bowed, then departed. Galya returned her fevered attention to Dane. "The session is about to begin."

"Rattan mentioned wine."

"Yes, wine will be provided during the session, wine made from our most succulent fruit. Dane . . ." She moved closer, placing her hand on his chest. Her fingers clenched greedily. "Before you leave, there are many delights I could show you."

Dane felt intensely aware of Batty's presence. "I will take great pleasure, I'm sure, in learning each one. Slowly." His words affected her like heated caresses. Dane wondered if he'd gone too far. "Yet Rattan has made a similar suggestion. I wouldn't want to cause contention between you."

Galya smiled. "Tseir women have learned how to share our pleasures. It won't be a cause of contention, but of increased pleasure . . . for you."

"Two of them, sir? How will you manage that?" Batty asked.

"I've never had a problem before." *As good an answer as any.* "In fact, rarely has one woman had the energy, shall we say, to endure my . . . attentions."

That was it. Galya quivered. Odd how unappealing it was. He was discussing the sexual intentions of two lustful females, and he felt nothing. But in Galya's condition, she might choose to delay the session.

"Unfortunately, I must put my duties as Candorian representative first. Perhaps later?"

"Yes." She growled the word. "Later. I should warn you, though, that Tseir women are . . . aggressive."

Dane shrugged. "I can handle it."

"I'm sure you can." Galya sounded breathless. She moved closer to him, allowing her breast to touch his arm. "The commanders will be waiting at the session hall. We must go."

Dane started out the door, past the guards. Galya stopped and motioned toward Aiyana's room. "Care for the Ellowan woman, please. She is violent, but her species lacks control. Be gentle as you awaken her."

The guards bowed, uniformly, then returned to Aiyana's room. "Don't worry about her, Dane. The guards will keep her safe."

"After her attempt on my life, I find myself worrying about her less and less." Dane placed his hand on the small of Galya's back. "Shall we go?"

She quivered beneath his touch, her lips parting. "I hope you aren't spent from your night with the Ellowan."

Dane sensed bitter envy, jealousy. "Not at all. The little Ellowan is fragile. Delicate. I had to take great care with her lest she be . . ." Dane paused. What was the term Aiyana used? "Rent asunder."

Galya gasped, her breath hot against his shoulder. "You need take no such care with us."

"That will be gratifying. For us all."

They entered the courtyard, and Dane caught his breath in the dry heat. "A moment, please, Galya."

"What's wrong?"

Dane shook his head, swaying. "The heat. I'm afraid the Thorwalian constitution adapts poorly to such weather."

Galya looked concerned. *Probably worried that the heat will inhibit my enthusiasm for later.* "Shall I bring you water?"

"No, no. That's not necessary. I'll just step into the shade." Dane leaned against the earthen wall, breathing heavily. "Perhaps you should inform Rattan that I'm delayed."

Galya hesitated. She glanced back toward the building where Aiyana was kept. Guards stood at the entrance. Dane noticed her suspicions, then seated himself on the dry fountain. "I'll just sit here and catch my breath." He pulled a drinking flask from his pack and held it to his lips.

"Very well. The entrance is there." Galya pointed to a large archway. "We will await you."

"I'm right behind you." Dane smiled, weakening her. She returned his smile, then headed through the archway.

"Never fails, does it, sir?"

"What, Batty?"

"The smile, sir. You use it well."

"Thank you." Dane set the flask aside. "Listen, and listen good, rodent. We don't have much time."

Aiyana woke to darkness. The air was thin, stark. She lay on the floor of her cell, her head throbbing. Nausea swarmed through her and she gagged. The potion they had used on her wasn't as effective as Rurthgar's concoction, but the side-effects were worse.

She struggled to sit up. Her hair fell in tangles around her face. Her meeting with Dane was skewed in her mind. She had shot at him, and she had missed. She wasn't sure he had understood her veiled warnings. She missed. Dane should know she wouldn't miss. But she couldn't be certain. Maybe he believed she really meant to kill him.

Aiyana rose to her feet and swayed. She braced herself on the rough-hewn wall. The jagged surface scratched her palm, drawing blood. She had forgotten how to tend her own wounds.

Aiyana sank down to the rock bench and bowed her head. She remembered cutting herself when she was a small child. Running tearfully to her grandmother. *Will I die?* She remembered the soft laughter, the hugs. *No,* damanai, *you won't die. Give me your hand and I will teach you to heal.*

Tears stung Aiyana's eyes as she healed her torn hand. She didn't remember her mother, but her grandmother had been everything to Aiyana. They were alike, in spirit and in appearance. And in the men they had chosen to love.

"Dane . . ." Aiyana's tears fell. She had been prepared to die. When she had begged for Arnoth's permission, she had considered herself ready. But not now. She had known life in Dane's arms. The joy and the passion, all that she ever wanted, at last within her reach.

"I can't lose you."

But she was alone, in a hot, dry cell, and he was above, with her enemy. While he remained on Franconia, Aiyana was safe. They wouldn't risk angering him by injuring her, or allowing their guards to misuse her.

But Aiyana also knew the Tseirs would never uphold their promise to return her to Arnoth. If Dane resisted, they would find a way to persuade him. Galya would force her to refuse, and invent some reason to motivate her refusal.

Did she want to go back to Keir, anyway? What could life be now? Arnoth would resume the ritual of endless survival. But could she face that now? How could she fight on, when she had lost her only hope of life with Dane?

The guards spoke outside the door. Aiyana hopped up to listen to their conversation.

"What was that? Something moved up in that corner."

"I don't see anything."

"I heard something move."

"You probably just heard the woman. Maybe she's getting ready for us."

The two guards laughed, and Aiyana grimaced in disgust.

"I hear the Ellowans like it whether they want to or not."

"We'll be lucky if the commanders let us keep her for long."

"Then make good use of her while we've got her. Maybe we should start now."

"Can't touch her till that ambassador leaves. Those are the orders, and if we don't stick to them, Rattan will have our heads."

"Worse than our heads . . ." The guards laughed again, but both sounded nervous at the prospect. "Looks like they'll be using the ambassador tonight. I'd rather be spending my time with that Ellowan, anyway."

"I'm aching just thinking of it. Curse Rattan for holding out on us."

"Our cherished Rattan wants it done in public, and she wants to watch."

Aiyana cringed and moved from the door. The Tseirs were vile, so . . . emotionless.

Aiyana returned to her seat, but her back straightened. Like Arnoth, she wouldn't give up. She had to fight. The Candorians needed her. Unknown systems needed her. Most of all, Dane needed her. She would find a way to live.

Dane entered the Tseir session hall and bowed to the seated commanders. Guards lined the hall, but none sat.

Every woman there looked at him as if he were some rare

morsel offered up at a feast. "I've had dreams like this. Surrounded by beautiful women, wine."

They reacted with predictable sighs and lustful gazes. Rattan rose from her seat. She had altered her attire since Dane had seen her last. Her neckline was lower, revealing large, full breasts. The fabric of her dress clung purposely tight.

"It may be difficult to keep my mind on our purpose, Rattan."

She sucked a swift breath through fleshy, thick lips. "We will state our case quickly so that you might . . . rest. Galya has indicated that you are in dire need of rest."

Dane smiled until his cheeks dimpled. The bat was right. It never failed. Rattan flushed with desire. Dane swayed, and shook his head as if to clear his senses, then sank down into a chair.

Rattan hurried around the table to check on his welfare. "What's wrong?"

Dane caught his breath. "The heat. Forgive me, Rattan. It is nearly unbearable to a Thorwalian."

"Bring water. At once!"

A guard rushed away at Rattan's sharp command. Dane held up his hand. "I'm all right. Usually my stamina is limitless."

Rattan's fingers clenched on his shoulder. "We must see that it is restored right away. Where is that water?"

Galya stood at his other side. "We don't notice the heat of our climate, so we've never taken measures to cool our buildings."

"I'll be fine, Galya." Dane straightened in the seat, though he winced as he moved. The guard delivered water, and Rattan passed a filled goblet to Dane.

"Thank you. This should help." Dane drained the goblet, then drew another tight breath. "I'm better now. Forgive the interruption, Rattan. Let us continue."

Rattan returned to her seat, Galya beside her. "As you

know, Ambassador, we have long been terrorized by the vicious and unpredictable Ellowans. They lured us to this system with promises of aid and protection, then enslaved us for their own vile purposes.''

Dane nodded. ''That sounds like the Ellowans.''

''I'm glad you have seen that. Perhaps your affection for Arnoth's mate isn't as great as Galya believed.''

Dane laughed, one brow angled. ''Affection? No. Can I speak plainly, Rattan? I don't want to offend you with my coarse nature.''

''Please, speak as you wish, Ambassador. I'm sure we won't be offended by anything you say.''

Dane allowed for a slow, sensual smile. ''I like women. Of any race. Maybe I should be more blunt. I like sex. When Arnoth offered me his mate, I leaped at the chance. It was sensual exploration, nothing more. The Ellowan woman wanted more from me. As you may know, the Ellowans are emotional creatures.''

The commanders looked uniformly weak and excited by his declaration. ''Go on.''

''The Ellowan nature is violent, as you also know. It pleased me to learn how this would translate in lovemaking.''

''And . . . did it?'' Rattan was breathless.

''What do you think?'' Dane didn't let her respond. None of the women looked capable of speech, anyway.

''But my purpose on Franconia, unfortunately, isn't sex.'' Dane paused to chuckle. Frightening, how easily he assumed this role. ''That has only been a side benefit of my trip. I'm afraid I can't resist pleasuring beautiful women, in the most bizarre and varied ways I can imagine. Sometimes I can be a little rough.''

One of the women uttered a low moan. He was getting carried away. Dane stopped, bowing his head as if dizzy, then filled his goblet with water. His hands shook from weakness and he spilled some.

Rattan drew a throaty breath. "I'm sure you are accomplished at . . . pleasure."

Dane just smiled.

"We need you." She paused and cleared her throat. "We need the Candorians to help us deal with the Ellowan problem."

"I will bring word of the genuine nature of Franconia's problem, and of the Ellowan capacity for treachery. I learned enough from them to know that they are a growing threat."

"What do you think the Candorians can do to help us? Will they send troops?"

"Candor doesn't have troops, as such. But they have effective ways of dealing with miscreants like the Ellowans. I, myself, might enjoy leading a group of able-bodied Thorwalians to assist you."

A shuddering gasp rippled through the women. "This bears consideration, Ambassador. Yes. If a group of your people came to our system, we could open better communications with Candor." Rattan paused. "Unfortunately, the Tseirs have never allowed females to take up arms. So it might be best if only Thorwalian men accompanied you."

Dane nodded, his expression serious. *I'll bet.* "That can be arranged."

"Good."

"The real purpose of my visit was to establish relations between Candor and Franconia. I think we've done that effectively. I learned more about the Ellowans than I wanted to know, firsthand."

"I'm pleased their lies didn't alter your opinion."

"When I return to Candor, I will tell their council what I've learned here. I feel certain they will respond as you deserve."

"Another matter demands our attention, Dane. The Ellowan female now in our custody."

"I understood she would be returned to Keir."

"That was our intention. Yet communication from Keir indicates that Arnoth, in league with the Keiroit rogues, has launched an assault on the Swamp of Keir. He is ever quick to battle."

"I noticed that. A grave situation, Rattan."

"Under these circumstances, it seems unwise to return the Ellowan female. It may be that we can use her to bargain with Arnoth. Even if he willingly shared her, his devotion to his mate is strong."

"I believe that it is, yes."

"Then you understand why we can't release her until this most recent attack is subdued."

"It would be foolhardy to release her, Rattan. I agree completely. I did hold myself responsible for her welfare, but matters such as defense take precedence."

Rattan breathed a muted sigh of relief, but Galya appeared skeptical. "Are you sure, Dane? You called her your mate."

Dane turned his sensual smile on Galya. He hoped the power hadn't faded. "To my race, mating is a grave matter, and the male swears fealty to the female. I consider it my duty to secure her welfare. But such bonds of honor go only so far. And of course, I have my Thorwalian mate to consider."

Galya's mouth dropped, and Dane reclined in his seat, enjoying the moment. "You have another mate?"

"Of course. I haven't seen her in a while, not since she had my second child. A Thorwalian can take as many mates as he can afford. Throwback to Ravager times. I didn't tell Kostbera much about that, naturally. Offends the Candorian sensibilities."

Dane sat forward, wide-eyed and innocent. "I hope I haven't shocked you."

"Not at all! The Tseirs abandoned formalized mating long ago, preferring to keep the pleasures of the flesh pure in their own right."

"A wise, and seductive, practice of handling a base function, Galya. Why place bonds around an act best kept freely enjoyed?"

Rattan exhaled a hot, hungry breath. "You understand us well. Maybe your race of Thorwalians and ours might find a more common ground than I imagined. You might enjoy life among our people, Ambassador."

"I already do."

"We will provide a flightship automated for your return to Candor. I hope you will return to Franconia, with your people. Soon."

"The pleasure of another visit intrigues me, Rattan."

"Perhaps we can give you a taste of that pleasure tonight." Rattan turned to the other commanders. "The session has concluded. Return to your posts."

The other women pouted, leaving slowly, casting appreciative glances Dane's way. "I'm afraid I can only handle a few at once, ladies. Yes, a group of Thorwalians would enjoy being stationed here . . . if they could get used to the heat."

"We'll find ways of alleviating the heat." Rattan placed her hands on Dane's shoulders. "You are magnificent."

"So I've been told."

Rattan's fingers clenched and trembled. She pulled his shirt apart and ran her hands over his chest, feeling the muscles. Rattan seized a wine goblet and took a sensual sip, then held it to Dane's lips. The wine was flavorless, quite unlike Thorwal's prized Ungan liquid.

He swallowed. "Delicious."

Rattan's dark eyes fixed on his lips, then his chest. She bent and pressed her hot mouth against his neck. Dane froze, his skin recoiling. But Rattan didn't notice his hesitation.

The touch of his flesh sent her into a wilder frenzy. She tore at her bodice, freeing large, fleshy breasts.

"You may watch, Galya, but I am first."

Rattan bent over Dane's chair, her breasts close to his face. "Or perhaps you would prefer to take us both at once."

Dane gulped. "Here?"

"Here, on the table, on the floor. You have aroused us past endurance. We can't wait."

Thinking fast had always been Dane's strong point—the ability to adapt to any situation. "My lust, too, knows no bounds. I will take you first, Rattan. Perhaps, when I'm finished with Galya, I will attend the others."

Dane rose unsteadily from his chair. "What . . . ?" He swayed, then braced himself on the table. "The heat . . . Curses . . ."

Dane collapsed forward onto the table, spilling wine and water. He hoped they wouldn't decide to make use of his unconscious state anyway.

Aiyana sat miserably in darkness. It was nearly dawn on Franconia, but she couldn't see the light. She had broken the blue lamp, because it was Tseir, and nothing else in her cell was breakable.

A flightship roared in the distance. Aiyana wondered why the Tseirs would send off a craft at night. A long-distance craft. She heard it depart, and her heart sank. She wasn't sure why, but she felt more alone now than ever before.

She had waited for hours, but Dane hadn't come to see her. At least he could have come to yell at her. She couldn't sleep, knowing how few hours might remain in her life. But wakefulness served no purpose.

Maybe sleep was better. If she didn't dream, it would offer a measure of forgetfulness. . . . Aiyana lay back on the stone bench and rested her head on her arm. She thought of her childhood, her life before the long stillness.

She remembered her grandparents telling her stories about when they first met. She remembered the young Elena pinning Arnoth to the floor while her grandfather tried to separate them. Then later, Elena shocked beyond words when she fell in love with her childhood nemesis.

A vision of the end flashed across Aiyana's mind. But she blotted out that memory, and forced her mind to the joys of her life. She thought of her long friendship with Arnoth. She thought of Rurthgar, and the day Arnoth made alliance with the Keiroits in the swamp.

"I lived well. There is no doubt."

Last, she remembered Dane. Strong and sure and confident, filled with life and boundless joy. She closed her eyes and saw his quick, teasing smile. She remembered his wit and the delight he took in conversation. She remembered him with Batty, arguing with a small winged rodent whose ability for speech came from Dane's own genius.

Aiyana sat up and burst into tears. "I want my life; I want you. . . . I want to see Batty get the better of you at least once. I want to see you beg his forgiveness and thank him. . . . I want you. Please, please don't leave me."

Aiyana contained her sobs, and wiped away her tears. She wanted so much. She wanted a life with Dane. She wanted to meet his beautiful, strong sister and Seneca, the man Dane idolized.

"I am free to want, and to want, and never to stop wanting. They can't take that from me."

She wanted to see Rurthgar, ruler of all Keir, once again. And Arnoth . . . She wanted to see Arnoth find life again. She wanted to see his beautiful face in love and happy, content at last with the memory of Elena, yet willing to accept his own future.

She wanted Batty to find She Who Leaps High again, and create a new subspecies of bat. And most of all, more than anything else, she wanted to give life to little "sirs." Forever after, she would live at Dane's side, while he grumbled about lingbats, when he commented with pleasure that Arnoth had turned old and feeble and toothless.

In her dreams, Arnoth *would* grow old, and he would be handsome and wise, and only Dane would find fault, but still, they would be the best of friends.

Aiyana collapsed back onto the bench and sobbed. She cried and cried, until her face stung from tears. Until her throat was raw. Deep in her misery, Aiyana knew she hadn't really cried since Elena's death. She'd never come close to losing what she had finally lost now.

So this is life, Aiyana thought. *Do you know how much it hurts,* damanai? "I know now. But I wouldn't exchange it, my friend. It was worth the pain, to know the beauty. For a little while."

Aiyana stopped crying. Her pain eased. Through the crack of her door, she saw faint morning light. A new day had come. Anything could happen. She was ready.

The morning grew fuller, and Aiyana's nerves tensed at every sound. Why hadn't Dane come? Surely he wouldn't leave her alone this long. He'd find a way to see her. He had promised. *I will protect you, Aiyana. I will give you all my heart. When you need me, I'll find a way to be there for you.*

Aiyana heard the guards at the cell door. She held her breath. *Dane* . . . The door opened and Galya appeared. Aiyana's heart crashed. Galya looked particularly angry and vengeful, and a tremor of fear replaced Aiyana's disappointment.

"What do you want, Galya? Where is Dane?"

"He's gone." Galya waited, pleased with Aiyana's shock.

Aiyana hopped up from the bench and faced Galya. "What do you mean, 'gone'?"

"We gave him a flightship last night, and he returned to Franconia."

Aiyana's breath caught; her throat tightened. "That can't be."

"Unfortunately, that's exactly what happened. Your rugged Thorwalian collapsed in the heat." Galya paused, her brow tight with displeasure. "He showed no signs of recovery, so we were forced to allow him to leave early."

"I could have helped him!"

"Rattan and I considered forcing you to do just that. But it seems likely that you communicate in your Ellowan trance, and that could work against us."

Aiyana turned away, shocked, defeated. "He's really gone."

"Don't mourn his departure too much, Ellowan. He easily took our side over yours, and promised to return with many strong Thorwalians."

Aiyana glanced over her shoulder. "Aren't you planning to obliterate their system as you did Valenwood?"

"We have reconsidered that option. Now, we will destroy Candor and take its power. But perhaps we will enlist the Thorwalian males to our service." Galya's eyes narrowed in evil mockery. "You were wrong about his desire. It's quite indiscriminate. Before he collapsed, he was willing and eager to pleasure us to the limit of his endurance."

"No wonder he fainted. Probably sick at the thought."

"His words spoke a more lustful tale."

"Did they?" Here, at the end, Aiyana felt jealous. *How dare he speak teasing, seductive words to the Tseirs!*

"He promised to take Rattan and myself . . . at one time."

"That's not possible. He has only one male portion."

"You wouldn't understand these things, Ellowan. Dane says you were too fragile for true pleasure."

"Fragile, indeed." Aiyana returned to her bench, but Galya entered the room after her.

"Don't bother to sit, Aiyana. Your day is just beginning."

Aiyana sat anyway. She felt odd, cold inside. What happened now shouldn't matter. Dane was gone. But she was scared. Life didn't disappear simply because the heart was broken.

"What do you mean?"

"Now that Dane is gone, we have no use for you. Well, that's not entirely accurate. The guards find admirable use for your body. Since Dane's incapacitation deprived us of pleasure, we will take it from watching you appease our guards."

"Appease?" Aiyana knew what Galya meant, but she couldn't accept it now that it was happening. "You mean you'll let them rape me and then you'll kill me. You did this to my sister. It must be an old sport for you now."

"But always enjoyable. In our homeland, such events take place in coliseums. They fill our need for—"

Aiyana rose to her feet and approached Galya. Now, at the end, she had some sense of the Tseir mystery. "For what? For life? You don't really have any life at all, do you, Galya? You're empty, and you fill it with others' lives. With my sister's misery, with Arnoth's grief, with my anger. You sought out Dane's lust because he's so filled with life. You're trying to contain life, to command it. And you never will."

Aiyana's words hit deeper than she expected. Galya swung her arm and struck Aiyana's face. Aiyana staggered back, but she smiled in a way that Dane himself would envy. "Even now."

"Enjoy the guards, Aiyana. I understand that the Ellowan female is inordinately sensitive to sexual union. You'll get a lot of that today."

Galya left the cell and called to a guard. "Bring her. If she resists, carry her. Many Tseirs await the pleasure of watching you, Aiyana."

"And when the day is over, Galya, you will be no more alive than you are now. I prefer my death to the sorry life you have."

"You will meet your death soon, Aiyana. If I am favored, then by my own hand." Galya paused, and her smile turned cruel and mocking. "I wounded your sister and left her to die. Didn't you know?"

Aiyana watched Galya head up the stairs. It wasn't possible. Not if the Tseirs were humanoid. But they had no children; they showed no signs of aging or any change. If that was true, much could be explained.

A guard entered her cell, and Aiyana backed away. "Shouldn't you have reinforcements, Tseir? Or didn't Galya allow it? They don't care much for your welfare, do they?"

He didn't answer. He just came closer. Aiyana backed against the wall, then steeled herself for one last battle. She fixed her eyes on his white visor. "Wouldn't you like to make your own decisions for a change, Tseir? You must tire of Galya giving orders." He came closer, and she slid her hand down to her waistband.

She had to keep him focused on her face, and she couldn't see the direction of his gaze beneath the visor. "All right! I'll walk. Just stay away."

He moved closer. *Ellowans don't touch Tseirs.* Aiyana slid her fingers beneath her waistband and stepped forward to pass him. He reached for her, but she whirled, her knife flashing in the dim light.

He dodged her blow, then jumped toward her. He grabbed her arm. "No!" Aiyana struggled wildly. "No, I will not fail!"

The guard towered over her, his strength insurmountable.

He held her wrist tight and pulled her close. "Love is sacred, Aiyana."

His whisper shot through her heart. Her knees gave way and she sank, but he held her up. Aiyana shook so much that she could barely stand up. She stared into his visor, seeing nothing. "Dane . . ."

"Fight me. Don't stop."

She swallowed. She knew what he meant. She knew what she had to do. She yanked away from him as two other guards entered the cell.

"Giving you trouble, is she? Want a hand getting her out of here?"

"Tried to knife me, the little demon." Dane seized the knife, then scooped her into his arms. "No trouble."

"Wonder if she's 'little' inside, too?" The guard chuckled, then followed Dane from the cell.

He climbed the stairs, bringing her to the open courtyard. Aiyana winced in the bright sun. The Tseir commanders were lined up around the fountain, hungry for the violence of her death.

Guards waited in the center of the square, vying for position. Aiyana struggled feebly in Dane's arms, drawing laughter from the other guards.

"You can do better than that." He spoke low, very softly. Aiyana tried. She kicked and he stumbled.

"Better."

Dane dropped her to the ground, but she leaped to her feet. *Now what?* She had no idea how he planned to save her.

"I'm first." The guard behind Dane shoved toward Aiyana, already tearing at his clothes. Another came forward, and shoved the first.

Rattan came to the center of the square. "You will all have opportunity at the Ellowan. Stop fighting. She's not worth that much."

''Worth a lot to me.'' Dane spoke. Aiyana was shocked at the change in his voice. He sounded admirably Tseir. Rattan glared at him, but sensed nothing wrong in his accent.

''You guards squabble and fight over a piece of Ellowan flesh. I will decide.''

''We could fight for her. Fight for who's first. Let us shoot for her. Best shot gets the first shot, right?'' Dane stopped and chuckled. Aiyana stared in astonishment.

Rattan considered his suggestion while Aiyana held her breath. ''That might be interesting. Like tournaments on the homeland.'' She looked around the square. ''Like a coliseum.''

''Right.''

''Very well. You will shoot for the female, and the best ten will vie for the first position.''

Rattan summoned the guards, then addressed the other commanders. ''We will watch our guards shoot, and the best will have the Ellowan. It must be an orderly event.''

Aiyana rolled her eyes. *Orderly.* The guards assembled and lined up. Dane looked around. ''We'll need a target.'' He left Aiyana and disappeared into the embassy. Aiyana waited, shocked, but he returned bearing a tray of goblets. He positioned them around the fountain.

''That should do, if we're back far enough.''

The guards lined up in a perfect row, but Dane remained beside Aiyana. ''Who's going to watch her while we shoot?''

Galya stepped forward. ''I will gladly stand guard.''

Aiyana looked up at Dane. ''What if you miss?'' She spoke in a whisper, but he didn't answer. Though she couldn't see his face, Aiyana knew he smiled.

Dane gave Galya the knife, and took his position among the guards. The Tseirs turned their attention to the target. ''One after another, shoot.''

The line shot laser blasts in perfect precision. When a guard struck a goblet, he stepped forward. Aiyana held her breath until Dane hit his mark, then relaxed. When the goblets were shattered, Rattan sent for more.

The line finished its shots, with at least twenty Tseirs successful. Galya held the knife to Aiyana's skin. "It takes time, doesn't it? It must be dreadful, waiting this way."

Aiyana looked at Galya. "Are you feeling alive now, Galya?" She turned her attention back to the shooting, pleased with Galya's fury.

The successful guards were repositioned farther back, and again shot at the goblets. Each time farther, narrowing down the ranks of the successful. Each time Dane was among them.

When only ten remained, Rattan took one glass and held it aloft. "I will move the goblet farther, and test you once more. As always, the skill of our guards has impressed the commanders."

Dane lined up to shoot last. Aiyana chewed her lip until she tasted blood. Only one Tseir hit the mark. Dane stepped forward. She closed her eyes. She heard him shoot. She heard the goblet shatter.

Dane turned to Rattan. "I tire of this infantile distance, Commander. Perhaps you would allow me to set the firing line this time."

"Are you so hungry for the Ellowan?"

"Starving."

Galya edged the knife deeper into Aiyana's arm. "They are beasts in rut, Aiyana. Not at all like your tender Thorwalian."

"I don't know, Galya. Dane could be a beast at times. You'd be surprised. A shame you didn't find out for yourself."

The knife pierced her skin, but Aiyana refused to flinch. Dane moved back twice the former distance, distracting her from the pain of the knife. *What are you doing?* Aiyana closed her eyes, then opened them. His confidence could be extreme. . . .

Dane shot and the goblet shattered. He stepped back for his opponent. The other Tseir fired, and missed. Aiyana drew a shuddering breath. *Now what?*

Dane walked toward her and took her from Galya. He hesitated when he saw the blood on her arm. Aiyana felt his anger, though he said nothing. "Let's go, female."

He hauled her across the courtyard, Aiyana tugging against him. "Stop! Where are you going, guard?"

Dane stopped at Rattan's harsh command. He glanced over his shoulder. "Where I can have a little fun."

"You will take her here, then pass her to the next. You know this."

"I'll bring her back when I'm finished."

Rattan came toward them. "Remove your visor, guard."

Dane edged Aiyana behind him. She looked up, desperate. "What do we do now?"

"I don't know." He really didn't. Aiyana fought panic.

"What do you mean, you don't know? Didn't you plan this?"

"The lingbat is waiting out beyond the square in a hovercraft. But I have to get you there."

"Oh!"

Dane stared down at her; she stared up at him. They were caught. "I love you, Aiyana."

Tears blurred her vision. "I love you, too."

"We can fight, but we won't get far."

"I'd rather die with you than live without you."

"Aiyana . . ."

A loud roar shook the embassy square. There, moving just above the ground, came a small, narrow hovercraft. Dane's mouth dropped. "It can't be. . . ."

The craft didn't stop. It edged toward them while the

Tseirs scrambled to locate the pilot. Nothing could be seen in the viewport.

Rattan shouted to her guards. ''What's going on?''

''Someone must have left the controls on.''

Dane grabbed Aiyana's hand. ''Now or never, love . . .''

''Stop them! Shoot, all of you!''

Dane raced toward the hovercraft, Aiyana beside him. Their steps clattered on the ancient cobblestones as they ran. He didn't let go of her hand, though she kept pace with his speed. The Tseirs' first shots skimmed by them, missing narrowly. ''We're almost there.''

The hovercraft kept moving toward them. Guards tried to block the oncoming craft. ''Stop!'' It jerked to one side, but didn't stop.

''Shoot the craft, fools! They'll never get away.''

A blast struck the craft, jarring it, but it righted itself. ''Aiyana, we have to jump.''

Dane didn't wait. As the craft drew near, he leaped onto the back and pulled Aiyana with him. He opened the shell and shoved her in headfirst.

Aiyana squirmed to the side, and Dane dove in after her. She righted herself and looked at the controls.

''Sir! I don't know how to stop! Help, help!'' Batty sat on a lever, trying to move it. ''It's stuck, sir.''

Dane yanked off his Tseir helmet and positioned himself at the controls. ''You saved us, Batty. Thank you. Your courage flames unexpectedly, but the timing was perfect. You are truly heroic, and I'm sorry for ever doubting.''

Aiyana burst into tears just as the hovercraft jerked into the sky. She couldn't see through the wash of tears, but Dane looked over at her. ''What's wrong, love? We made it.''

Aiyana sniffed and wiped her eyes. ''You thanked him.'' Her voice caught on a sob. ''You really thanked him. And you begged forgiveness. . . . Oh!''

Batty sighed. "So he did."

Dane frowned. "I wouldn't call it 'begging,' exactly."

"That's all right, sir. My forgiveness is granted. By the way, they're still shooting at us. And they'll be after us, too."

"I know."

Aiyana realized they weren't free yet. "We could steal a shuttle, if we're quick, and if you're able to send them on a false trail first."

"No problem. I can do anything."

Aiyana sighed. "I know."

Dane concealed the hovercraft behind a shuttle bay, then led Aiyana and Batty toward the nearest vehicle. Outside the bay, the Tseir hovercraft raced wildly, trying to regain his trail. "We don't have much time, Dane. They'll guess what we want."

"Over here." Dane forced open a shuttle ramp and helped Aiyana inside. He took the helm and fired life into the vehicle.

The shuttle roared into the sky, followed by the blasts of their pursuers' ships launching. "They're sending more after you, sir."

"Good. All the easier to lead them astray."

Dane guided the craft through the thin atmosphere, then slowed when they entered black space. "What are you doing? They'll catch us!" Aiyana gripped her seat and looked back from a rear window. "They're coming, Dane! And Tseir shuttles have armaments."

Dane checked the panel. "It appears we do, too. Unfortunately, the weapon unit is empty."

"Perfect. Well, I'd prefer to die here, in space, then endure what they had planned."

Dane angled his brow doubtfully. "You won't die, Aiyana Nidawi. I won't let you."

"Isn't that Keir, sir?"

"It is." Dane increased the speed of the craft, then angled toward Keir.

"They're getting closer, sir!"

Dane looked around. His gaze fixed on the distant, dark globe of Valenwood. The Midnight Moon. "They think we're headed for Keir. They'll be on us the minute we land. No . . . I've got a better idea."

Dane sped the craft back around the far side of Franconia out of sight of his pursuers, then aimed for Valenwood. Aiyana looked on in amazement.

"What are you doing? We can't go there!"

"Why not?"

She hesitated. "It's lifeless. What will we do on Valenwood?"

"We'll rest, eat . . . talk. Then we'll return to Keir and enlist your crazy former mate into saving my system from the Tseirs."

Aiyana exhaled a long breath. "Then you finally believe me."

"I do."

"Why?"

"They made you lie to me; they forced you to shoot at me."

"I'm glad you realize that." Aiyana hesitated. "What does that prove?"

"They had to use persuasion, Aiyana. I assume they threatened my life. Yet they didn't want to kill me. The only plausible explanation is that you're right about their plans for Candor."

Batty hopped to Dane's shoulder. "Don't follow, sir."

"Also, the Tseirs are under no threat from the Ellowans. True, you've been an irritation to them, but hardly a threat. Certainly not one they couldn't handle."

Aiyana's brow furrowed. "I don't follow, either."

"Clones, Aiyana."

Aiyana and Batty looked at each other. "Sir?" They spoke at once.

"The Tseirs are clones." Dane glanced at Aiyana and Batty, baffled by their confusion.

"Clones? Do you mean . . ." Aiyana paused. "What do you mean?"

"I mean they're copies. Not machinery, you understand. I assume at one time in their history, they were genuine humanoids. But they don't reproduce as we do. It's probably done in a cloning unit."

Aiyana sat back in her seat and stared at Dane in utter astonishment. "Clones?"

Batty chirped excitedly and hopped up and down on Dane's shoulder. "That explains the Tseir-allied Keiroits, doesn't it, sir? They're clones, too."

"That seems a reasonable assumption. Rurthgar told you they don't mate."

Aiyana's mouth remained open. "Clones?"

"Yes, Aiyana. You have a hard time with this, I see. But it really was obvious from the beginning."

"Clones?"

Dane laughed and patted her knee. "That explains their lust, which produces nothing. By this time, those copies are probably infertile."

"Is that why they suck life from us?"

"Exactly. I came a little too close to that facet for comfort."

Aiyana frowned. "So Galya told me."

"I was concerned that they'd grab at my . . . male portions, and find a lot less than they were looking for."

"You weren't aroused?"

Dane grimaced. "No." He eyed her in a condescending manner. "I'm not a machine, Aiyana. It's not as easy as pushing a button. A man's arousal is a sensitive thing. Entwined with his heart and soul and imagination.'' He sat back in his seat, looking both thoughtful and smug. ''An arousal is one of the great wonders of the universe.''

Batty coughed. ''Maybe I should take a nap in the gear, sir.''

''Gear . . . What do we have for gear, Batty?''

''Your pack is all, sir. And you've got that rifle. And the Rurthgar explosive strips.''

Aiyana studied Dane's expression as he contemplated their assets. ''Are you going to use the strips, Dane?''

''I'm not entirely sure. But the key to survival is adaptability, Aiyana. We use what we've got.''

Chapter Nine

"Wake up, love. We're preparing to land."

Dane touched Aiyana's hand and she jerked in her seat. He pointed to the viewport as Valenwood filled the screen. Half the globe looked dark.

"We'll land just before the nightline. That way, in case any Tseirs were able to track us, they'll have to start on the far side of the planet. Gives us time. Any particular suggestions for landing areas?"

"I can't tell from here." Aiyana studied the distant landscape. "That's odd. There are clouds. Valenwood shouldn't have clouds."

"Why not?"

"Well, after the destruction, the atmosphere thinned into a poisonous layer. There were no clouds."

"That was four hundred years ago, Aiyana. Ecosystems seek balance. Thorwal endured a sudden ice age, thanks to a miscreant comet. But the planetary systems did finally balance, if a little on the cold side."

"If Ariana was right, a lot on the cold side. I wonder how Valenwood has balanced?"

Dane watched as Aiyana's face knitted thoughtfully. A strange chill centered inside him. He had found only half the truth on Franconia. He had solved the mystery of the Tseirs, but the secret of Valenwood still eluded him.

"We'll soon learn."

"I suggest you land near the equator. Our largest city was there, and should still have flat surfaces for landing."

Dane nodded. "As you wish, my love."

Dane lowered the craft toward the surface of Valenwood. He saw long, winding rivers that stretched from one pole toward the equator. He saw an inland sea, and a large ocean below the equator. Many islands dotted the water.

"Even the planet is artistic."

"It is." Aiyana sighed, her expression wistful. "And it's not uniform, either. The Ellowan cities of the desert are similar to the old buildings on Franconia, made of hardened clay, in unique shapes. In the forest, our earliest ancestors lived in thatched homes, or even in the trees, just as we live in Valendir.

"By the sea, the Ellowans constructed perhaps the most beautiful city of all. White tile, with mosaic patterns, built on the edge of the water, extending over it. They crafted ships and sailed across the sea to the islands, long ago. Later, they used the obsidian craft to fly there."

"It sounds . . . like paradise."

"It was."

Dane guided the craft toward the ocean's edge. Far below, he saw scattered ruins. Light glistened off white, perhaps the remnant of the tiled city.

Aiyana's face changed as they drew near. Dane saw her sorrow; he felt it. She averted her eyes and looked out across the blue ocean. "It might be wiser to land elsewhere, Dane.

The City of Tile was our most populous region. The Tseirs would search there first."

Dane knew that she battled emotion. But Valenwood had been gone for centuries. Why was her pain at the sight of its destruction so bitterly intense?

"The desert is just beyond, slightly to the northeast. The forest is probably gone."

"There appears to be some green returning to your world, Aiyana. And the atmosphere is thin, but the shuttle controls indicate pure air. It might be that Valenwood will be inhabitable again. Arnoth's band might prefer life here to the cold climate of Keir."

Aiyana's eyes glistened with tears. "The Ellowans will never return to Valenwood. It is a giant, endless graveyard to us. So many faces that we remember, gone forever."

Dane watched her, and his heart ached. He was beginning to understand the Ellowan mystery. Maybe he had always known.

"I see a crop of hills there below. The desert stretches beyond. This might be the best area for landing."

Aiyana swallowed, then nodded. "Yes. Obsidian was found in those hills, ages ago."

"And the ships constructed of that substance are still in use today."

"They will exist forever. They are strong."

"Like the Ellowans, Aiyana. Like you."

Dane concealed the shuttle behind a large, arched rock formation, then pulled out his pack. He gave a wafer to Aiyana, then handed another to Batty.

"The whole thing, sir?"

"The whole thing. And if you desire another, good rodent, I will see that you get one."

Aiyana took a bite of her wafer and drank from Dane's flask. "I owe you, both of you, my life."

Dane smiled. "Think nothing of it. You saved me once, Aiyana. I promised that I would do the same for you."

"Dane Calydon, you gave me life in Valendir. Didn't you know?"

Dane studied her small face. The mists that concealed the secret of the Ellowans slowly lifted. Aiyana averted her eyes, looking nervous. He guessed she feared his reaction to the truth.

"So . . . what happened while I was imprisoned? How did you manage to mislead the Tseirs into thinking you'd left?"

"Simple enough. I sent their flightship on automatic pilot through the wormhole, then took a shuttle back to Franconia. Batty had been keeping an eye on you."

Aiyana turned to Batty and patted him fondly. "Were you, Batty? I am grateful. I heard a guard say he'd heard something. Was that you?"

Batty puffed with pride. "It was. Afraid I coughed a little. Thirsty . . ." Batty eyed the flask and Aiyana held it to his small lips. He swallowed, dribbling water over his cheeks.

Dane shook his head, but he smiled at the rodent's new hero status.

Aiyana peeked up at him. She seemed a little shy. "How did you convince the Tseirs to trust you? Galya seemed quite sure you were under their control."

"That was simple, too. I agreed with their assessment of your 'threat.' I agreed with everything."

Aiyana's eyes widened. "Not . . . ?"

"No, not that. I did have them eating out of my hand, though." Dane grinned. "Incidentally, should you ever hear information to the contrary, I don't have a mate and children on Thorwal."

"What?"

"Had to convince them mating wasn't a serious concern to Thorwalians."

"Oh." Aiyana sighed and shook her head. "How did you keep them from . . ."

"That was close, too. I built them up over my stress in the heat, then collapsed before Rattan could strip off any more of her attire."

"How much did she take off before you collapsed?"

Dane grimaced. "You don't want to know."

"Probably not. Are you sure they didn't fondle you after you collapsed?"

Dane hesitated and Aiyana's eyes widened into fierce pools. "Dane!"

"Well, I couldn't do much about it, could I? I was pretending to be unconscious. I suppose they groped my 'admirably formed buttocks.' "

"Nothing else?"

"Gave that a squeeze, too."

"Dane! Oh!" Aiyana clenched her fists. "I shall return and obliterate them!"

"Lucky thing they considered me out cold. Otherwise I'd have had some explaining to do over my lack of arousal."

"Well, that's something. Good." Aiyana's frown subsided. "So you impersonated a guard. . . ."

"I learned from the expert. You. Unfortunately, I didn't get back to Franconia before morning. I intended to incapacitate your guards, and slip away with you before anyone noticed. But by the time I arrived at the embassy, Batty told me they were already bargaining for the sport of you."

"They are truly evil. Is that because they're clones?"

Dane laughed. "I don't know. I haven't known any clones. But I'd say that if a race clones over and over, as the Tseirs must have done, they must lose something that can't be regained. They appear to seek out more and more violent pleasures."

"And more violent conquests of other systems. Galya

says they have a homeworld. I shudder to think what damage they've caused in the galaxy."

"One system at a time, my love. For now, we need to find a way to protect Candor."

Dane lowered the shuttle ramp and checked the air. "Seems clean, Aiyana." He looked out across the desert. The sun faded over the ocean, over the remnants of the tiled city. "It truly is beautiful here."

Aiyana joined him, her face taut with emotion as she looked out at her ancient land. "Once, this world was a garden. The desert bloomed with life. Multitudes of creatures lived here. Bright red and green reptiles, giant pink birds that mimicked human speech. Fish flew over the water, birds dove. Amber whales sang. In the forest, there were deer and winged sheep."

"Any lingbats?"

"No such creatures, Batty. I'm sorry to say."

Dane took Aiyana's hand and they watched the sun set together. Batty perched wistfully on Dane's shoulder, and they fell silent.

Dane glanced down at her as she stared across the desert. "If only . . . If only I had fought . . ." Aiyana whispered the words, but Dane heard, and he knew.

"You have been here before, haven't you, Aiyana?"

She looked up at him. He saw everything in her eyes, and his heart ached with a pain he'd never known before. "I was born here."

Dane shook his head, denying what he already guessed. "That's impossible."

Aiyana looked back at the disappearing sun. Only a purple glow remained as it sank away. "Hakon was my grandfather."

Dane's breath caught sharply, but she didn't look at him. "Hakon lived four hundred years ago."

"Approximately. Closer to four hundred and fifty. But

still . . ." Aiyana glanced at him and she smiled. "I told you I was older than you."

Dane stared down at her, shocked. If she had lived so long, he must seem a child to her. "Four hundred years, Aiyana! How can this be? How could any race be that long-lived?"

"We're no longer-lived than Thorwalians. At least, I don't think so."

"We live at most a hundred and fifty years, woman. Not centuries."

Aiyana turned to face him. "I told you once that I was a ghost, that all Ellowans were ghosts."

"You're . . . dead?"

Aiyana laughed at his horrified expression. "Not exactly. You know that the Ellowans can heal each other. That art can also be modified to reverse the body's growth."

"Oh, thank you." Dane bowed his head. "You're not dead. Just . . . modified."

"Exactly."

"And Arnoth?"

"He's modified, too."

"I take it you modified each other."

"We did. At intervals, we perform a sacred ritual. It involves touching. . . ." Dane's eyes narrowed, and Aiyana laughed. She seemed different after speaking her hidden truth. Older, yet happier. Free. "Of the temple. So Arnoth has touched me, often, as I told you."

"As long as he kept his fingers to your temple only, that is an endurable image."

"I touched his, too."

Dane's lip curved, but he saw the pleasure she took in teasing him. Their dynamics hadn't changed; he'd just finally seen them for what they were. "The ritual, Aiyana. Is this how you've . . . prolonged yourselves?"

"It is, and also those Ellowans who wished to continue

the fight with us. The only survivors of Valenwood were those who had been off-planet at the time of the destruction."

The final truth dawned in his awareness. He wondered if, somehow, he'd known all along. "Aiyana . . . it was you. You and Arnoth. You were the pacifist ambassadors who convinced Hakon. . . ."

She looked away. "We were fools."

Dane stared at her as she stood in the fading sunlight. He had never seen anything more beautiful or more tragic. Tears filled his eyes; his throat tightened. He reached for her and drew her into his arms.

"You weren't fools, Aiyana. You did what you thought was right."

Tears glittered in her eyes, too. "If we hadn't convinced Hakon . . . He loved me, you see. He loved Arnoth. He gave us time, though he was adamant about destroying them. Elena agreed with him. She wanted to fight. Now both are dead—" Aiyana's voice broke, and she paused while she contained her emotion.

"The last words spoken between Arnoth and Elena were in anger. He has never forgiven himself."

"Oh . . ." Dane endured an intense wave of pain and sympathy for his dark-eyed nemesis. "But he saw her again. She went to Franconia with him."

"No, she came after. I've never known why, or how."

Dane held Aiyana close, her head against his shoulder. "The poor man. My sweet Aiyana . . . What can I do for you now?"

Aiyana drew back and looked at him. "You can give me back the Rurthgar strips and let me return to Franconia."

"No! Aiyana, that is madness. I won't give you up."

"I see no other way. The Tseirs will guess it was you who rescued me. They will waste no time preparing for an assault on your system. With the strips, I can create an explosion in their power core. It's kept on the far side of their planet. It would wreak havoc in their atmosphere, and stop them from attacking you."

"For how long?"

"Not forever, I know. But for a while."

"Aiyana, these aren't the only Tseirs. I saw little evidence of a full fleet. It's my guess that they rely on a much larger fleet, somewhere beyond this system. There must be a better way."

"Such as what?"

Dane hesitated. "I'm not sure. But I'll think of something."

"We don't have time."

"Sir!"

"What is it, Batty?"

"Thought I heard something, sir. Lots of somethings."

Aiyana's brow furrowed at the bat's alarm. "Nothing lives on Valenwood now, Batty."

"There's something, sir. Over there!"

Dane looked around. "Are you sure, Batty?"

"There's a lot of them, sir, and they're coming this way."

"A lot of what?"

Aiyana squinted as she surveyed the barren landscape. "It's not that dark, Batty. I don't see anything."

"They're disguised, but they're coming." Batty gulped. "Shall I defend you?"

"Stay put, Batty. What are they, can you tell?"

"Don't know, sir. They're all covered up, moving slowly, stealthily. Bent over, hunched. Creeping along. But they're all around us."

"There can't be anything alive on Valenwood. They must be Tseirs."

Dane squeezed Aiyana's shoulder. "Stay here." He eased into the shuttle, and seized his rifle.

A loud, tremulous yell erupted from the hills. From all

sides, cloaked and covered humans raced toward them, bearing spears. ''Tseirs don't wield spears, Aiyana. What's going on?''

''Sir! Shouldn't we get back into the shuttle?''

''Good idea.'' Dane pushed Aiyana toward the shuttle, but the strange warriors appeared out of nowhere, cutting them off from the vessel. ''They must have sent a few in first. Even Batty missed them.''

Aiyana moved close beside Dane. ''Are you going to shoot?''

''I have no idea.''

The hordes of warriors surrounded them, still issuing the wailing war cry. Then they fell deadly silent as their circle closed in around Dane and Aiyana. They wore earth-colored cloaks, hooded, their faces concealed by cloth. When they stood upright, they were tall and slender.

Dane held up his rifle, then tossed it to the ground well in front of him. Aiyana gripped his arm. ''What are you doing? That was our only weapon!''

''I know.''

One robed warrior stepped forward, a rough-hewn lance aimed at Dane's heart. The tip was obsidian. The warrior approached Dane until the pike touched his chest.

Dane didn't move. The warrior assessed him, then turned to Aiyana. For a long time, no one moved. ''Tseirs do not throw aside weapons. They shoot. Who are you? Not Tseirs.''

The warrior was female . . . and Ellowan. Aiyana stepped toward the woman. ''I am Aiyana Nidawi. This is Dane Calydon. He disguised himself as a Tseir guard to save me.''

''Nidawi is known. I am Nidawi also.'' The warrior pulled back her hood, and Aiyana gasped.

Dane stared in astonishment. Though her face was dirty, painted with odd streaks of red and blue, the warrior woman resembled his own sister more than Aiyana. Her hair was blond, but her face was finer-boned than that of a Thorwalian. Dane guessed Aiyana's sister had looked the same.

Aiyana clasped her hand over her breast. "You're Ellowan. . . . Dane, she is Ellowan. It can't be."

"Ellowan means 'People of the Elf Wood.' That is a term used by our ancestors. We are the Stone People now."

Aiyana touched the young woman's face. "You are so beautiful." Tears spilled to Aiyana's cheeks as the other Ellowans drew back their hoods.

The other warriors moved silently closer, watching her with bright, curious eyes. Many had blue and green eyes. A few even had blond hair like their leader.

They varied in age. Some were even younger than the leader. Some were aged and gray. Both males and females wore their hair loose, faces painted in individual style, with dark beads strung around their necks.

Aiyana fingered the girl's hair. "You really are Ellowan. How can that be?"

The young woman looked confused, but Dane smiled. "It appears some of your people survived, Aiyana. And left descendants." He glanced at the other warriors. "Many descendants."

Aiyana shook her head. "But I see Thorwalian blood. That's not possible. Hakon's descendants are all accounted for."

"Hakon? Hakon is the father of the Stone People."

Aiyana's breath caught and she leaned against Dane. "Hakon? You know of Hakon? He was my grandfather."

"I'd save that story, Aiyana. I don't think they can understand how you've managed to exist for four hundred years."

The young woman's brow angled. "If she is Nidawi, she used ritual."

Dane rolled his eyes. "I should have known. I suppose prolonging life is common."

"Quiet, Dane! It isn't common. It never was. It offers no joy. Intimacy, for instance, is impossible during the time. It is an infertile period."

"Do you mean Arnoth hasn't had sex in four hundred years?"

"Must you be so graphic? You will shock them."

Aiyana turned back to the woman. "He is also Thorwalian, like Hakon. They don't understand restraint."

Dane watched Aiyana in amazement. She had changed. She sounded almost . . . motherly. To appearances, they were the same age. But Aiyana treated the warrior like a child. She patted the young woman's cheek.

"What is your name, my dear?"

No, not motherly. Grandmotherly . . .

"I am Nidawi, too. Helayna Nidawi. I am the leader of the Stone People warriors."

"I see that." Aiyana spoke proudly. She glanced back at Dane. "Aren't they beautiful?"

Dane hesitated. "A little dirty."

Aiyana frowned reproachfully, then turned back to Helayna. "Dane is grumpy. Never mind him. How have you survived? We thought all Ellowans were destroyed when the Tseirs attacked Valenwood."

"Tseir . . ." Helayna's dirty face furrowed in displeasure.

"You know of them. They come to Valenwood still?"

"They come to take our black rock."

"Obsidian?"

"Yes. They take it, and leave. Sometimes . . ." Helayna paused to chuckle, and Dane decided she resembled Aiyana more than he first thought. "Sometimes they don't leave at all."

"Do they know you exist?"

"A few found out. But they never told the others."

"Can you be sure of that?"

Helayna fingered her spear. "I'm sure."

Dane assessed her spear. "What good is that primitive weapon against Tseir rifles?"

Helayna positioned the spear tip on Dane's chest. She pushed slightly, and he backed away. "It's sharp. Up close, it is very effective."

"It's more primitive than a Ravager battle-ax."

"When thrust through an opponent, the result is the same as a rifle blast."

Aiyana tapped Dane's shoulder. "She's right, you know."

Dane remained skeptical. "If you get that close . . ."

Helayna seemed pleased with herself. "We get as close as we wish, Man of Hakon."

"Dane."

"Man of Hakon *Dane*. You failed to notice our approach until we were upon you. Even your guardian missed our scouts." Helayna studied Batty, who looked puffed and proud. "What is this creature?"

"I am a lingbat. *Ling*bat. One of the larger specimens."

Dane resisted the impulse to correct the rodent's assertion. "And amazingly adept at piloting hovercraft."

Helayna accepted the lingbat's existence without question. Her lack of curiosity suggested a weak imagination to Dane. He wondered if Aiyana might be disappointed in her descendants. She stood beside him, hands clasped over her breast, tears in her eyes, smiling.

Dane guessed Helayna's flat nature hadn't bothered her, after all. Or maybe Aiyana saw only what she wanted to see. Finding her people alive must have been a shock. It might take a while to place them in perspective.

Helayna gazed up at the darkening sky. "Other ships follow yours."

Dane groaned. "Tseirs. Curses! They followed sooner than I expected."

Aiyana shook her fist. "We can't let them discover Helayna's Ellowans. We must leave."

"We'll be shot down before we reach the first clouds!"

"Can we hide the shuttle?"

"No time, Aiyana. They're coming through the clouds now."

Helayna seized Aiyana's arm. "We will hide you. But you must leave your sky ship."

Aiyana looked desperately at Dane. "We can't. Without it we'll never get off Valenwood!"

"Must you leave, Nidawi? This is your home."

"It was. But not anymore. The Tseirs destroyed my world. And I must stop them from destroying Dane's. If we can't leave Valenwood . . ."

Dane looked up at the sky. "We don't have a choice, Aiyana. We've got to get out of here. Now."

The Ellowans moved across the desert like hunters, bent forward as they ran. They ran faster than Dane expected. Helayna led them into the hills, then stopped. "The Tseirs won't see us now." She held up her hand, then looked carefully back at the shuttle.

"They didn't see us. See how they center their blasts on your craft?"

Dane looked around the corner and groaned. Tseir shuttles hovered above his craft, sending blasts of blue plasma into its hull. "It's going to explode, sir." Batty closed his eyes. "Going to be loud."

An immense boom shook the ground, and the shuttle erupted in blue-white flames. The Tseir craft elevated, remaining to shoot at any survivors. Dane shook his head and turned back behind the rocks.

"Wonderful! Perfect! We're stuck on a barren planet, among people the Ravagers would consider primitive. . . . Without a ship. Curses! Why did I land on Valenwood?"

Helayna's eyes narrowed. She fingered her spear. "You

issue many complaints, Man of Hakon Dane.''

Aiyana chuckled. ''That much is certain.''

Dane was furious. ''Now what? If I had time, and mobility, I would have found a way to stop the Tseirs. Perfect!''

''Don't worry, Dane. We'll find a way.''

Dane eyed Aiyana doubtfully. She spoke lightly, in a casual manner. He wondered if her senses were rattled. Dane watched the Tseir shuttles rise again into the sky and disappear.

''Well, at least they think we're dead now. That might make things easier for us in the long run.''

Helayna touched Aiyana's arm. ''You need a sky ship, Nidawi?''

''We do, very much.'' Aiyana paused. ''Do you know where to find one?''

''I know where to find many. The Tseirs that came for our black rock, they left ships. We didn't leave them in the open, because other Tseirs might wonder what happened to their people.''

Dane eyed the young warrior. ''What did you do with them? I find it hard to imagine you could pilot a spacecraft.''

''We took them apart and brought them to the Stone City.''

''Took them apart? How 'apart'?''

''What we could separate, we separated. Some parts are one piece. It took many warriors to move those parts.''

Aiyana glanced up at Dane, her brow knitted doubtfully. ''We'd have to put one together.''

''No trouble.''

''Are you sure?''

''I can do anything.''

Helayna looked at Aiyana, her dirty face knitted in doubt. ''He is very sure of himself, isn't he?''

Aiyana sighed. ''He is.''

Her small jaw was set hard, her expression determined. Dane watched her, knowing what she was thinking. If he couldn't come up with a better idea, Aiyana would attempt to blow up the Franconian power core. Learning her race survived, after all, might be the final provocation.

He had to think fast. "Show us to the shuttle parts, Helayna. We have no time to lose."

Helayna led her group along the hillside. Night deepened around them. Aiyana didn't speak. She seemed overwhelmed with emotion. Dane imagined returning to Thorwal, four hundred years after its destruction, and finding that his people had survived. No wonder she couldn't talk.

Dane held her hand as they walked. The other Ellowans remained silent, moving without sound. Stealth seemed inherent to their nature, to their survival.

Helayna stopped and the other Ellowans gathered around her. "Here is the entrance to our world."

Dane looked around. They stood by a sheer cliff wall. "What entrance?"

Aiyana jabbed him in the ribs. "Hush . . . She will tell us."

"Nidawi is trusted. But these entrances are secret. You, Man of Hakon Dane, must speak vow before entering."

Dane set his jaw, feeling unusually stubborn. "Just who do you think I'm going to tell?"

"You are stubborn, so it pleases me. Speak the vow, or you will remain out here tonight."

Aiyana repressed a smile, but Dane glared.

Helayna twisted her spear back and forth, idly. "It would be a shame if the sand-scorpions found you alone at night."

Dane drew an impatient breath. "What's the cursed vow?"

"You acknowledge Stone People's mastery, and will keep this entrance secret forever after."

"Fine."

Dane's brief reply wasn't enough. Helayna waited for more. Dane clenched his teeth. "I acknowledge your mastery, and won't tell anyone ever, as long as I live and the sun burns in the sky. Does that suffice?"

"Adequate." Helayna turned to the wall while Dane eyed her with growing dislike.

"Irritating woman."

Aiyana sighed happily. "She takes pleasure in life."

"In tormenting me."

"That, too."

"Obnoxiousness comes naturally to your people, Aiyana. She's nearly as infuriating as Arnoth."

Aiyana looked up at him, her eyes wide. A small smile curved her lips. "She is, isn't she?"

"That's not a compliment, woman. Those with temperaments such as Arnoth's and that of this warrior-maiden-fiend quite often end up strangled."

"Arnoth has lived nearly four hundred years without being strangled by anyone."

"Only because I left Valendir before I had the chance. . . ."

Helayna touched tiny indentations on the cliff wall, and a doorway opened. "This way."

Dane studied the passage as he entered. "Clever. It opens inward, and leaves no trace. Well done."

The door closed behind them, leaving them standing in total darkness.

Batty whistled. "Beautiful tunnel, isn't it, sir?"

"Only for those with lingbat eyes."

"Makes me pine for home, sir."

Helayna lit a small torch and held it to the wall. It puffed to life, firing a long trail of torches down the tunnel.

Aiyana beamed with pride. "It's beautiful!"

Dane wondered if she'd lost her mind. "It's a tunnel,

Aiyana. I see no doors, no caverns, no halls. Nerotania on Candor was beautiful. This is a mine.''

Helayna nodded. ''It was modeled after the old mines, yes. This is an outer entrance. We must travel far to reach the Stone Caverns.''

Dane sighed. ''Walking?''

''Well, you must walk to the transports, yes. Perhaps you are unused to walking, Man of Hakon Dane?''

''Dane. Just Dane . . . And I have made the physical mastery of my body a top priority in life.''

Helayna glanced at Aiyana as if to be certain Dane was serious. ''Indeed. I find that odd. You are strong by choice. We are strong from necessity.'' Helayna shook her head and turned away. She headed down the tunnel and the others followed.

Dane muttered under his breath as he walked beside Aiyana. ''I don't know about these descendants of yours, woman. It wouldn't surprise me if they're bringing us to a feast . . . and we're the feast.''

''My descendants aren't cannibals.''

''Don't speak too soon.''

The tunnel was long, as Helayna said, but downhill. Aiyana looked on in wonder, still shocked to be among her own people. Helayna brought them to a mine shaft and indicated small, black carts, each attached to each other.

''These make the journey down easier. Get in.''

Aiyana climbed into a cart beside Helayna. Dane and Batty followed, though Dane looked intensely suspicious. ''It is wisest to hold on, Nidawi and Dane.''

Aiyana gripped the cart's side, and Helayna released a lever. The cart plummeted downward. ''Sir! My ears . . .''

Aiyana glanced at Batty. His ears were plastered back, and he clung to Dane's shoulder. Dane's hair flew straight back, too. Aiyana laughed. ''You look just alike.''

Dane glared and started to speak, but the cart whipped around a corner, and he gasped instead.

The cart dropped down again, seemingly over a cliff, then angled left. It reached a flat surface, then slowed. It ground to a halt, stopping the carts behind as well. Helayna hopped out, unaffected by the dramatic ride.

Aiyana hopped out, too, but Dane clenched his teeth. "The sand-scorpions would have been more enjoyable. Probably more accommodating, too."

Helayna looked at Aiyana. "You spoke truly, Nidawi. He is grumpy."

Aiyana took Dane's hand. "But he's beautiful, and very brave."

The mine shaft opened to a large, rough hall. Aiyana heard many voices, pleasant conversation, sounds of work. She followed Helayna into the hall, staring spellbound at the vast room.

"I have brought you to the outer hall of the Stone City. You are welcome here, Nidawi." Helayna paused. "And your Dane."

Aiyana couldn't speak. Ellowans moved through the hall, pausing to nod to her, then hurrying on. Children played, or helped the older Ellowans. A small boy stole a hammer from an elderly Ellowan, then darted around a corner.

Helayna sighed. "Seraphin will be a warrior, I suspect." She pointed to an arched gateway. "I will take you to the inner hall. There we will give you sleeping chambers, and you may rest. Tonight we will feast in your honor."

Dane looked impatient. "We can't stay here long, Helayna. Where are the shuttle parts?"

"They are stored in another outer hall, beyond the inner hall, beyond Hakon's Tomb."

Aiyana's face drained of blood, her eyes widening with shock. "Hakon's Tomb?"

"It is a sacred place of ritual. We do him honor there."

Dane nodded as if this clarified something. "Of course. These tunnels and caverns are similar to those on Thorwal. Used for mining, even growing food. Mushrooms in particular. Hakon's doing, I suppose?"

"Hakon started the Stone City."

Aiyana caught her breath, tears flooding her eyes. "He survived. . . . My grandfather survived."

Helayna studied Aiyana's face. "He was a great man. He was my ancestor also."

"He was?" Aiyana's emotion altered. "That's not possible. He would never have taken another mate."

"His mate was called Ariana. She was Nidawi."

Aiyana closed her eyes and clenched her fists at her sides. "Ariana survived, too?"

"Her tomb is beside Hakon's."

Aiyana looked at Helayna, seeking in her young face a memory of Hakon, of Ariana—of the life she knew, and believed forever gone. "They had another child?"

"They had a son. He was Karanoth, and he was leader after Hakon. His children, and their children, are the Nidawi clan of the Stone People."

"Was he prince? Do you have a priestess?"

These terms appeared to confuse Helayna. "We have leaders, leaders of each clan. Each clan offers builders and warriors. Some few are breeders."

Aiyana's mouth dropped. "Breeders?"

"The Stone People's world is not so big, Nidawi. Only when an old one passes is a young one brought forth."

Dane patted Aiyana's shoulder. "It makes sense. There are limits to underground building."

"Why don't you live above ground?"

"We hide, and we survive. If we were to exist in the upper world, we would be killed."

Aiyana's brow knitted. "The Tseirs keep you from returning. Their evil never ends."

"The need for survival has become ritual to them, Aiyana. Although maybe they're right. I don't think the Tseirs would allow the Ellowans to flourish again."

"No, they probably wouldn't."

The halls of the Stone City stretched endlessly, heading off in every direction, opening to feasting halls, to storage units, to living areas. Despite the enclosed surroundings, the Ellowans they encountered seemed happy, content in their underground life.

Aiyana took special pleasure in watching the children. Many wore paint on their small faces, emulating their heroic warriors. Some sat thoughtfully, building toys. Several children had pale blond hair. Hakon's blood still ran strong in her people.

Aiyana watched the children play. Helayna watched, too. "They are strong and brave. Some walk in Hakon's image."

"I see that." Aiyana's voice quavered.

"You are in haste, Nidawi. But perhaps you would like to visit Hakon's Tomb."

Aiyana glanced up at Dane. He smiled gently. "We have time, love."

Aiyana nodded, but she couldn't speak. She followed Helayna into a dark chamber. Helayna lit a row of torches, which blazed into sudden life.

The ceiling was higher here than in the outer halls, and it glowed with ancient tiles. Wide, low stairs led to a black case. Hakon's Tomb. Aiyana walked alone up the stairs, while Dane and Helayna waited below.

Her breath came quickly, raggedly as she approached the tomb. It was long, to accommodate a tall man's height. Aiyana reached her shaking hand and touched the smooth surface. "Grandfather . . . I love you so."

Aiyana bent and kissed the tomb, her tears dropping to form tiny circles on the black surface. "I'm sorry I didn't listen; I'm sorry we didn't fight as you told us. You were right."

Aiyana straightened. Behind his tomb was another, smaller, but adorned with carved images—dancing figures, an Ellowan harp. Aiyana closed her eyes, and saw her beautiful grandmother, her deft fingers plucking the strings while she sang to Hakon.

"You had another baby. I wish I had known him. He must have made you very happy. And he had children, and they are so strong and so beautiful. Oh, but I miss you so."

Aiyana brushed her tears away, but more followed. "I miss you so."

A firm, gentle hand touched her shoulder. Dane wrapped his arm around her and she cried against his chest. "They lived. Dane, I can't believe it. Arnoth and I came back after we escaped, and there were so many dead. Nothing could have survived in the atmosphere. We couldn't leave the ship, because the air was poisonous. But they lived somehow."

Dane ran his fingers through her tangled hair. "Quite a few must have survived the blast. Perhaps Helayna can tell us how."

Aiyana laid her palm on Ariana's tomb, a gentle farewell. Then she turned away. Helayna waited at the bottom of the stairs. No emotion showed in her face, just pride and courage. Aiyana took her hand. "Thank you, Helayna. It means so much to me to know they survived. To see where they lie."

"They lie in honor."

Aiyana nodded. "They do."

"Hakon led my ancestors in courage. We have not failed him."

"I see that. Are there records of how Hakon managed to save so many of his people?"

"It is said that he foresaw the Tseir attack, but too late to ensure mass survival. The Ellowans of the forest all perished, as did many in the City of Tile. Hakon ordered them into the mines, but most failed to reach their destination."

Aiyana closed her eyes, remembering the corpses strewn across the desert, shattered hovercraft everywhere.

"How did they survive the poisoned air? And the water must have been undrinkable, too."

"The mines had filters that cleaned the air. Hakon improved those air filters, and designed wells that purified the water also." Helayna paused. "Water still is precious to us."

Dane's brow tilted. "Apparently you don't use it much for washing."

"Only the breeders wash frequently. But the warriors wash at every cycle."

Dane bent to Aiyana. "Just how often is a cycle?"

Aiyana hesitated. "Approximately every six weeks."

Dane nodded. "I guessed as much. Your water must be pure now, Helayna. Perhaps you could make more liberal use of it."

This suggestion didn't appeal to Helayna. "I see no need. Washing removes the paint. A warrior needs to blend with the ground."

"By wearing it?"

"Yes."

Helayna removed her cape and Dane's eyes widened. The warm underground required little clothing. Helayna's breasts were covered with an earth-colored fabric, but her midriff was bare. The same fabric covered her hips, but reached no farther than her thighs.

Aiyana chuckled. "I assume you have no complaints about their clothing?"

"None in particular. Perhaps you, my dear, would feel comfortable dressed thus."

"How do you think I dressed in Valenwood?"

"Like that?"

"Similarly."

Dane sighed. "I'm sorry I missed it."

Helayna eyed them doubtfully, as if she didn't understand their interaction. "You would learn more of the Stone People in Hakon's book."

"His book?"

"Hakon recorded the fall of Valenwood, but my people understand little of his script."

"If it's written in Thorwalian runes, I should be able to decipher it."

Aiyana turned to Dane, her eyes wide with hope. "You can read my grandfather's book?" She paused, biting her lip. "Do we have time?"

Dane hesitated. "We need to assemble a shuttle, love. If we can't secure the future, the past has no meaning." He turned to Helayna. "Can you give us Hakon's book?"

"I will ask our old ones, who keep our records, and I believe they will surrender the book to you. I hope one day you will return it."

Aiyana nodded. "If I survive, I will. Thank you, Helayna. You can't know what it means to know you exist. And to another, one I love, the value may be infinite."

Helayna left to consult with the old ones, but Dane took Aiyana's hand. "You're thinking of Arnoth, aren't you?"

"I am. As much as I've blamed myself, he has blamed himself more. We have to return to Keir to tell him about these people. It may give him some comfort."

Aiyana's tears dried. She felt strong again. Alive. Anything was possible. Even for Arnoth. "If we phrase it just so, it may give him a lot more than that. It may give him a reason to live."

* * *

Aiyana stood amidst heaps of control circuits and obsidian siding, disengaged panels and speed levers. "This is impossible. It would take years. Dane, I'm no technician."

Dane kissed her cheek. "Ah, but fortunately, I am."

"Can you make sense of this rubble?"

"Rubble, my love, is just parts of the whole. Envision the whole, each part to its own device, and we'll soon have a workable shuttle."

"Assuming you can put one together, how will we get it out of here?"

Helayna overheard the question. "The east gateway is large enough for the sky ship. The distance is short from here to there."

Dane rummaged through the shuttle parts. "I could use assistants, Helayna. You mentioned builders."

"We have craftsmen. They are builders. They keep the water clean, the air free of poison. They fix and maintain and build more. But I will request their assistance."

Helayna left the storage chamber, and Dane took Aiyana's hand. "They're not what you remembered, are they?"

"I don't know. . . . The old customs have changed, but life was sweet and easy for us then. But they still value freedom. Did you notice that even though she is leader, Helayna never gives orders? She said she would 'request' the builders' assistance. My people are still good."

Dane considered this. "Come to think of it, I didn't hear Arnoth giving many orders, either."

"He never had to. Our people valued his word. Rurthgar's Keiroits came to value it, also."

Dane returned to his task, sorting through shuttle parts. Aiyana watched, unsure how to help. "What will the Tseirs do now? Will they believe we died?"

"Maybe. But that poses an even greater problem for

them. If I don't return to Candor, it will awaken suspicions."

"They'll probably say we killed you."

"Kostbera won't take their word for it. She'll send another ambassador. Candorians never act in haste."

"The Tseirs hate the unknown, Dane. The situation has gone beyond their control."

Dane straightened, his expression thoughtful. Then he smiled, very slowly, until his cheeks dimpled. Aiyana's heart took an odd little leap at the sight.

"What are you thinking, Dane Calydon?"

"There's an old saying on Thorwal: 'There's more than one way to skin a wortpig.' Ever heard it?"

Aiyana grimaced. "No, but it isn't an appealing image."

"No, my sister forbade me to ever repeat it again. She was sensitive about wortpigs."

"I thought they were food. Hakon often mentioned wortpig stew."

Dane stood up, laughing. Aiyana wondered what had brightened his mood. He stooped and kissed her forehead. "When you meet Nisa, don't mention Hakon's taste for wortpigs. She would not be amused."

By morning, a fully assembled, working shuttle sat by the eastern gateway of the Stone City. Tired builders milled around it, patting its surface, admiring Dane's handiwork. From the assorted pieces, Dane had assembled a telescope, and set Helayna's warriors on a watch in the hills.

Aiyana stood beside him, exhausted, but feeling strong. The Ellowans were an intelligent race, swift to learn. Dane had found instructing them easy, and did little more than supervise the reconstruction of the vessel.

"What do you have Helayna watching for?"

"It's my guess that the Tseirs are expecting reinforcements from their homeworld. I don't want to leave Valenwood while there's a chance of being spotted."

"I don't understand. I thought we were going to Keir to get Arnoth's flightship, then head through the wormhole to warn the Candorians."

Dane's brow angled doubtfully. "That plan had many flaws, Aiyana. For one thing, our passage through the wormhole would be noted. An attack would soon follow. I don't know how much power the Tseirs manage. Maybe Candor couldn't resist an attack."

"So what are we going to do?" Aiyana resisted panic, but it wasn't easy. Dane remained so calm, confident.

"We're going to Keir, of course. Unfortunately, I need your infuriating former mate to assist me in the operation of the flightship. I could also use Rurthgar's assistance."

"What about me, sir?"

"I couldn't possibly succeed without your assistance, good rodent."

"Proud to be of service, sir!"

"Carob will be proud, also."

Batty looked wistful. "I hope so, sir. My sire always said my size would be a hindrance, but my courage would see me through. I thought he was making that part up to make me feel better."

"Carob knew, Batty. You're as brave as they come."

"Still wish I was bigger, sir."

"She Who Leaps High might be intimidated by a large rodent. I'm sure she prefers your size to that of a brawny lingbat."

"Now, that is a truism, sir. She Who Leaps High considered me immense."

Helayna returned from the upper world alone. She approached Dane, looking disgruntled. "Watching your telescope is tedious, Hakon Dane. I have left another to the task for a while."

"I take it you saw nothing."

"No. Franconia turns in the sky, golden, then half dark, then dark. But I saw no streaks of light. That is what you told me to look for, yes?"

"Many streaks of light. So you didn't see anything? Good. Their fleet isn't assembled yet."

Aiyana relaxed. "Maybe we can eat, then. And rest."

"A good idea, my sweet. Once Helayna's scouts spot the fleet, we'll need to work fast. We might as well be rested."

A twinkle in Dane's blue eyes indicated he had more on his mind than rest. Aiyana's stomach fluttered.

Helayna looked between them. "I take it you are breeders."

Aiyana blushed. "We are mates." She peeked up at Dane. "Aren't we?"

"I believe I vowed my eternal love, yes."

Helayna shook her head. "A shame. You would have made fine warriors."

"Unfortunately for the Tseirs, Aiyana has been a fine warrior for a long time."

Aiyana recognized Helayna's confusion. "In our worlds, people can be both, my dear."

Helayna remained skeptical. "I did not choose to be a breeder. They spend much time gazing into each other's eyes, as you do. They sleep overlate, and their emotions run too high. Males are good companions, but I can't imagine having one around all the time, especially not in the same bed."

Aiyana patted Helayna's arm. "Maybe you'll find someone one day who will change your mind."

"I know every male in the Stone City. None has changed my mind so far."

"There are other men, Helayna. Many Ellowans live on Keir. Perhaps they will return here, after all. Maybe they can show you how life was when the Ellowans lived above ground."

"Can they fight?"

"Arnoth is the best fighter I've ever known." Aiyana noticed Dane's dark expression, and she smiled. "Though Dane is a better shot with the rifle. But Arnoth battled the leader of the Keiroits, green, scaly creatures with terrible jaws, and he won. Then they became our allies."

"That is impressive. I would like to battle green, scaly creatures, too."

Aiyana smiled innocently as Helayna walked away.

Dane shook his head, but he was smiling. "You certainly built him up to heroic proportions."

"I don't know what you mean. Arnoth has always been heroic."

"Umm."

Aiyana peeked up at Dane, and her innocent expression faded into a devious smile. "I thought Helayna might enjoy hearing some of our deeds, since we're a kindred race."

"Helayna seemed more interested in fighting Keiroits than in seducing Arnoth. Not that I blame her, of course."

"You be still, Dane Calydon. The world didn't end, and I can plan, and hope, and want, can't I?"

"You can."

"Good. Because there's something I want now."

"And what would that be, my beloved?"

"I want you."

Dane lay alone in an Ellowan sleeping chamber. Naked. Helayna had given him the use of a room, but Aiyana hadn't appeared. Dane frowned. His hands folded on his chest, then unfolded. He sat up.

"Where is that woman?" Dane lay back down, annoyed. "Probably launched into conversation with her 'descendants' and forgot me."

Dane adjusted his position. "I'll teach you not to make me wait, woman!" Dane considered how. He pictured her soft, supple body bent to his will. He hardened at the image.

"I'll make her wait." He drummed his fingers on his hard chest. He didn't want to wait. "There must be a better way."

Dane sat up again, and looked toward the door. The Ellowan sleeping chambers were built around central halls, but they were well sealed. Hakon's touch, no doubt. Apparently technical skill had been inherent even in the Ravagers.

Dane glanced around the small room. There was only one bed, low and wide. Covered by thin, handwoven blankets.

The door was arched, carved with strangely sensual yet abstract figures. Even here, dwelling in exile, underground, the Ellowans had spent time on sensual detail. He flopped back down in bed.

The door swung open, and a hooded woman appeared. Dane gulped. Her face was covered with a cloth. "Helayna?" She closed the door behind her, but she didn't speak. No, it couldn't be Helayna. This veiled female wasn't tall enough.

Also, she had no spear. He had never seen Helayna without her spear, and doubted the warrior would easily relinquish it. The woman just watched him from beneath her veil. Then she moved toward him. There was no mistaking her intentions.

"I think you may have the wrong room."

A soft laugh was the only response. Dane noticed his burgeoning arousal. *Curses!* The woman would misunderstand his reaction. He lurched upright and adjusted the sheets over himself.

"Just waiting here for my mate." Dane tried to sound casual. "She'll be here any moment. We're quite weary. Exhausted."

She laughed again, then knelt beside his bed. Dane wondered if she intended some odd Ellowan custom such as foot washing. "That's not necessary. . . ."

She pushed back his blanket, seized his erect staff, and took it into her mouth. He froze, shocked beyond motion. Her little tongue swirled over the tip; she suckled. . . .

"Help!" Dane leaped off the bed, naked in the warm light. His staff glistened with her mouth's soft moisture. His pulse raced to dizzying heights.

The woman laughed—a delighted, wicked laugh. Dane stared, aghast, his heart pounding. Then she sank to her knees in front of him, and seized his staff again. She massaged him fiercely, kneading, squeezing, her grip strong.

"Stop that!" His voice shook; his knees quaked. She laughed, soft and low, then touched her small, pink tongue to the underside of his shaft, running upward, over the tip. Dane nearly crumpled.

No woman had such nerve. Except one. He pulled back her hood and tore away her veil.

"I should have known. You are a demon, woman."

Aiyana peered up at him, her eyelids half-closed. "I think you liked it."

"I think you're right."

She fingered the blunt tip of his arousal idly. Dane quivered. She kissed him gently, then sat back. She pulled off the cape and it sank to the floor behind her. She wore the revealing, glorious attire that had graced Helayna's body.

Dane caught his breath at the sight. "I'm pleased you chose only the clothing, and not the dirt."

Aiyana ran her hand along Dane's hip, down his thigh. "I think I have made up for all your teasing, Thorwalian. I like playing with you. It is satisfying."

"You have natural ability. Your combining shock and pure, unadulterated lust . . . Well done."

"And if the woman beneath the cape had been someone else?"

"We'll never know, will we?"

"I think you would have screamed 'Help' again, and fled."

Dane laughed. "You may be right."

Dane scooped Aiyana into his arms and carried her back to the bed. He held her for a moment, then kissed her mouth. "I don't know what will happen, Aiyana. I don't know if we'll succeed or fail. But tonight, I'm going to give you something that will last through all eternity."

Aiyana's eyes widened, but Dane didn't let her speak. He lowered his mouth to hers, delving between her lips with his tongue. He placed her gently on the bed. His gaze traveled her slender body slowly, taking pleasure in each subtle curve, each hidden morsel.

The sight was tempting, teasing to his eye—what he saw, and what he didn't see. "You are a delectable temptation, my love. Sweet . . ."

Dane licked his lips and her green eyes darkened. He slid his finger beneath her breast-covering, just grazing the small peak. It hardened against the fabric, and he smiled. "You respond well." He bent and ran his lips over the concealed bud.

The fabric wrapped over one shoulder. Dane kissed her bare flesh, making small circles over her breast with his palm. He tasted her skin, murmuring softly, "You know, you have a sweet taste, Aiyana Nidawi."

"Do I?" She sounded breathless. Dane swept his tongue along her inner arm.

"Mmm." His thoughts transformed into erotic bliss and he gave himself over to her pleasure.

Aiyana quivered beneath Dane's skilled touch. He kissed her taut stomach, tasting her flesh. "You're sweet here, too." He kissed her navel, lower. Then he ran his hand down her leg. He raised it and kissed the inside of her calf muscle. Then her ankle. He kissed her toes and she giggled.

"Don't tell me my toes taste sweet, Thorwalian."

Dane nipped at her toes. "Such pleasing little toes."

Aiyana laughed again. "Stop that! You're tickling me."

"Am I?"

He was a demon—far worse than she could ever be. Mostly because he looked so sweet while inflicting his blissful torment.

"It so happens that I enjoy tickling you." Dane knelt at the end of the bed and pulled Aiyana down, positioning her legs over his shoulders. "But I think I'll find another spot. I must sample all of you, lest I miss something particularly delectable."

Aiyana braced herself, looking down at him. He ran his fingers up the inside of her thighs, and she held her breath in anticipation. He touched her warm, slippery flesh and she exhaled sharply.

"You do enjoy playing with me, don't you? I think it excites you as much as it devastates me." His fingers toyed in her moisture as he spoke.

Aiyana shuddered. "I can't deny that, Thorwalian. The sight of you, naked, so perfectly hard . . . And forcing you to react thus . . . Oh, it was sweet pleasure!"

His teasing finger found her small, feminine bud, stopping her words, stopping her breath. He circled it, thoughtfully. "Here is a morsel worth sampling."

"What?" Aiyana stared in astonishment as he kissed her. There. Well, she had kissed him in the same way. She wondered if he would like kissing her there as much as she liked kissing him that way.

She held her breath, waiting for evidence that this pleased him. She felt his breath, warm against the sensitive spot. Then she felt the smallest tip of his tongue. It circled, tasted. And then he moaned, low and hoarse. He liked it, too.

Aiyana lay back. He teased and tasted and suckled until she thought she would go mad. She wrapped her legs tight around his neck, arching and moaning, grasping his hair. He treated the small spot like a sweet fruit, and he devoured the taste and the feel and her pleasure.

Aiyana felt like a rich delicacy. She felt savored. He increased the intensity of his savoring. She thought she might shatter into wild delirium. His tongue swirled and circled and tickled. He really was tickling her. There.

Aiyana's whole body spasmed. She cried out, bit her lip, and cried out again. Thousands of tiny contractions rippled through her, demanding and devastating. . . .

Aiyana pulled Dane's hair, trying to drag him above her. Instead, he pulled her down until her hips reached the end of the bed. He cupped her hips in his large hands, elevating her to his hips. Then he thrust deep inside her.

Aiyana moaned, low and raggedly. She was fire inside, every nerve ending afire and pulsing around his length. Her wild delight intensified and burst and spread through her whole body. He drove inside her, full and strong, and she watched him as the blissful sensation overtook him, too.

His head tipped back, his neck strained. His wide chest glistened, every muscle taut. He moaned her name over and over as the hot waves of pleasure seared through him. Aiyana felt every one.

He looked down at her, wonder on his beautiful face. He withdrew from her body and straightened. He stood above her like a young king, tall and strong and powerful. Then he moved around the bed and picked her up.

"I love you, Aiyana." He kissed her, then lowered her back upon the bed. He climbed beside her and she rested her head on his shoulder.

Neither spoke for a long while. Aiyana listened to his strong, even heartbeat. She felt his life, and she felt her own. Small twitches of pleasure radiated through her in passion's aftermath. She looked into his face, into his sleepy eyes.

"You looked surprised. Why?"

"I was astonished." Dane kissed her forehead. "You and I have made love before. But today we were truly one. I know all of you; you know all of me."

Aiyana's eyes misted with sudden tears. "Maybe I should have told you sooner."

"It was right to tell me here. Kostbera gave me only one instruction. She said, 'Find the reality of Franconia.' On Keir, I learned the secret of the Keiroit rogues. Among the Tseirs, I learned the secret of their evil. And here, my sweet love, I learned the secret of you."

"Then you've done what you came to do."

"I have. And now we will use all those secrets to save Kostbera's world."

Chapter Ten

"Nidawi and Dane, wake!"

Aiyana woke with a start. Helayna stood by the bed, her spear gripped in both hands. "What is wrong, Helayna?"

Dane groaned and rolled over, then sat up. "Couldn't just let us sleep, could you?"

"You said I was to tell you about streaks in the sky. There are many, like lightning around the Tseirs' star."

Dane reached for his tunic while Helayna watched suspiciously. "You sleep unclothed. This is odd."

Dane pulled it over his head, leaving the tie unbound. "I suppose you sleep in your clothes."

"Of course."

"I knew that. I didn't have to ask." Dane glanced at Aiyana. "Just out of curiosity, does Arnoth sleep clothed?"

"When I shared his bed, he wore clothes."

Dane's eyes narrowed. "Just how often did you sleep together?"

Aiyana shrugged. "We shared chambers for a long while. He offered great comfort."

Dane's narrow eyes became slits. "I'll bet."

Aiyana patted his arm. "But not in the way you comfort me."

"Only because I have proof of your body's innocence can I possibly accept this." Dane paused to shake his head. "The man always was crazy. That much is certain. He probably sleeps in armor."

Aiyana paused, considering the significance of what Arnoth wore in bed. "I believe he didn't bother with clothing when he slept alone. Once, I went to his chambers when I had a nightmare. He was unclothed then. Why do you care what he wore?"

"I wondered if his private nature is sensual. I should have known he's as crazy in private as anywhere else."

Aiyana glanced at Helayna, who listened without interest. *It may take some doing to . . .* "I believe that he is very sensual, underneath. Once, when we were very tired, he started to kiss me. He stopped. He didn't sleep with me after that."

"Good." Dane looked around. "Where did I put that Tseir uniform?"

Helayna picked it up and passed it to him. "Had you remained clothed, you would leap quicker to the task."

Dane gritted his teeth, but Aiyana chuckled as she dressed. Dane put the Tseir uniform over his own clothes. "Why are you wearing that? It's warm here. And it doesn't suit you at all."

Dane grinned, then turned to Helayna. "Did you keep any Tseir helmets? I'm afraid mine was in the shuttle when it exploded."

"We keep helmets, for trophies."

"I'll need one."

Helayna shrugged, then left to find one. Aiyana waited for an explanation. "Are we returning to Franconia?"

"Not necessary, my love. I have a better plan."

"You might tell me about it."

"I'd rather mull it over a little first. I'll explain when we reach Keir."

Helayna met Dane and Aiyana in the central hall. She held a Tseir helmet and an aged, hand-bound manuscript. Dane took the helmet and tried it on. "All the same size, naturally."

Helayna placed the book carefully in Aiyana's hands. "Hakon wrote much. I would like one day to know his words."

Aiyana held the large book against her chest. "I want to know, too."

"Your sky ship is ready. The lingbat is there already. I hope he is able to locate She Who Leaps High again."

Dane sighed. "I take it the lingbat has been talking. Not that this should surprise me."

"He was the chief speaker at our evening time, where the old ones usually tell stories and play music."

Aiyana studied Helayna with interest. "Do you play music, Helayna?"

"Music is not for warriors. It is unseemly for a fighter."

"Arnoth plays the harp, and he's a warrior."

Helayna remained doubtful. "Not when he's playing the harp. I am a warrior always." She paused. "Who is Arnoth?"

Dane chuckled. "Funny you should ask. If we had time, believe me, Aiyana would tell you more than you, or I, could ever want to know."

Aiyana frowned at Dane, then smiled pleasantly at Helayna. "Arnoth is the prince of Valenwood."

"We have no prince."

Dane sighed. "Something tells me you will."

Aiyana stood on the shuttle ramp and looked back at Helayna. She stood among warriors young and old, the enduring power of the Ellowans. The builders stood apart, but equally proud, still admiring the shuttle. A few couples, the "breeders," stood behind with the children. They smiled and waved, happy.

Aiyana watched them for a timeless moment. Her heart filled with a painful joy. They had survived. They would always survive. Helayna held her hand to her breast and bowed, a warrior's farewell.

Aiyana waved, though her face was wet from tears. *Hakon ensured your survival. Now, at last, I will ensure your future. . . .* She bowed, too, then turned and went up the ramp.

Dane engaged the shuttle engines as the Ellowans pulled the great doors open. "You'll miss them."

Aiyana sniffed and nodded. "I will."

Dane looked out the viewport at Helayna. "I don't know about your scheme to unite that woman with Arnoth."

"Why not? She resembles Elena. She's strong and intelligent. She's beautiful."

"Maybe so. But Helayna wouldn't like taking orders."

"Probably not."

"Nor would Arnoth. They both like issuing 'requests' a lot more. And quite frankly, though she's well built, Helayna doesn't have Arnoth's spirit."

"I knew you liked him!"

"Not at all."

"You don't think Helayna is good enough for him. That means you like him, Dane Calydon."

"It only means I don't think they're right for each other." Dane touched Aiyana's cheek. "You and I found love, so we want those we . . ." He paused to sigh. "Oh, all right! Those we *care* about, to find love, too."

Aiyana frowned. "I suppose that's true. Still, I think Arnoth could fall in love again."

"I think so, too. But it's not up to you and me to arrange it for him."

Aiyana's frown became a pout. "Don't you think he should come back here?"

"I don't know, Aiyana. His world is gone. I don't know how I'd feel, returning to Thorwal in these circumstances. I wonder if perhaps Arnoth's fate lies beyond this world, beyond any we know."

"I hope it involves a woman. But I don't know about 'other worlds.' "

Aiyana didn't like the idea of a stranger seducing her former mate. She preferred Helayna, a woman she knew—a relative, who looked like Elena. What if Arnoth fell in love with a beautiful, sweet alien? One with charms Aiyana couldn't guess. She didn't like the idea at all.

Dane chuckled at her expression. "It's not for us to decide, my dear. It will take one unusual female to crack through Arnoth's armor. I don't think, to be honest, that Helayna is crazy enough for him."

"Arnoth isn't crazy."

Dane angled a brow. "Where to begin?"

Aiyana wanted Arnoth to find love. Helayna was obviously the perfect choice, despite Dane's skepticism. "We must all learn to compromise. Think of what I've had to restrain in your company."

"Such as what?"

"I'm letting you pilot the vessel."

Dane sat back. "You have a point, my dear." He stood up and bowed. "Aiyana Nidawi, the controls are yours."

Aiyana's eyes widened. Then she smiled, sure and satisfied as she seized the controls. "I, of course, am a much better pilot than you."

"Prove it."

The shuttle engine roared, then blasted from the Ellowan gateway like a rocket. Dane jerked back in his seat, clinging to the side bars. Batty tumbled from the viewport and rolled down the aisle toward the rear.

Aiyana didn't bother with leveling. She headed straight into the sky, bursting through the clouds, then increasing the speed as they reached the outer atmosphere. Dane tried to speak, but his words stuck in his throat. A small squeak resembling Batty's most terrified voice came instead.

From the rear of the craft, Batty echoed Dane's squeak. "Sir! Oh, I thought you were bad. . . ."

The shuttle burst from the atmosphere, then slowed. Aiyana sat back, pleased with herself. "In a race between us, Thorwalian, you would lose."

Dane exhaled a long, tight breath. "But I'd still be alive at the end of the day."

"Shall I aim straight for Keir?"

"No . . . Set the course around Franconia, then take a trajectory resembling that of a scout ship. The Tseirs send scout ships back and forth to Keir. Hopefully, we won't be noticed. Their communication is automatic."

"How do you know these things? It took us years to decipher their communication systems."

"You're not technicians. I am. The Tseirs have little to fear from other craft. You have acted in sabotage, but not with your own fleet. They're not watching for us anymore. I'm sure they think we were destroyed on Valenwood, or at the very least are marooned there. But it's wise to keep to their usual route, just in case."

Aiyana programmed the vessel for Dane's route, then tried different magnifications through the viewport. She focused on Franconia. "Look! So many ships!"

Dane studied the vessels. "Odd that they're all black. Those were your ships first, weren't they?"

"They were. But we didn't have many. The Tseirs must have built more. Yet there isn't enough obsidian on Valenwood to construct that many vessels."

"It seems they clone more than just their bodies."

"Can you clone a flightship?"

"Why not? They're copies. And copies have flaws."

"Is that why the Tseir females wanted you and Arnoth? Because you're real?"

"Well, I don't know why they'd want Arnoth. But Rattan requested that on my return to Franconia, I bring 'strong Thorwalian males' with me."

"Your strength seems to have impressed them a great deal."

"And my stamina." Dane chuckled. "Like most women, they focus on my looks and miss my real strength."

Aiyana glanced down at Batty, who had made his way to the front of the craft again. She was sure she saw the lingbat roll his eyes. "And what is your 'real strength,' Dane Caldon? The color of your eyes?"

"No. Vivid blue is common on Thorwal."

Aiyana repressed a giggle. "And vanity."

"Not at all. No, my dear, my real strength is now as it's always been. Adaptability. Seneca told me that once. He said I could get along anywhere. And I can."

"What has that to do with stopping the Tseirs?"

"Everything. I am strong where the Tseirs are weak. They don't adapt, Aiyana. They control. I see things as they are. They force whatever's there to a shape they can dominate. You see, then, why I am the perfect person to shatter that domination?"

"No."

"You and Arnoth, and all your people, could never adapt to the Tseirs. They knew they couldn't control you, so they tried to annihilate you entirely. You weren't controlled, and you survived like an bee to eternally sting them."

"I don't see your point, Thorwalian."

"Don't you? I made them think they controlled me; I made them think I was destroyed. And now . . ."

"And now?"

"I'll give them what they hate most."

Aiyana held her breath. "What?"

"Lack of control. In the worst place imaginable. In themselves."

Aiyana guided the ship toward Keir while Dane studied Hakon's book. "Can you read his words?"

"It's simple once you know his pattern. He did well at using Ravager runes to form meaning."

"What does it say?"

Dane hesitated. "Let me read first, Aiyana. Much is here."

Aiyana puffed an impatient breath. "Hurry up! I want to know my grandfather's words. I want to know what happened."

Dane read further, then looked up at her. "There are things that may be painful for you. And for Arnoth."

Aiyana looked over at him, her face growing pale. "Does he mention Elena?"

"He does." Dane turned back to the book. His expression turned sorrowful as he read. Sometimes he smiled. Aiyana's heart ached, though she didn't know what Dane was learning from Hakon's words.

He read a long while, then closed the manuscript. Aiyana waited. "Well?"

"I would prefer to tell you and Arnoth what I've learned together. It might be easier for both of you. I will say, however, that his depictions of his mate match very closely what I would say of you."

"Were they flattering?"

"Let's just say she was a demon, too."

Aiyana's chin angled proudly. "She was. He worshiped her."

"That, too."

Aiyana turned reluctantly back to her controls. "We're entering orbit around Keir, Thorwalian. What now?"

Dane sighed. "Head for Rurthgar's marsh. We'll find out where Arnoth moved your village, and enlist our scaly amphibian. I hope you don't land the way you take off."

"Sure, I'll go. If you need a Keiroit, I'm the best one."

Dane rolled his eyes at Rurthgar's boast. "We need Arnoth, too. Do you know where to find him?"

"I'm here."

Arnoth appeared out of the swamp mists, his hood thrown back behind his dark head, an Ellowan rifle slung over his shoulder. He looked . . . heroic. Dane grudgingly accepted the inevitable. Arnoth was now, and always would be, a hero.

"The Tseirs are assembling their fleet. My guess is that they'll head for Candor before Kostbera learns of my death."

Arnoth's dark brow angled. "Death?"

Dane felt smug. "If you can live without life, I can die without death. Rurthgar has offered to join us. Unfortunately, I need you, too. I assume you have knowledge of flightship armaments."

Arnoth smiled slightly, equally smug. "Who do you think designed them?"

Dane deflated. "I thought your people opposed violence."

"Their original purpose was the destruction of asteroids . . . but they serve well in battle."

"Never let me get the last word, do you?"

"No."

"Your time will come, Arnoth."

"Maybe."

Aiyana puffed an impatient breath and positioned herself between them. "Behave, both of you. Where's the flightship, Arnoth? If we're going to blend in with the Tseir fleet, we've got to move fast."

Arnoth's dark eyes glittered. "Follow me."

"It's old and it's decrepit." Dane rummaged through the supplies on board the Ellowan flightship while Rurthgar fiddled with the aged controls. The ageless Ellowan raced around, removing unnecessary furnishings as Dane grumbled about the ship's condition.

Arnoth shrugged. "It works."

"Maybe."

Aiyana growled. "Stop that!"

Both Arnoth and Dane looked at her, innocent and surprised. "My dear, what do you mean? Stop what?"

"You know, both of you. You're trying to get the best of each other, and you never will. You're both handsome, you're both brave, and you're both vain. Accept it, and get to work."

Arnoth looked puzzled. "I'm not vain."

Aiyana decided not to mention that Arnoth had offered no objections to *brave* and *handsome*. Aiyana reached up and fingered his hair. "Perhaps we should cut your hair, for practicality's sake."

His eyes narrowed. "I see no need—"

Dane laughed and tried the engine, interrupting Arnoth. "It seems to work. For now. Let's go."

The engine came silently to life, and Dane guided the ship into the sky. Arnoth stood behind him, scrutinizing Dane's operation of the controls. "Now that you've got us here, maybe you'd like to tell me where we're going, and why."

"We're going to join the Tseir fleet, of course. What else?"

Arnoth shook his head. "It's certainly been a lifelong ambition of mine."

Dane ignored him, but Aiyana touched Arnoth's arm and drew him aside. She had told him on the way about her imprisonment, about Dane's rescue. She told him about Batty's brilliant piloting. But one thing remained.

"There's something you should know, Arnoth. Dane and I went to Valenwood when we escaped."

Arnoth's face darkened. He started to turn away. He didn't want to hear. Aiyana touched his shoulder. "The surface is still barren. But underground . . ."

Arnoth turned back to her. "What, Aiyana? Are you going to tell me there's life again on Valenwood? Worms?" He waved his arm, his rare anger surfacing. "Small reptiles?"

"Ellowans."

He froze. Aiyana took his hand and kissed it, tears sparkling in her eyes. "At least a thousand, maybe more. Arnoth, they're so beautiful. . . ." She glanced at Dane. "Aren't they beautiful, Dane?"

Dane hesitated. "A little dirty."

Arnoth appeared stunned. "How did they survive? The Tseirs devastated the entire planet."

"Hakon . . ."

Arnoth caught his breath. "Hakon survived?"

"He did, and Ariana, too. He brought as many people as he could into the mines. He filtered the air and the water, and they survived."

"The mines . . ."

"They're giant caverns now, beautiful halls and tunnels."

Dane nodded. "And they have a very interesting manner of mine shaft transportation."

Arnoth grasped Aiyana's shoulders. "Is this true? Hakon survived? Our people . . ."

"They live underground, and when the Tseirs come for obsidian, they . . . well, their hunters make the Tseirs think twice about coming back."

"Do the Tseirs know they exist?"

"Helayna says not."

"Helayna?"

Dane coughed, casting a pertinent glance Aiyana's way. Aiyana tilted her brow in warning. "She is their leader. A very sweet, lovely young woman."

Dane coughed again, louder. "We're assuming she's lovely, from what you can see beneath the grime and paint. Well built, though. But as for calling that demonic warrior-maiden 'sweet' . . . that's a bit of a stretch, Aiyana. She almost rammed a spear through my heart."

Aiyana ignored Dane. "She is descended from Hakon and Ariana."

Arnoth looked between Aiyana and Dane. "That's not possible. You and Elena were Hakon's only heirs."

"They had another child, a son. They named him Karanoth."

"It means 'dream of Arnoth.' "

Aiyana's tears fell to her cheeks. "I know."

"I can't believe it, after all this time."

Aiyana hugged Arnoth, then touched his face. "They thrive, Arnoth. They've changed our customs a little. . . ."

Dane cleared his throat. "A lot. Unless you divide your people into warriors, builders, and breeders."

"They had to do that, to keep the population down."

Arnoth's brow angled doubtfully. "Breeders?"

"Parents . . . If they're ever safe from the Tseirs, they'll start living above ground. They may wish to learn the old ways."

Arnoth looked shocked, but not quite as happy as Aiyana

expected. Of course, he hadn't met Helayna yet. Aiyana remembered Dane's warning. Maybe Arnoth would feel no more than duty. *No, I want more for you.*

Dane guided the flightship through the atmosphere, then set the controls toward Franconia. He rose from his seat and faced the others.

"We're headed for Franconia, my friends. Once we join the fleet, we'll have to keep our minds on our task. I don't know what will happen when we enter the wormhole. Nothing is certain."

Dane stopped and retrieved Hakon's book. "I've managed to decipher Hakon's words, and I think you'll both want to hear them. You might not get another chance to know what he thought of you."

Aiyana stood beside Arnoth, both silent as Dane opened the book. "He writes about his life on Valenwood, and about meeting Ariana. He also clears up a few Thorwalian misconceptions about Ravager history. . . ."

Aiyana nodded in satisfaction. "Good. I hope he corrected your impression of his brother."

"Actually, he admired Haldane. Even loved him. There were other elements involved in their war. . . . But that may be more interesting to Thorwalian historians. As far as the Tseirs, you're right. He distrusted them from the beginning."

"We know that, Dane. What else did he say?"

"He said he almost made the greatest mistake of his life. He almost stopped you from going to Franconia."

Arnoth looked skeptical. "He must have written this before the destruction."

"No. He wrote it years after. After the birth of his son."

Aiyana shook her head. "That can't be. He warned us."

"He did, and he was wrong. He loved you, Aiyana. Apparently he loved Arnoth just as much. He said you did what was right, and nothing . . . *nothing* the Tseirs did could change the value of your lives.''

Arnoth's gaze drifted to the viewport. ''Hakon was noble. I wonder if his praise is deserved.''

''There's more. And it may be painful for you to hear. But I think he'd want you to know.''

Arnoth turned back, reluctant. Aiyana just stood, her small face blank, but wet with tears. Dane longed to hold her, but she had to face the past alone to ever be free of its grip.

''He speaks of Elena. Though he loved her, he seems to have feared for her for a long time. Since childhood.''

Aiyana glanced at Arnoth, then back at Dane. ''Why? Elena was stronger than anyone.''

''Too strong, according to Hakon. Apparently she reminded him of Haldane, whom Hakon considered bent on self-destruction.'' Dane paused. ''He was right, too. Our history tells that Haldane died a brutal death at the hands of his enemies. Haldane's son was the first to unite the warring tribes.''

''What has that to do with Elena?''

''I've debated revealing this portion of Hakon's account. It may cause you both pain. But maybe it's necessary to know the truth, even when it hurts.'' Dane paused and drew a long breath. ''Elena feared if alone together, you and Arnoth would become lovers.''

Aiyana's mouth dropped, but Arnoth looked away. Aiyana's chin firmed. ''That's not possible. Grandfather was mistaken.''

Dane didn't respond. He waited for Arnoth. Arnoth sighed heavily. ''It's true, *damanai.* Elena loved you, but she was jealous. It was a source of bitter conflict between us. Nothing I said convinced her that I didn't secretly prefer you.''

Aiyana shook her head fiercely, injured. Dane saw her

pain; it drove into him like a knife. She fought tears. "Why didn't you tell me?"

Arnoth touched her shoulder. "I knew it would hurt you, Aiyana. And it wasn't your fault. Elena was jealous of any woman who came near me. But she loved you. Her jealousy worked both ways. Because you and I were friends, she often accused me of taking you from her. It wasn't entirely rational." Arnoth glanced at Dane. "Which is why I know your sister's claim on logic is tenuous at best."

Dane smiled. "I'm afraid Seneca would say the same. But on Nisa's behalf, I will say she valued his freedom more than her claim on his life. For that reason, their union is strong."

"I believed that as Elena matured, her fears would ease."

Dane met Arnoth's eyes. "Hakon said you called her a Ravager. He said you were right. He believed there were two kinds of Ravagers. Some would adapt, and some would die. Those like himself, and those like Haldane. It had been his fear, always, that Elena would die."

Dane paused, knowing his words would cut, and cut deep. "Though Hakon forbade it, Elena took a flightship to Franconia. You believed that she came to offer herself for your release, didn't you?"

Arnoth didn't speak, but he nodded.

"Hakon says otherwise. She left Valenwood before the battle, because she couldn't stand to think of you and Aiyana together."

Aiyana clenched her sides and squeezed her eyes shut. "No . . ."

Arnoth said nothing; he didn't move, didn't cry. He just stood like stone, finally knowing why his young mate had gone to Franconia.

Tears dripped down Aiyana's cheeks. "How could she think that?"

Aiyana's grief tore at Dane's heart. "She wasn't thinking,

Aiyana. She was reacting to fear and to doubt. Hakon says that Haldane was the same. Their passion was too large to contain, both compelling and destructive."

Arnoth nodded. "That was true of Elena."

"Hakon tried to protect her. When reason didn't work, he resorted to orders and forbade her to leave. He told her to have faith in you both. She wouldn't listen. She held him at rifle-point and stole a shuttle."

Dane set the book aside. "Elena's capture wasn't your fault, either of you. She made a choice, and it was a bad one."

Arnoth clenched his teeth. "If I hadn't gone . . ."

"Maybe. But Hakon questions here, years after he thought he'd lost you all, whether a man should subdue his own soul to protect another. For Hakon, the answer was clear.

"He loved you both, and he admired you. Apparently you were both held up to his people as models of Ellowan courage. I'm awfully afraid Helayna has taken 'courage' to unforeseen heights, but either way, you were part of what the Ellowans became."

Aiyana stood quietly and her tears dried. Dane held out his hand. Aiyana took his hand and buried her face against his shoulder. He held her, gently stroking her hair.

"Aiyana, you can't change the past. Neither one of you could change what Elena thought or feared. You did what was right."

"Sir! Light flashing on the panel, sir."

Dane turned back to the controls. The golden orb of Franconia lay before them, surrounded by Tseir ships. "There are still vessels arriving. With luck, they'll think we're just one more."

Arnoth shook his head. "The Tseirs communicate on visual screens, Thorwalian." He indicated a panel inset in the viewport. "They'll expect to see you."

Dane placed the Tseir helmet on his head. "And they will. They'll see a faithful guard and his loyal Keiroit clone."

Arnoth's eyes widened and Rurthgar gurgled. "Clone?"

Aiyana nodded. "That's another thing we forgot to mention."

Dressed as a Tseir guard, Dane eased the Ellowan flightship in amongst the Tseir assembly. Rurthgar sat positioned beside him, operating the controls. Beyond the sight of the viewport monitor, Aiyana handled the communication panel, while Arnoth sat at the weapons control with Batty on his shoulder.

"Dane, there's a message coming in. . . ."

Dane took a deep breath. "Set it to the screen."

An image flickered on the inset monitor. Rattan's face appeared. She looked composed. "Fellow Tseirs, I am pleased to announce that the fleet is assembled."

The image switched from Rattan to a Tseir guard. "All panels should be set for automatic entry into the wormhole."

Dane glanced at Rurthgar. "Are we set?"

Rurthgar shrugged. "Guess so."

From behind the panel, Arnoth sighed.

"All controls will work in unison, standard procedures followed. Proceed to the wormhole. Final check-in of the ship controllers now."

The image of the guard disappeared, and Rattan returned to the screen. Galya stood just behind her. "The fleet assembly was successfully accomplished in double-quick time. This is the benefit of cohesive action. Proceed as directed, and we will soon subdue the Candorian aggressors."

The image flickered and disappeared. Aiyana peeked around the screen. "Aggressors?"

Dane shrugged. "Maybe to the Tseirs, anyone who is

strong and who can't be controlled is an aggressor."

"What did the guard mean by 'final check-in'?"

Rurthgar gurgled. "Figure it means we're to check in."

Aiyana chewed the inside of her lip. "What if you check in wrong?"

Dane considered this. "Aiyana, try to pick up other ships' communications. See how they handle it."

Aiyana placed headphones over her ears and listened. "I've got something!" She frowned and shook her head. "I should have guessed. You respond, 'Under control.' "

"That's it?"

"That's it."

"Message incoming!"

"Screen, love."

Aiyana held her breath and transferred the signal to the viewport.

"Z-one zero four three, report in."

Dane faced the viewscreen. His image was transferred to the Tseir in the command vessel. "Under control."

Silence. Dane waited. Aiyana's heart throbbed in her chest.

"Take position, Z-one zero four three."

Dane looked back at Aiyana, silently questioning his response. Aiyana shook her head, advising him to say nothing.

The image disappeared, and she breathed a long sigh of relief. "What now?"

"We take our position, of course. What else?"

"We're coming up on the wormhole." Dane swiveled his seat to face the others. "When we arrive on the other side, we'll have to act fast. Aiyana, are communications locked on the command ship?"

"Yes, sir."

"Rurthgar, is the control panel operative?"

"Yes, sir."

"Arnoth . . ."

"Yes, sir."

Dane repressed a smile. "And you, honored rodent . . . I trust you're faring well."

"I'm all right, sir." Batty paused to sigh. "Sorry I couldn't have seen She Who Leaps High just once more."

"I'm sorry, too, Batty. We didn't have time."

"I know. But I've been thinking, if we disable the Tseirs, we're doing a favor for the Dwindle Bats, too. The pollution of the swamp is spreading. It already infects the air. I'm helping She Who Leaps High, even if I never see her again."

Dane looked back at the lingbat, perched on Arnoth's shoulder, his small face scrunched thoughtfully. "You're right, Batty. If we can deal the Tseirs a setback here, it might be that we're helping systems beyond ours. Systems that now suffer Tseir domination."

The wormhole grew closer in the viewport. Dane was near the middle of the Tseir formation. It moved forward in a three-dimensional wedge, moving in perfect precision. He looked around at his strange companions.

Rurthgar sat beside him, hooded, his webbed feet in metal support shoes. He made gurgling noises as he adjusted the controls. On the next station, out of his enemy's sight but forever potent, forever strong, Arnoth readied the weapon panel.

Batty sat on Arnoth's shoulder, overseeing the procedure. The lingbat didn't look scared. Maybe he'd proven to himself that he'd earned his given name.

He Who Flames With Courage, I am proud to serve with you.

At the rear of the cockpit, her back to Arnoth, sat Aiyana. Dane rested his gaze on her profile. Her brow furrowed; her lips were tight as she concentrated on the Tseir communications. Her long, black hair fanned softly over her shoulders, down her back. She wore the same cape he'd first seen her in, the same snug bodice and tight leggings. The same thonged boots.

"You are the most beautiful woman in all existence."

Aiyana looked over at him, surprised. A faint blush tinged her cheeks, and her lips curved in a shy smile. Dane smiled, too.

"I just wanted you to know, before we go in."

Rurthgar gurgled again, then wheezed. "Going in now, Thorwalian. There goes the first Tseir!"

Dane returned his gaze to the viewport. One by one, then by twos, the Tseir vessels disappeared into the wormhole. They disappeared as if sucked down a black tube.

Dane watched the perfect precision of the Tseirs' movement. *You've gone too far this time. You go forth to conquer. You fear freedom. This time you'll learn how powerful freedom really is.*

The vessel in front of them vanished and Dane leaned back in his seat. He closed his eyes. The man who emerged on the other side would be a Ravager. He wouldn't wield a sword or an ax. He merely wielded himself.

"Sir! Sir, wake up!" Batty perched on Dane's chest, hopping madly, wings flailing. Dane emerged into consciousness, but Batty didn't notice. He filled his lungs with air, then hurtled himself into Dane's face.

"Watch it, rodent!"

"Trying to wake you, sir. We're here."

Dane shook off the heavy effect of wormhole transition and poked Rurthgar's cloaked body. "Keiroit, we have emerged."

Rurthgar startled and gurgled, then sat upright, returning to his controls as if nothing had happened. Dane rose and shook Arnoth. "We're here."

Arnoth held Dane's gaze for a moment. They both knew

what could be lost, and they knew that they were the only ones who could alter the dark course. Arnoth engaged the weapon system and a red light flashed ready.

Dane knelt beside Aiyana and kissed her hand. She stirred and opened her eyes. ''Are you ready, love?''

She swallowed, stretched, and then bent to kiss his forehead. ''I'm with you. That is what I wanted.''

Dane rose to his feet. He touched her chin, then bent to kiss her mouth. ''Whatever happens, know that I will love you throughout time.''

''As I love you . . .''

Dane drew a breath and returned to the helm. He replaced the Tseir helmet, covering his face. Aiyana watched him. He was strong and confident. If anyone could thwart the Tseirs, it was Dane Calydon.

She looked out the viewport at the assembled Tseir fleet. So many, and so strong. Maybe they were stronger; maybe nothing could stop them. But she knew, suddenly and with force, that what really mattered was that with Dane, with Arnoth and Rurthgar, with Batty, she was doing the right thing.

''Aiyana, are you still locked on to the command vessel?''

''I am.''

Dane drew a long breath and exhaled. His blue eyes glittered. ''Then we're ready. Rurthgar, transfer command vessel communications systems . . . to us.''

''Done.''

Aiyana trembled—from fear, from excitement. She reminded herself of all her acts of sabotage. She'd had no fear then. Her gaze drifted to Dane. She'd had nothing to lose then. Now she had everything she'd ever wanted in her grasp.

''Are you sure this will work?''

Dane's brow angled. "I arranged the circuits myself. I'm sure."

Arnoth sighed as he checked the weapons code. "You're right, *damanai.* He is vain."

Batty sighed, too. Dane turned in his seat, eyes narrowed. "I hope you're not agreeing with him, Batty, my *honored guide.*"

Batty straightened. "Oh, no, sir! Not at all. Not in the least. You're not vain." He paused, struggling with conscience. "More vainish."

Aiyana laughed. A strange warmth grew inside her. They were on the edge of war, and she laughed. A fleet of evil, cruel clones surrounded them, and she sat on a ship with four males she loved. Each one distinct. Individual. The Tseirs didn't stand a chance.

Rurthgar belched. "We're coming up on Candor, Thorwalian."

Aiyana leaned around the panel to look out the viewport. The giant gas planet of Candor blazed in the sky, red and orange and purple. "Where's the moon?"

"On the other side. They'll have to enter orbit around the gas planet before they can center on the moon."

"Message incoming, sir." *If I die, I will die happy. I will die among those I love. I will die at the best of life.*

"Put it on the monitor, then." Dane sounded cheerful, too. *Maybe, when you love and are loved, nothing else matters.* "And keep yourselves hidden. We don't want them sighting an Ellowan. Or a lingbat."

Aiyana transferred the message. *"Assume orbit around the Candor planet, cross formation."*

"Got it?"

Rurthgar chuckled. "Got it."

Aiyana turned to Dane. "The commanders' message didn't go out to the other ships."

"It shouldn't have. But let's see if they start moving."

Aiyana held her breath, not daring to look at the viewport for fear her face would show up on a Tseir commander's monitor. "What are they doing?"

Dane breathed his relief. "Nothing. We've got to act fast. Aiyana, open communications out from my port."

Aiyana's hands shook, but she punched in the code. "Done."

Dane seized a microphone and assumed a Tseir accent, perfectly mimicking the previous transmission. "Assume orbit around the Candor planet, wedge formation."

The fleet moved at once.

Aiyana's panel buzzed. "They're sending confirmation codes back to the command ship."

"Very good."

"We've got another message from the commander."

Dane chuckled. "Let's have it."

"This is not cross formation! Assume cross formation!"

"Do I reply?"

"Wait, then open my port again."

Aiyana waited a moment, then opened Dane's line.

He spoke. "Well done, commanders. Break wedge into double-file. Vanguard ships should see the Candor moon now. Assume orbit."

Aiyana bit her lip until Dane finished. She closed his port. "Why don't you just send them into the gas planet and be done with it?"

"They'll only take my orders so far, woman. They know why they're here."

The light on Aiyana's panel flashed. "I don't think the Tseir command is at all pleased. . . ."

"Stars forbid they should be displeased. Patch them through."

"This is not the correct approach pattern. Check programming at once. It may be flawed."

Aiyana snapped off the message. "What if they guess they've been sabotaged?"

Dane lifted the microphone. "We'll reassure them, shall we? Open my line."

Aiyana did, though her nerves felt so tight that it hurt to move.

"All ships, send confirmation of accurate programming to command vessel at once."

Dane lowered the microphone and waited.

Aiyana's panel buzzed again. "They're doing it, Dane. It must drive the commanders crazy!"

"That's the idea."

"More coming."

"Enter orbit for attack."

Aiyana's heart banged against her chest. "They're still planning to attack. Dane . . ."

"I knew they would. In fact, I counted on it. Now, open my port again, my dear."

Aiyana obeyed, but she felt dizzy.

"Command vessel order change: All vessels alter programming at once. Surface scan indicates live Candorians have been warned of our attack. They have taken refuge on the gas planet. Candorians will be found concealed in . . ." Dane hesitated, then shrugged. "In orange bubbles. Attack must commence close to the surface."

Dane stopped and Aiyana switched off his port. "Do you think they'll do it?"

"We'll see."

"What if they question the commanders?"

"Some will."

"But Dane, if they do . . ."

"We want them to, Aiyana. Rurthgar, move the vessel slowly away from the moon. Edge us to the rear of the fleet."

Rurthgar cackled happily, proving Dane's prediction accurate. ''Half of 'em headed off with us. Other half . . .''

''I'm getting a lot of signals, Dane.''

''Yes, but they won't get a response. Except from me. Open port, Aiyana.''

Aiyana shook, but she snapped open Dane's port.

''Attention: all vessels. Half our fleet is disobeying the first commander's instruction. Sabotage is suspected. Those remaining in orbit are under alien control.''

Dane sat back, impossibly pleased with himself. Aiyana closed the line and waited. '' 'Alien control?' ''

''I'm an alien of sorts. . . .''

Arnoth laughed. ''That much is certain. Do we fire, Dane Calydon?''

''We'll hang back awhile. Let them do the damage first. We'll deal with what's left.''

Aiyana beamed with pleasure. She liked chaos. ''Dane, my sweet love, we're getting another message from the command vessel. Shall I patch them through?''

''Do so, my dear. Can't keep the commanders waiting.''

''The fleet is dividing! Stop at once. Sabotage is suspected. Fire on the defectors.''

Dane chuckled. ''Accurate, but too late.''

Arnoth looked out the viewport. ''They're bound to notice that the command vessel isn't moving, Dane.''

''So they are. Good point. Aiyana, open my port.'' Aiyana did so, and Dane continued.

''Attention! Command vessel under attack! Power core disrupted. Suspected terrorist involvement. Engage fleet to—''

Dane set the microphone down and nodded to Aiyana. She shrugged, then turned off the communications. ''Why did you stop?''

''I want the fleet to think the command ship is under attack from within. Send a code to that effect.''

Aiyana beamed with pride at Dane's ingenuity. ''Done!''

Rurthgar chortled at the sight of Tseir vessels firing at

their own. "I'll edge us back farther. The Tseirs remaining around the moon outnumber 'our' side."

"I'm afraid that's true."

Dane seized the microphone and Aiyana opened his line. "System on-line . . ." He tapped the mike to indicate a power glitch. "Point-blank firing will be necessary. Move in on the disruptors."

Aiyana stilled the line and waited. "They're doing it! Look, they're moving in on the other line."

Dane stood up and stretched. He removed his helmet and ran his fingers through his hair. "I'd say we've rattled them admirably." He looked out the viewport. Tseir ships shot blue rays of deadly plasma through black space. Hulls burst and shattered, exploding in the vacuum of space.

Rurthgar leaned forward. "Our defectors are losing, Thorwalian."

Dane furrowed his brow, mimicking disapproval. "As it should be. Disloyal, disobedient, uncontrolled . . ."

Aiyana shook her head, but she smiled. "Now what? They'll regroup, and we're the only ones left."

"So we are. We've rattled them effectively. Now it's time to remind them of fear."

"How?"

"You, my sweet, will remain at the communications panel. Arnoth, I'll need you, and bring your rifle."

Arnoth grabbed his rifle. "And now that I'm armed?"

Dane seated himself and replaced his helmet. "Now, if you'll kindly announce yourself. And make it grand."

"With pleasure."

"Aiyana, open port to the command vessel."

"I'm not sure this is such a good idea." Aiyana held her breath and opened the communications line to the commanders.

Arnoth took the microphone and positioned himself in view of the monitor. "I am Arnoth of Valenwood. This fleet is under my control. Your feeble response was no match for the skill of my warriors. Surrender or die."

Aiyana closed the line. Dane chuckled. "Now, get ready to patch him through to the fleet. Arnoth, be sure that rifle shows in the monitor." Dane flopped forward on the panel. Rurthgar hesitated. "Play dead, Keiroit." Rurthgar growled, but complied.

Aiyana transferred the port and waited for Arnoth's next speech.

"I am Arnoth of Valenwood. I have sabotaged your command vessel, and hold your commanders hostage. Surrender, or die."

Aiyana closed communications and Dane sat up. "Well done! Hostile, arrogant. Perfect."

Arnoth smiled, then resumed his seat at the weapons panel. "The Tseirs don't value their commanders' lives. I assume you expect the ships to commence firing on the command vessel."

"Exactly."

Rurthgar waved his concealed paw in the air. "You were right. There they go! The commanders don't stand a chance."

Beyond the viewport, the Tseir vessels fired at the command vessel, then at each other. Aiyana watched with a strange mixture of horror and hope. "Why don't they flee? At this point, I'd head back through the wormhole and go home."

"You would, my love, because you're real. You value life. Even Tseir life. They act on a different level. They want control, because they fear the lack of it. They want their immediate needs gratified, because there's nothing beyond themselves that they desire. It is horrible, but it's what happens when a race becomes empty of individuality, of aspiration, and of the value of life."

Arnoth looked over at Dane, a strange expression on his

aristocratic face. "That is what Hakon meant. It's better that we acted on our value for life than to deny it because we were afraid."

Tears welled in Aiyana's eyes. "And that's the beauty of the Ravagers, isn't it? It isn't that they're brave and strong and wise, as I once believed. It's that they wanted something beyond themselves; they wanted to grow and build and create."

Dane's eyes glittered with tears, too. "That is the soul of my people, just as the value of life is the soul of yours. Neither one of us will ever be beaten, Aiyana, because we want and we love, and that matters."

"It matters."

Batty hopped to Rurthgar's shoulder, straining as he watched the final battle. "Sir! Isn't that the command ship pulling out? What are they doing?"

Dane turned his attention back to the viewport. His heart held its beat. "They're landing on the Candor moon! Rurthgar, set an interception course. Arnoth, we'll need to shoot our way through. I hope those old weapons of yours work."

"Age has its benefits, Dane Calydon. And I should know."

Dane took control of the flightship helm and moved at full speed through the battling Tseir craft. They had turned on each other, firing at random, refusing to leave, bound in chaos by the lust to control. Ultimately, they were attempting to control each other.

"They're firing at us." The ship lurched, cutting off Rurthgar's words. He steadied himself and locked in an irregular course.

"Arnoth . . ."

"Ready. Fire one."

Aiyana left her station and watched through the viewport. A blue line of liquid fire burst from the front of their vessel.

A perfect shot. A Tseir vessel spiraled out of control from the blast.

"I was wrong when I told Helayna that Dane was a better shot than you. You're equal in that, too."

"Fire two."

Another blast shot from their vessel, striking the middle of another Tseir ship. The small hole widened, then burst open as the ship collapsed on itself, spewing debris like a fan through space.

The debris smashed across the viewport, but Dane kept the ship straight. "If they land on Candor . . ."

"I don't understand. What do you think they'll do? Aren't they just trying to get away?"

"You misunderstand the Tseirs, my love. They're angry. Even if they blame Arnoth, their real target remains Candor. They *must* exert control, or lose their identity. In a very real sense, the Tseirs do fear annihilation. Their ideas mean more to them than reality. If they lose their sense of domination, they lose themselves. To the Tseirs, and to those unfortunate humanoids like them, that is worse than death."

"Then the Candorians are still in danger."

"We've lessened the threat. But Galya is certainly with them. She has been in Nerotania. Kostbera will be her target."

"They want vengeance. . . . Vengeance for nothing."

Arnoth fired another shot, then sat back. "That is all they ever wanted, Aiyana. They took it on me, on Elena. They would have taken it on you, if not for Dane. Let us deprive them, shall we?"

Aiyana nodded, her heart set and determined. "We shall."

Dane lowered the ship through the Candorian atmosphere, searching out the land below for the Tseir vessel. "Look! There, on the horizon. They're firing!"

Aiyana stood behind his chair. "What are they firing at?"

"The pyramid gateways, probably. Good. If they waste their time that way, we have time to stop them."

Dane guided the ship over the amber, cratered terrain of Candor. "They're landing." Another vessel caught his attention. It was on the ground, near a destroyed pyramid. His heart took a sick leap, his stomach clenching. "No . . ."

Aiyana gripped his shoulder. "What is it?"

"It can't be." Dane aimed for the vessel.

"What?"

"I know that vessel. I helped design it myself."

"Is it Thorwalian?"

"Partly. And part Dakotan. Aiyana, it is the shuttle Nisa and I designed. It belongs to Seneca."

"They're here?"

"They must be."

Dane's hands shook as he guided the craft to a landing. "We've got to go in, to warn them."

The ship stopped, and Rurthgar lowered the ramp. Dane didn't wait. He grabbed a rifle and jumped out. Aiyana and Arnoth followed, then Rurthgar with Batty on his shoulder. They ran across the dry surface, racing toward the shattered pyramid.

The multihued gateway shimmered before them. Dane leaped through, and the others followed. They emerged in the colossal halls of Nerotania. Candorians raced along the hallways, shocked by the attack.

Dane caught an older Candorian man. "You're being invaded. Where is Kostbera?"

"She's in the council chamber. Dane, it's you. What's happening?"

"No time. Get under cover; get everyone under cover in the lower tunnels. You're under attack."

The man raced away, and Dane continued down the hall, running until his lungs burned. Aiyana ran beside him, as did Arnoth. From behind, he heard Rurthgar's metal shoes clanking on the ancient tile.

Dane ran into the council chamber, but no one was there. "Curses! Where are they?"

Arnoth held his rifle ready. "There's blasting ahead, Dane. They're coming in there. Would this Kostbera flee, or stay and fight?"

"I don't know. She must have her guards readied by now." Dane started off toward the noise, clutching his own rifle, around a corner, through another vast hall, into the atrium that was Kostbera's pride.

A large group of Candorians were assembled at the far end, nearest the gateway. The gateway collapsed inward, and Tseir guards leaped through the opening. They bounded through the rubble. There, at the farthest end of the hall, Dane saw his sister.

He heard himself shout, drowned out in the blast. "Nisa! Get out of here! Kostbera, get them out of here!"

The Candorian guards appeared behind Dane. Aiyana choked back a scream.

Dane turned and saw the Candorian globs as they entered the hall. "It's all right. Those are Kostbera's guards. Just stay out of their way."

Dane stopped to let the globs pass. They oozed toward where Kostbera's group stood huddled together. Nisa and Seneca were among them. Dane's heart nearly stopped when he saw a small boy clinging to Seneca's hand.

"Nisa!"

Nisa turned. "Dane!"

Dane leaped forward, but Galya appeared through the opening. She wore Rattan's robe, and it was stained with blood. Galya saw Dane and Aiyana, and she saw Arnoth beside them. From across the hall, Dane recognized her fury when she realized that they, too, had escaped her power.

The globs moved toward the Tseirs. Dane stopped, waiting. Aiyana stood beside him. "What are they? What will they do?"

"They live deep inside the planet. They come out when Kostbera needs them. These same globs destroyed invaders when I first came to Candor. And those invaders outnumbered the globs."

The Tseirs fired into the globs, just as Dane remembered the earlier invaders had done. At that time, the globs had absorbed the energy and destroyed the invaders. But not now. The Tseirs' rifles fired plasma, and it seared through the amorphous guardians. Unlike in the earlier battle, they didn't rise again, or merge together.

The Tseirs blasted again, and the globs began to retreat. Dane leaped forward. "We've got to stop them!"

He fired as he ran, and Tseirs fell. Arnoth and Aiyana fired beside him. Rurthgar leaped forward, firing a short, blunt rifle with perfect aim. Galya took cover behind her guards, easing around toward Kostbera's group.

The Tseir guards faltered before Dane's attack. In mindless chaos, they shot at each other, into walls. Though the guards lay dead around her, murdered by their own hands, Galya kept her self-control. Her normally bland face burned red with hatred.

She snatched a rifle from a dead guard and aimed into the Candorian group, toward Nisa. Nisa, who so closely resembled Elena, the woman Galya herself murdered. Dane saw the blast. It moved so slowly, as if time held still. . . . It struck Nisa in the chest. She fell and Dane heard a child's scream. He heard himself scream, too.

He ran. As in a dream, his legs seemed too heavy to carry him with enough speed. Behind him, Arnoth knelt and fired, and Galya crumpled to the ground. Dane raced to where Nisa lay. Her son sobbed; Seneca held her in his arms, crying, too.

"Nisa . . . No." Dane knelt beside her, surrounded by

shocked Candorians. Aiyana knelt beside him, then took Nisa's hand and checked her wrist.

"She's alive, Dane."

Dane's heart beat again. "Can you save her?"

"Possibly. But I am not the Ellowans' best healer." She glanced toward Arnoth. He shouldered his rifle and came to her side.

Dane rose. "You can save my sister, Arnoth."

Arnoth looked down at Nisa's stricken face, and Dane knew the Ellowan prince was seeing his own dying mate. "Please, you can save her." Dane was crying; he clutched Arnoth's shoulder.

Arnoth didn't move. He just stared down at Nisa. Aiyana turned back to Nisa. "I will try."

Arnoth broke free from his dark memory. "No, Aiyana. This is for me to do."

Aiyana moved back and Arnoth took Nisa gently from Seneca's arms. Seneca seemed reluctant to release her. Arnoth met his eyes, and Dane saw a mirror of one man in the other. "I will heal her."

Dane touched Seneca's shoulder. "He can. . . . Trust him."

Seneca released Nisa's body, and drew his son into his arms. They waited together, helpless and shocked, enduring the greatest pain of their lives.

Arnoth placed Nisa on her back. Only then did Dane notice that she was pregnant. The Candorians gathered around, silent. The globs returned and seemed to watch, too. Arnoth touched Nisa's smooth forehead, then her temples. He hesitated. Dane knew the prince warred with his own memories. If those memories won, Nisa would die.

Arnoth entered his trance. He didn't speak aloud, but Dane knew what he spoke to the depths of Nisa's mind. *Do you desire life*? There was no doubt. Something in Arnoth relaxed at Nisa's answer. He nodded, slightly.

Nisa would live. Dane exhaled a long, shuddering breath. He looked at Aiyana and saw her small face wet with tears. She knew what this moment meant to Arnoth. Dane knew what it meant to her.

For a timeless while, Arnoth taught Nisa's strong body to heal itself. Arnoth sat back, weakened by his effort, his head bowed. Nisa stirred, then opened her eyes.

She reached up and touched Arnoth's face, a strange expression of wonder in her eyes. "Thank you."

Arnoth took Nisa's hand and kissed it. "It gives me more pleasure than you can know to see you healed and well, my lady."

"My baby . . ."

Arnoth nodded, then placed his palm over her round stomach. "Your daughter is unharmed."

Nisa's eyes widened. "Daughter? Seneca . . ."

"I'm here, maiden." Seneca helped her to sit up, tears streaming down his face. The little boy hugged Nisa.

"Mama . . ."

Nisa held her son on her lap. "I'm all right. Your sister is all right, too."

"That man made you better, Mama. He looks like Father."

Nisa looked up at Arnoth. "I noticed that."

"Who is the other, Mama? He looks like you. Only bigger."

Nisa met Dane's eyes. She pressed her lips together to keep from crying. "This is your Uncle Dane, Ananda."

Dane knelt beside the little boy. "Ananda. I hope we will be friends."

Ananda considered this possibility, but hesitated before entering a formal agreement. "Do you like wortpigs?"

Dane hesitated, then nodded vigorously. "Of course."

"I am nearly as good at TiKay as my father. Do you like TiKay?"

"I practice daily. Almost."

"A daily effort is required, Uncle."

"Daily from now on."

"Then we will be friends." Ananda leaned his small, proud head on his mother's healed chest. "He likes wort-pigs, Mama."

"Of course. I taught him well." Nisa reached for Dane's hand. "I see that you have become a man. I should have known it wouldn't happen without drama."

"This isn't quite the way I intended to return."

"No, but it's certainly typical of you." Nisa sighed, then braced herself on Seneca's shoulder. She propped herself up, then stood. "I'm not so graceful in this condition."

Seneca's mouth dropped and he looked at Arnoth. "Should she be standing?"

Arnoth rose to his feet and stood back. "She is healed."

Dane slid his arm around Nisa's expanded waist. "I've been through it myself. It's an effective technique."

"Do you mean you've been injured, too?"

"Of course."

Nisa shook her head. "I don't think I want to know."

"Probably for the best, dear sister. I'm alive now, and you're alive, and your daughter is alive. But I'm curious; why are you on Candor, especially in your condition?"

"When your ship returned without you, Kostbera sent us word. We didn't want to wait for news on Dakota."

Seneca touched Nisa's shoulder. "When your sister is determined, nothing stands in her way."

Nisa nodded proudly, then turned her attention to Aiyana. "You didn't come back alone, I see." She waited expectantly, but Dane held up his hand.

"First things first. I have a report to issue."

"Oh!"

Dane turned to Kostbera with a wry smile. "I have sought out the reality of Franconia. It wasn't an easy trail to follow.

But I'm afraid I have to advise against aiding the Tseirs."

Kostbera nodded thoughtfully. "I find I must agree with you. You have done well, Dane."

Kostbera turned to Seneca. "So well that I think it's time you both be admitted to the Intersystem Council. I shall recommend you both to the prime representative on Nirvahda. You shall represent your worlds with honor."

Seneca bowed. "It is my honor."

Dane glanced at Nisa and shrugged. "Mine, too."

Kostbera's daughter emerged from the crowd. Selena looked to where Dane stood with Arnoth and Seneca. Her lips parted; her eyes widened, then softened into a blissful expression of admiration.

Selena turned to Kostbera. "I have fallen in love upon sight, Mother, and I am ready to choose my mate. Here before me stands the most beautiful image of masculinity that I have ever seen or imagined in my mind. I will have him."

Kostbera smiled, though she didn't seem surprised. "I thought so. . . . As you wish. It will be done, Selena."

Dane's mouth dropped. He held up his hand and shook his head. "I'm sorry, Selena." Seneca looked nervous and eased to Nisa's side. Arnoth paled and backed away. Selena shoved past Dane, past Arnoth and Seneca.

Arnoth, Dane, and Seneca stared in shock as Selena pulled back Rurthgar's hood. "I will mate with you."

Before Rurthgar could respond, Selena transformed. Her willowy, translucent body altered until it became green. Scales emerged on her green flesh, and her head changed to a Keiroit shape.

Rurthgar issued a loud squawk. Ananda covered his ears. Aiyana looked at Dane and burst into laughter.

Dane stared at Selena, then back to Kostbera, who remained sublime and calm. "You're . . . Keiroits?"

"We're anything we want to be. Our original form was

similar to what you termed 'orange bubbles' on the Candor gas planet. But that was millenia ago. We choose our own shape. But so do you, Dane. Don't you know that your body is a temple, your soul its master? We choose. You chose, too."

"Oh."

Kostbera sighed. "That is the odd thing about the Tseirs. They behave as if they had no choice."

"Maybe they didn't. You'll find that the Tseirs are actually cloned beings, Kostbera. Franconia wasn't their main world. Their homeland still poses a threat to the Intersystem."

"The Nirvahdi believe that the Tseirs in Franconia are part of the same race of clones now assailing the inner-galaxy worlds."

"If Franconia was only a Tseir *outpost,* the danger is great."

"It is. But for now, the Tseir threat here has diminished. Our scanners indicate that they are destroyed entirely. No Tseir ship will return to Franconia." Kostbera studied Dane's face and she smiled.

"I questioned my judgment in sending you, a young man from a primitive race. . . . But it is wiser to judge a person for what he is, and not outside factors. I'm not sure how you accomplished such a resounding victory, but you managed to turn the Tseirs against each other."

Nisa and Seneca looked on with pride, and Dane resisted the impulse to grin foolishly at Kostbera's praise. "I didn't do it alone." He turned to his companions. "Allow me to present Arnoth, the prince of Valenwood."

Arnoth bowed. "I am honored."

Kostbera assessed Arnoth intently. "You are the Ellowan leader. We have been told that you are ruthless and without heart."

Arnoth offered no denial. Dane refused to accept this description. "Ruthless, maybe, but not without heart. If not for the Ellowan resistance, the Tseirs would long ago have invaded our system."

"That seems to be their nature. They are driven to subdue others."

Dane gestured toward Rurthgar. "And here is the rightful ruler of Keir, Rurthgar. His swamp has been overtaken by cloned Keiroits, and polluted by Tseir weapon manufacture."

Kostbera frowned at this. "We can offer you aid in this, Rurthgar. The wanton destruction of nature disturbs us deeply. If you agree, we will bring our guards to assist restoring your swamp."

Rurthgar reluctantly drew his attention from the transformed Selena. "Do you mean those squishy, oozing blobs?"

Dane winced at Rurthgar's lack of tact. "They're intelligent beings, Keiroit."

"They're ugly."

"I would hesitate to ask them what they think of you."

"Ha! It's been established that I'm the handsomest male here, Thorwalian. As if there were any doubt . . . Well, if the blobs are interested, I'd be grateful for their service."

Kostbera clasped her hands together, then bowed in formal agreement. "It will be done." Her attention shifted to Batty, perched straight and proud on Rurthgar's shoulder.

"And you, little one, how did you fare in Franconia?"

Batty cleared his throat, and Dane waited for the inevitable recitation of glory. "I found several moments direly unnerving, Kostbera. But Dane is a wise leader. Our mission was successful."

Dane's jaw dropped. "He Who Flames With Courage is modest, I fear, Kostbera. Using his own ingenuity, he operated a hovercraft and saved Aiyana and me from certain death. I am proud to serve at his side."

"As you say, sir."

Kostbera's gaze shifted to Aiyana. "We have met before, you and I."

Dane took Aiyana's hand. "You were right, Kostbera. I spent a great deal of time in Aiyana's company. And she wasn't at all what I expected."

Kostbera touched Aiyana's face. "When I first saw you, you were wounded in the soul. You are healed now."

Aiyana's eyes puddled with tears. "I am healed. The power of Dane's life reminded me of my own."

"I hoped it would be so. He takes great joy in life."

"He gives it, also."

Dane's face felt hot. He cleared his throat. "What about the Tseirs, Kostbera? We've shaken their control, but their homeworld still poses a problem. The loss will leave a great unknown to the Tseirs. And they hate the unknown. They may redouble their efforts toward control."

"For that reason, an Intersystem conference has already been called."

"Already? Then you received my message."

"A Franconian vessel emerged from the wormhole. Yes, we received your message."

Aiyana turned to Dane in surprise. "You sent a message? Why didn't you tell me?"

"I forgot."

"Forgot!"

Dane took Aiyana's hands. "A lot was going on, my dear. It slipped my mind. Not unlike your four-hundred-year mating with Arnoth."

"True. It happens."

Nisa looked between them expectantly. "Well?"

"Well, what?"

Nisa glared, and Dane guessed his teasing had overstepped its bounds. Dane drew Aiyana forward to meet Nisa.

"This is Aiyana." He paused, allowing the moment to build. "My mate."

Nisa beamed. "Your mate!" She turned to Seneca. "I told you so!" She clapped her hands together, then patted Dane's cheek as she had when he was a small boy. "When you came racing in, and those guards in helmets were shooting at us, I informed Seneca that you had a mate."

Seneca nodded. "She did. I thought her timing odd. Perhaps, maiden, you should have ducked instead."

"I'm fine now. Aiyana." Nisa seized Aiyana's hands. "I have always wished for a sister. Thorwalians were only allowed two children. Until now, of course. Now that I'm ruler, we can have as many as we want." She patted her stomach.

Aiyana looked up at Nisa, her small face more vulnerable and younger than Dane had ever seen it. "I had a sister once. She looked like you."

Nisa touched Aiyana's face. "We are sisters now." She kissed Aiyana's forehead. "Life was too easy for my brother. I trust you will keep him on his toes."

Dane bent and kissed Aiyana's cheek. "There's no question about that. I haven't been off my toes since I met her."

Epilogue

The Candorians hosted a great feast in a hall designed ages before by the Ellowans. Aiyana cleared up the mysteries of Nerotania by explaining the Ellowans' history of space travel. Nisa seized Hakon's book to learn on her own.

"To think! A Ravager became king on another world."

Seneca patted her hand. "And survived catastrophe. Yours is an indestructible race, maiden."

Aiyana noticed Arnoth's distant expression. Seeing Nisa and Seneca together had to remind him of himself with Elena and what might have been. Seneca was handsome, like Arnoth, and clearly in love with his mate. He touched Nisa often, and she smiled back at him with the same blissful expression.

Aiyana knew she was seeing her own future with Dane. Perfect ease in each other's company. And just below the surface, a desire to slip off to privacy . . . Arnoth must see this, too, and it must hurt beyond anything she could imagine.

She wanted him to heal, to find that perfect bliss, and at last know peace. If she had her say, he would find it far sooner than he imagined.

Arnoth rose from the table, bowed, and left. Aiyana started after him, but Dane stopped her. "Let me." She wasn't sure why, but if anyone could reach Arnoth, it was Dane Calydon.

Dane found Arnoth in the hall, staring absently at a mosaic image. "Yours was a glorious civilization, Arnoth. It has changed, but it's not lost."

"It is lost to me."

"It doesn't have to be."

Arnoth glanced at Dane. "Aiyana is high priestess. You are her mate. Like Hakon, you are now king of the Ellowans."

"Am I?" Dane considered this. *King.* Dane knew, clearly, that once, far in his soul's past, he had been a king. A king without love. Now he had Aiyana. "I don't want to be a king, Arnoth."

"Hakon was a great king. I believe you would be, too. You and Aiyana will have children, and the line of Nidawi will continue."

"We'll have children. But they'll be more Thorwalian than Ellowan."

"The line of the high priestess has never been sundered, Dane. Aiyana is the last Nidawi."

"She isn't the last. There's another. Helayna would make an admirable priestess."

Dane hesitated, resisting setting Aiyana's unlikely scheme into motion. He felt certain it wouldn't work as she imagined. But Arnoth needed to accept life again. Maybe he'd find it in the shadow of duty. "All right, she might make a better military commander. . . . Either way, those Ellowans on Valenwood could use your help."

Arnoth turned back to the wall, avoiding Dane's suggestion. ''It's up to you to help your people, Arnoth. Whether you like it or not. You are still prince, because I won't be their king. Aiyana is my mate, and she will stay with me. I think she wants that.''

Arnoth started to argue, then shook his head. ''I think she wants that, too. It's what she always wanted. A Ravager of her own.''

''Aiyana needs me. But Valenwood needs you.''

''I have nothing left to give. Certainly not as prince.''

Dane sensed Arnoth's hesitation. ''You mean, not as a mate.''

''Yes.''

Dane considered this. Arnoth could be stubborn, too. ''So return to Valenwood, straighten it out, set Helayna up as priestess, and then . . . do whatever you want.''

Arnoth sighed heavily. ''I suppose that is my duty.''

''Duty can be rewarding, my friend. For duty, I went to Franconia, and found Aiyana. I wasn't expecting it, but these things happen, my friend. Maybe even to you.''

Dane slapped Arnoth's shoulder, then returned to the hall. He seated himself beside Aiyana, smiling. ''Well, my love, if you have no objections, I've surrendered your position as priestess, and relinquished my role as king.''

''That was good of you. Handling those little decisions.''

''Do you mind, Aiyana?''

She laughed, then kissed his shoulder. ''I want to be with you. I want to know your world. If Arnoth returns to Valenwood, my task is complete.''

''He'll return. He's none too cheerful about it, but then, he's none too cheerful about anything.''

''We've given him a chance, anyway.''

''I hope he finds a woman who shatters all that irritating restraint. And I hope I get to see it.''

Aiyana smiled as Dane rubbed his hands together. "I hope I like her, whoever she is."

"What about us, love? Where would you like to live?"

Kostbera overheard their conversation. "I have a suggestion."

Dane looked up, curious. "What?"

"The Candorians will leave soon for the Intersystem conference. We came here to learn of your system, and to meet our kindred race."

Dane sighed and nodded. "The orange bubbles. Yes." He eyed the globs waiting in the corner. "I suppose you're related to the globs, too."

"Of course." Kostbera grinned. "But so are you. All things are related, Dane."

"That's very comforting."

"You have represented your worlds well, and we no longer fear for you. Other worlds demand our attention, especially in light of the Tseir threat."

"You're leaving?"

"We are. But Candor is a beautiful world. Much has been built here. An outer planet could serve your united system well."

"That's true."

"Then I suggest you remain, Dane Calydon, as leader. There may be Thorwalians and Dakotans who would like to join you here."

Dane looked at Aiyana. "What do you think?"

"I would like to live here. With you, with lingbats . . ."

"By the way, where is Batty?"

Kostbera rose from the table. "He went to see his sire, Dane. You may wish to do the same. Carob doesn't have much time left."

Dane's heart sank. "I'll go now."

* * *

Nisa and Seneca followed Dane to the lingbat tunnels. Aiyana stood beside him as he called for Batty. Batty emerged from the small tunnel, looking sad. "He's pretty much gone, sir."

Dane bowed his head. "Carob . . ."

Aiyana touched his shoulder. "Can you bring him to us, Batty? I might be able to ease his pain."

"I'll fetch him."

Aiyana waited while Batty dragged Carob's limp body to the edge of the tunnel. Dane lifted his body and held him to his chest. Carob's breath came shallow and uneven; he looked thin and drawn. Beside Dane, Nisa wept silently.

Carob opened his eyes, wincing as if even that effort caused pain. "You came back. . . . I knew you would."

"Of course."

"Did you bring the Ellowan?"

Dane was confused. "Yes."

Carob tilted his head to Aiyana. "Dropped the disguise, did you?"

"You knew!" Dane and Aiyana spoke at once.

"Lingbats . . . have superior senses." Carob coughed, then went weak.

"Let me take him, Dane."

Dane placed Carob in Aiyana's hands. She touched his small, round head, then entered her trance. Dane watched, wondering if her skill extended to easing the misery of old age.

Aiyana smiled, and Dane guessed Carob's answer to her question. She worked over him silently. Then she set him back in Dane's hands. "Well? How is he? Did you ease his pain? What can you do for old age?"

"It was much more than old age, Dane. His body was infected with a spreading cell alteration. I believe he was subjected to strange substances."

Nisa nodded, wiping tears from her face. "He was a lab

specimen. I freed him. Dakota has stopped such practices, but too late.''

Carob's eyes popped open and he squirmed upright, then scratched his way to Dane's shoulder. ''Not too late, girl. Just needed a little realigning. Subtle touch . . . So, you mated, did you?'' Carob turned his head toward Aiyana. ''I hope you didn't make it easy for him. Where is my litter son? Did he prove himself adequate?''

Dane's mouth dropped at Carob's sudden vigor. Then he laughed. ''More than adequate, Carob. He saved my life, and Aiyana's. And he operated a hovercraft by himself.''

Perched on the tunnel's edge, Batty puffed with pride. Carob eyed his son. ''Did you, now? Good lad.''

''Thank you, sire.''

''You'll be a good leader. Set you up after myself.''

''I'm sorry, sire. I've got other plans.''

''Other plans? What other plans? If I say you're leader, you're leader!''

Though Carob braced for attack, Batty shook his small head. ''Can't do it, sire. I'm going back to Franconia, to the glorious planet of Keir. The prince will take me. She Who Leaps High is waiting.''

Carob looked at Dane in disbelief. ''He found a female? You . . .'' Carob pointed his wing tip into Dane's face. ''You are a bad influence!''

Aiyana slid her arm around Dane's waist. ''He's right, you know. You have a way of changing everything. You changed me.''

''Love is sacred, Aiyana. It changes everything.''

Aiyana and Dane sat together on a boulder, watching the gas planet of Candor sink below the horizon. The sky was a deep, rich red, the horizon streaked with orange and purple. Aiyana leaned her head on his shoulder.

''It's beautiful here. Warm and peaceful.''

Carob adjusted his position on Dane's shoulder. "So, Ellowan, did you tell him yet?"

Aiyana glanced at Carob. "I was waiting for privacy."

Carob's round eyes narrowed. "You're not going to get it, girl. I've waited a long time for this."

Aiyana sighed while Dane waited expectantly. "Tell me what?"

"You're going to be a sire, boy."

Aiyana rolled her eyes and groaned. "I was hoping to tell him that myself."

"Took too long about it, girl. I'm an old lingbat. I don't like waiting."

"You're not so old, Carob. You'll live many years now that I've cured you of your cell disintegration."

"A sire?" Dane's voice sounded very small.

Aiyana took his hand and kissed it. "I bear your child. Its life began on Valenwood, when I disguised myself and seduced you."

Carob issued a derisive snort. "I don't need to know these details."

Dane's face revealed utter bliss. " 'Little sirs!' The little fellow will be almost the same age as Nisa's daughter. We'll have to visit them often, my dear. Children need playmates. When we have this one, we'll have to start right away on the next."

"Maybe you'd like me to give birth to triplets, to save time."

"Can you?"

"No."

Dane pondered his upcoming role as sire. "I hope I know what to do. I wasn't very close to my own father."

Carob hopped down to Dane's knee. "I'll teach you, boy. You've got to know your litter. Know when to push them, know when to leave them alone."

"And if they don't obey, smack them with a wing tip."

"Exactly."

Aiyana kissed Dane's shoulder. "You'll be a good father, Dane. You'll adapt. That's what you do best."

Dane's blue eyes darkened, his lips curving into the sensual smile that had stolen Aiyana's heart from the first moment she saw him. "I'll adapt. But as for what I do best . . ."

Dane stood up and took Aiyana's hand. "I thought I reminded you last night, but it bears repeating."

Aiyana stood, too. "I haven't forgotten. But the memory needs refreshing. Daily."

Carob groaned loudly, but they ignored him. "If you two keep up this pace, you'll have a litter of forty."

"We keep our aspirations high." Dane bowed to Aiyana. "Shall we return to Nerotania, love? A woman in your condition needs a great deal of rest."

Carob huffed. "As if she gets any sleep at all . . ."

Dane and Aiyana started away, walking hand in hand toward the reconstructed pyramid gateways. Carob bounded after them. "Trying to lose me, were you? Not a chance, humanoids! I missed one adventure; I don't intend to miss another."

Dane laughed, then stopped to wait for Carob. He accepted the lingbat's grumbling, then helped him up to his shoulder. Aiyana scratched behind Carob's pointed ears, and his complaints subsided.

The red sky deepened toward black as they entered the multihued gateway. Bright stars appeared in the sky, one by one, heralding the night. Near and bright shone Thorwal, a white star, never fading, constant. Warm Dakota glittered just beyond, where Nisa would give birth to her second child.

Far in the distance, almost beyond sight, a tiny pin of light shone. The sun rose on Valenwood, and it was no longer midnight. Morning had come at last.

Dear Reader,

I hope you enjoyed *The Midnight Moon.* I loved writing it! Dane Calydon is certainly one of my favorite characters. He first appeared in *The Dawn Star,* and demanded a story of his own. Similarly, Arnoth is a hero I couldn't forget. His story continues in an upcoming novel, *The White Sun,* where Arnoth finds love with a most unexpected woman. (Yes, the lingbats are on the scene to offer their own peculiar brand of wisdom.) Look for *The White Sun* in the spring 1999. My first time-travel romance, *Free Falling,* coming later in 1999, is a fun-filled adventure in Apache territory, where a shy, awkward woman finally gets to be a hero to the man who saved her one too many times.

If you would like to receive my newsletter, please write to: Stobie Piel, P.O. Box 1305, Suite 194, Brunswick, ME 04011. I'd love to hear from you.